Republished in 1970 by
LITERATURE HOUSE
an imprint of The Gregg Press
121 Pleasant Avenue
Upper Saddle River, N. J. 07458

Standard Book Number—8398-0170-X
Library of Congress Card—78-104421

Printed in United States of America

THE

MAMMON

OF

UNRIGHTEOUSNESS

Hjalmar H. Boyesen

LITERATURE HOUSE / GREGG PRESS
Upper Saddle River, N. J.

THE MAMMON

OF

UNRIGHTEOUSNESS

BY

HJALMAR HJORTH BOYESON

AUTHOR OF

"GUNNAR," "IDYLS OF NORWAY," "THE LIGHT OF HER COUNTE
NANCE," ETC., ETC.

NEW YORK

UNITED STATES BOOK COMPANY

SUCCESSORS TO

JOHN W. LOVELL COMPANY

150 WORTH ST., COR. MISSION PLACE

PREFACE.

A GOOD friend of mine, who has read this novel in man-
uscript, is of opinion that every book of any consequence should have a preface. A prefatory flourish of
bugles announcing the approach of the procession arouses
attention, he thinks, and tunes the mind into a mood of
expectancy. Now if he had offered to sound this heraldic
blast for me he would have relieved me of the embarrassment of blowing my own trumpet. If I buckle on my
brazen armor of self-esteem, and with naïve frankness
blare forth my conviction that this is a very remarkable
novel, of the realistic kind, I shall challenge the pugnacity of the whole field of critics, and run the risk of being thrown by some particularly adventurous free lance.
Wishing to avoid this risk I will omit the trumpets, and
for the sake of appearances sing small :

"Pastorem, Tityre, pingues
Pascere oportet oves, deductum dicere carmen."

In fact, this is partly a pastoral narrative, devoid of sensational incidents, and it behooves me to content myself
with a very slender prefatory note.

What I have chiefly at heart is to guard against misap-
prehension. I have used a definite locality which many,
no doubt, will recognize (it is impossible for me to write
a novel without having a distinct and real topography in
my mind), and to some the conclusion may not appear un-
warranted that my characters have also their originals
among the inhabitants of that region. It is this inference
I wish to guard against. My life and daily intercourse
with people supply me with constant hints, which form, as
it were, *nuclei*, lying dormant for a period in my mind,
drawing from my experience and observation such nourishment as may prove organically assimilable, until they

are ready to step forth as characters into the light of publicity. But it never occurs to me to put an acquaintance bodily into a book with his appearance, peculiarities, and the circumstances of his life. I have known during the twenty-two years of my sojourn in the United States four or five founders and conspicuous benefactors of institutions of learning, and they all had certain pervasive traits in common which constitute a type. This type, which I have endeavored to present in the Honorable Obed Larkin, has borrowed something from all of them, but is not a copy of any of them. If they were all to sue me for libel, I should have to plead equally guilty and equally innocent toward all.

My one endeavor in this book has been to depict persons and conditions which are profoundly and typically American. I have disregarded all romantic traditions, and simply asked myself in every instance, not whether it was amusing, but whether it was true to the logic of reality—true in color and tone to the American sky, the American soil, the American character.

COLUMBIA COLLEGE, NEW YORK,
    May, 1891.

THE

MAMMON OF UNRIGHTEOUSNESS.

CHAPTER I.

A KEYNOTE.

"I mean to be true to myself—true to my convictions," ejaculated Alexander Larkin, impetuously, and the echo flung back the words with the same impetuosity from the rock opposite.

"I mean to succeed," said Horace, his brother, and the echo immediately asserted, with the same positiveness, that it meant to succeed.

"Do let us row further up the lake, where we can escape that ridiculous echo," said Alexander, striking the water with his oars.

"All right," assented his brother.

They rowed rapidly, for about fifteen minutes, past green, smiling slopes, covered with wheat-fields and meadow-land, intersected here and there by deep, pine-clad ravines, through which swollen creeks poured their muddy waters into the lake. It was one of the minor geological basins, in the middle of the State of New York, thirty or forty miles long, and but a few miles in width. The lake which received the surface water of this basin was also long and narrow ; but the creeks, three of which had united at its southern end, were, with their deposits of mud, forming a fertile but malarious delta, which was constantly encroaching upon the territory of the lake. It was upon this delta that the town of Torryville was situated.

The two brothers, as they skimmed along over the shining waters, paid little heed to the beauty of the landscape,

with its softly undulating lines against the blue horizon.
They were both intent upon the subject of their late dispute, and each was thinking of the argument with which
he meant to checkmate the other, when the discussion was
to be resumed.

Horace, the elder, was tall and strongly built, with a
large, bony frame, and a countenance which expressed
shrewdness and determination. It was not a handsome face,
but it was strongly individualized and interesting. It was
the face of a clever man—a face which bore the impress of
a self-reliant spirit. There was a look of shrewd observation in his gray eyes, and in their glance something disrespectful and good-natured, which was distinctly American. The mouth was rudely drawn and partly covered by
a coarse, reddish-brown mustache, innocent of all ornamental purpose. The chin was strong, self-assertive, argumentative, and was often thrust forward with a peculiarly combative air. The brown hair, approaching the
color known as ashy-brown, was rather short, parted on
the left side, and coarse as a brush. The whole face was,
perhaps, a trifle crude, and, to a fastidious person, not
wholly agreeable, but it was a face which took hold of you
—which it was difficult to forget. It was full of force and
rude energy. It was said in the village that Horace Larkin was a thunderin' smart chap; and no one who saw
him would be apt to dispute this verdict.

Alexander Larkin, who was two years younger than his
brother, was slighter in figure and more delicately made.
There was something frank, open, and youthfully charming in his appearance, which Horace entirely lacked. Out
of his clear blue eyes spoke a soul in which there was
no guile. In the soft contour of his face, in the fresh,
handsome curves of his lips, in the blondness of his hair—
nay, in his whole personality—there was something chaste,
and sweet, and virginal. It was impossible not to like him,
as one likes spring, and youth, and all things fair and per-
ishable. That way of looking out into life through a pair
of unclouded blue eyes, with frank curiosity and delight,
somehow arouses a pathetic pleasure, tempered with compassion, in hearts which have long since forfeited this
privilege. You would not for the world disillusionize the
dear boy; life will soon make havoc of his illusions. In
youth it is, after all, pardonable to have no very well-de-
fined individuality—to swim joyously in the broad, universal current, without having any urgent cause for di-

verging. It was so with Alexander Larkin ; he was what most young men are whom corruption has not touched ; only he was rather handsomer and cleverer than the majority.

The two brothers had gradually struck out into the middle of the lake, where the echo from the shores would not mock their conversation.

"You were saying," began Aleck, as he was familiarly called, leaning forward and resting on his oars ; " you were saying that you meant to succeed."

"Yes," replied Horace, "and you were saying that you did not."

"I beg your pardon," exclaimed the younger brother, with animation ; " I said nothing of the kind. I said I meant to be true to my convictions."

"Well, it amounts to the same thing."

"Of course, I know you say that to tease me. But, seriously, Horace, for a man of twenty-eight, you are an inveterate cynic. You have no poetry in you, no ideals."

"You could not pay me a greater compliment. Life's substance is prose, and it is this prose I mean to master."

"Life's substance is just as much poetry. It is only to the average unideal man that it looks like prose."

"The average unideal man you will usually find to be the successful man, at least in a democracy. The world is made by average men for average men. Civilization cripples great characters and lifts up the small, in order to strengthen the average. This American democracy of ours—what is it but the triumph of the average ? Look at the men we send into public life now! Compare them to those we sent fifty or a hundred years ago ; compare their very faces, and you see how the type has degenerated. What does that mean, if not that the average fool who formerly took pride in being represented by a wiser man, now prefers to be represented by as great a fool as himself ? The average American, fifty years ago, was poor, and he paid the homage of admiration to greatness, moral and intellectual ; but now his prosperity has turned his brain ; he feels big enough to kick up his heels on his own account, and he dislikes the man whom he suspects of being his superior."

"I should be ashamed if I were you," exclaimed Aleck, with youthful ardor, "to be slandering my country."

"That depends upon what State we are talking in," said Horace, dryly ; "as you know, slander in New York is actionable only in case it is a lie ; while in New Jersey it is actionable if it is of a derogatory character, whether it be true or false.   I am not in the least ashamed of slandering my country in the New Jersey sense."

Aleck listened with visible impatience, took a few strokes with the oars, then lifted them again and looked intently at his brother, who had, in the meanwhile, lighted a cigar and faced him.

" In what you have just been saying," he began, "you have sealed your own doom.   You certainly are above the average, intellectually, whatever you may be morally ; and you have the ambition to distinguish yourself in public life.   I should think your chances were poor if Americans only chose fools to represent them."

The elder brother blew a couple of rings of smoke into the still air, and smiled as only a strong man smiles.   It was a smile full of amusement and impregnable self-confidence.   "My dear fellow," he said ; "you go too fast. Let us admit, for the sake of argument, that I am no fool. How do you suppose a clever man would set about winning public favor?   By demonstrating his cleverness?   By inadvertently letting his wisdom out of the bag, and impressing his countrymen with his intellectual greatness?   No, my dear boy; if he did that, he could not be elected a commissioner of highways, far less a member of Congress. No, if I am intellectually superior, I mean scrupulously to conceal the fact from my fellow-citizens, unless, indeed, they choose to apply a degree of ingenuity to the interpretation of my personality far beyond any with which I credit them.   As I have said, I mean to devote my life to the study of reality, at close quarters, and to reach my conclusions without regard for rose-colored traditions. By applying these conclusions to my conduct I mean to rise, and rise I shall.   If you live long enough, you will verify my predictions."

" I should not wish to succeed at that price," Aleck rejoined, seriously ; "you think character is a barrier to success ? "

" I haven't said that ; though, as the world is now constituted, a great elevation of character might interfere with success.   In the modern world tact is the accepted substitute for character."

" You think, then, that principles and convictions are needless encumbrances, and should be thrown overboard by every man who aspires to enter public life ?"

"One thing at a time, if you please. Let us begin with convictions. What are convictions at the age of twenty-eight? Untried axioms, accepted on trust, which experience is likely to upset. Well, I admit a man who means to succeed cannot afford to equip himself luxuriously with that kind of commodities. At forty, a man may have convictions that are, perhaps, worth something. A public man now-a-days is no more the leader of public opinion, but its follower. He is not an embodiment of knowledge and experience in public affairs, but merely a register of the public ignorance."

The younger brother sat silent for some minutes, and gazed dreamily toward the distant horizon. "Horace," he said, at last, "I am too fond of you to wish to quarrel; but excuse me for saying that I believe you talk for effect. You experience a pleasant sensation when you shock. You like to have people believe you a deep and cold-blooded schemer. I fear you are too clever for your own good—so clever that you are in danger of outwitting yourself."

Horace, so far from resenting this uncomplimentary analysis, looked up with genuine pleasure.

"Good for you, brother," he exclaimed, heartily; "cleverness evidently runs in the family. You, too, are a good deal deeper than I gave you credit for."

Instead of answering, Aleck again struck the water vehemently with his oars, and sent the boat skimming away over the glassy surface of the lake. His brother was a most unsatisfactory disputant, he thought, who would try the patience of a saint. He talked not to convince, or to arrive at a conclusion, but rather as a feat of intellectual gymnastics, and because he liked to exhibit his wit. He was a lawyer first, and afterward an individual; counsel for the prosecution or the defence, as the case might be, even in the bosom of his family.

CHAPTER II.

A SELF-MADE MAN.

The Hon. Obed Larkin, the uncle of Horace and Alexander, was the great man of Torryville, and felt the responsibility of his position. Not only by his wealth was he eminent, but his philanthropy was proportionate to his millions. He had founded the Larkin University, a far-famed co-educational institution, situated on the beautiful hill overlooking the town. He had endowed it with a cool million in cash, as he was wont to say, when any of the professors rebelled against his authority ; and he averred that he would never have had that amount of money to spare, if it had not been for the fact that he had never used tobacco or whiskey in any shape, during his entire life. He, therefore, had a strong prejudice against professors who smoked ; and if he had had his own way, would have given them twenty-four hours' notice to quit the town. But, as he reluctantly admitted, there were other considerations to be taken into account ; and though he stoutly maintained that a man who smoked would also, on occasion, get drunk, and accordingly was unfit to be an instructor of youth, he was yet obliged to tolerate some of these objectionable characters in his seat of learning. He could not forbear, however, to lecture them, not overbearingly, but with many and awkward pauses, on the error of their ways ; and when they beat him in argument, as they often did, he did not blaze up instantly, but he went home, and chewed the cud of reflection, and grew angrier the more he thought of the disrespect they had shown him.

The conceited beggars, didn't they owe everything to him? Didn't they live on the fruits of his labor? Where would they have been, if he had not founded his University, and given them employment at extravagant wages ?

It was scarcely to be wondered at that the Hon. Obed Larkin took this view of professors who dissented from his opinions on the whiskey and tobacco question ; for his townsmen had long nourished his self-esteem by deferring to him in everything. The influx of students and instructors had given a great impetus to the growth of the town, and raised the value of real estate fully five hundred per cent. For this the town was naturally grateful. The greatness and goodness of Mr. Larkin were, therefore, articles of faith in Torryville. The fact that he, who was rich enough to live in magnificence anywhere, chose to live in Torryville, showed plainly enough that Torryville was a most desirable place of residence, and that investment in corner lots was sure to prove profitable.

As far as his outward semblance went, the Hon. Obed Larkin was not very imposing. He was a tall, lank, raw-boned man, with a large head and strong, homely features. He had the shrewd, self-confident look of the successful, self-made man ; but under it all lurked a vague discontent which was emphasized by three deep perpendicular wrinkles in his forehead. He seemed always to be thinking of something unpleasant, always ready to take you down a peg or two, and play ducks and drakes with your self-esteem. He stooped somewhat in his walk, and his coarse gray chin-beard then concealed a part of his shirt-bosom. His upper lip was usually covered with stiff white stubble, giving the impression that he had been shaved two or three days ago. Two deep longitudinal wrinkles, like boundary lines on a map, divided the region of the mouth from that of the cheeks. His grayish-blue eyes, which were shaded by heavy, upward-curling eyebrows, expressed shrewdness and sagacity. Sometimes there lurked in them a gleam of humor which was like a genial commentary to a forbidding text. But ordinarily they had a scrutinizing look, which to strangers was often embarrassing. "However clever you pretend to be, I am going to find out just what you amount to," they seemed to say ; and as politeness rarely imposed any restraint upon Mr. Larkin, it is not strange that many found his society less congenial than it was prudent to admit. Applicants for positions in the University were apt to go away with a very unfavorable opinion of him. In the first place, the questions he asked seemed often (to a man of scholarly education) absurd ; and secondly, the steady scrutiny of his eyes seemed directly intended to embarrass. Though his manner was plain and devoid of pretence, it had yet that air of patronage which the practical man in the United States is apt to assume toward the scholar, and which the successful millionaire assumes toward all the unsuccessful

creation. When Mr. Larkin's gaunt, stooping figure arrayed
in a rusty dress-coat, with a slight deposit of dandruff on his
collar, appeared on the University campus, professors and
tutors, unless they had an axe to grind, took care not to
cross his path. There was a number of anecdotes related
sub rosa and quietly chuckled over, illustrating his views
concerning educational affairs ; but these were only for
private consumption. If occasionally he bored a professor
with his talk concerning things which he knew nothing
about, he was apt to mistake the deferential silence with
which his victim listened for admiring astonishment and approval. He had, on the whole, no very flattering opinion
of the practical sense and judgment of scholars ; but he
had not the remotest idea that they regarded his own de-
liverances on educational subjects with similar disrespect.
When a professor, on one occasion, urged upon him the
necessity of a larger appropriation for the library, Mr.
Larkin cornered him with this remark :

"You want more books, eh ? I'll bet you a dollar you
hain't read all those you've got. Read those, and then
we'll talk about getting more."

And chuckling at his shrewdness, he strolled off to but-
tonhole an instructor, whom he took to task for having
failed to pass some applicants at the entrance examina-
tions.

There was no gainsaying his arguments, especially
when he came along with the rejected applicants, personally insisting upon their admission. He had never been
in a college himself, and could not be made to understand
that some things have to be known before others can be
taught with advantage. He was a self-made man, and as
Lawyer Graves, the wit of the town, said, having made
himself, he had enough left over to make a brother. The
brother in question, however, would not stay "made."
Ezekiel Larkin was one of those sanguine men who
plunge headlong into enterprises, without properly considering the probabilities for and against success. He was
a cleverer man than the Hon. Obed, but would have sunk
into absolute penury if the latter had not taken him under
his wing. There was a story told which nobody pretended
to believe, and yet did not wholly disbelieve, that Obed
owed his fortune to an invention made by Zeke. However that may have been, there was something in the relation of the brothers which gave color to the suspicion.
That they did not love each other was perhaps not so very

wonderful; but that so shrewd a business man as Obed
should consent, again and again, to invest in Zeke's enterprises, which he must have known were foredoomed to
failure, and patiently bear his elder brother's erratic behavior, could only be explained on the supposition that
the latter had a " pull " on him. Obed was not otherwise
noted for indulgent judgments, and he apparently respected no idiosyncrasies but his own. He had risen, by slow
degrees, from nothing, and he maintained that that was
the only proper way of reaching eminence. His brother
and himself had both commenced life as stone-masons,
and would perhaps have remained stone-masons, if the
improvement in bridge-building, which Obed patented,
had not thrown profitable contracts for public works in
his way by enabling him to underbid competitors. The
subsequent steps in his advancement followed naturally
with his increasing wealth and influence. He made vast
sums during the war in his legitimate business, besides
being interested in army contracts which also yielded him
handsome profits. At the close of the war he settled in
Torryville, where he established a paper mill, a national
bank, and in the course of time a flourishing university.
Without any apparent effort, he absorbed all the dignities
which his fellow-citizens had to bestow, went to the legislature, became a State senator, and had repeatedly been offered the nomination for governor. On his brother's death,
in 1867, he took his nephews into his house, made them
enter his university, and in due time established them in
what promised to be a profitable law practice. He made
the firm of Larkin Brothers his legal representatives
whenever, in his various enterprises, his interests collided
with those of others, and managed to throw a great deal
of business in their way.

As regards Mr. Larkin's domestic relations, they were
in all respects exemplary. There was but one drawback
to his happiness : his wife had no children. It was to
repair this deficiency that he had adopted his brother's
sons, and moreover, a little girl named Gertrude, whom, in
a Quixotic mood, he had picked up in an asylum or alms-
house, or some such institution. That was, at all events,
the legend in its official version. Miss Gertrude herself,
who was now seventeen years old could neither confirm
nor deny it, as she was but three years old when she was
removed by Mr. Larkin from her original habitat. The
fourteen fat years of her life had swallowed up the mem-

ory of the three lean ones. And yet, the obscurity of her origin remained a most potent fact in fashioning her character. She knew, or imagined she knew, that it was remembered against her, and this consciousness gave to her bearing a certain reserve which many mistook for pride. She was tall of growth and large-limbed. The expression of her face was vague, groping, unawakened, but withal soft and maidenly. It was this sweetly bovine expression which Homer attributed to Hera when he called her heifer-eyed. Gertrude's wide-open, infantine gaze carried out the same suggestion. Its virginal shyness alternated, however, at times, with the liveliest animation and enterprise. But if anyone presumed upon her sympathy to become confidential, her manner instantly changed to a cold and haughty unresponsiveness. Her dark-blonde, wavy hair was subject to continual experiments in the manner of arrangement, but whatever was done with it seemed incapable of spoiling the noble contour of her head. Taking her altogether, she was quite as much a mystery to herself as she was to others; and if it had not been for the fact that she was beautiful, and moreover Mr. Larkin's adopted daughter, nobody would have troubled himself to solve her riddle. As it was, the sentiment which the town entertained toward her was anything but favorable, and Gertrude, feeling the latent hostility, returned it with interest.

"You can't make out that girl," was the remark most commonly heard; "but what can you expect of a person that has been picked right out of the gutter? Mr. Larkin's kindness to her has turned her head."

Tea-sipping, middle-aged Cassandras were never weary of prophesying disastrous consequences to Mr. Larkin from his generous conduct to Gertrude. If these prophecies, in a mitigated form, reached Mr. Larkin's ear, they made no impression upon him. He was, by nature, too sanguine to believe that anything in which he was concerned could turn out disastrously. Girls, to be sure, were queer things, and you couldn't always tell what they would be up to. But he had observed that they generally came out all right in the end. He had known lots of girls in his day, and most of them had had a period when all sort of antics and tomfooleries came sort of natural to them; but for all that, they had slipped as meekly as any into the matrimonial harness, and then they were of course all right. If Gertrude was a little hifalutin', why, it didn't

signify. She was a pretty girl, and he had observed that
pretty girls were apt to have more antics, and were harder
to manage, than the homely ones. But they were sure to
come out all right, he repeated, confidently.

If Mrs. Larkin did not share his confidence in this, as in
many other respects, it was with her a matter of temperament rather than of conviction. Mrs. Larkin had a propensity for lugubrious predictions, and cherished a subdued aversion for her husband's optimism. She never
contradicted him, chiefly because, with her natural indolence, she felt unequal to the effort of arguing; but she
sighed her dissent and expressed it in mournful glances
and shakings of her head. She was a large, blonde, good-
looking woman of about forty, with sad blue eyes and a
healthy complexion. She had a slight stoop in her shoulders and walked heavily, not so much on account of stout-
ness as on account of the weight of woe that oppressed
her. Frequently she paused, as if endeavoring to recollect
where she was going. There was a perceptible inequality
between the two sides of her face, though not enough to
attract immediate attention. On the left side there was
an odd contraction of the muscles which drew the corner
of the mouth a little downward, giving to the face a chronic
air of dissatisfaction. She could therefore only smile on
one side of her mouth, while the other seemed to deprecate
such levity. She dressed without style or pretence of
style, and her garments hung about her with Quaker-like
rigidity. As she had equal difficulty in keeping warm in
winter and cool in summer, fretful comments on the
weather formed the staple of her conversation. A red
worsted shawl was either drooping from her shoulders or
depending from her arm, and, as malicious critics asserted,
served the purpose of concealing the bad fit of her dresses.

What Mrs. Larkin, above all things, hungered for was a
mission; not a mere self-imposed task, but an unmistakable call from on high, such as came to the prophets of
old. She was in her way a religious woman, but believed
religion to consist in a general disapproval of everything
pertaining to the earth, and a predilection for lugubrious
conversation. It was a source of grief with her that she
had never heard God's voice calling her in the stillness of
the night, as it did the child Samuel; though she had remarkable dreams, in which her pastor, Rev. Arthur Robbins, was disposed to discern divine warnings and commands, she was a little bit too conscientious to agree with

him. Her spurts of enthusiasm for this or that cause
which the church endorsed, were usually due to the influence of Mr. Robbins ; but either because, as she was fond
of asserting, she was a frail vessel, or because her worldly
sense was not quite so dead as she liked to believe, her
zeal was apt to flag before much was accomplished. She
had had her Indian craze, during which she had gone to
considerable expense in having Mr. Robbins's tract,
"Science and the Bible Reconciled," translated into something which she innocently believed to be "the Indian
language." She had been in correspondence with officials
in Washington and Indian agents, regarding the expedi-
ency of having this tract distributed along with the sup-
plies from the government agencies, and had been much
gratified at the interest which her correspondents displayed in the project. An army officer who was her husband's guest for a few days, had, however, the cruelty to
disillusionize her, and from that time forth her interest in
the Indians was at an end. A project for the conversion
of the Catholic converts in China to the Evangelical religion, and another for spreading the gospel among the
Mohammedans, were equally short-lived and expensive.

The more remote a mission was to Mrs. Larkin, the more
it fascinated her. It was owing to this peculiarity of hers,
that her nephews, Horace and Alexander, with whom she
came in daily contact in her own house, never presented
themselves to her mind as possible objects of missionary
zeal. Horace had an imperturbable self-confidence which
made her half afraid of him, and his disrespectful laugh
discouraged all interest in his spiritual welfare. Alexander,
on the other hand, seemed too incorrigibly light-hearted,
and refused to sympathize with her solicitude for the fate
of the heathen in the hereafter. He treated her with
humorous affection, made fun of her projects in a good-
natured way, ran against her in the doorways, embraced
her by accident, and made profuse apologies.

"You only imagine me to be an Arab or a Zulu-Kaffir,
aunt," he would exclaim, laughingly ; "and then you won't
mind."

She could not help liking him, in spite of his frivolity ;
but influence him she could not. It was, in fact, not Mrs.
Larkin's *forte* to influence anybody. Even Gertrude, her
adopted daughter, had long since emancipated herself from
her authority. When, therefore, her husband expressed
his confidence that Gertrude would turn out all right, she

would lift her eyes to heaven and sigh, as if oppressed with forebodings of disaster. When she had occasion to address the girl, she never looked at her or spoke to her directly, but dropped her words, as it were, inadvertently in corners and around the walls, and left Gertrude to pick them up if she chose. Whatever her daughter said or did seemed to have a strange power to shock Mrs. Larkin, who then, instead of expressing her disapproval, appealed with devout eyes to the ceiling and shook her head in dismal apprehension. It was scarcely to be wondered at that Gertrude felt uncomfortable under this treatment, and sometimes was guilty of unfilial language. But when, in the spasms of remorse which followed these outbursts, she flung herself on Mrs. Larkin's neck and begged her forgiveness, the latter's unresponsive manner, her virtuous disavowal of all her personal feeling, and her references to heaven as the only source of forgiveness, would suddenly chill the passionate girl and make her feel hard and wicked. If, with a vague hope of consolation, she sought refuge with her father, his well-intentioned obtuseness was scarcely easier to bear. He was so irritatingly confident that everything would come out all right, that nobody meant any harm, that all resentment and sorrow were mere mistakes, and as such easily corrected. He had always occupied this neutral ground between her and her mother ; he had refrained from committing himself to any definite judgment, and was therefore equally unsatisfactory to both.

2

CHAPTER III.

FOUNDER'S DAY.

It was the trustees of the University who had put down Mr. Larkin's birthday as a holiday on the calendar, under the name of Founder's Day. Larkin' Day the students called it, and celebrated it in the spirit of their own interpretation. The opportunities for " larkin' " were, however, limited in Torryville, and in the dearth of amusement the young men had recourse to all sorts of desperate inventions. They contrived by superhuman efforts to get one of the founder's cows up into the bell-tower of the chapel, and there proceeded to paint it green. They put a fine collection of live mice into the desk of one of the professors, who was very near-sighted and nervous, and they dyed with blue ink the marble bust of a certain opulent, but unpopular, college officer which adorned the library. Sometimes they descended upon the neighboring villages and played all sorts of rude pranks upon the citizens ; and occasionally a party of them would visit credulous farmers, to whom they would introduce one of their number as the son of General Grant or some other celebrity, and be entertained accordingly.

The principal ceremony of the day was, however, the founder's Reception, which took place in a large forlorn, jail-like dormitory, called the Barracks. Here students of both sexes gathered in a great dreary, imperfectly lighted hall, with bare plastered walls, and dingy white-painted woodwork. In the middle of the floor stood Mr. and Mrs. Larkin, and shook hands with a multitude of people, the former with his head on one side and mildly jocose, the latter stiff and awkward, with her elbow against her side, and holding out one limp hand which made no response to any pressure. Her one-sided smile, with which she greeted those of her visitors whom she knew, looked sadder than ever ; and her feeble and tentative remarks, which for lack of confidence in their propriety, she rarely finished, made one realize, as he went away, that life was a melancholy affair. Young men with crude but earnest faces, and in all varieties of costume, walked up, some with a stoop and some with a swagger, to exchange some awkward remarks with the man who regarded himself as their benefactor; and their features showed the relief they felt when the ordeal was well over. A few of them, braving the prejudice which yet existed against co-education, had female students, in prim or helplessly aspiring toilets, loosely attached to their arms, as if they feared contact; while others, glorying in their prejudice, came striding along with village beauties who clung to them with delightful confidence.

A dozen Brazilians, with dark and indolent faces, formed a group near the door, from which the most adventurous among them made excursions in the direction of the prettiest girls, and again returned to render an account of their exploits, which were then discussed with southern gestures and animation. Two small, yellow-faced Japanese, with bristling black hair and bead-like eyes, had been cornered by some resolute female students, and were being subjected to a rigid cross-examination concerning the government and social customs of their native land. A Servian, two Russians, and a Bulgarian completed the collection of alien tribes, as far as the undergraduates were concerned.

There were professors, however, whose wives represented several nationalities and strikingly varying types. There were men who looked as if they came directly from the plough, and expected to return to it, with wives whom toil and child-bearing had made prematurely old; and there were recent graduates of Harvard and Columbia, in correct evening attire, and with an ease of manner which became slightly ironical when they conversed with their rustic colleagues. There was the stout, squatty, and melancholy Professor Dowd, who for some inscrutable reason had wooed a sprightly little Viennese lady, and for some equally inscrutable reason, had won not only her hand, but her affection. She was so dainty and *petite*, and looked, as she came tripping along through the crowd, like the very incarnation of delightful frivolity—as a wasp-waisted pink shepherdess *à la* Watteau would have looked in the meeting-house of the Pilgrim Fathers.

"Ach! I am so glat to see you, Mrs. Larrkin," she exclaimed, with an inimitable foreign accent and vivacious gestures. "You are well, yes? Ah, yes, I see you are well. You look so fine and radiant. And your husbant, he is well—how you must be proud of him on a day like this, dear Mrs. Larrkin—to see all he has accomplished—to have brought the plessing of knowledge into so many young lives. He looks so proud and commanding—like a sheneral on a field of pattle."

Mrs. Dowd went on with unblushing mendacity pouring forth her compliments, until something in Mrs. Larkins's wondering eyes showed her that she was throwing her pearls before swine. Then suddenly, with an impatient shrug of her shoulders, she pinched her husband, who in the meanwhile had been conversing with the founder, and whispering with suppressed wrath: "*Ah, mon Dieu, qu'elle est bête,*" dragged him reluctantly away. They were followed by Professor and Mrs. Wharton, whom the founder greeted with handshakes that tingled in their toes. Professor Wharton gave instruction in some practical branch of study, not usually embraced in a university course, which Mr. Larkin had especially at heart. He was a man with a shrewd, homely, coarse-featured face, coarse brown hair, and rims of dried tobacco juice on his lips. His wife, who was tall, lean, and flat-chested, with remnants of faded comeliness, looked as if, on proper provocation, she could scratch your eyes out.

"Well, Professor," Mr. Larkin began, as he released Mrs. Wharton's hand, " it looks rather different on this hill-top from what it did ten years ago, when you first came here."

" It dooes, indeed," said Mr. Wharton, with the emphasis of conviction.

" You wouldn't know it was the same place, eh ?"

" I wouldn't believe you on your oath, if you were to tell me it was the same place, if I hadn't been here myself and seen everything change from day to day."

Mr. Larkin chuckled delightedly. That was the kind of talk he liked to hear.

" It does seem wonderful, Mr. Wharton, don't it ?" he went on, loath to drop the congenial topic.

" It does, indeed," Mr. Wharton said once more, looking as if the thing just struck him in a new and surprising light.

" You have reason to be proud of your work, Mr. Larkin," remarked Mrs. Wharton, in a shrill, grating voice.

" Not proud, but gratified, Mrs. Wharton," answered the host ; "a man can't do more than his best, you know, and God's blessing must do the rest."

"A true word is that, Mr. Larkin. But it ain't everyone of us that God gives the chance and the will to do
such great things in his service."

Mr. Larkin was about to reply, when he observed at
his elbow the Rev. Arthur Robbins, with one daughter
clinging to his arm, and four more following close behind
in his wake. They were all, with one exception, plain, and
were attired in brown dresses with an innocent pink bow
at the throat. There was something in the looks and
small, abrupt motions of the four undistinguished ones,
which reminded one of mice or squirrels. Their small
heads, their shy, dark, and alert-looking eyes and receding
chins, emphasized the resemblance. Only Arabella, the
youngest, for whom Mr. Robbins was just endeavoring to
secure a share of Mr. Larkin's attention, had her father's
features, though in a somewhat cheapened and weakened
edition. For Mr. Robbins was a fine-looking gentleman,
with gray, well-trimmed mutton-chop whiskers, dark, intelligent eyes, and an air of well-bred worldliness, which
made him a trifle conspicuous in Torryville, where the
clerical profession was expected to conform to quite a different type. His youngest daughter had the same fine
eyes and the same warm pallor, but there was something
feverish and uneasy in her expression ; and her manner
alternated between a weary languor and an almost hysterical vivacity. There was an anxious sweetness in her
smile as she caught sight of Horace Larkin, who was
standing with his back against the wall, submitting to a
cross-examination by one of the co-educational ladies, in
regard to his opinion of Alexander Hamilton and that
statesman's influence in moulding the destinies of the republic. As the young man suspected, she had chosen
this as the subject of her commencement thesis, and was
talking with a strictly practical purpose. Miss Robbins's
anxious smile afforded Horace an opportunity, which he
was not slow to seize, of breaking off this conversation,
and from the asperities of barren learning to plunge into
the soft embrace of caressing compliments. He did not
entirely approve of Miss Robbins's die-away airs and exaggerated behavior, as he had been known to remark on
more than one occasion, but for all that her evident approval of him did much to modify his opinion. She
listened to his most trivial remarks with devout attention,
and was disposed to find even a profounder meaning in
his comments upon men and things than he had himself

divined. A man has to be preternaturally pachydermatous to be proof against such insidious flattery.

"It is an age and a half since we have seen you, Mr.
Larkin," said Miss Robbins, as she pressed the young
man's hand with effusive cordiality. "Is it co-education
or the law which has been absorbing you?"

"It is both, Miss Robbins," replied Horace, with that
air of brusque candor which was habitual with him.
Whatever he was charged with he always admitted for the
sake of argument, and it was therefore impossible to tease
him.

"So you really approve of co-education?" Arabella
went on, with a caressing cadence in her voice which seemed
to implore confidence and friendship.

"I approve of everything that it is for my advantage to
approve of."

"Then why don't you approve of me?"

The remark was made in the spirit of daring banter,
but there was a sudden adventurous light in the girl's
eyes which was like the glare from a furnace door that is
for an instant ajar.

"Naturally, because I do not think it would be for my
advantage," he replied, smiling; "because it might be
even dangerous."

"I scarcely know how to interpret that," she replied,
with a nervous little laugh; "but I have an impression
that it is not exactly polite."

"Politeness is nothing but judicious mendacity," he remarked, sententiously.

"Well, women are so accustomed to being treated with
judicious mendacity, as you call it, that you can't blame
them if they have come to expect it as a sort of right."

"I will lie to you to your heart's content, if you desire
it," he retorted, giving a twist to his mustache, under
which his ironical smile was lurking.

"Do you know, Mr. Larkin," she ejaculated, as if resolved to emulate his bewildering tactics; "I sometimes
have a suspicion that you are a desperate flirt?"

"Has that never occurred to you before?"

"No, I confess it hasn't."

"Then put it down in your note-book for future reference."

A perceptible ripple of excitement passed through the
assembly, as Alexander Larkin entered with his tall cousin
on his arm.

"How lovely Gertrude looks!" exclaimed Arabella Robbins; "she looks like the Queen of Sheba!"

"Permit me to question that," her interlocutor replied. "The queen was, no doubt, a trifle more *décolletée.*"

"I am not up in the fashions of those ancient times, of course, but I merely mean she looks queenly. And your brother—he looks like Aladdin in the fairy tale."

"That is rather a better comparison, apart from the costume; for my brother, I regret to say, passes most of his time in a fairy tale."

"You mean to say he is in love."

"Oh, no! nothing as bad as that. I merely mean to say that he looks at life through rose-colored spectacles. And like Aladdin, he has a child-like confidence in the wonderful lamp which he carries hidden under his coat."

Alexander, tall, blond, and radiant, was advancing through the crowd, making his frank and fearless gaze wander around the room, as if in search of somebody. In striking contrast to the youthful animation of his features, was the listless apathy of Gertrude's face.

"Do liven up a little, Gertie," he said, with an impatient shake of her arm; "you look cross."

"When I am cross, why should I not look it?"

"Is it I who have displeased you?"

"No more than anybody else."

"Who, then, is it?"

"Everybody."

"That is amazing for a girl of your age to be dissatisfied with everybody."

"It is more amazing for a man of your age to be satisfied with everybody."

"Perhaps. But I was made that way."

"So was I—made my way."

"That's very unfortunate."

"Perhaps, but it can't be helped."

Alexander's wondering glance had by this time lighted upon a dark-haired young man, who, by some kind of nervous sympathy, turned about as if someone had touched him.

As their eyes met, the dark-haired man advanced rapidly and made a ceremonious bow to Gertrude. He had a grave, refined face, of the Edwin Booth type, full of nervous mobility and melancholy resignation. One lock of his black hair hung with an appearance of studied negligence down on his forehead, and a pair of hazel eyes strayed with a look of weary hauteur over the variegated company. There was an air *à la* Hamlet in the way he carried his head ; and only doublet and hose were needed, instead of a neatly-fitting dress suit, to complete the resemblance.

"Well, Archie," exclaimed Alexander, as he eagerly shook his friend's hand, "you concluded to come, after all ? "

Dr. Hawk—for that was the friend's name—ran his fingers through his curly hair, and fixed a dreamily adoring glance upon Gertrude before he answered.

"We are weary, my heart and I," he quoted, rather irrelevantly.

"You mean you are bored," said Gertrude ; "a sympathetic soul at last ! "

The Doctor bowed again in acknowledgment of the compliment. "What a pity, Miss Gertrude, that you and I were not born before the world had yet grown old," he sighed, translating his adoration in another ardent glance.

"Yes, before the world had yet been made," the girl sighed, in mock imitation of his sentimental tones.

"You are cruel, indeed," he said, with an offended air.

"Pardon me, Doctor, but you know that is a forbidden topic."

He turned half about, gazed sulkily at the walls and the ceiling and finally, recovering his equanimity, faced her once more.

"Humanity, in my opinion, demands too little of life," he said. "It is satisfied with the mere questionable privilege of existing. As Schlegel says, 'Living for the mere sake of living is the source of all vulgarity.' As for me, if I have not the delusion of a pursuit that appears in some way worthy, I regard breathing as a pure waste of energy. I would just as leave give my air-pumping apparatus a rest—forever."

Gertrude had listened with a slowly kindling animation to this discourse ; the pleasure she felt shone out of her eyes. Every word seemed as if spoken out of her own heart.

"But what would you have us do, Doctor ?" she said. "What is the good of rebelling against what you can't help ? "

"There is nothing which we can't help," he replied, transfixing her again with his direct gaze ; "or I should say, there is nothing which you can't help, Miss Gertrude."

"If, for instance, Gertie has a stupid partner," Alexander remarked, "can she take him by the ear and command him to be interesting?"

"No ; but let her take him by the heart, and he couldn't help being interesting."

"I should find him more intolerable than ever, Doctor," ejaculated Gertrude, laughing.

"You mean that Gertie should go about making people fall in love with her," said her cousin, "so as to give them an object worth living for ? But wouldn't that in the end make a considerable muddle in the town, when they should all come and claim her?"

"They should not claim her," cried Hawk, with sudden warmth ; "the privilege of being in love with her would be its own reward."

"With all due respect for Gertie, I doubt if you will find many who will take that view."

"So much the worse for them," said the Doctor.

It was his habit to pay audacious compliments of this sort with a solemn face, and in a sad, melodious voice which had a curiously penetrating resonance. Gertrude had to make a physical effort to shake off the spell which he threw over her. She liked him, because she found him entertaining, but she had a vague distrust of him, and felt the need of being on her guard.

"Do let us invent something to prevent these people from boring each other to death," she said, with sudden revival of energy. "I feel a kind of responsibility for them. I would like to take them by the shoulders and shake them."

"That is not a bad idea," said Alexander, "only you have got to do it to music. Otherwise they might not like it ; or rather, you must let them shake you."

"You mean we ought to dance."

"Yes, why not?"

"Isn't that rather undignified at a founder's reception?"

"Not half so undignified as standing around in a chilly room, uttering dreary platitudes about the weather and the progress of the University."

"Then will you speak to father?"

"We'll both speak to him."

Mr. Larkin, who prided himself on his liberality, was never disinclined to entertain any proposition. He was at first rather dubious as to the propriety of dancing on

the present occasion, but when he found that his wife objected to it on religious grounds, he veered around and
maintained that there was nothing he liked so much as to
see the young people amuse themselves.

"What do you say, parson?" he asked, turning to Mr.
Robbins, who was explaining to Mrs. Larkin how recent
geological discoveries had confirmed the biblical story of
the creation.

"Don't ask me," said the clergyman, jocosely, "I have
nothing to do with your conscience, you know; I am only
the keeper of Mrs. Larkin's."

"Well, she is my conscience. I have no other. She kinder
supports one for the benefit of the family."

"Then you ought to refer the question to her."

"No, I have observed her conscience is out of repair;
kinder worn out by too much use."

The permission being given, a hysterical piano with
some kind of internal disorder was procured from a student's room across the hall, and a young man who played
the violin emphasized the waltz measure by hoarse and un-
melodious scrapes on his strings. The Presbyterian and
the Baptist ministers took their departure very pointedly
(though not on musical grounds) when the noise began,
and expressed to Mrs. Larkin their regret that her husband
should countenance such sinful amusement; but the founder, for whose ears the regret was intended, laughed a
shrewd, contented laugh at his ability to "rile the parsons."

The music persevered for ten minutes in producing
scraping and rumbling noises in three-quarter measure,
before anyone ventured to swing out upon the floor. Then
Aleck and Gertrude, for philanthropic reasons, resolved to
take the initiative; and a dozen couples immediately followed in their wake. Soon the upper half of the hall was
filled with dancers whose heads bobbed up and down with
small regard for the music. There were many who danced
well, but a far greater number who did not know whether
they could dance or not, but thought they would like to try.
There were young girls, with nice innocent faces in which
there was no guile, laboring conscientiously to keep their
feet in rhythmic motion; and young men who, with one
arm loosely encircling their partners' waist, jerked solemnly
about with their eyes fixed on their boots. There was
young Professor Ramsdale, of Harvard antecedents, who
held the girls tightly clasped and conversed leisurely with
them, while he gyrated about with reckless ease, "revers-

ing " every moment, and winding his way skilfully among the thronging couples without ever risking a collision. The frivolous-minded among the seniors hated him, when they saw him waltzing, and would have found some way of avenging themselves, if his popularity with the serious-minded had not shielded him from molestation. Among the female students there were many who reviled him in unmeasured terms, but none who had the heart to refuse, when he asked them to dance. Handsome he was not, though tall and athletic, and his conversation, as a rule, was jerky and fragmentary. His blond hair was cut very short, and a mustache of indefinite color curled over a strong, sensuous mouth. His blue, serious eyes, the white of which was veined with yellow, protruded from their sockets, and with their stiff and solemn stare reminded you of fish-eyes. Whether he joked or was in earnest, no one could guess by the look of his countenance ; which, if it was the mirror of his soul, was certainly a very imperfect one. In spite of this disadvantage, he made the impression of being a sturdy and trustworthy personality ; whatever he said (perhaps because he said so very little) was well received, and seemed to admit of no dissent. He was known in the town as a persistent adorer of Gertrude Larkin, and it was told of him that, when someone accused him of having proposed to her seven times, he answered that he would persevere even unto seventy times seven. But that sounded so unlike him that his friends refused to credit it. That Gertrude, for some reason, objected to him was generally believed, though it was hinted that her objections could scarcely be serious, since she continued, after having refused him, to accept his attentions.

From the moment Gertrude entered the reception-hall with her cousin, she had felt the eyes of her indefatigable admirer upon her. While she danced with Aleck, they followed her with their calm, expressionless gaze.

" Do get that Ramsdale to look at somebody else, Aleck," she said ; " I assure you he is burning a hole in the back of my head."

" Who else is there here worth looking at ? " asked Aleck, in the spirit of gallantry.

"Oh, Aleck ! That from you ! It is too much."

" Not at all. Don't mention it. Or rather put it down to my credit, as a fund to draw against when my mood changes."

" Why doesn't he stare at Bella Robbins ? "

"That would be a thankless task. She has eyes for no one but Horace."

"But for him she has a great deal."

"Of eyes?"

"Yes."

They danced aₗong with leisurely swings and caprices for some minutes.

"Oh, dear, what a mixed up world this is!" sighed the girl; "why can't everybody let everybody else alone?"

"If he did, the world would fall into a million pieces."

"So much the better."

"Civilization would come to an end."

"Better still. I have always felt in myself a taste for savagery."

"Man is a gregarious animal."

"I am not a gregarious animal."

"Oh, yes, you are; you are only a trifle fastidious in your gregariousness."

She raised her large, dark-blue eyes slowly to her cousin's face, and he looked smilingly into them, and saw the little flame-like lines in the iris radiating from the pupils, and little cloudy dots in the blue which made it look doubly blue.

"Aren't you just a little bit unendurable, Aleck?" she asked, with ominous gentleness.

"Oh, yes, I am a little bit—anything you like. But you look so lovely to-night, Gertie, that you can afford to be magnanimous."

The music came to a stop in the middle of a bar, by the breaking of the violinist's fourth string; but several couples still hopped about in a dispirited way, until they became aware that they were having the floor to them-selves. Then they ceased half-wonderingly, and walked apart, with no pretence of ceremony. Doctor Hawk and Professor Ramsdale both hastened from opposite sides of the hall toward Gertrude; but the athletic Professor, in his blind zeal, knocked down a freshman, to whom he stopped to apologize. Thereby the Doctor gained an advantage, and Gertrude gained another. For she preferred, on the whole, the Doctor's society to that of the Professor. The latter, finding that he had lost the race, stared with his calm fish-eyes at his rival's back, which was turned toward him with defiant bravado; then without trace of ill-will or discomfiture, walked off and consoled himself with a little co-educational damsel, who received his attention with undisguised gratitude. The music presently started up again, minus the violin, and the measure of her bliss was full, when he asked her to dance.

"Do tell me, Professor," she said, as he put his arm about her waist and swung her out upon the floor, "what is the substance of Schopenhauer's Ethics? Do you regard Hartmann as a fair expounder of Schopenhauer?"

"No," answered Ramsdale, stolidly; but he refused to commit himself further. He was asking himself bitterly, if life was worth living. His fortunate rival was apparently troubled with the same query.

"Life, life, life!" he exclaimed, dramatically, when Alexander had betaken himself off. He made a point of never saying what was expected of him, and to Gertrude, who seemed to herself to be daily smothered in commonplaces, it was this element of surprise in his speech which made him attractive. He was one of the few men she knew who did not bore her.

"Have you been jilted, Doctor, or what is the matter?" she asked, laughing.

Hawk contracted his brows with displeasure.

"I could well imagine a woman refusing me, Miss Gertrude," he said, deep down in his melodious bass, "but jilt me, never."

"Why the one any more than the other?"

"The measure of a woman is the man she loves—the man she is capable of loving. The woman capable of loving me would for that very reason be incapable of jilting me."

"That is a neatly turned compliment to yourself."

"I should say it was a neatly turned compliment to you."

The audacity of his repartee prevented her for a moment from fully comprehending it. As its meaning dawned upon her, however, an indignant blush mounted to her cheeks, and the animation in her eyes was suddenly quenched, leaving a chilly vacuity. The Doctor perceived that he had made a mistake, but instead of blaming himself for it, he blamed Gertrude. For a moment he fairly hated her. Ramsdale, whose watchful stare had never been averted, perceived that now was his opportunity. With imperturbable seriousness, he took leave of his co-educational damsel and presented himself at Gertrude's elbow at the very moment when she was wishing for a convenient escape. She seized his arm almost with alacrity, and responded with freezing hauteur to the Doctor's mock-ceremonious salutation. The Professor was fairly aglow with pleasure and pride. He bore his charge away in triumph, while the floor seemed to undulate under his feet. His face, however, betrayed no trace of agitation.

"May I have the pleasure of dancing the next waltz with you, Miss Larkin?" he inquired, in tones of the solemnest prose.

"You may, Mr. Ramsdale."

"Thank you."

The orchestra, which in the meanwhile had been enriched with a piccolo flute, struck up the desired waltz, and he lost no time in placing his arm firmly about Gertrude's waist and sailing out upon the unoccupied floor. Here he was in his element. He danced as naturally as a fish swims, and almost as gracefully. It was a luxury, after the exhausting conversation of Dr. Hawk, to rest in the clasp of an athletic arm and be guided passively on and around and about in all sorts of surprising turns and swings, and feel no responsibility and no need of effort, but a mere instinctive surrender to the rhythm of the music. It was with regret that she heard her partner's voice, in which there was a thick, "grouty" tone, uttering something which, though it was far from abstruse, she failed to comprehend.

"Have you seen the new 'varsity crew?" the Professor repeated.

"No."

"They row in very good form."

"Indeed!"

"Heavy men, all of them. I believe in heavy men, don't you?"

"Believe in heavy men? Well, I don't know. I have known some slender men, too, whom I have liked very well."

"I mean in a boat."

"In a boat? Oh, yes. But a man whom I like on dry land I am also apt to like in a boat."

The fact was she had scarcely listened, and answered at random. She was rehearsing in her thoughts Dr. Hawk's insolent remarks, and was wondering what he really could have meant by them. If he was in love with her, that was certainly not the way to tell her of it. If it was mere vanity on his part—or a constitutional inability to refrain from uttering whatever came into his head—then he deserved to be punished, and punished he should be. How she was to punish him she could not decide, but she had time enough to think of that before they met again.

"The coxswain weighs only ninety-four pounds," Ramsdale observed, as he suddenly changed his step from a slow gliding motion to a quick three-quarter measure.

"Indeed!" she answered, absently, "how remarkable!"

"Oh, no, it isn't very remarkable; he is only sixteen years old."

"He must be very large for his age," she said, in order to say something.

"Why, no, he is very small for his age," her imperturbable partner replied.

"I thought you said the crew were all heavy men."

"So I did; but the coxswain isn't the crew."

She had to laugh in spite of her vexation, and he, though not comprehending why she was amused, joined her with a good-natured grunt. He admired her so abjectly that he did instinctively whatever he believed would please her. He cudgelled his brain for some time to find another topic of conversation, and hit finally upon one which seemed appropriate.

"Don't you think the scenery about Torryville is beautiful?" he inquired, feeling sure that here, at last, was a bond of sympathy.

"No," she answered, wilfully; "I think it is hideous."

"The waterfalls and the ravines seem to me quite handsome," he continued, not in the least disconcerted.

"They seem to me frightfully wearisome."

"You mean to climb?"

"No, to look at—and talk about."

"I see you are not fond of nature."

"I am not fond of anything—or anybody."

"Isn't that rather an uncomfortable state to be in?"

"No, I thank you; it is a very comfortable state—the only comfortable state."

A slow wonder began to stir in the interior of Mr. Ramsdale's brain, but it did not affect his immobile features. He had but a slight acquaintance with the fair sex, and felt incompetent to interpret its moods. He thought of Virgil's famous *mutabile et varium*, etc.; and it occurred to him that Dido, very likely, had cut up in this style with Æneas. There were plenty of historic examples to account for it, and all classical writers agreed in the opinion that it was not to be taken seriously. But for all that, such rash and inconsequent speech could never lose its power to inflict pain and discomfort. Nevertheless, Gertrude in a disagreeable mood was better than no Gertrude at all, and Ramsdale held her doggedly in his firm semi-embrace as long as the music continued to supply an excuse for such felicity. When that excuse ceased, he offered her his arm and conducted her to a long table of unpainted boards, upon which were piled up coffee cups, plates, and pyramids of sandwiches. It was all of a coarse and substantial kind. From one end of the table something was served which was euphemistically called ice-cream, but tasted like frozen corn-starch or custard. Here they ran against Horace and Miss Robbins who, with her pathetic smile, was listening to his authoritative discourse. They were talking of Miss Kate Van Schaak, a young lady from New York, whom Bella had recently been visiting.

"You would be sure to fall in love with her, Mr. Larkin," she was saying, in her languidly caressing tone. She had frequently before exhorted him to fall in love with this or that girl, whom she suspected him of liking, merely for the comfort of hearing his blunt refusals.

"Kate is such a charming girl," she continued; "she is a perfect angel."

"Then she wouldn't do for me," Horace replied, with gratifying decision.

"Why so?"

"Angels, as a rule, have no money."

"There you are mistaken. Kate is a rich angel. She has a great deal of money. But you surely don't intend to marry for money, Mr. Larkin?"

"Not exactly. I intend to marry first health, then wealth, and thirdly a good temper!"

Bella's heart sank within her; she was conspicuous neither for health nor wealth; nay, was rather lacking in both. She hoped, however, that her good temper might suffice to compensate for her deficiencies.

"Then you do not intend to marry for love?" she said, looking up into his face with her imploring smile.

"No," he answered, briefly.

"But that is a terrible declaration, Mr. Larkin."

"I don't see why it is terrible. If I have a healthy and good-tempered wife, who, moreover, has a material claim upon my gratitude, I shall be sure to love her."

"But would she be sure to love you?"

"I shall demand very little of her in that direction. To

be frank, Miss Bella, I think all this talk about love is nine-tenths twaddle. We talk of love as if it were a tremendous, overwhelming, inexorable power in our lives which we have got blindly to submit to. But, as a matter of fact, does such a passion invade the lives of many modern men and women in the United States? In the Middle Ages, when men were more passionate and less rational—more barbaric, in other words—I know that love and hate, and avarice, and all the savage, animal instincts were the tremendous forces they have been represented to be. At the present time, too, we have savages of this kind, incapable of restraining their natures ; but most of them are in jail, and those who are not, ought to be."

"People who are capable of loving passionately ought to be in jail!" exclaimed the girl, horrified.

"Yes, if you like," Horace replied, delighting in the paradox.

"And you would like to be their jailer?"

"If I had nothing better to do, I might ; but for the moment I find the law business more profitable."

"Mr. Larkin, I don't believe you mean what you are saying," she exclaimed, pathetically. "You said yourself a while ago, that you intended to love your wife after marriage."

Horace twisted his mustache for a moment, and looked at the earnest and somewhat agitated face of the girl with his quizzical smile. It amused him to see what a power he had over her, and how completely he could sway her by his words ; calling up any emotion he might desire. At the same time he was conscious of a little twinge of conscience and a sort of supercilious kindness for her helplessness. That she was in love with him he had long known ; but while formerly this unrequited devotion had appeared half ridiculous, it now suddenly became a meritorious thing and a claim to consideration. He had shocked her enough for one evening ; he could now afford to humor her sentimentality, as far as his dignity permitted.

"The fact is, Miss Bella," he began leisurely, tossing the charm of his watch-chain up and down on his index-finger, "love, before marriage, has a hard struggle for existence, through a long engagement with its lovers' quarrels, experimental flirtations, and other fatalities. You know yourself——"

"Indeed I do not, Mr. Larkin," she interrupted, eagerly.

"I mean by observation, not from experience," he

3

rejoined, with laughing eyes. "You know how often it dies prematurely, and its little corpse is, after marriage, decked out pathetically into a semblance of life. Husband and wife walk on tiptoe, as if afraid to disturb it, though they both know that the trump of doom could not rouse it into life. If, on the other hand, love is born after marriage, it is such a delicate little thing and so much depends upon its survival, that no sane person would expose it to the rough and haphazard treatment which it often has to suffer at the hands of ignorant lovers. By such tender care, applied during its infancy, love has a much better chance of survival, and soon grows strong enough to take care of itself."

The young man sipped his coffee leisurely out of a thick cup of white crockery, and made two or three sandwiches disappear under his moustache, while he delivered this fanciful discourse on the nature of love. He looked solid, reliable, and aggressively masculine, as he stood there in his closely-buttoned frock-coat (he had a stubborn prejudice against the swallow-tail), and uttered sententious phrases which obviously delighted himself as much as they did his listener. He stood with his legs somewhat apart, and occasionally, while speaking, balanced himself upon his toes. The four fingers of his hands, when they were not occupied, were usually in his trousers' pockets, while the thumbs moved slowly up and down on the border of his waistcoat, keeping pace with the labor of his brain, as a pendulum does with that of a clock.

Miss Robbins, who watched him with the same devotion when he ate as when he talked, did not attempt to conceal the pleasure she felt at having him make concessions to her sentiments.

"Then you do believe in love?" she exclaimed, joyfully, arresting a teaspoon with ice-cream on its way to her dainty mouth.

Horace put his coffee cup on the table, brushed some crumbs from his coat with his napkin, and having relieved Miss Robbins of her saucer, offered her his arm.

"You do believe in love, don't you?" she repeated, coaxingly.

"I have said nothing of the kind," he answered, gazing at her with an amused expression. "I am afraid we shall have to begin all over again."

It was but a little after ten when the guests began to take their leave, and both host and hostess indicated by half-suppressed yawns that they had no objection to their departure.

"I do hope you have had a pleasant evening," or "I hope you have enjoyed yourself," they said to each one as he came up to shake hands; and the reply was, "Yes, I thank you very much," or "I have had a perfectly lovely time," according as the departing guest was of the male or the female gender. While a few vivacious couples were still lingering, a rough-looking functionary in shirt-sleeves came in and began to remove the table and put out one gas-jet after another. So far from being offended, they took it in good part, and joked familiarly with him on his lack of hospitality.

Outside the air was chill and raw, and the moon, whose face was entangled in misty cobwebs, was vainly trying to unveil. A white mist hovered over the surface of the lake, and drifted in shreds up the hill-sides. But out of the mist came the gay voices of young people; shrill little laughs, petulant cries, and hysterical shrieks, which held the same proportion to their provocation as a hen's cackle, with all the sympathetic commotion of the poultry-yard, does to one little innocent egg. It was regarded as perfectly proper in Torryville for young men to escort the young girls home from parties, and to linger as long on the way as they saw fit. The chaperon was an unknown character, and parents felt like awkward intruders, if by chance they dropped in upon their daughter when she was "having company." It did not occur either to Mr. or Mrs. Larkin, as they drove down the hill-side in a high buggy (which was a monument of discomfort) to inquire about Gertrude, or to trouble themselves about how or when she reached home. They knew that young men were apt to be more entertaining to a girl of her age than her parents, and they saw no impropriety in having her consult her preferences. The gainer by this arrangement was Professor Ramsdale, who in a state of tranquil bliss marched down the steep slope, holding Gertrude's arm as tightly as formerly he had held her waist. He made some spasmodic efforts to be poetical, hoping thereby to induce her to talk. He related soberly how on one occasion, when he was in college, he had felt a strong impulse to write a poem to the moon, but after two hours' labor had got no further than the first line. She then naturally inquired what the first line was, to which he replied: "Oh, moon!" but could get no further.

This seemed so irresistibly funny that she began to laugh, and she continued to laugh nearly all the way, until they reached the streets of the village. Ramsdale was so elated at her appreciation of his unintentional humor, that he seized the opportunity to mention something that he had long had at heart.

"Do you suppose you have the courage to share a scholar's quiet and uneventful life, Miss Gertrude?" he asked, with an eloquence which bore marks of preparation.

"That would largely depend upon who the scholar was," said Gertrude, maliciously.

There was something in the tone of her voice which discouraged him, but after a reflective pause he again began :

"Suppose it was one who loved you?"

"Oh, that wouldn't make so much difference," she answered, recklessly; "the question would rather be whether I loved him."

"Well, suppose you did?"

"That is a very daring thing to suppose, Mr. Ramsdale. It is one of the things which in the Latin grammar they would have put in the imperfect subjunctive."

"Why so?"

"Because it is contrary to fact."

The bantering tone in which she spoke seemed yet to leave a little hope that she might not be in earnest. And determined to have the subject finally disposed of, he took courage, after another pause, to remark :

"A vine-embowered cottage in a quiet university town would not satisfy your ambition, Miss Gertrude, would it?"

"That would all depend upon who lived in it."

"Suppose I lived in it?"

"Then I don't see what it has to do with my ambition."

"I mean, of course, in case we were married."

"Ah, there you are again in the imperfect subjunctive," she ejaculated, laughing; "but to be serious, Mr. Ramsdale, you are so good a man that you deserve a wife who will love you in the present indicative. I cannot."

CHAPTER IV.

THE SCHOLAR IN POLITICS.

The town of Torryville was originally built on low, swampy land, where a couple of small streams flow into the lake. The first settlers, as well as their descendants, were soundly shaken for this piece of folly ; for the ague came and made its home among them, though it was regarded as high treason to recognize its existence. It had been known to exist in the neighboring county, but in Torryville not a case had ever occurred that was not imported from elsewhere. This belief did not prevent those who had real estate in the town from selling at a sacrifice, and rebuilding their homes up along the eastern hill-side, which had a natural drainage and was free from malarial influences. It looked from a distance as if the whole town, in the effort to escape from the disadvantages of its original position, was climbing "the hill ;" and stately houses of wood, brick, and sandstone, surrounded by pretty garden-patches, dotted the green eastern slope, on the crest of which lay the great piles of masonry which collectively constituted the Larkin University. Half-way down the slope, a little to the north of the inhabited portion, the white obelisks and broken symbolical columns of the cemetery gleamed among the foliage of elms and chestnuts and maples. Although medical experts had proved again and again that the dead, in their picturesque resting-place, were engaged in slaying their descendants—that, in other words, the cemetery poisoned the wells of the town —it took twenty years of agitation before a reservoir was built and the water saved from contamination. And even then, it would not have been done, if Mr. Larkin had not, for the welfare of his University, championed the cause, and demonstrated with irrefutable figures that it was a paying investment. The clerical argument (which had hitherto had most weight) that the building of a reservoir would imply distrust of Divine Providence, then gradually disappeared and was heard of no more. The same fate befell the ghastly joke which originated in student circles, that the Torryvilleans were cannibals, because they drank their ancestors.

One evening in October of the year in which our narrative opens, a crowd of citizens of all degrees was gathered in the Main Street, outside of a great barn-like building which looked like an exaggerated cigar-box, and rejoiced in the name of "Tappan's Opera House." The street, which was lined at irregular intervals with hitching-posts for farmers' horses, had the ragged and shabby look of the main business street in most country towns. Tall angular brick buildings devoid of style loomed up between one-story wooden shanties, exhibiting big glaring signs, with the names of job printers, book-sellers, hardware dealers, dentists, and saddlers. Whether you looked up or down, the irregular line of the roofs resembled that of a broken-toothed comb. The middle of the street was muddy, and full of holes, showing here and there remnants of a pavement ; but the stone sidewalks were dry and would have been comfortable for walking, if they had not been encumbered with empty boxes and barrels, which in fair weather served as seats for that part of the male population which was socially inclined. To-night they were occupied by boys who in the dearth of other amusement hooted, yelled, blew fish-horns, and cheered or groaned as the prominent citizens of the village filed into Tappan's Hall. For there was going to be a Republican primary for the nomination of delegates for the county convention. The little clique of six men who "ran" the politics of the town had suffered a defeat at the last election, and had therefore found it advisable, in the words of the Torryville *Herald*, "to rally the business interests, the virtue and the intelligence of the community about the grand old banner." They had therefore issued a ringing appeal, full of warlike similes, to the Republican voters of the county, and invited their active participation in the primaries and nominating conventions of the party. Even the quiet professors on the Hill, who rarely voted in off-years, unless a candidate sent a buggy to bring them to the polls, were summoned "to save the county from the ruin and disgrace of a Democratic victory ; " and as there had recently been a good deal of discussion in the press as to the political duty of scholars, most of them braved the jeers of the hilarious boys on the dry-goods boxes, and entered the hall where the destinies of the republic were to be decided.

"Shoot that hat!" someone yelled, as Professor Dowd came in sight, wearing an unseasonable white hat ; and a tremendous chorus of hooting, whistling, shrieking, and Indian war-whoops followed.

"Hooray for old Grant!" a small boy shouted irrelevantly, and the same ear-splitting chorus again rent the air.

When Mr. Larkin appeared, accompanied by his two nephews, the crowd went wild with enthusiasm ; but through the noise all sorts of disrespectful remarks might be heard.

"How are you, old chap?" "Pull down your vest!" "Give us a chaw of tobaccer, will yer?" were some of the observations which greeted the old gentleman's ears, as he elbowed his way to the door of the hall. He nodded smiling to the boys over his shoulder, feeling no resentment, but rather pride, at their affectionate familiarity.

The political wire-pullers, who were present in force, received him with effusive cordiality. Horace and Aleck were likewise heartily welcomed, but declined to take seats among the party managers. One of the latter, an alert little red-whiskered man, named Mr. Dallas, called the primary to order, and made a speech about the poor negroes in the South, who were slaughtered like cattle if they ventured to exercise their political rights. The Democrats, he said, were traitors and copperheads, and it was an outrage for the people of this county to have allowed them to elect their candidates last November. He spoke throughout as if the Democrats were not citizens, but a hostile, invading force, which plotted destruction and the overthrow of the liberties of the land. In order to prevent further mischief in the South and elsewhere, it was necessary to elect only Republicans to office in Talbot County. He felt confident that in presenting the following names to the primary he was giving voice to the feelings of every voter to whom the principles of the grand old Republican "pairty" were sacred and precious. He then read the list of the delegates, accompanying each name with an eloquent eulogy ; and, as the evening was already far advanced, and he was confident of the unanimity of sentiment which prevailed in the meeting, he felt justified in asking the nomination of the five gentlemen he had named by acclamation, and that they be left unpledged as to their votes in the convention.

A generous round of applause rewarded Mr. Dallas's eloquence, although he spoke through his nose and occasionally got into conflict with the English grammar. He was followed by a bilious-looking tanner, named Graves, who spoke in the same strain, only more excitedly. It appeared that the very destiny of the nation was at stake, and that unless the candidates proposed to the primary were elected, he—Mr. Graves—would not like to be answerable for the consequences. He hinted at the direst calamities — business disturbance, national bankruptcy, the re-enslavement of the negroes, general anarchy and ruin. As he took his seat with a perspiring countenance, flushed with noble excitement, a few cat-calls were heard, but these were immediately drowned in a burst of applause, which showed that the temper of the assembly was patriotic rather than critical. A few there were, however, who failed to be carried away by the general enthusiasm.

"What impudence !" whispered Horace Larkin to his brother. "That fellow Dallas and his gang, after having conferred with Senator Harkness, meet in his back office, and make up a slate, consisting without exception of political bummers. Then they try to make sensible people believe that the country will go to the dogs, unless they are elected."

"But why don't you say that, Horace ? You would be doing a good thing if you could open people's eyes."

"Say it ? What's the good of saying it ? If people are such fools as to believe such buncombe, I am not the one to undeceive them. Moreover, those fellows have the political machinery in their hands, and I don't care to make them my enemies."

"I didn't think you were such a coward, Horace," said his brother, reproachfully.

"Coward ! No, I am not a coward ; but neither am I a fool."

"You mean to say that you may yourself some day want a nomination ? "

"Well, I don't mind telling you that some day I may."

"And you would consent to run on the same ticket with such a disreputable shyster as that fellow, Burton, whom they are going to put up for circuit judge in the place of a learned and honorable man like Judge Wolf ?"

"What does the rest of the ticket concern me ? I don't assume responsibility for anybody's morals but my own."

The brothers were yet talking when they heard the

chairman put the motion to nominate the ticket by acclamation. There was no question but that it would have
been overwhelmingly carried, when suddenly, to everybody's surprise, Alexander Larkin jumped up and addressed the chair.

"I cannot but think, Mr. Chairman," he began, "that,
whether intentionally or not, you have on the present occasion shown small respect for the intelligence of the Republican party, which you have just, in such eloquent
words, exalted. You have invited here the best citizens
of our town, under the pretence of wishing to consult with
them as to who ought to represent them in the legislature
and conduct their public business during the ensuing year ;
and when the citizens accept your invitation, you first treat
them to a tirade concerning the condition of the negro in
the South, as a preparation to springing upon them a
ready-made slate, which you and a few of your friends
have agreed upon in your back office."

The consternation of the gentlemen on the platform, at
this unexpected attack, was almost ridiculous to behold.
They at first scarcely knew what to make of it ; but when
loud cheering for a moment interrupted the daring orator,
Mr. Dallas, white with excitement, stepped forward and
called out :

"The gentleman is out of order."

It was astonishing with what quickness the temper of
the meeting had changed ; the unheard-of boldness of the
young man had won its sympathy and admiration. A derisive shout greeted the chairman's declaration.

"May I inquire," asked Aleck, much emboldened by
the cheering, "in accordance with what rule of Cush-
ing or any other recognized manual of parliamentary proceedings I am out of order ?"

"You have made no motion," cried Dallas.

"But I supposed your motion was debatable ; indeed, I
should judge it was very much so."

"I rule you out of order, sir," shouted the chairman,
quickly changing his tactics, "because you are not talking
on my motion ; your remarks are personal and irrelevant."

"Then I offer this amendment to your motion," Aleck retorted promptly, "that the delegates be elected by ballot,
not by acclamation. This amendment naturally takes
precedence of your motion, and I presume you will not rule
me out of order if I proceed to give my reasons for offering
it."

Mr. Dallas was at his wits' end. He stood staring with a look of astonishment and disgust upon the applauding multitude. He had to head this incipient reformer off, at all risks, or the spirit of rebellion would spread, and the occupation of himself and his comrades would be irretrievably gone. While he was cudgelling his brain to invent an expedient, one of his colleagues, Mr. Watson, stepped forward and whispered something in his ear ; whereat his troubled countenance brightened. Mr. Watson then descended into the audience, and was seen no more. But suddenly, from the part of the hall which he was visiting, a man jumped up and moved an adjournment.

"It appears," said he, "that this primary has been packed by the Democrats, and I move, sir, an adjournment, subject to the call of the chair."

That was a bold move, but a little too bare-faced to succeed. Three men jumped up from different parts of the hall, and excitedly demanded the floor.

"The gentlemen are out of order," Mr. Dallas again declared ; "a motion to adjourn is not debatable. It has been moved and seconded that this meeting adjourn, subject to the call of the chair. Those in favor of the motion will signify it by saying 'aye.'"

A dozen spiritless 'ayes' popped up irregularly, here and there, like frogs out of a pond.

"Those opposed——"

The "nays" came with a volume and a determination which made the result unmistakable. The overwhelming decision made Mr. Dallas afraid of resorting to his last expedient, viz., to declare that "the ayes have it," and before anyone could raise a question, leave the platform and the hall. There was always the danger of alienating the party and being defeated at the polls, instead of conciliating it and winning a victory. In pure despair and to gain time, he declared that "the chair was in doubt ;" but that was an awkward move, and it was greeted with derisive shouts of laughter.

There still remained one possible remedy. Mr. Dallas gave the chair to the bilious-looking tanner, and after a whispered conversation with Mr. Larkin, descended from the platform and walked up to where Aleck and Horace were sitting. He shook hands with both the brothers, as if they were his dearest friends, quite forgetting that he had already greeted them on their entrance. After a smiling inquiry regarding their health, he asked Aleck if he would not have the kindness to accompany him to the committee room, behind the stage. Aleck, though he had no desire for a private interview, arose and was amazed to see Mr. Dallas put his arm through his and begin to talk to him with a sort of laughing cordiality which seemed to imply that they understood each other perfectly. It began to dawn upon him that, perhaps, the wily politician meant to discredit him, by raising at least a doubt in the minds of the assembly as to whether he was not himself in the ring, and had made this little row at the instigation of the very men whom he was pretending to antagonize. The thought drove the blood to his face and made him pause for a moment at the door of the committee room, which Mr. Dallas had opened before him. He knew that he could not match himself in cunning with this accomplished trickster, and felt, as he was about to enter his den, an uneasy expectation that in the end he would manage to outwit him.

As soon as they were inside the room, which was decorated with campaign portraits and littered with torn paper and envelopes, Mr. Dallas handed his young friend a box of cigars, and asked him to help himself.

"My dear young fellow," he began, with affectionate deliberation, as soon as they had both seated themselves ; "you stand upon the threshold of a career which you can make almost anything you like. I mean what I say, sir," he continued, as he observed in Aleck an inclination to contradict ; "I mean it literally. With your opportunities, your fine appearance—yes, sir, I must insist upon it—with your fine appearance, and your commanding talents, there need be nothing which, in this grand republic of ours, you might not legitimately aspire to."

This affectionate tone had, at first, the effect of half disarming the young man, and if he had only had confidence in Mr. Dallas's character he would, no doubt, have surrendered. But as he recalled the situation clearly to his mind, and his own purpose never to compromise with evil, he felt his courage rise.

"I shall aspire to nothing, Mr. Dallas," he said, a little hotly, "which will compel me to put my self-respect in my pocket."

"Oh, of course not, of course not," rejoined the politician, suavely ; but, after a pause he added, laughing, "though, to be sure, that is not a bad place to have it— ready to be hauled out whenever there is call for it."

Though he was not sure it was good policy, he could not deny himself the luxury of the joke.

"What I mean to say," he continued, as if eager to brush the little Mephistophelian hint out of sight, "is that you have a great political future before you, if you make a prudent use of your opportunities. I may as well tell you at once that if you care to go to the legislature, I think we can make a niche for you. We only put up that fellow, Greene, because we had no one better. But I'll see that he is taken care of, anyway."

There was to Aleck something very insinuating in Mr. Dallas's speech; something well-meant and elder-brotherly, which would have made an abrupt refusal on his part seem little less than brutal. There could be no doubt that he meant what he said; he had it in his power to make the nomination, and Aleck flattered himself that, if nominated, there could be no doubt of his election. It was no very grand thing, to be sure, to be an assembly-man; but it was necessary to begin on the lowest rung of the ladder if he meant to climb to the highest ones. He had a sudden widening of vision, and all sorts of alluring things rose up, one behind another, in the dim distance.

"I believe, without flattering myself," he remarked, with a slight embarrassment, "that I have a considerable aptitude for public affairs."

It occurred to him, when he had uttered this sentiment, that in all probability it must have struck his interlocutor as very fresh. Possibly he was sitting and laughing at him in his sleeve. But the kindly gravity with which Mr. Dallas answered precluded such a suspicion.

"Yes," he said, "I haven't a doubt of it. I wonder at myself that I never thought of you before."

This adroit flattery was like music to Aleck's ears; it put him off his guard and, in his agreeable exhilaration, made him seem at peace with all the world.

"I may say," he observed, guilelessly, "that politics has always had a great attraction to me. I studied political economy in college, and have since collected a very fair library in that science and in constitutional history."

He could not tell why his ears burned so uncomfortably, why such a terrible awkwardness stole over him, before these words were fairly out of his mouth. He looked anxiously at Mr. Dallas, and thought he detected a ghost of a smile lurking about the corners of his mouth. At that very moment a great laugh, followed by hooting and cat-calls, reached him from the hall. He sprang up, knocking over his chair, and darted toward the door.

"Hold on !" cried Dallas, "what's your hurry ?"

"I must go."

"No, don't go yet. I have got to make some little arrangements with you before presenting your name to the convention."

"I won't make any arrangements with you, Mr. Dallas."

"Now, don't go off the handle like a goose. I thought we understood each other perfectly."

"Yes, we do. That is to say, I understand you perfectly ; you got me in here in order to keep me away from the meeting, where I was interfering with your plans. You have been sitting here trying to bribe me to desert my convictions, simply because you were afraid I should make trouble for you and smash your slate if I stayed in the hall."

"Aleck Larkin, look here !" cried the politician, springing forward and placing his back against the door ; "if you open your d—— mouth again to-night, I'll—I'll make you regret it until your dying day."

"All right ! Only, please, get away from the door, so I can get out."

"You've got a minute to decide in."

"Go away from the door, I say, or I'll knock you down."

Mr. Dallas looked, not angrily, but with shrewd scrutiny at the young man's face ; then thrusting his under lip contemptuously forward, moved away. As the door closed upon Aleck's retreating figure he gave a whistle, then broke into a long and picturesquely composite oath.

It was in a curious frame of mind the young reformer re-entered the hall. Had he, or had he not, been on the point of yielding ? He had always, in speculative moments, imagined himself repelling temptation with heroic decision and contempt ; and here he had actually entertained the proposition to accept a bribe as the price of his silence ! What was doubly humiliating, he was not now positive whether his sudden indignation had been due to outraged moral feeling, or to the discovery of the trick which the politician had been playing upon him. But if he had been weak, he would seize the opportunity to retrieve himself. He felt his breast swelling with leonine courage. Now let them come, and they should find out whom they had to deal with. Happily, Professor Dowd

had been occupying the time, while he was behind the
stage, with a lecture on Kleon and the Athenian democracy, the purpose of which was to show that a democracy was only strong as long as it was truly representative, but that its days were numbered as soon as it fell
into the hands of an oligarchic clique. He had the courage to declare that the six party managers who carried
out the behests of the all-powerful, office-dispensing senator in Washington, were such an oligarchy, and that it was
high time the people rebelled against their rule. This
declaration had occasioned the mingled shouts of approval
and dissent which had recalled Aleck to his senses, as he
was sliding along the broad and slippery way which leads
to office and political distinction. The air as he entered
the hall was thick with the smoke of cheap cigars, which
hung like a bluish mist above the heads of the people ;
and the light from the globeless gas-jets shone dimly, like
signal-lights in a fog. The glare of the hideous white
plaster on the walls hurt his eyes, and there was not an
object anywhere the contemplation of which could have
afforded pleasure to the most easily contented. The
crowd, which consisted of all sorts and conditions of men,
but in which the farmer element predominated, vaguely
repelled him, not 'because he was afraid of it, but because
it was ill-dressed, ill-mannered, ill-looking. Under the
stress of a mere æsthetic antipathy, he felt the courage
which his indignation had kindled in him slowly ebb
away. But, if he did not mean to disgrace himself, he
could not afford to yield to any such feeling. He hastily
ascertained that his amendment had not yet been voted
upon, and in order that there might be no mistake as to
his own attitude, he arose when Professor Dowd had sat
down and demanded the floor.

"Mr. Chairman," he said, "I have not had the privilege of hearing all the remarks of the last speaker, but
from his eloquent peroration I conclude that he is in
favor of the amendment which I have submitted. I think
it is time for the Republicans of this county to wake up
and take a look at their political affairs. What does your
privilege of voting at present amount to, gentlemen ? Is
it not the privilege of choosing between two sets of men,
in the nomination of which you have had no hand, and the
one of which is usually no better and no worse than the
other. Do we not all go to the polls with a protest in our
hearts, or with a discouraged or an outraged feeling, as if

we had been shrewdly circumvented and outwitted ? Are
these the men we want to carry on our public business—
men whom, with one or two honorable exceptions, we
would never think of intrusting with any private business
in which we had large interests at stake ? This sprinkling
of respectability, fellow-republicans, is an old trick, and it
can no more redeem a bad ticket than a sprinkling of salt
can make a rotten fish wholesome. The opportunity
which is to-day presented to you, of showing your influence in favor of a ticket which shall be clean throughout,
and representative of the best intelligence and manhood
of our county, may not soon return, and I therefore beg of
you to support me in this effort to reject the names which
have been proposed, and to nominate others worthy of
your suffrages, both as regards ability and character. I
therefore urge you to favor my amendment, that each
candidate be voted upon separately, that the nominations
be made by ballot, not by acclamation."

When the customary noise of shouting, clapping, stamp-
ing, and hissing had subsided, an old round-backed farmer
arose, and in a raucous and solemn voice accused "the
young feller as has been makin' the rumpus to-night" of
being a paid emissary of the Democrats—those arch-plot-
ters and enemies of the State—charged with sowing the
seed of dissension among the Republicans, and thereby
breaking up the grand old party which had freed four
million slaves, and saved the Union. The managers on
the platform and their friends, in the meanwhile, were
circulating among the crowd and privately laboring with
each man, alleging that Aleck Larkin was nothing but a
sore-head ; that he had been wanting the nomination for
the Assembly, and that he was kicking up a row simply because the managers had refused point-blank to consider
his name. At the end of about half an hour, during which
speeches had been made on both sides of the question,
they were sure, by actual count, that the amendment would
be rejected, and the chairman felt safe in putting the
question. Tellers were appointed and the ballots were
deposited in two old stove-pipe hats which were placed on
a table in front of the platform. It was nearly eleven
o'clock when the vote was finally declared, and what was
the amazement of Mr. Dallas and his colleagues, when it
was found that their calculations had been all wrong ! One
hundred and ten votes had been cast for the amendment ;
ninety-seven against. Their slate was accordingly broken,

and they were discredited with their master who dispensed favors from Washington. Yet, pending a consultation, they had no choice but to make the best of a bad situation.

Aleck, flushed with victory, stood with his back against the wall, listening to the tremendous applause that greeted the announcement of the result. Dowd, Ramsdale, Dr. Hawk, and a number of other friends made their way through the crowd, and overwhelmed him with praise and congratulations. All prophesied for him a great political future ; some, in their enthusiasm, even hinted that it would not surprise them, before long, to see him in Congress. Of course, he deprecated their zeal and laughed at their prophecies ; but in his heart of hearts, there seemed in that moment nothing beyond the reach of his power. He felt like some strong creature, endowed with wings which can and must bear him higher and higher. It was not the mere accidental result of the vote which buoyed him up ; but the excitement of the struggle itself had something expanding and exhilarating. He had stood shivering on the brink of his resolution, but like a powerful swimmer, when once he has taken a header, he felt a healthful glow pervading his frame. He was enlisted on the side of the powers of light in their world-old struggle with the powers of darkness. He was destined to be one of the leaders in the conflict. Was not such a consciousness enough to consecrate a life, and make it beautiful ?

But here was no time for dreaming. Here was practical work at hand. Mr. Dallas, who again occupied the chair, had, with the best grace possible, declared that nominations were in order, and one of his lieutenants on the floor had made a speech recommending the original nominee on the broken slate. Mr. Burton was an obscure young lawyer, without any other practice than such as his political affiliations brought him. No sooner had the lieutenant sat down than Aleck was again on his feet ; but the chair took no notice of him, and gave the floor to another of his sympathizers who endorsed Burton. A second and a third time Aleck demanded the floor, but each time failed to be recognized by the chair. At last, seeing that the oversight was intentional, he walked up and placed himself right in front of the platform, demanding the right to speak.

"Oh, my dear sir," said Mr. Dallas, smiling ; "why, I

wasn't aware you wanted to speak. I thought, after your
recent effort, you needed rest."

"You evidently mistook your own feelings for mine,"
responded Aleck, promptly, and the audience, always ap-
preciative of a joke, and sympathizing with opposition,
laughed and applauded. The politician had to swallow
the bitter pill ; he gave the floor to his opponent. It is
needless to report the speech which the latter made in
favor of pledging the delegation to vote for the renomination of Judge Wolf, who by his rigid interpretation of the
law and his unaccommodating spirit, had given offence to
the "boys." When, after much discussion and exchange
of acrimonious repartees, a ballot was taken, there proved
to be a majority of fourteen in favor of the proposition.
Pandemonium now broke loose ; everybody seemed bent
upon speaking, while no one cared to listen. In the
midst of this confusion, Aleck made his way to Professor
Wharton, and induced him to nominate his brother Horace as the head of the delegation ; for his name, everyone
would admit, would be a guarantee of good faith. But no
sooner had the Professor revealed his purpose, than Horace rose, and, in a few conventional phrases, thanked for
the honor and declined it. His business engagements, he
said, were of such a nature as to make it impossible for
him, at the present time, to accept any public trust. The
Professor sat down, a trifle disconcerted, and sent bewildered glances in the direction of Aleck, who, as he later
expressed it, had persuaded him to make a fool of himself.
Aleck, however, who in the intoxication of his triumph
had gloried in the opportunity to fulfil one of his
brother's secret wishes, was completely at a loss to account
for his refusal. The sense of power and the thirst for
beneficent activity which had animated him during the
entire evening, suddenly deserted him. There was something utterly disappointing, almost humiliating, to him in
the thought that Horace was unwilling to accept an
honor which he had been instrumental in bestowing.
That subterfuge about private business affairs he knew to
be an invention.

The discussion became interminable and aimless, and
interested Aleck no more. He saw plainly that it was
the chairman's intention to tire out the professors and
their sympathizers in the audience ; and that the departure of but a dozen of them would secure the triumph of
the rest of the slate. The professors were vaguely con-

4

scious of Mr. Dallas's intention, and for this reason stayed until long after midnight ; but gradually hunger and bad air oppressed their lungs and exhausted their patience, and one by one they stole out and pegged up the hill-side. When Mr. Dallas, who had a trusted lieutenant stationed at that door, felt confident beyond peradventure that his friends were in the majority, he cut discussion short; and the result of the ballot this time showed that he had made no miscalculation. His candidates got their required majority. There was now nothing more to be done. Aleck, seeing that he could not prevent the election of the machine delegates, sauntered out and was soon followed by his brother. Old Mr. Larkin, after having refused to keep his nephew in order, had betaken himself home early in the evening. He held Aleck's performances to be as futile as the somersaults of a wooden monkey over a stick, but he liked, for all that, to have him show pluck and readiness of resource. From an educational point of view he approved of " the row," and was entertained by it.

The two brothers walked along in silence, while the dry leaves rustled under their feet. The air was damp, and there was a close, mouldy smell of decaying vegetation. Now and then an aimless gust of wind came careering along and swept the leaves into a whirl, or chased them along like a panic-stricken army.

" Horace," said Aleck, looking up at the waning moon, " why did you refuse that nomination as delegate ? "

" For several reasons," answered Horace.

" Let's hear them."

" Well, first, because I shouldn't care to make Dallas and his gang my enemies."

" Then you mean to enter political life under their auspices ? "

" Theirs are the only auspices in this county, under which political life can be entered."

" Then you really declined because you knew that the nomination came from me ? "

" Well, if you insist upon it, I did."

Aleck glanced toward his brother's averted face, in the twilight ; it looked calm, prudent, and determined. It was the face of a man who was bound to succeed. He felt a sharp pang of regret, of self-pity—of disappointment—he scarcely knew what. He dimly divined the spiritual gulf between himself and Horace. The triumph in which he had exulted had been, after all, but a bonfire of blazing illusions ; and now there was nothing but the ashes left. If it be true that wisdom consists not so much in knowledge gained as in illusions abandoned, his elder brother started with a great advantage over him ; for he was wise already : he had no illusions to abandon.

CHAPTER V.

A FOX AND A TRAP.

Aleck Larkin's political rebellion, the old man's neutrality, and Horace's shrewdness, were the chief topics of
conversation during the two weeks which preceded the
election. In the book-stores and corner groceries, which
were dedicated to the discussion of public events, there
were found not a few who admired the young man's pluck
in taking up arms against so formidable, widely ramified,
and completely organized a power as the Republican machine. But there were many more who laughed at his
presumption, and praised the foresight and self-restraint
of his brother, which before long would have their reward.
About the railroad depot, where the leisured class of the
population sat on trunks and boxes, betting on anything
that turned up, from a dog-fight to a presidential election,
the latter view generally prevailed, and odds were offered,
but never taken, favoring Horace's prospects at the expense of those of his brother.

It was not the public disapproval, however, which
troubled Aleck, but he was bitterly disappointed at his
failure to accomplish what he had set out to do. After
the departure of the University contingent, the regular
machine slate had been elected ; and Judge Wolf, as the
solitary representative of respectability, would, he feared,
be more obnoxious to a convention constituted of office-
holders and their satellites. This latter fear, however,
turned out to be groundless ; for a strong influence in
favor of the Judge made itself manifest from other parts
of the county, and he carried the convention in spite of
the opposition of the machine influence. It was an open
secret, however, that the managers had determined to
knife him on election day because they resented his being
"crammed down their throats," and longed for a chance to
inspire the obnoxious reformers with respect for their
power. Aleck, in spite of his mortification, resolved to
accept the challenge and, if possible, elect his Judge. He

confided his plan to Horace, who laughed at him, called him a visionary, but ended with giving him, under the pledge of secrecy, valuable advice. If he had set his heart on electing his judge, he said, there was but one way to accomplish it, and that was not to say a word about it, but, early on election day, organize a squad of his friends upon whom he could rely, and send a couple of them to each polling place in the county. While these watched the polls, others should be sent about with buggies to hunt up out-of-the-way voters, and on the road persuade them to vote for the Judge.

Election day dawned still and smoky, full of sad autumnal feeling, over the Torryville valley. There was a smell of burning in the air. Elms and maples, half denuded of their foliage, stretched their ragged branches against the sky ; and now and then noiselessly dropped a leaf which went gyrating downward, and softly alighted among the rustling heap which covered the roads and filled the gutters. The silence in the streets had no swelling undertone of chirruping locusts and bird-song ; it seemed dead and heavy ; only interrupted at times by the falling of a chestnut-bur which burst open, revealing the richly brown fruit within, or the crackling of dry branches as an early voter came shuffling along, inspecting the tickets which he had received by mail the night before. Among the very earliest to exercise their civic rights, when the sun had shown his dim and sleepy countenance above the eastern hills, were Aleck and his fellow-conspirators, Hawk and Ramsdale. The latter, though they were, for obvious reasons, not fond of each other, professed a warm friendship for Aleck, and were quite ready to work for the same end where his interests were at stake. They were met on the sidewalk outside the shabby cigar store, upon the counter of which the seven ballot-boxes were placed, by half a dozen electioneering agents who buttonholed them, and tried to pull them aside to urge upon them the claims of different candidates. They were not noisy and argumentative, but mysteriously confidential ; hinting in an undertone at deals and all sorts of nefarious things committed by the opposing party. There was also a middle-aged woman in Bloomer costume, covered from the shoulders to the knees by two huge placards on which was printed, in mammoth letters :

No License ! Vote the
Prohibition Ticket !

She elbowed her way boldly through the crowd of electioneering agents, and presented the three young men with a set of tickets and handbills, bearing the legends : "A Vote for License is a Vote for Hell!" and "Vote for Christ and no Rum!"

"Now, Mr. Larkin, you want to be on the right side in this election," she began, seizing both Aleck's hands and staring straight into his face.

"I am already on the right side, Mrs. French," he answered, laughing ; "you will excuse me, until some other time ; then I'll be happy to discuss the matter with you."

She began, in a sermonizing tone, what was evidently a set speech in favor of prohibition ; and held him at the same time so tightly by the hands that he found it difficult to tear himself away.

"Another time, Mrs. French, another time," he cried, in laughing vexation, as he escaped into the store.

"Another time, you rogue, I shan't want to waste my words upon you," she answered, shaking her clenched fist after him.

He had already prepared his ballots the night before, and lost no time in depositing them. Among the inspectors of election who sat behind the counter and checked off the names in their poll-books, there was apparently one who could not read writing, and another who, if he could write, was unwilling to display his accomplishment. But Mr. Graves, the bilious-looking tanner, who was also seated at the table in an official capacity, was kindly assisting them, and was every moment having his pen over in their books. He nodded with a malicious smile to Aleck, as his name was called, and licking an unlighted cigar, one end of which he had been chewing, observed pleasantly : "Good Republican weather, Mr. Larkin! A heavy vote means a Republican victory."

"Shouldn't wonder, Mr. Graves. I suppose you conclude from that, that Providence is on your side."

"If I did not believe that He was on our side, sir," Graves responded, with great earnestness, "I'd be d—d if I'd ever cast another ballot in my life."

Aleck had, in accordance with his brother's advice, organized his plot with great secrecy. He had made arrangements with about twenty of his friends, several of whom were students in the University, that they were to take early trains to the other towns and villages in the county, hire buggies (which had already been telegraphed for in advance) at his expense, and spend the entire day, laboring by all legitimate means for Judge Wolf's election. He had reserved Torryville for himself, as he knew that the influence of his name would be more potent there than elsewhere. He had just separated from his friends and given them the last instructions, when he espied his brother's close-buttoned figure approaching from the upper end of the street. Horace was walking along with a deliberate step, gazing straight down before him, as his habit was when he was absorbed in thought. It struck Aleck again what a solid, weighty, and definite personality his brother was. He never looked aimlessly about him, like most men, but had his eyes as his thoughts clearly fixed upon some exact object. Though he admired him greatly, he never could get quite near him; he could not deny that he was a little bit afraid of his pitiless logic and cold worldly sense.

"Hallo," said Horace, taking his cigar out of his mouth; "why did you run away from your breakfast?"

"Oh, I forgot!"

"Forgot to eat breakfast! I had no idea you were so unscrupulous."

"Unscrupulous?"

"Yes, unscrupulous. A man who, in order to accomplish his designs, gets up at five o'clock in the morning, forgetting even to pay the flesh its due, is unscrupulous."

He looked so serious that Aleck, for a moment, was in doubt whether he was joking or in earnest. "But I acted on your advice, Horace," he said, with an uncertain smile.

"I did not advise you," responded his brother, imperturbably; "I did not pronounce upon the morality of your undertaking. I merely said that if you wished to elect your man, you would have to employ the very methods which you condemned in others. I wished to catch you in inconsistency, in order to give you an illustration of the impracticability of your high moral standards applied to politics, or in fact, to anything."

"Then you mean to say that you intentionally laid a trap for me?"

"Yes, if you like you may call it that. I did it, because I have your welfare at heart, and wish to teach you the road to success, while you are yet young enough to profit by the lesson."

A strange strident sound, like the grating of an iron gate, came from the sky above them; on looking up, they saw a flock of wild geese following in horseshoe-shaped flight their leader, who, with his long neck outstretched, was guiding their way to a sunnier clime. A silence fell upon the two brothers, while they stood watching the winged troop, as it vanished in the smoky air beyond the towers of the University buildings.

"What a happy time they have of it," said Aleck, "to be flying so high above all moral perplexities."

"In that respect you resemble them," answered Horace ; "it is just that which I object to in you, that you are a high-flier whose actions have no root in facts, but in fond imaginings."

There was a real distress in the younger brother's face, as he listened to this unfeeling criticism. "What have I done, Horace, that displeases you so?" he asked, with touching simplicity.

"Displeases me! You make me sick with your slipshod habits of thought. I have not said a word about my own displeasure. I have merely said that, as a political reformer, you have adopted the very methods of the organization you have set out to reform."

"Why, I have distinctly said to all my friends that they are only to influence the voters by honest persuasion——"

"And free buggy rides."

"I have told them to refrain from all abuse and slander——"

"But you have yourself employed intimidation."

"Intimidation!"

"Have you not called upon the family butcher and baker and candlestick maker, and told them why you intend to vote for Wolf?"

"Well, what wrong is there in that?"

"Though you have not said it, you have led them to suppose that the influence of our family, which, you know, counts for a great deal in the town, is thrown on the side of your candidate, and that the loss of our patronage may result from voting against him. That is what I call intimidation."

"Why, Horace, I assure you——"

"My dear boy, don't defend yourself. I am not blaming you. I am merely holding up a looking-glass to you. A truthful looking-glass is often the severest of censors. Good-morning."

He struck a match on the sole of his boot and lighted his cigar, which had gone out during the discussion.

"By the way," he said, between the puffs of smoke, "you have done some very valuable work for the machine."

"For the machine?"

"Yes. I shouldn't wonder if by your work for Wolf you have saved the whole ticket. And, between ourselves, I quite agree with you that it is bad."

He nodded, with a gleam of amusement in his eyes, to the unhappy reformer, and strolled toward the polls, striking his heels against the wooden sidewalk. Aleck, half stupefied by this parting shot, stood gazing after him with a look of bewilderment and distress.

"I have made a fool of myself," he muttered; and, in a mood of bitter disillusion, sauntered homeward.

CHAPTER VI.

A QUEER FATHER CONFESSOR.

The Reverend Arthúr Robbins, estimable though he was, and anxious to be of help, was not the kind of man to whom you would naturally resort in hours of tribulation. He could be, at times, mildly pastoral; but he was never priestly. When, for all that, Alexander Larkin, after a day spent in keen misery, betook himself in the evening to the Congregational parsonage, it was chiefly because he felt an acute need of sympathy, and Mr. Robbins was equally agreeable as a talker and a listener. He was always delighted to see you, made you feel as if you conferred an honor upon him by calling, expended his best cigars upon you, and, as long as you were not in obvious conflict with the ten commandments, approved of everything you said and did. He could even, when the humor took him, tell mildly improper anecdotes in a hushed voice and with a delicious sense of their wickedness, while he glanced half anxiously toward the door which separated his study from the virginal bower of his daughters. There was the story of the clergyman who, at a bachelor's funeral, prayed for the sorrowing children, and half a dozen others in the same strain. Clergymen and deacons were invariably their heroes.

It was this kind of gently soothing entertainment which Aleck needed to heal the bruises which his brother's pitiless words had inflicted. He had spent the morning, since his return from the polls, in his room, torturing himself with doubts and self-examination. He had been making a journey of exploration into the untrodden regions of his heart, and he had come back filled with distress at the things he had seen. Now, without directly making a confidant of Mr. Robbins, he wished to be made to feel that his humiliating conclusions regarding himself were all wrong, that he was in reality a good and estimable fellow.

The clergyman had hastily divested himself of his dress-

ing-gown and was adjusting the collar of his coat, when
his visitor was ushered into his study.

"Ah, my dear Mr. Larkin, I am delighted to see you,"
he said, extending a soft, warm hand to Aleck ; "pray sit
down—here, this chair is more comfortable—and what
kind of a cigar can I offer you? Mild, middling, or
strong? Here, take your choice. If you'll allow me to
advise you, I would recommend these Almansors ; they
have the real flavor that rejoices the soul."

It was Mr. Robbins's habit, when he liked a man, to take
him, as it were, by storm—to overwhelm him with cordiality ; while he possessed in the same degree the faculty of
chilling those whom he disliked to the marrow of their
bones. As a clergyman in a small country town, he could,
of course, not have indulged the latter luxury, if he had
been pecuniarily dependent upon his congregation. But
the fact was, Mr. Robbins had, in his callow days, married
a rich but preternaturally homely wife, who, after having
presented him with five daughters, four of whom had inherited her lack of chin, betook herself to that realm where
a lack of chin is not incompatible with happiness. But
during her earthly career an excess of nose and the
above-named deficiency made her life a martyrdom. She
had hungered for her husband's admiration with a hopeless and unwearied passion. She knew that, however
much he endeavored to conceal it, he disliked the sight
of her. He was something of an epicurean, with æsthetic
tastes and inclined to luxurious habits. The very instinct
which had prompted him to woo her prevented him from
loving her. The birth in rapid succession of four daughters, whom according to their profiles you would have
classed in the order of Rodents, was accepted by their
father as a chastening discipline, or a reminder from Providence that the unworthy motive of his marriage was yet
unforgiven. But when No. 5 came and developed a clean-
cut, well-proportioned countenance, he freely forgave her
her sex and took her to his heart. Though his suspected
difference with Heaven had never greatly troubled him,
the reconciliation expressed in this child's fair features
seemed a great and momentous event, worthy of a special
celebration. After having pondered various ways of
worthily commemorating it, Mr. Robbins sent to New
York for a case of fine old Madeira and a dozen boxes of
Almansor cigars. He kept these treasures strictly for himself, knowing that there were neither palates nor nostrils

in Torryville capable of appreciating them. He made an exception of Aleck, first because he liked him, secondly because he cherished a secret ambition to make him his son-in-law, and thirdly because his face and his talk showed him to be a man of fine senses.

The conspicuous way in which Mr. Robbins favored his handsome daughter at the expense of the unattractive ones occasioned a good deal of comment in his congregation, and more than one sister had attempted to give him a realizing sense of the disapproval with which his unfatherly conduct was regarded. But here the advantage of a bank account became manifest. With the moral support which it gave him, Mr. Robbins became obtuse of comprehension and freezingly and uncomfortably polite ; and his monitresses became ill at ease, and wished themselves on the other side of the door. If there were mutterings of discontent in his church (as sometimes there were), he pursued the even tenor of his way and refused to be annoyed. If he had been a poor man, he would, of course, have been remonstrated with, and perhaps requested to resign. But a pastor who himself subscribed to the raising of the church debt could not be treated in that off-hand way ; and everything considered, he was a good and fairly eloquent man, not quite sound on eternal punishment, perhaps, but otherwise highly acceptable. His sermons had also at times shown a dangerous laxity in other doctrines, and for months he seemed to be drifting, Sunday by Sunday, ever further toward all sorts of modern heresies and "liberal" interpretations. But just as he seemed to be on the point of taking the fatal plunge, he would pull up suddenly, as you stop a run-away horse, and return the next Sunday to the bluest and fiercest Calvinism. The flames of the pit fairly blazed with their sulphurous fumes through those discourses, and "the old people" were comforted. As a matter of fact it was mere fright at the results toward which he was drifting which led Mr. Robbins to call a halt in that energetic fashion. But when his fear was over, he began again to drift, preached about seven geological periods, which were evidently what was meant by the seven days of creation, and involved himself in all sorts of futile ingenuities to prove that the Bible had anticipated all the discoveries of science. Since his wife's death, nine years ago, he was more frequently subject to these attacks of liberalism, possibly because, her sinister presence being removed from his life, he acquired a greater faith in the general benevolence of Providence. On the whole, he felt himself on good terms with the Ruler of the Universe, being confident that he was rather a meritorious creature, and unquestionably, in morality and intelligence, above the average of his kind. Even his four "Rodents" were not the affliction they once had been ; and he was able, without much effort, to treat them with kindness. They apparently accepted their fate with stoicism, as being in the inscrutable nature of things, regarded their father with shy respect out of their bead-like eyes, and gave him at times an uneasy feeling that all sorts of curious things might be going on inside of those heads, of which he had not the faintest conception. The alertness of their black eyes, which nothing escaped, their queer mute communications, as they sat with him at the table, and their mysterious, suppressed titters when nothing had occurred that seemed to anyone else ridiculous, strengthened in him the impression of their alienism—as if they were mere sojourners in his house rather than his children.

Alexander Larkin, being a frequent visitor at the parsonage, had been acquainted with the peculiar relations of the household from his boyhood. He was what the Germans call a "house-friend," with a definite place in each one's estimation. He marvelled at nothing and needed no explanations ; and half of the charm of his society consisted, in his host's eyes, in this easy and natural familiarity. If Mr. Robbins, in his heart, hoped that he came to see Arabella, he was not on that account less inclined to claim his full share of his attention. Arabella's preference for the elder brother her father professed to regard as a caprice which he was at a loss to understand. He had, indeed, the highest respect for Horace's ability, but he was a trifle afraid of him, and could not persuade himself to like him.

"Pardon me, parson," Alexander was saying, as he settled back luxuriously in his easy-chair, "but are not these cigars of yours rather unclerical?"

"You mean to say," his host replied, "that a clergyman should smoke to mortify the flesh?"

"Oh, I don't profess to have any opinion as to what a clergyman should do and not do," rejoined the young man ; "and, anyway, the time is past when heretics were smoked."

"Yes ; now they smoke instead of being smoked. But I hope you don't mean to say that I am a heretic?"

"No; I am aware that this is one of your orthodox weeks."

"Hush, my dear boy, what are you saying there?" ejaculated Robbins, with hushed anxiety.

"Oh, I am not going to take you to task. I like your heretical sermons better than the orthodox ones."

Robbins laughed gently to himself as, with keen enjoyment, he blew the cigar smoke toward the great lamp on the table.

"You are a sly dog," he said, "but I'll admit there is a grain of truth in your insinuation. The fact is, the old people in the church get alarmed occasionally at my advanced views, and I am obliged, now and then, to set them at rest in regard to my orthodoxy."

Aleck had no desire to press the subject further, as he saw awkward possibilities in it.

"Mr. Robbins," he began, after a pause, "I came here to ask you a favor."

"My dear boy, I shall be delighted if I can be of service to you."

"I want you to bolster up my self-esteem. I am in an uncomfortably humble mood."

"What has happened?"

"I have made a fool of myself, that's all."

"How so?"

Aleck told him the story of his efforts to re-elect Judge Wolf, and of his brother's discouraging comments.

"I can't see but that you have been doing exactly right," said Mr. Robbins, when he had finished; "you have tried to save a worthy and upright man from being punished for his uprightness, and whether you succeed or not, you deserve credit for having made the effort. When we have done our best, we can only leave the result to Providence."

"Ah, no, Mr. Robbins! Who ever leaves anything of that kind to Providence without himself getting left? Providence is, in politics, on the side of the cleverest schemer, or, as Napoleon said, 'on the side of the heaviest battalions.'"

"The triumph of the wicked is in itself a punishment," said the pastor, with professional didacticism.

"Then I shouldn't mind being punished in that way, Mr. Robbins. I am hungering for success—of some kind. I have no talent for obscurity. You have preached righteousness to me so long that I am beginning to rebel a little

against the limitations which it imposes. Was it not
Christ himself who told us to make friends with the Mammon of Unrighteousness?"

There was a sudden vibrating cry of the soul in these
recklessly uttered words, which did not fail to impress the
clergyman. He put away his cigar, leaned forward, and
looked sympathetically at his young friend.

"Alexander," he said, "I did not know until now that
you were in earnest."

"I scarcely knew it myself, Mr. Robbins, but the fact is,
I am a little bit heart-broken. I feel wounded and hum-
bled down in the very depths. I have tried to live consistently—in accordance with my conviction—and I only
succeed in getting hopelessly muddled and accomplishing
nothing. And when I feel sore at my own inconsistency
and incapacity, then Horace comes and tells me, in cutting sarcasms, what I have dreaded but not dared to say to
myself. And that breaks me all up, and makes me miserable."

The note of keen youthful distress, with its unconscious
emotional luxury, appealed to the pastor's tenderness;
and yet it made him, for a moment, almost envious. There
was a time when he, too, had felt like that—oh, so long,
long ago. He threw a glance into the mirror at his iron-
gray hair, and sighed. What a finely attuned instrument
a human soul must be, to be quivering with aspirations
like these! He hungered for success—he had no talent
for obscurity. The pastor smiled. He remembered the
days when he, too, had been troubled with a similar repugnance. But as the straight and narrow path to eminence had appeared too laborious, he had striven to reach
it by the short cut of a wealthy marriage. And like most
short cuts to glory, it had led in quite an unexpected direction. He was so fond of this young man that he would
like, if he could, to save him from similar errors.

"If my power to help you were as great as my desire,"
he said, "I should surely not send you away uncomforted.
But it seems to be a fact that a certain amount of bung-
ling, and fumbling, and blundering is not only necessary
in youth, but, within certain limits, an absolute boon. A
correct young man is either a prig or a fool. A youth
who, in the generous tumult of his blood, commits errors
and repents of them, is to me a more sympathetic creature. He has growth in him, while the former has not.
No one is born in the light. Only through twilight can

we grope our way to clearness. Only through doubt can we gain certainty. Only through combat can we grow strong. The light, as far as each individual is concerned, can never be a free gift from on high ; it has to be fought for and prayed for. A certainty that has never known doubt is worthless, like a fortress that has never been exposed to hostile assault. Strength that is not the result of struggle is not strength, but pretentious weakness. It is inevitable that you should fight your battles now and make humiliating experiences, if your manhood is to carry out the promise of your youth ; and even if your plans miscarry, they will nevertheless yield you a profit in practical knowledge of life."

"Ah, but, my dear Mr. Robbins," Aleck exclaimed, passionately, "it is just here where my trouble lies. The lesson that these experiences teach me is the very opposite of what you have taught me. It is that, in order to succeed, you must surrender your convictions, prove unfaithful to your ideals, and apply a code of morality on Monday quite different from the one which you profess on Sunday. Now, where the issue is clear—where you have to choose —what would you do ? Give up success or surrender your convictions ?"

"But I cannot admit that such a choice is necessary, except in very rare cases ; and then you cannot doubt what my advice would be."

"If you'll pardon me, that shows that your own experience is limited. You look down from this peaceful study upon the slender stream of life that flows past you. And you judge by that. That's where clergymen, in my opinion, are at a disadvantage. They have to pilot men through waters with which they are but imperfectly acquainted. They know whither they are bound, but they have no reliable chart to steer by. They have a light at the masthead which throws more of its illumination backward than forward, and flashes only faint gleams down upon the unexplored waters about the bow."

It had grown late, while the pastor and his friend had been discussing these serious problems, and Aleck was interrupted in his indictment of the clergy by the entrance of a chambermaid, who placed a bundle of letters and newspapers upon the table. About the same time the door-bell was heard to ring ; the maid vanished, and on returning, announced Mr. Horace Larkin. Mr. Robbins, though he was not agreeably surprised, forced his features into a conventional smile, and pressed Horace's hand with proper cordiality.

"I am very happy to see you, Mr. Larkin," he said; "will you, please, be seated."

"I really came to see my brother, Mr. Robbins," Horace replied, without polite circumlocutions; "I was told he was here. I was so rough with him this morning, that it is only fair that I should be the first to tell him that his man is elected, without doubt. All the returns are not in yet, but, though he has been largely scratched, he is yet in a fair way to run ahead of his ticket."

"There," cried the parson, delightedly; "didn't I say it? Righteousness has triumphed."

"No," retorted Aleck, dismally, "scheming intimidation and free buggy rides have triumphed. Horace is the triumpher, not I."

"Well, whoever it be, I mean to celebrate his victory," said Robbins, pulling a bunch of keys out of his pocket; "I have some old Madeira of '58 which is good for the blues. For you know, it is not right to pour new wine into old vessels like you and me, Mr. Larkin," he went on, addressing Horace. "You know what Scripture says?"

"Oh, yes," the latter responded, promptly. "It is not meet to put new wine in old bottles, lest—lest they turn and rend you."

The pastor laughed a hushed and guilty laugh, but looked in the next moment at his visitors with a mildly reproving air in which there yet lingered a spark of amusement. He opened a small, richly-carved cabinet of teakwood which hung on the wall above the low book-cases and brought out three dainty wine-glasses and a yellow-sealed bottle, the dust on which was carefully preserved. While he pulled the cork, he told the old joke about the twenty Episcopal clergymen who at a social gathering got into a dispute about a passage in Scripture; but not one of them had a New Testament or prayer book at hand, whereby to verify the text. When, however, there happened to be a call for a corkscrew, everyone of the twenty plunged into his pocket, and hauled out the required article.

"You wouldn't do for a candidate on the prohibition ticket, parson," said Horace, as he gulped down, without visible emotion, the precious liquid.

Mr. Robbins fairly winced at such barbarism, and

5

thought: "Another time I shall not throw pearls before swine."

"No, Mr. Larkin," he said, aloud ; "I approve of good wine and disapprove of bad wine."

"Isn't that rather a pagan creed for a clergyman?" Horace inquired, in a spirit of pleasantry.

The remark grated a little on the pastor, but he repressed his irritation and answered, soberly :

"Life must have a certain gloss, to me, or it is not worth having. You cannot set up the same standard for all men. Frowsy evangelical poverty would never do for me ; I should sink under it into hopelessness and lethargy. I should lose my usefulness ; because I should lose my self-respect."

Happily Horace was relieved from the necessity of answering by the opening of a door and the appearance of a piquant blonde head between the folds of its heavy maroon curtains.

"What a horrid lot you are !" said the blonde head, with a pretty pout, as it nodded to each of the visitors ; "here you are sitting laughing and having a good time, while I am perishing with loneliness."

"Come in, dear, come in, if you can stand the cigar-smoke," said Mr. Robbins, holding out his arms to his favorite daughter. He had, perhaps, a suspicion as to whose voice it was which had made her solitude unendurable ; but, indulgent as he was, he could not find it in his heart to deny her any pleasure.

"Oh, I don't mind the smoke," ejaculated the girl, tripping lightly over the carpet and seating herself on a footstool at her father's elbow.

"Have you been confessing to papa, Mr. Larkin?" she said, with transparent deceit, lifting her languishing face toward Horace, for she knew well enough that he had just arrived.

"No, he has been confessing to me," he replied, "that pagan luxury agrees better with him than evangelical poverty."

"Has he confessed that? Why, you have succeeded in getting into his confidence better than I ever did. I have always been accusing him of that very thing, but I could never make him own up."

"That is because he was afraid you would make him pay too heavy a penance—in bonnets and things," answered Horace.

"Bonnets and things! Aren't you horrid? You evidently think girls have no thoughts beyond bonnets and things!"

"Perhaps not. But then you know *things* may embrace anything you like. It may include flirtations, matrimony, novels, and moral philosophy. Or what do you think, Mr. Robbins? Are you in favor of the higher education of women with Greek and astronomy and German philosophy? Do you like the soaring kind or—or——"

"Why don't you say the boring kind?"

"All right," interposed Arabella, "the boring kind, if you like?"

"Oh, I am an old-fashioned sort of man," Mr. Robbins rejoined, listlessly; "I don't believe in going too far in anything. But if education could be so arranged as to give more elevation to the thoughts of women—something beyond flounces and trivialities——"

"Why, papa, what are you saying?" his daughter interrupted; "Don't you see, you are on my side against Mr. Larkin——"

"Oh, am I? All right then—I believe—I believe in whatever my daughter believes in—whatever that is."

"Now that is worse still. Do you know, gentlemen, if I was clever enough what I would do? I have thought of it many times, but never, somehow, had the courage to commence it. I have thought of writing a play, giving the woman's side of these questions that everybody is writing about nowadays. I mean to introduce a young married couple who love each other dearly——"

"Oh, that would never do. It would be too sensational," said Horace.

"Now, Mr. Larkin, I wish you would just behave," protested Arabella, in a staccato whimper, in which there was more coquetry than remonstrance. The spoiled child was visible in all her attitudes, and audible in her inflections, which began with a little jerk like an *appoggiatura* in music.

"Well, let us suppose, for the sake of argument, that they did love each other dearly," laughed Horace. "What else did they do?"

"Nothing."

"Why, they must have had some other occupation, surely, besides loving."

"No, they didn't."

She was now really half offended, and without looking

up, sat playing with her father's fingers which rested upon the arm of the leather-covered easy chair.

"Then they couldn't have made much of a living," Horace observed, dryly; "for loving, unless you love an heiress, has never been held to be profitable."

"Look here, sir," cried the girl, a smile breaking through her vexation; "I'm not going to waste my ideas on you any more. I'm going to speak to your brother. He's much more agreeable."

She arose from her footstool, flounced across the floor, and with ostentatious friendliness seated herself in a chair which she drew close up to Aleck's side.

"Now, my dear Mr. Aleck," she began, dramatically, glancing toward Horace to observe the effect of her manœuvre, "don't you think your brother is just a little bit—horrid?"

"Quite a good bit, I should say," replied Aleck, with a faint smile.

"You bet your boots on that," the subject of their criticism interposed, laughing; "when a girl says that a man is horrid, she means to compliment him. I consider that I have points about me that money can't buy."

"What a happy man you must be to be so well aware of your advantages!" exclaimed Bella, addressing, in spite of her resolution, all her remarks to Horace.

"Well, I can't complain; though I should be happier if I were President of the United States."

"You are not one of those who would rather be right than be President," observed Mr. Robbins.

"Scarcely. It is a very pleasant thing to be right; but it is, in my opinion, still pleasanter to be President."

"There I don't agree with you," said Aleck, gazing solemnly through his cigar smoke.

"You are not an expert, Aleck," his brother replied; "you have never tried either."

The retort was meant for pleasantry, of course, but there was that lack of tact and fine feeling in it which often wounds without intention. The opportunity was ill-chosen for that kind of banter, when Aleck was sore with disappointment and bent down with troubles which Horace's coarser nature was incapable of comprehending.

"Have another cigar, gentlemen?" said Mr. Robbins, passing across the table a fragrant box, from the cover of which a Cuban señorita with beau-catchers was archly smiling.

"No, thanks," they both answered, and rose to take their leave.

"Why, don't be in a hurry," the pastor remonstrated, feebly ; "I didn't mean to drive you away."

"You don't. We flee voluntarily from the world, the flesh, and the parson. Good-night."

CHAPTER VII.

TOWN TALK.

In a small town, where nothing of any consequence ever happens, talk becomes a power, and in a certain way takes the place of events. What people say appears so very important because, outside of their routine of business and domestic tasks, they do nothing. If an eccentric man, to relieve the monotony of life, thrashes his wife, he becomes something of a hero ; and suns himself in the light of publicity. Though his act is not commended, it is so hungrily, so exhaustively, discussed, that he may be excused if his vanity mistakes notoriety for fame and objects to a relapse into the obscurity of commonplace behavior. Nor does he lack apologists who, in the corner groceries, declare the rod to be the proper exponent of domestic authority, and quote Scripture to sustain their position. The other bad characters in the town have in a confused way the same reckless pride in furnishing food for discussion. The town drunkards, who as a rule have large families, claim the additional merit of keeping the charitable impulses of the people in activity.

The fact was, the possibilities of doing anything, without transgressing, were limited in Torryville. Once in a while, when a second-rate show arrived, all that part of the population which had fifty cents to spare and no religious scruples flocked to Tappan's Opera House, and watched the primitive performance with stolid attention. But religious scruples were quite prevalent, and the profits of the shows were never very encouraging. Lecturers and elocutionists usually rejoiced in a better reception ; and spiritualistic mediums often stayed for weeks, gave *séances* in private houses and reaped a golden harvest. Several professors in the university were known to be interested in spiritualism, professing to investigate the phenomena in a purely scientific spirit. But their claim to scientific impartiality was vitiated by the zeal of propagandism which they displayed, and their readiness to be deceived by the

most transparent frauds. It was particularly Professor
Wharton who discredited himself with sober-minded people
by championing the cases of every medium whose tricks
had been exposed. One or more of these persecuted saints
was usually entertained at his house, and invitations to
séances were issued in his name, at a charge of fifty cents,
to those who were supposed to be "open to conviction."
For want of other amusement he was said to spend long
nights with mediums, in edifying converse with Indian, nau-
tical, and other illiterate ghosts, who slapped and caressed
him and took all sorts of liberties with his dignity. Occasionally he quarrelled with his mediums and dispatched
them to the railroad depot at short notice; not because he
saw through their frauds, but because, encouraged by his
forbearance, they would shock him, in their mundane
capacity, by a too great familiarity or freedom of manners.

It was early in December, about four weeks after the
election, that the younger members of the Larkin family
received invitations, at the usual price, to attend a *séance*
at Professor Wharton's house. The old man it would have
been of no use to invite, as he was known not to be open
to conviction. Horace and Alexander, too, were more
than sceptical, while Gertrude was restrained from betraying her credulity by the fact that a kind of dingy disre-
putability was associated in her mind with the very name
of spiritualism. Dr. Hawk, who was a half-avowed believer, had told her so many wonderful things which
he had seen, and which it was useless to try to account
for, that her prejudice was conquered and her curiosity
aroused. In the state of what might be called passionate
vacuity, in which, ever since her return from school,
she had found herself, anything that broke the monotony
of life seemed a godsend. Even Professor Ramsdale's
perpetual wooing, inconvenient though it was at times,
had a faint aroma of adventure about it which made it
"better than nothing." A proposal, even if unacceptable,
was yet an event, and an event, in Torryville, of whatever
sort, was attended with some excitement, and as such not
to be discouraged. Her two years' sojourn at a fashionable school in New York had ill fitted her for the empty
monotony of existence in her home. She felt a deadly
ennui which oppressed her like a positive burden. Her
father and her mother were equally uncongenial to her, and
her two cousins, though they were good enough in their

way, troubled themselves very little about her. She was unfortunately so constituted that she could do nothing with moderation. When she took a fancy to read, she shut herself up in her room from morning till night, had her meals sent up to her, and devoured book after book with hungry avidity. Then there came a reaction, during which she hated books and could not bear to look at one. At such times, she rode horseback with the same immoderate vehemence which she had formerly expended on literature. And when that craze was over, a weary lethargy followed, and the demon, called the Blues, knocked at her door and became her constant companion. In the midst of a luxurious life, which knew no ungratified want, she seemed to herself the most miserable of beings. Her education had given her a smattering of knowledge in all directions, but it had given her no real interests. It had taught her to bow and courtesy, but it had not taught her to think ; it had drilled her in all the arts of deport-ment—how to enter and leave a room, how to grade her greetings with admirable precision, all the way from cor-diality to a snub ; but it had furnished no intellectual contents to her life, which might give it purpose and dig-nity. At times a passionate hunger for pleasure came over her ; and it seemed as if something cried out within her, impelling her to brush aside all restraints. But, on the other hand, there was, in the depth of her soul, a respect for the conventions which she thought she despised. Filial affection and the ties of blood which keep so many turbu-lent natures within bounds she scarcely knew, and of parental guidance she had had none. Mr. Larkin was too busy a man to occupy himself with her ; and, as we have seen, he was of opinion that girls, if they were only let alone, would be likely in the end to come out right ; and Mrs. Larkin, although she inclined to the opposite belief, was only repelled by Gertrude's passionate vacillation ; and her constant fretting was vexatious rather than help-ful. The only pronounced talent which the girl possessed and which, with proper cultivation, might have become a source of happiness, was discouraged by both, and became thereby a source of deeper discontent. From her earliest childhood she had had a taste for drawing ; and her eye caught with unerring instinct the characteristic phase of whatever attracted her attention. But this correct eye invariably condemned what her untrained hand produced. Her finest intentions her obstinate fingers refused to carry out. She drew with a certain bold inaccuracy and dash which were wholly unfeminine, but there was a taking quality in these rough sketches and that indefinable charm of touch that distinguishes the artist from the *dilettante.* When the blues came upon her, like a shower that suddenly sweeps across a clear sky, the first thing she destroyed was always her sketch-book. She tore out each separate leaf with fierce satisfaction, and saw it curl in the grate in fiery torture, then glow and quiver, until the draught caught it and hurried its ashes up the chimney.

She went through with this process three or four times a year, and felt after each *auto da fé* a desolation which was terrible. It seemed to herself that she could have wept blood ; as if her whole life stretched out before her in long, barren vistas, unrelieved by a single gleam of joy. But so curiously complex is our nature in youth, that this very despair was, in a way, its own consolation. There was something in it which gratified her pride and appealed to her sense of the picturesque. She was not insincere ; nor was she coquetting with unreal woes. But she maintained that defiant erectness which was characteristic of her, even in her misery ; she had a feeling of being an exceptional creature, because she had such exceptional sorrows. If she was not like other girls, it was because other girls were so far below her. She envied them, and yet would not have been one of them.

It was in her eighteenth year that Gertrude woke up one morning with a kind of creative itching and tingling in her brain, as if she must do something or perish. She got out of bed and dressed in a misty tumult, brimming over with a sense of dim energy which made her happy and miserable by turns, but would not leave her in peace. The desire possessed her, she could not tell why, to fashion something with her hands—something grand and beautiful—she did not know what. She had seen several statues in New York, both in plaster and in marble, and she had surreptitiously taken a few lessons in a sculptor's studio. But the thought of emulating him in his art had not then occurred to her. It seemed such an easy thing to do—merely to fashion your thoughts in such a pliable substance as clay, with your fingers and a couple of modelling sticks. While yet aglow with this desire, she improvised, with the aid of Tom, Mr. Larkin's stableman, a studio at the top of the house, and for a week shut herself up, taking her meals in her room. The family were so well accustomed to such caprices on her part that no one marvelled ; and when Mr. Larkin occasionally asked what had become of her, the answer that she was not well seemed to call for no further inquiry.

It will thus be seen that Gertrude managed to lead an agitated life in the midst of the general monotony. She led a life of her own, though not a happy one. Her original nature and her vigorous blood impelled her to rebel against her lot, and to grope in eager uncertainty for something to lift her thought and fill her empty existence. She had found something, at last, which, for the time, filled her with satisfaction ; but even while, in a happy intoxication, she was working away, shaping, changing, and reshaping, she was half conscious that she was only the victim of some new delusion. She feared contact with her wonted surroundings, lest she should discover that she had again deceived herself. The stimulus of an artificial excitement enabled her, as it were, to inhabit only the upper stories of her mind, and kept her from descending to the ground floor where sobering criticism dwells. It was Dr. Hawk's note, offering her his escort to the *séance*, which finally compelled her to make the descent ; and she was by no means grateful to him for it. She felt like a bat that had tumbled out into the sunlight ; like a reveller who wakes in the glare of day in the empty banqueting hall. Dr. Hawk seemed as indifferent to her, in this moment, as if he had fallen from the moon. Everything seemed pale and dreary and insignificant. But since the spell was once broken and she had to face another period of desolation, she might just as well put up with Dr. Hawk as with anyone else. He had, at all events, the merit of being unusual, and sometimes entertaining.

What, above all things, made Dr. Hawk interesting was the fact that he had a history, or was suspected of having one. He had come to the university some eight or ten years ago, and had struck up a great friendship with Aleck Larkin. He was then a slender and round-shouldered youth with large black eyes and a sallow complexion. Though he scarcely had any money, he dressed with care, and always managed to look striking in his threadbare habiliments. The attention he bestowed upon his appearance, and particularly his picturesquely tumbled hair made him the butt of the undergraduates, and there was scarcely a week that the student papers did not contain some gibe at him. It had been the fashion in the earlier days of the university rather to affect roughness, in deference to the majority, to whom it came without affectation. Nothing was more unpopular than "putting on airs," and Archibald Hawk, who was adjudged guilty of this offence, acquired the reputation of being everything that was objectionable. He was a hard student, and yet failed to gain the favor of the majority of the instructors, although Professor Dowd was known to expect great things of him. In the class rooms, his answers, which were always out of the common run, were often greeted with derisive laughter. There was an effort at originality in them which made them seem forced. The professors, who were themselves mostly commonplace men, failed to see anything but vanity in them, and secretly sympathized with the undergraduate view of their author.

It was in the second year of their college life that Aleck Larkin, whose generous nature was shocked at the maltreatment of Hawk, began to champion him; and from that time forth his martyrdom was at an end. He blossomed out in the literary societies as an orator of a high order; and though it was not always easy to decide what he was talking about, he enjoyed a certain degree of consideration. But it was in a congenial *tête-à-tête* that he was at his best. Then clever fancies and surprising ideas rose spontaneously to his lips, like the bubbles in a champagne glass. Only a little sympathetic shake was needed to start them, and they bubbled on delightfully. He could sit for hours in Aleck's room and rhapsodize about science, and poetry, and religion; and Aleck, to whom unusual ideas were always welcome, feasted on his eloquence and rewarded him with the heartiest admiration. After his graduation Hawk went to New York to study medicine, and thence to Vienna. How he managed to support himself during these years was a mystery to his friends, and a legend gained currency that he had engaged himself, in his boyhood, to a young girl who had a little money, and that he had speculated in her devotion with a strict eye to his own advantage. That she was uncultivated and unattractive, but desperately fond of him, followed, as a matter of course, and that he remained reluctantly faithful, for fear of an *exposé*, seemed also in keeping with the situation. What made his dilemma still more tragic was the surmise (based upon some sort of shadowy evidence), that he had, during his European sojourn, fallen in love with an exalted lady, whose rank was an obstacle to passionate avowals. Another conjecture was that he had committed some interesting indiscretion, and was now suffering from remorse.

However that may have been, it was obvious that he was suffering from something. His large dark eyes looked as if they hid a sad secret, and it was impossible to talk long with him without wondering what this secret might be. To young ladies particularly, his vague, sad smile was tantalizing, suggesting all sorts of clues, but furnishing none. To Arabella Robbins, who, under the stimulus of a torturing curiosity, had ventured to banter him on his mysterious sorrow, he said with a sigh of dolorous reminiscence :

" My dear child, if there is one thing your sex is incapable of comprehending, it is its own power for mischief."

That was a concession, at least, that there was a woman in the case ; but, in other respects, left the field of conjecture as wide as before.

It was his friendship for Aleck Larkin which was understood to have induced Hawk to return to Torryville. When, during his stay in Vienna, his resources (whatever they were) had failed him, Aleck had induced his uncle to advance him a loan ; and when his studies were at an end, he was nothing loath to accept his friend's advice and begin his professional career in Torryville.

He counted upon the Larkin influence to bring him into vogue, and in this he was not disappointed. Mr. Larkin, to be sure, could not be induced to dismiss his old leech, Dr. Sawyer, who wore no necktie, and prescribed quinine for all ailments that Torryville was heir to ; but Mrs. Larkin submitted the whole list of her ailments to Dr. Hawk, and found him very sympathetic. He treated all her symptoms with respect, and discussed them with professional gravity. Mrs. Larkin had not, during her entire life, known the luxury of such tender and considerate treatment. She longed for the doctor's visits, and sent for him whenever she sneezed, as her husband humorously averred. Other ladies followed her example, and Hawk soon rejoiced in the reputation of being the ladies' doctor, *par excellence.* As he was not " a man's man," so no more was he professionally agreeable to the male sufferers of Torryville, who demanded an explicit diagnosis with a name, strong remedies, and quick recoveries.

CHAPTER VIII.

A HISTRIONIC WOOER.

When Dr. Hawk, on the evening of the *séance,* sauntered down Elm Street toward the Larkin mansion, he did not immediately enter. He remained outside in the twilight for some minutes, and stood gazing up at the dusky façade of the house as if he were appraising its value. It was a large, square, unpretentious-looking brick building, painted a light slate-color, with bulging bow windows, and a flat roof. It had once impressed the doctor as a wonder of magnificence, but since his return from Europe he had a conviction that its style was bad. For all that, it represented a good deal of money, and that was always impressive.

"Rather a comfortable box," Hawk remarked to himself, as he mounted the steps and rang the door-bell.

A servant girl admitted him into the spacious hall, the floor of which was carpeted, and the walls painted a yellowish gray, marbled, and divided into geometrical squares. There was a table for the reception of hats and overcoats, and above it hung portraits of the Father of his Country and his spouse. A wide staircase led up to the second floor, and a door in the rear afforded an exit into the yard. A distinct atmosphere of homely comfort and patriotism pervaded the house. Crude likenesses in oil of Grant, Seward, Stanton, and Sumner asserted the latter quality, while the former was a combined impression of spaciousness, pleasant temperature, and absence of display. The first objects which met the doctor's eye, as he entered the parlor, were Rogers's group of Beecher, Garrison, and Whittier, which stood upon a marble-top table at the window, and a mediocre copy of Carpenter's picture of Lincoln and his Cabinet, which hung over the piano. The furniture (which had not the faintest touch of æstheticism) was of black walnut, upholstered in red rep. The window curtains were of the same color, and apparently of the same material, but they were much faded where they had been exposed to the light. The walls were plastered and painted gray, with long bars and scrolls of a vaguely decorative intent in the corners. On the mantel-piece, which was of marble and glaringly white, a severe-looking black clock, representing the portico of a Greek temple, was ticking demurely, and on each side of it was a large bouquet of wax flowers under a glass bell.

Dr. Hawk, from the height of his foreign experience, was regarding these objects with compassionate contempt, and was imagining the tactics he would employ to get them removed, when he should have gained an intimacy in the house which entitled him to be critical. He had almost made up his mind how to set about it, when a faint sweet odor and a heralding rustle from the other end of the room gave another turn to his fancies. He arose and bowed with that foreign flourish of manner which he often assumed where he thought it would impress. Gertrude returned his greeting with an indifference which a weary smile prevented from being impolite.

Dr. Hawk, in cases of abnormal behavior in his patients, was apt to take a pathological view and refuse to be offended. But Gertrude had always declined to recognize him in any but his private capacity, and was disposed to repel his medical solicitude as an impertinence.

"Miss Gertrude," he said, fixing his sad and tender gaze upon her countenance, "you have been cruel indeed."

He disliked so much saying what was expected of him, that he often omitted to say "Good-morning," or "Good-evening."

"Cruel?" repeated Gertrude; "how have I been cruel?"

"You might have the generosity to comprehend without compelling one to be explicit," said Hawk, in his clear, vibrant bass.

"I would if I could," the girl replied with a little more animation; "but I fear, doctor, you overrate my power of intuition."

> "True genius and true woman! Dost deny
> Thy woman's nature with a manly scorn?"

he quoted, rather aimlessly, from his favorite poet, Mrs. Browning. He did not discover until it was too late that the verse did not apply to Gertrude's case.

"Let us be sensible, doctor, and talk prose," she said, in a vain effort to comprehend. "If I were what you say, I should not be so disheartened and miserable at my incompetency as I am to-day."

"Your incompetency—at what?"

"At everything I undertake."

"But if you were commonplace—like all the rest—you would undertake nothing. You would be vulgarly content with vulgar inanities."

"Vulgarly content with vulgar inanities. I must remember that," ejaculated Gertrude. "It is a very consoling phrase for one who, like me, is inclined to discontent."

"Discontent is the Promethean spark in the human breast," the doctor sententiously rejoined ; "if it were not for it we should all be howling savages to-day, instead of civilized beings."

"Then the blues must be highly civilizing, and the bluer we are the better."

"That is perhaps a little paradoxically stated. But it is plain that the contented man is conservative and invents nothing. It was the savage who was discontented with the flint axe who dug for iron and paved the way for the steam-engine. It was the men who were dissatisfied with monarchy who invented the republic."

"But those who are dissatisfied with the republic, what are they to do?"

"They will have to wait for the millennium—and work for it."

"Dear me ! That'll be a long work. I feel already the gray hairs sprouting."

"Give them to me, and let me keep them as a souvenir of your divine discontent."

"Divine discontent ! I am obliged for that phrase, too, doctor. It is a charming phrase. It's worth more than a lock of gray hair. But the *séance*—I had nearly forgotten it. It's time we were off."

She arose full of animation and moved toward the door. It was marvellous how this man, even when she had determined to be disagreeable to him, tuned her up and restored her self-respect. She took his arm as they descended the steps, and felt his appealing eyes resting sadly upon her in the dusk. A strange feeling rippled down her back—she scarcely knew whether it was a thrill or a shiver. Why did she distrust him ? Was it not an unreasoning prejudice which impelled her to treat him as she did ? What had he ever done to merit her displeasure, except to pay her rather audacious compliments, which might, perhaps, be more sincerely meant than she suspected? To look upon him in the light of a potential lover was, of course, out of the question, as it was a well-known fact that he was by duty, if not by love, bound to another. There was such a sense of security in this knowledge that she might, without danger to her own peace of mind, take pity on his remorse and console him with sympathy and kindness.

A strange tremulousness came over her, as she began to meditate the possibilities of the situation. She shivered repeatedly, and before she had walked far, a curious light-headedness made her fearful to open her lips; while at the same time a leaden weight oppressed her chest and momentarily impeded her breathing.

"You are not well, Miss Gertrude," cried Hawk, stopping and firmly seizing her wrist.

"Oh, it's nothing," she replied, with forced lightness. "I have been shutting myself up too much of late, I fear, and taken too little exercise."

"Don't you wish me to take you home?"

"No, thank you. It'll be over in a minute."

CHAPTER IX.

BETWEEN LIFE AND DEATH.

When Dr. Hawk, on the following morning, called to inquire about Miss Gertrude's health, he was informed by Mrs. Larkin that "she guessed she was all right ; but she hadn't got out of bed yet. She's a queer girl," Mrs. Larkin continued, "and you can never tell about her whether she's well or sick. But I'm glad you called, doctor, for I ain't feeling particularly scrumptious myself to-day."

Whereupon Hawk was regaled with a long and detailed account of Mrs. Larkin's ailments.

His uneasy conscience impelled him to repeat the call in the afternoon and the following morning ; but Mrs. Larkin attributed each time his presence to solicitude for her own health, and repeated the story of her curious symptoms. She had not seen Gertrude since the day of the *séance*, but she felt confident that she was all right, though it had not occurred to her to inquire.

"She often takes a notion to stay in bed for days together," she said, in her usual plaintive accents ; "but if we was to bother about that we shouldn't get much else done in this family. She's a headstrong and cantankerous girl, and it's past finding out what she'll take into her head to do next."

Mrs. Larkin had always, on general principles, disapproved of Hawk's attentions to Gertrude, not because she looked upon him as an undesirable son-in-law, but because she could not comprehend how anybody could find Gertrude attractive. A little unconscious jealousy also mingled in her disparagement of her adopted daughter, and her calm appropriation of her admirers, when they came to pay court to her, was perhaps ascribable to the same source. Dr. Hawk, to whom Mrs. Larkin's favor was worth a thousand or more a year, did not therefore dare to betray his predilection. He timed, however, his next visit so as to avoid meeting the elder lady, and by interesting

6.

Aleck in his errand gained the intelligence that Gertrude was lying in a sort of stupor, and that apparently she was not at all well. He then demanded admission to her bedroom in his professional capacity, and Aleck, in the absence of any other authority, took the responsibility of admitting him. Nettie, the chambermaid, conducted him up to the second floor and ushered him into a large, high-ceiled room, the furniture of which was covered with crayon boxes, half-finished drawings, sketch-books, and articles of feminine apparel. On the sofa a white starched skirt was lying in friendly proximity to a box of charcoal; on the pegs of an easel which stood in front of the north window, hung a big Gainsborough hat, a corset, and bonnet ; shoes of various descriptions were lying about the floor, as if they had been tried and kicked off in disgust. A couple of reduced antiques in plaster struck superb attitudes upon the mantel-piece and tables, and half-finished crayon and charcoal repetitions of them, from many points of view, were nailed with tacks to the walls. A paper shade, which could be rolled from below upward, regulated the light from the large western window ; and the afternoon sun, which made it half translucent, showed the bold fragments of arms and legs and experimental physiognomies with which it was covered.

Dr. Hawk gained a distinct impression of the unconventionality of this curious boudoir, as he approached the bed, where Gertrude lay in feverish, uneasy slumber. Her face was flushed, and there was a distressed expression in the frown upon her brow, and the strained lines about her mouth.

"I reckon she ain't quite right in her head," observed the maid, who remained standing at the door. "She took on mighty hard last night, talkin' and cryin' and makin' a big racket."

"And did you tell the family that she was ill ?" asked the doctor, sternly.

"No. She's sorter queer most of the time, and the family don't bother much about her."

"Yes, blood *is* thicker than water," murmured Hawk, half to himself ; and yet it seemed odd to him that a girl so beautiful as Gertrude and so well endowed could be of such small consequence in her own home. He looked at her for some minutes with a wholly unprofessional glance, and wondered where she got those large, Titianic lines— that splendid throat—those stately shoulders. He took

hold of her hand, which was large and of noble shape
with long, supple fingers; he could not help feeling that
the pulse beat with abnormal speed within it, but he
staved off all medical reflections until he had filled himself with the impression of her loveliness. It was unprofessional conduct, as he well knew, but after all, even a
doctor was a man first, and only secondarily a physician.

"Where the deuce does she hail from?" muttered he,
staring at her flushed features, as if endeavoring to read
in them the riddle of her birth. "I'll be hanged if I believe that story about the orphan asylum. One doesn't
pick up that kind of specimens in orphan asylums. She
was born to the purple and in some way defrauded of it,"
he continued, mentally; "that is unless her mouth and her
chin and her eyes and every instinct of her nature have
entered into a conspiracy to lie."

It struck him in the midst of his meditations that he
was, perhaps, taking an unfair advantage, in thus peering
into a young girl's soul through the transparent mask of
her unconscious face. But this thought did not greatly
trouble him; he was more of an æsthetician than a mor-
alist. The maid's presence, however, began to arouse his
torpid conscience. He beckoned her to come nearer,
and addressed to her a series of professional questions;
then wrote a couple of prescriptions and begged her to
hurry to the apothecary and return with the medicines.
Having made this concession to duty, he pulled an easy
chair up to the bed and became once more absorbed in
genealogical conjectures. The groping, undirected artistic instinct which revealed itself in the chaotic adorn-
ments of the room—the perpetual start toward something
acutely felt, but never attained—suggested a soul-history
full of pathetic incidents. Discouragement—disgust at
recurrent failures—passionate vacillations between all extremes of feeling—could, by the aid of a little ingenuity,
be read in the fragmentary sketches of limbs, heads, tor-
sos, and landscapes. "But such aspirations must have
an ancestry of some sort," Hawk reflected; "they do not
start out of the ground like toadstools."

He let his glance roam slowly about the room, and by
the time it returned to the bed it met that of his patient,
staring at him with a puzzled frown, as if she was trying
to determine whether he might not, after all, be a mere
fever vision.

"I am sorry to see that you are ill, Miss Gertrude," he said, in as solemn a tone as he had at his command. She rubbed her eyes, first with one hand then with the other; but did not answer.

"I took the liberty to admire your artistic efforts," he went on, a trifle embarrassed. The discovery that he had been stared at, he did not know how long, annoyed him; it gave him a sensation of having been surprised in undress. It required always a moment's preparation to compose his face into its tragic folds.

"Am I very ill, doctor," she asked, after a pause, during which she had convinced herself of his reality.

"I cannot tell yet. Your pulse is 130."

"Is that much or little?"

"It is a good deal more than it ought to be."

"Then you think I am going to die?"

"Not at present."

"You needn't spare me. I don't care."

"My dear Miss Gertie, you know I do not believe in death. When a person's time comes, he merely passes out of the body—the soul, which is he, moves into another house——"

"Well," she interposed, impatiently; "don't you think I am going to pass out—move into another house?"

"Not until you have seen a good deal more of life than you have yet."

"I don't think I care to see a great deal more. What I have seen has not been particularly pleasant."

He noticed an hysterical quivering of her lips and saw that her eyes were full of tears.

"You mustn't talk," he said. "You are weak from the fever. I'll give you something to reduce your temperature."

"I *will* talk," she answered, with determination. "Who cares whether I live or die?"

"I care, for one."

She looked at him with large, solemn eyes.

"Ah, life, life, life!" she sighed.

"Why do you say that?"

"Because I sometimes suspect that you are a great humbug," she answered, gravely.

He gave a start at her words and gazed back at her with a sad, reproachful glance.

"I know you are not accountable for what you say in your present condition," he murmured.

She lay for a while breathing heavily and staring vaguely at the ceiling.

"Why do you live here, anyway?" she asked, abruptly.

"I have to live somewhere."

"But with your talents and your great knowledge, I should think you could make your living anywhere."

"It is not all of life to live," the doctor quoted, impressively.

"I know that, but it is apt to be a very important part."

Hawk sighed and looked out of the window.

"Why don't you answer?" asked Gertrude, striving to catch a glimpse of his features.

"My dear Miss Gertrude," he replied, turning his melancholy face toward her; "there are some things—in fact, you should not try to peer into any one's soul; it is not kind of you."

There was a tone of appeal in his voice which took the sting away from the rebuke, and aroused interest and curiosity.

"It is true, after all, he has a secret sorrow," thought Gertrude. "It must be a very low woman who would hold him to a promise which he gave as a boy, when he has since come to repent of it."

And she lapsed into conjectures as to the appearance of this obnoxious woman, her age, and the circumstances of her life; and the longer she meditated the more she grew to hate her. The doctor, as a victim of affectionate persecution, which he had incurred by his love of learning, became a more interesting person than he had ever been before. She became convinced that she had been unjust to him in attributing the dramatic accent in his conduct and speech to an uneasy vanity and desire to impress. He was, no doubt, more genuine than she suspected.

Presently Nettie returned with the medicine bottles and interrupted her reflections. The doctor felt Gertrude's pulse once more, took her temperature by means of a thermometer placed in her arm-pit, asked her a few medical questions, poured out a teaspoonful of medicine, which he gave her, and left minute instructions as to her diet, the ventilation of the room, etc. There was something in his professional conduct which was distinctly agreeable. His grave tenderness, his soft, unhesitating touch and resolute motions inspired confidence. Though the physician seemed so distinct from the man, he yet reflected a little of his character upon his unprofessional brother.

On the stairs Hawk was met by Alexander, who inquired with some anxiety what was the matter with his cousin.

"I can't tell for a certainty," answered his friend; "but it looks very much like typhoid."

"Typhoid!"

"Yes."

The word struck terror to Aleck's heart. He had never appeared to be extravagantly fond of Gertrude, but they had, in a way, grown up together, and through all their superficial bickerings had been boon companions. Habit had fostered between them an attitude which was not that of devotion; but under it all smouldered a feeling which was warm and genuine. At all events Aleck was conscious of a sudden faintness at the thought that Gertrude's life was in danger; and as soon as he recovered from the first shock began to think in a bewildered way what he could do to save her. Hawk, feeling it incumbent upon him to apprise the rest of the family of the young girl's condition, secured an interview with Mrs. Larkin, who, in the meanwhile had returned from a charitable errand, and repeated to her the instructions he had given the chambermaid.

"I would recommend you to engage a professional nurse," he said; "it will be an affair of six weeks or more, and a great deal depends upon the nursing."

"All right, doctor," Mrs. Larkin replied, with an injured air; "you get her. She charges twenty-one dollars a week to be sure, and if that ain't outrageous, I don't know what is, but I guess I ain't good enough to take care of the girl; and if you say I ain't, I won't say I am. Though, when I was a girl, nobody thought of engaging a nurse at twenty-one dollars a week for anybody, no matter how sick he was."

Mrs. Larkin seemed altogether more offended than grieved at her adopted daughter's illness, and Hawk had to talk to her for an hour, before he could persuade her to withdraw her opposition to the measures he thought necessary. He struck the right chord, however, when he argued that the extremely delicate condition of Mrs. Larkin's own health would make it absolutely dangerous for her to expose herself to the toil and fatigue of attending to the wants of an invalid who was often inclined to be unreasonable and exacting. This little drop of implied censure of Gertrude set Mrs. Larkin's scruples at rest, and induced her, after much cavil, to give the doctor *carte blanche.* As soon as he had removed the impression that he entertained the least solicitude for Gertrude's fate, or swerved in his undivided loyalty to Mrs. Larkin's ailments, he could have twined his patroness about his finger. When Mr. Larkin came home and heard the word typhoid mentioned, he grew very serious. He scratched his head frequently, and rubbed his forehead. Sometimes he took hold of his bushy eyebrows and pulled them, then looked at his thumb and forefinger to see if he had extracted any hairs. He grew more and more restless the more his wife talked to him. Her lugubrious forebodings and Biblical quotations irritated him. His sanguine nature could not bear to contemplate an annoying thought, and yet all his efforts to throw it off were unavailing. He made a feint of eating when supper was served, and before the meal was at an end, arose and mounted the stairs to Gertrude's room. The creaking of his boots made an intolerable racket, and he sat down on the topmost step and pulled them off. Just then the Dutch clock in the hall struck seven, and every stroke seemed to resound through the still house with distressing distinctness. Mr. Larkin walked down in his stocking feet and stopped it. The canary bird in the library, who was in a shockingly hilarious mood, he sent down into the kitchen. It was a satisfaction to be doing something which gave him a respite from harassing thought. When at last he had nerved himself to open the door of the sick-room, he found Mrs. Rasher, the hired nurse, already sitting at the bed-side. He looked about the room in wonder and again scratched his head, while a curious grimace, half of amazement, half of disapprobation, distorted one side of his face. He inspected the plaster casts, the charcoal and crayon boxes, and the naked men who struck attitudes on the walls, before he turned his attention to his daughter.

"Poor thing, I reckon she is a little loony," he murmured, and remained standing, lost in reverie, in the middle of the floor; "her mother was so before her," he added, after a long pause.

He walked on tiptoe up to the bed and seated himself in the easy chair which the doctor had occupied. Gertrude, under the influence of the drugs she had taken, was lying in a heavy stupor. There was no trace of feeling in his hard, gray eyes, as he sat gazing at her flushed, motionless features, but he glanced now and then uneasily at the nurse, as if he feared that she might suspect him of being emotional. The latter, divining that she was *de trop*, got up and gave herself an errand out into the hall ; and Mr. Larkin seized the opportunity to stroke his daughter's listless hand, and heave a big sigh which shook his whole frame. There was something shy and awkward in the way he pulled his hand away the moment the nurse re-entered.

"Do you reckon she has any chance?" he asked her, a trifle huskily, as she resumed her seat at the foot of the bed.

"It is too early to tell yet," she replied ; "but she is young and strong, and I should say she had ten chances to one."

Mr. Larkin did not trust himself to speak a second time. He feared to imperil his dignity.

During the eight or nine days that followed Gertrude had but few conscious moments. She raved in her delirium about the doctor, Professor Ramsdale, Mr. Robbins, and particularly about some imaginary creature whom she addressed as "mother."

"Come, mother," she cried again and again ; "you look cold and miserable. Come, let me warm you up. Don't run away from me that way. I am Gertie, don't you know? I won't harm you. They have been bad to you, mother. Who is it has been bad to you? You need not be afraid of me. It is I who am afraid of you, sometimes, but I'll try not to be. I'll try to love you. But oh, don't look at me with those horrible eyes!"

And she would start up with a scream and bury her face in the pillows. Sometimes she reached the middle of the floor in her effort to escape from the ghostly eyes, and help had to be summoned to get her back into bed. Hawk made two or three visits a day, but did not seem quite satisfied with the turn the disease was taking. He would have liked to call in another physician for consultation, but he lived on a war footing with his medical colleagues in the town, and had, moreover, so low an opinion of their acquirements, that he felt unequal to the solemn farce of asking their opinion. As something had to be done, however, he induced Mr. Larkin to telegraph for a renowned specialist in New York City, to whose judgment he could subordinate his own without humiliation. But the renowned leech, who arrived promptly, had very little to say. He approved, on the whole, of everything Hawk had done, but he decided to remain for some days, while his assistance might be of value. The fever had, on the ninth day, reached its crisis, and an atmosphere of dumb excitement pervaded the house. Swift and low orders were issued from the sick room, now for ice, then for brandy, camphor, hot or cold water, sponges, towels, etc. Every now and then the sick-nurse, with her sleeves rolled up to the shoulder, flitted noiselessly across the hall to the head of the stairs, where the chambermaid sat weeping, and hastily wiped away her tears with her apron, to attend to her orders; and Gertie's canary bird, who, somehow, had found its way back into the library, lay dead from starvation on the bottom of its darkened cage; the big clock in the hall, with its motionless pendulum, gave the impression that time itself had come to an end.

Alexander, who was seated before the open fire-place, staring into the smouldering embers, felt weary and oppressed. He had been walking about for days in a state of anxious expectancy; the calamity which loomed up before him seemed to throw its gloom over his entire life. It seemed to him as if he must forever walk in its shadow. Could life be the same to him when Gertrude was dead? Well, life has a heartless way of adjusting itself to all changes, however radical; of closing, with unruffled surface, like the sea, over its dead, and swiftly obliterating their footsteps. Alexander, though his heart rebelled against this order, knew that it was merciful. Even now there was something remote and mysterious in his thought of Gertrude. It was as if she were already half way out of his life. What were they doing to her, those strange doctors, in whose hands she was left, isolated from all the familiar world which had hitherto surrounded her? She underwent a singular transformation in his thought, and he found it difficult, even in fancy, to realize their former relation of easy, bantering familiarity.

He spent the entire night in his chair before the fire, receiving now and then a visit from his uncle, who was restlessly hovering about in his stocking feet from room to room. He seemed to have something on his conscience which he wished to confide to Aleck, but which apparently, on second thought, he concluded to keep to himself. He looked haggard from loss of sleep. The lines of his face had lost their resolute firmness, and drooped pathetically. He stood long at the window, the shutters of which no one had thought of closing, and gazed at the great dark clouds which hurried away over the tree-tops.

"The—the wind is veering northward," he observed, as he resumed his seat at the fire; "it feels like snow."

CHAPTER X.

A FATAL ENTANGLEMENT.

"It was like fanning a spark," said the renowned physician, as he pocketed Mr. Larkin's check, two days after
the critical night ; "a moment's abatement of vigilance and
all might have been over."

"Tell me, doctor," said Aleck, who was standing at his
desk in the library regarding the great man with grateful
admiration, "do you think a great excitement could induce
typhoid fever ?"

"If it did not actually produce it," the doctor replied,
"it might yet be the proximate cause of it. By prostrating
the body, and reducing its vitality, it would make it more
liable to succumb to a fever, the germs of which were
already in the blood."

Aleck drove the doctor to the depot in the family buggy,
and by pursuing this subject further became convinced
that it was the spiritual *séance* which had brought Gertrude to death's door. An intense bitterness toward Dr.
Hawk filled his soul. It was he who, in case Gertrude
had died, would have been her slayer. All that morbid
hunger for excitement ; all that owlish nocturnal traffic
with its mystic nonsense became so abhorrent to him, that
he felt an itching to attack with his fists the first spiritual-
ist that came in his way. The little dramatic touch in
Hawk's behavior which had hitherto seemed but an expression of his intensity of nature, seemed now of a piece
with the ghostly charlatanry in which he was mixed
up, and put him on a par with mediums and quacks who
found it necessary to depart from ordinary standards of
conduct.

It was a mettlesome beast Aleck was driving, and he did
not in his indignation give due heed to its management.
As they crossed one of the three railroad tracks which it
was necessary to traverse before reaching the depot, the

buggy leaped so high that it was only the doctor's two
hundred and thirty pounds which saved him from a bath
in the gutter.

Gertrude's recovery was slow, but proceeded for a while
without interruption. In order to avoid agitation she saw
no one except the nurse and Dr. Hawk ; and when the
latter arrived, the former usually seized the opportunity
to absent herself. It was in the second week of her con-
valescence that Hawk one day took his seat at her bed-
side, in an exceptionally lugubrious frame of mind.
His hair was more than ordinarily rumpled and the scowl
on his handsome brow more than ever recalled Booth in
" Hamlet."

Gertrude, cut off as she was from all communication
with the world, found herself pondering in the long idle
hours on the causes of his discontent, and spinning long
romances, of which he naturally was the hero. She imagined he grew sadder in the same degree that she regained
her strength, and she came to the conclusion that there
had probably been some new development in relation to
that odious woman who persisted in loving him—in demanding a return in affection for her expenditure in
money.

This gnawing heart-sorrow—"this worm that never
dieth"—became a wonderfully vivid and interesting thing
to her in her meditations ; it trailed its course through
the long procession of vacant hours and grew larger
and fiercer from day to day. The only event which interrupted the train of her morbid imaginings was the arrival every morning of a fresh bouquet of roses with a little
sympathetic message from her cousin Aleck. But the roses,
though they flamed in a variety of gorgeous colors, gradually paled beside the intenser hues of Hawk's romance.
She did not know, of course, that they arrived fresh in
moss by the morning train from Rochester ; but it is questionable if even this circumstance, if it had been known,
would have enabled them to hold their own against the
doctor's lurid passion flowers.

" It is well with you to-day," he was saying, as he pushed
back the lace wristband of her *robe de nuit* and felt her
pulse ; " yes, yes, yes ; it is well with you."

"But it does not seem to be well with you, doctor,"
Gertrude remarked. " Let me give you this flower, the
odor of it will refresh you."

She handed him a half-opened deep-crimson bud, and

he took it with his disengaged hand, and stared at it, shaking his head mournfully.

> "I sometimes think that never blows so red
> The rose, as where some buried Cæsar bled," *

he declaimed, with his mellow, gently vibrating bass.

The words thrilled like a light shiver through Gertrude's frame.

"You spoil the flowers for me," she said, with half-assumed petulance ; "it is horrid to think that they draw their color from anybody's blood."

"There will grow a redder rose than that out of my blood," he murmured, half absently.

"I don't believe it. You couldn't get a redder one than that."

The doctor stood silent for a moment, then began slowly to pick the rose-bud to pieces. His lips began to move, and with low and exquisite intonations he declaimed,

> "Ah, love, could you and I with Him conspire
> To grasp this sorry scheme of things entire,
> Would not we shatter it to bits—and then
> Remould it nearer to our hearts' desire?"

The passionate energy with which he thrust forth the third line made again the girl quiver with sympathetic excitement.

"You don't mean that, doctor," she whispered ; "it is only poetry you are reciting."

"Ah, child," the doctor responded, "you do not know what you are saying."

And with a stage frown and gesture he flung the stripped rose-bud into the fireplace.

"Yes, I would shatter it to bits," he repeated through his clinched teeth ; "and then " (here he raised his eyebrows and fixed a darkly penetrating glance upon Gertrude) "remould it closer to my heart's desire."

He took up his hat and walked rapidly out of the room.

A thought dawned upon Gertrude—a thought which shook her being to its very core. It came over her with the force of a sudden conviction. She was not sure whether it gave her joy or pain—a joyful pain, or a painful joy seemed more nearly to express her sensation. In the tumult of feeling which convulsed her feeble frame

* Omar Khayyam's "Rhubayat."

there was something overwhelming, inexorable, like Fate
itself. How was it possible that she had not thought of it before? How wilfully blind she had been not to see what, for
conscientious reasons, he had endeavored to conceal from
her ; but which now had broken down the barriers with
which timid scruples had hedged it in. He loved her ;
had loved her silently and patiently for years ; though she
had availed herself of her power by alternately attracting
and rebuffing him. He was bound to another, who, no
doubt, was base enough to resort to any measure to keep
him ; who had mortgaged his affections, and meant to foreclose, if she suspected him of a disposition to alienate them.
Hence his melancholy—his tendency to brood upon the
darker sides of life. And to think that she, who had been
the cause of his sorrow, had been cruel enough to ridicule
him. She did penance to the doctor in her heart, and
determined, in the future, to make amends for her bad
behavior in the past. That he was culpable in having, by
his unguarded conduct, agitated her, when her very life
was intrusted to his care, did not for a moment occur to
her. The mighty passion in his breast, of which she had
caught a glimpse, seemed to her feminine mind relentless as a force of nature, and it would be absurd to demand of him that he should restrain it.

She scarcely had the heart to attribute her general prostration during the afternoon, and the return of the fever
toward evening, to the fatal discovery she had made in the
morning. She could not find it in her heart to blame a
man for loving her, even at the peril of her life. This
accidental betrayal of a vital secret (for she firmly believed
it to be accidental) under the stress of irresistible feeling
seemed lifted above the common prose standards of
judgment. It seemed like a passage from Shakespere—a
glimpse of that world of lofty thought and action for which
she had hungered. She looked forward with a palpitating
eagerness to the doctor's arrival, heedless of the fact that
every winged thought, every accelerated heart-beat, was
draining the ebbing remnants of her fountain of life.

When Hawk finally did arrive there was something a
little shamefaced in his appearance which displeased her.
So far from coming like a conquering hero, riding rough-
shod over all paltry considerations, he did not quite dare
look her in the eye, but stole quick and half-guilty glances
at her when he imagined himself unobserved. He acted like
the very personification of a bad conscience. The return

of her fever disturbed him, and the recurrence of other unfavorable symptoms caused him an alarm which he could
not conceal behind a non-committal, professional mask.
Mrs. Rasher, the nurse, who, contrary to her custom, had
remained in the room, saw in his conduct a confirmation
of suspicions which she had long entertained. She had
heard snatches of the extraordinary poetry he had recited,
and had resented, moreover, the lofty scorn with which he
had rejected her medical suggestions. The story of the
séance was also, by this time, a matter of common gossip,
and Mrs. Rasher, who put her own construction upon it,
had declared emphatically in the kitchen, that in case Miss
Gertrude died, she wouldn't like Dr. Hawk's conscience
for a bedfellow.

Apparently the doctor shared her opinion, for he did
not go to bed that night. After a brief interview with
Mr. Larkin he telegraphed again for the famous specialist,
who replied that he would arrive by the morning train,
The patient, in the meanwhile, after a restless, drugged
sleep, had become delirious, and Mrs. Rasher, brimming
over with indignation against Hawk, felt the need of free-
ing her mind to some member of the family. She accordingly seized the opportunity when Aleck, his handsome
brow knitted with distress, mounted the stairs to inquire
about his cousin's condition. Mrs. Rasher, standing on
the topmost step, gave her version of what had happened
in a hushed voice, but with much spirit.

"He's been a-comin' here every mortel day, sweet-
heartin' with her, and talkin' poentry and stuff, and a-cuttin'
up like a young cub, as hasn't got no more conscience
than I have hair on the back of my hand," said Mrs. Rasher, illustrating her comparison by a rapid stroke of her
right hand over the back of the left. "And she, poor
thing, lyin' there on her back, and seein' nobody but him,
it ain't no wonder if she takes on hard about him, when
she's out of her head, and gets flustered when he speaks
to her ; and he, all the time, a-wrigglin' about like a snake
in the grass, jest to be aggervatin', and tearin' her roses to
pieces and flingin' 'em into the grate, and actin' up generally, and pertendin' to forget that he's a-holdin' her
poor life between his fingers, like a candle that's a-splut-
terin', that he kin blow out with one little breath of his
mouth."

Mrs. Rasher was so moved that the tears rolled down
over her cheeks, She took her clean, white apron, blew

her nose surreptitiously under it, and wiped her eyes. The young man was so stunned by her recital that for a while he could do nothing but stare at her with a face full of dismay. There was something in what she said which jarred harshly within him and set all his being painfully astir. If he had had the doctor at that moment under his hand, he felt as if he could have murdered him with rapture. The vague distrust he had felt of him, since the spiritual episode, deepened into hate. That jealousy had anything to do with his emotion he did not himself dream ; for his uppermost feelings were condemnation of the doctor's abuse of the trust confided to him, and a trembling anticipation of the calamity which would overtake the family in Gertrude's death. It did not occur to him to question Mrs. Rasher's veracity (as his brother Horace under similar circumstances would have done). As soon as he gained control of his voice he thanked her briefly and descended into the library, where he found Hawk seated before the fire, smoking a cigar. Three gas-jets were dimly burning under the roof, and there was a drop-light with a green shade standing upon Mr. Larkin's writing-table. In the embrasure of the bow-window Horace was sitting with a newspaper over his face dozing. Aleck's entrance awoke him, and merely to signalize the fact that he was awake, he observed in a voice which grated terribly upon his brother's overwrought nerves :

"You don't think she has much of a chance, doctor, do you ?"

"All we can do," responded Hawk, solemnly, "is to labor 'hopefully against hope.'"

That irritating little epigram, the insincerity of which was now palpable, fell into Aleck's mind as a spark into a powder magazine. There sat the man upon whom he had lavished the guileless affection and faith of his youth ; the man to whose glittering paradoxes he had listened devoutly as to the inspirations of genius ; the man whom he had befriended when others turned their backs upon him, and revered as something nobler and finer than common clay. Each one of these thoughts was a pang of anguish and humiliation. A savage rage took possession of him. He shook like an aspen leaf. He felt an impulse to seize the doctor by the throat, to knock him against the wall, to stamp on him with his feet. But even in the midst of his agitation there was a still small voice of reflection, which, like a sober commentary, accompanied the

excited text.   Even while he yearned to strangle the doctor, he knew that he would never do it.   The remark
which he finally made was several octaves below the pitch
he had intended to strike.

"Dr. Hawk," he said, with unsteady voice, "you are
playing an underhand game here."

Hawk turned his head quickly with a vague alarm in his
face.

"What do you mean by that?" he asked, with surly indifference.

"What would you call a physician," continued Aleck,
struggling to master his agitation, "who in order to gratify
his own vanity, sacrificed a life entrusted to his care?"

"I would call him a d——d scoundrel," cried Hawk.

"So would I," Aleck retorted hotly ; "and that's what I
call you."

The doctor started up with a livid face, and made a
motion as if he intended to grab the fire-irons.   But suddenly he bit his lip, thrust his hands vehemently into his
pockets and took a couple of long strides across the floor.
He nearly ran against Horace, who, by this time had got
his paper down from his face and was watching the scene
with the same kind of interest with which a man watches
a dog-fight, simply to see who will beat.

"You are my witness," Hawk burst out, "that your
brother has insulted me."

"You wish to retain me as counsel, do you?   Well,
business is business."

"I suppose you have heard the language your brother
has used toward me?"

"I shall have to ask for a retainer before I commit myself to any such testimony," Horace replied, with mock
gravity.

"I tell you I'm not fooling," cried the doctor, angrily.

"Nor am I," answered Horace, coolly.   "You know an
attorney never likes to take the witness-stand in favor of
his own client.   It is a thing that is only resorted to in extreme cases."

The doctor turned around on his heel, and muttering an
oath walked across the floor to the mantel, where Aleck
was standing with his back to the fire.

"Will you or will you not apologize for what you have
said?" he asked, breathing hard.

"I will not."

"Then you are prepared to take the responsibility?"

"What responsibility ?"

"The responsibility of life and death."

Aleck stood as one petrified. That had not occurred to him when he gave way to his indignation. He did not know that the New York specialist had been telegraphed for ; and even if he had known it, would he have been willing to leave Gertrude without medical aid for one night, when her life was every moment trembling in the balance ? The floor seemed to be gliding away from under his feet, leaving him standing in mid-air. His legs seemed numb, his senses frozen. "If she should die, if she should die," he kept mechanically repeating to himself ; "if she should die to-night, what would become of me ?"

He murmured the question half aloud, and with a singular coolness, merely to keep hold of the situation which threatened to slip away from his grasp. All of a sudden a flash broke through his mind. He saw himself fleeing through the long years of the future, in storm and darkness, pursued by the terrible phantom—Remorse. The vision of Gertrude dead—with cold, upturned face, sunken eyes, and white, unfeeling hands folded upon her breast— sent another pang to his heart. With a face eloquent with anguish he stood for a while staring at Hawk. "I apologize, doctor," he said, huskily. "I beg your pardon."

7

CHAPTER XI.

A SANGUINARY EPISODE.

A week of anxious suspense followed the arrival of the
renowned leech, who, after a stay of two days, sent on a
younger colleague from New York, who took full charge
of the case, practically superseding Hawk.   It was obvious
to the latter that the elder practitioner had taken in the
situation, and had intended to make him superfluous ; but
lest others should hit upon this opinion, and his prestige
in the town suffer, he exalted Dr. Manson's ability to the
skies, and treated him with distinguished consideration.
If he gnashed his teeth in private and resented the polite
but unmistakable rebuffs which he received, whenever he
attempted to interfere, he was clever enough to adjust his
public mask so as to disguise his feelings.   The mood of his
favorite poet, Omar Khayyam, always came to his rescue,
dulling the edge of pain, when his resentment was keen-
est.   It was all vanity of vanities.   In a hundred years
what would it matter ?   He would then pace up and down
the floor of his sitting-room, with his head bent, and now
and then glancing half surreptitiously at himself in the
mirror, while he murmured :

> " When you and I beyond the vail are past,
>   Oh, but the long, long while the world shall last,
>   Which of our coming and departure heeds
>   As heed the seven seas a pebble cast."

Heine observed that he wore out the patience of all his
friends in dying, and Gertrude, if she had been aware of
it, might have had the same experience.   Mr. Larkin,
genuine though his grief had been, had gradually grown
callous, and in a vague way had accustomed himself to
the thought of Gertrude's loss.   Horace, whose sympathies were never very acute, felt an annoyance (of which,
to do him justice, he was ashamed) at having the house
turned upside down for so long a time ; and Mrs. Larkin,
in order to give vent to her accumulated sense of wrong,

scolded the servants, discharged one cook after the other, and threw out accusations of a grave nature against everyone who displeased her. Only Aleck followed the progress of the disease with undiminished anxiety, and hailed with inexpressible relief the first decisive turn toward recovery. Of the many townspeople who had been in the habit of inquiring at the door about the patient's condition, only Professor Ramsdale persevered until inquiry seemed superfluous.

It was remarked in the town, as the winter progressed, that the friendship between Aleck and the doctor had cooled. They had before been constant companions, and were now never seen together. On his long afternoon tramps Aleck was now accompanied by the taciturn Ramsdale, who paced with a long, business-like stride like a professional pedestrian. The professor had not a spark of humor and was not exhilarating company. But there was something solid and trustworthy about him which compensated for his lack of conversational brilliancy. Moreover, his serious solicitude for Gertrude, and his dog-like devotion in spite of rebuffs, filled Aleck with kindness for him.

The story of Aleck's quarrel with the doctor had, by this time, gone abroad in several distorted versions. It was told that Hawk had attacked his patron with a poker, because the latter had accused him of making love to Gertrude under the guise of professional attention. Another version was that Hawk had wished to engage Horace Larkin as counsel in a libel suit against his brother, but that Horace had insisted upon having his retainer in cash, and had asked a larger sum than the doctor could raise. Nobody felt any hesitation in asking the participants in the affair about their share in the proceedings ; but their answers tended in nowise to settle the disputed points. Horace told grotesque Munchausen yarns with the soberest face in the world. The doctor gave only dark hints as to what might happen, and in the presence of his lady friends wrapped himself in an impressive cloak of mystery. Only Aleck declared frankly that the subject was painful to him, and that he preferred not to discuss it.

Gossip is a form of energy which many of us are inclined to deprecate. It fulfils, however, an important mission. It keeps many a wearisome community from absolute stagnation and decay. The tendency to gossip is a venerable Aryan inheritance. Cæsar tells us that in an-

cient Gaul the stranger was surrounded in the market-
place by the curious inhabitants, and assiduously pumped,
until he had delivered up the last scrap of news he possessed ; and one can imagine how long the poor isolated
villagers lived on these precious bits of intelligence, exer-
cising the ingenuity of their dull brains in adorning and
varying them *ad infinitum.* When this gossip has grown a
hundred years old we call it tradition ; a little extra dis-
tortion makes it folk-lore and poetic. Every century that
slips away adds to its value, until, in due time, mytholo-
gists make sun-myths of it, and invest it with a profound
and beautiful meaning.

If this Torryville incident had occurred in an earlier
century, when events crowded each other less, some such
fate might indeed have overtaken it. As it was, it must
content itself with its place in the present unpretentious
chronicle. It did, however, prepare the way for a sensation which shook the town to its very foundation, and
caused the local daily to issue an extra in the middle of
the afternoon.

Early in the morning of February 23d, the day after
Washington's Birthday, hackman Tommy Colt, driving to
the depot to catch the 7.15 Western express, found, in the
middle of the road, a Derby hat with a hole in the crown,
which had evidently been made with some sharp instrument. On picking it up he found that it was bloody, and
that a tuft of blonde hair and a substance resembling brain
and crushed bone adhered to the inside of the lining, where
it had been pierced by the deadly weapon. A further inspection revealed to his horrified eyes the initials A. L.
stamped in gilt letters on the lining, and he was not slow
in jumping to the conclusion that the hat belonged to
Alexander Larkin.

The whole story of the latter's quarrel with Dr. Hawk,
with all the latest embellishments, darted through Tommy
Colt's brain. He reflected briefly on the consequences of
his discovery, and whether he would like to see the doctor hung on his testimony. He concluded, after a while,
that he would rather not, but feared that, in case he pre-
varicated, he might cast suspicion upon himself. In order, however, to share the responsibility of discovery with
the next comer, he put the hat back where he had found
it, jumped up on his box, and drove to the Larkin mansion. There he demanded and obtained an interview with
Horace, who was just coming down to breakfast.

"Is Mr. Aleck at home?" Tommy Colt inquired, with chattering teeth, by way of overture.

"No; he went to New York last night by the 11.15 express."

Tommy Colt, with great deliberation, took the quid out of his mouth and put it in his vest pocket. His teeth chattered so that he could hardly speak.

"You hain't heard from him sence?" he managed to stammer.

"No; why do you ask?"

"I reckon you'd better come outside with me," Tommy observed, taking the lawyer familiarly by the arm. He felt a pity for him which obliterated all sense of social station.

"Good Lord, man, what do you mean?" cried Horace, his face white with horror. "Has he come to harm?"

"Mebbe he has," answered the hackman, clenching his teeth hard after each word, "and mebbe he hain't."

Horace grabbed a hat from the hat-rack and rushed into the street. He seemed to be wrestling with a frightful nightmare, and half-suspecting that he might wake up and find that he had been dreaming.

"Now tell me what has happened," he thrust forth, breathlessly.

Tommy Colt related the incident of the finding of the hat, and volunteered to drive Horace to the spot, where it was probably yet lying. Three laborers and half a dozen unkempt children had, in the meanwhile, scented the sensation, and a dozen more were coming, at an uneven trot, across the empty lots.

It was a raw morning with slate-colored skies, dripping roofs, and dirty patches of snow melting in the hollows of the brown fields and along the edges of the ditches that skirted the black railroad tracks. Here and there a bit of meadow was half submerged and mirrored the dismal skies in its shallow pools. A cold, shivering moisture pervaded everything. It silvered your mustache with tiny water-drops; it stole through the texture of your thickest ulster; it insinuated itself into your very bones, and made you feel as if you never could grow warm again. The roads, which were a sea of slush and mud, expanded in many places into the neighboring fields, and every railroad hack that came along cut its deep ruts a little beyond the semi-circle made by its predecessors. Two ugly squatty buildings, looking as if they had been soaked in filthy water, surrounded by dripping lumber piles, débris of coal, and a network of tracks and "switches," exhibited half-obliterated signs which indicated that they were railroad depots ; and the proximity of two elevated water-tanks, a multitude of freight-cars, a smoke-begrimed grain-elevator, and some white-painted structures resembling gallows, and warning you to "Beware of the Locomotive while the Bell is Ringing," served further to emphasize the suggestion.

It was to this scene of desolation that Horace was conducted by Tommy Colt. He sat drearily staring into the murky air, striving vainly to shake off the numb despair which held him in its clutch. The calamity seemed so inconceivable, so cruel, so overwhelming. Tommy Colt had to speak twice to him, as he stepped into the middle of the road, where the railroad laborers and the children were standing, gazing with a vague gratification at the interesting object. Horace stepped out at last and stared with a hard, old-looking face at the people. He shuddered with cold and with horror. Then he stooped to pick up the hat. The circle around him narrowed, and with craning necks and straining eyes they pressed as near as possible to watch for exciting developments. Tommy Colt, with a proud sense of his prominence in the affair, elbowed his way to the centre and obligingly raised the hat on the handle of his whip. "If that ain't Aleck's hat I'll be blowed," he said, rather unfeelingly ; "it's got Barber & White's mark on it. It's a two dollar and a half Derby, and I seen Aleck buy it myself at Barber & White's, a year ago last election."

Tommy had by this time conquered his tendency to shiver, and was ready to assert himself as his importance warranted. His words, however, had an unforeseen effect upon Horace. They pierced his benumbing lethargy and aroused his faculties. The question whether it was actually Aleck's hat began to interest him, and having determined that it was, he asked himself whether it was probable that he would choose an old Derby, of last year's fashion, when he was going to New York. He remembered that Aleck had been in the habit of keeping this hat at the office, where anybody might have carried it off without attracting attention. He had even a faint suspicion that the hair adhering to the clotted blood was a shade darker than his brother's. Was it not possible that the person who had been murdered had stolen Aleck's hat, or possibly in some other way gotten possession of it? These theories, whatever they were worth, appealed to his judicial ingenuity, and though not dispelling his fears, eased the intolerable sense of oppression. Without uttering a word he took his seat again in the hack and ordered Tommy to drive him to the telegraph office. There were but two hotels in New York to which Aleck would be likely to go, and if he was at either of them, he would be prompt to answer.

"Ain't yer goin' to take that hat to the police?" inquired Tommy, anxiously.

"No."

"I'll be blowed ef it ain't Aleck's, he repeated, eagerly. "Didn't I tell ye I seen him buy it?"

"You did."

Tommy had acquired a sense of proprietorship in the sensation, and was determined not to have it belittled or explained away. He was not going to be defrauded of his glory by any lawyer's trick.

"I guess ye don't feel good," he observed, as he tightened the reins and whipped up his sorry nags.

Having despatched his two telegrams, Horace discharged the hackman and returned home. He found his uncle seated alone at his breakfast. His strong molars were laboring over the beefsteak with a business-like regularity, showing the working of the muscles at the base of the jaws and a sympathetic movement in the temples, whenever he brought his teeth together. He nodded to Horace as he entered, but gave him no other greeting. The combined odors of beefsteak, buckwheat cakes, and maple syrup, which at other times were so agreeable to the nephew's nostrils, made him now almost faint. He took his seat, however, and ordered a cup of coffee. He strove to exhibit no sign of excitement in the old gentleman's presence, because he meant to have him finish his breakfast in peace.

"Did you foreclose that Ruppert mortgage in Wayne County?" Mr. Larkin inquired, pulling some papers out of his pocket and making some memoranda with a pencil on the back of a letter.

"It was attended to, sir," Horace replied, gazing vaguely at the Three Christian Graces, with the abnormally big eyes, which hung over the mantelpiece.

"Do you think that $2,500 mortgage on the Hallett farm in Wisconsin is good?" the uncle went on, while he folded the buttered buckwheats with his fork and made

them disappear with absent-minded despatch. Like most
Americans, he ate in order to live, and was as remote as
possible from reversing the proposition.

"I wrote to the lawyer in Racine about it, and expect
a reply to-day," the nephew answered. He, too, had
fallen to eating, in order not to make himself conspicuous
by abstention. But he seemed to be having an immoderate labor in swallowing ; he would have put syrup on his
steak, if the waitress had not prevented him ; he could distinguish no difference in taste between meat and buck-
wheats. When the old gentleman had finished simultaneously his second cup of coffee and his memoranda, he
got up and walked, with a slight stiffness in the knees,
toward the library. Horace, too, pushed his plate away
and followed him. A little business conference after
breakfast was a regular incident of the day, and Mr.
Larkin did not trouble himself to look up, as his attorney
seated himself on the other side of his desk.

"There's some little excitement in town this morning,"
Horace began.

"What's up ?"

"It may concern us, and it may not," Horace replied,
without a tremor in his voice ; "a hat has been found on
the road to the depot."

"Well, what of that ? Some drunken fool probably
lost it."

"The hat appears to be Aleck's."

Mr. Larkin raised his head slowly and stared at his
nephew with a strained expression. Through the rigid
lines of his face struggled a vague demand to know the
worst at once and have it over.

"Don't try to spare me," he said ; "is he dead ?"

"I don't believe it," Horace rejoined, energetically. "I
have a feeling that he is not dead."

"Anyway, don't let Gertie know anything about it ; it
would be an awful set-back to her. Tell the servants not
to say a word to her."

At the mention of Gertrude's name, the same thought
flashed through the old and the young man's brain, and
their eyes met in a significant glance of understanding.
It was a sickening thought, and one which they would
willingly have repelled.

"God have mercy on us, miserable sinners," Mr. Larkin sighed, as he stalked out into the hall and pulled on
his overcoat.

Outside of the house the street was black with people. The usually quiet town was all excitement and commotion. All along the board sidewalks poured a dense stream of humanity down toward the scene of the tragedy. There was an animation in their gestures and bearing which contrasted with their wonted dulness and lethargy. Elderly men who usually moved at a snail's pace, ran ; slow-witted grocers and drygoods and hardware men grew bright under the stimulus of the excitement, and exhausted themselves in ingenious conjectures as to manner, motives, and circumstances of the murder. Dr. Hawk's name was freely bandied about ; and what had at first been whispered as a remote suspicion was soon discussed as a probability which admitted of no cavil. Aleck was a universally popular man, and was known to have had no enemy in the world but Hawk. The latter, it was maintained, was, nobody knew who—a suspicious character of mythical antecedents. Nobody ought to be surprised if such a man turned out to be a criminal. It was demanded by several influential citizens that the doctor be forthwith arrested ; but Judge Wolf, who was the only judge in town, cooled their zeal, and begged them to wait until some positive proof had been obtained. In the meanwhile he consented to have two policemen detailed to watch Hawk and prevent his escape, in case he should attempt to leave the town.

Old Mr. Larkin's gray head, surmounted by the inevitable rusty beaver, made a sensation wherever it appeared. It was thought strange at first that he was not too prostrated by grief to interest himself in tracking the murderer. But the sentiment gradually predominated that the vindictive enterprise he displayed was more in keeping with his character, and therefore commendable. He was not a man who loved to sit still ; all his sentiments, whether painful or joyous, acted as a propelling force to set him in motion. Discarding his nephew's arm, he started at a brisk pace down the plank-walk, elbowing his way through the dense throng of people who stood ankle-deep in mud, seeing nothing except the backs of their neighbors' heads, and yet animated and buoyed up with a half-gratified excitement. There were a thousand people at the very least, and more were constantly arriving. The stores on the main street had been closed in order to give clerks and proprietors an opportunity to assist at the clearing up of the mystery ; and the professors in the University had dismissed their classes and given a general holiday. In acknowledgment of this concession they were greeted, wherever any of them appeared, with the peculiar University yell, and sometimes inadvertently pushed into the gutter by a company of students who came storming, four abreast, along the crowded plank-walks. But they were well accustomed to such amenities, and usually bore them without display of temper. When, however, the founder collided with such a squad of noisy under-graduates, threatening demonstrations were apt to follow. Mr. Larkin having founded the University with his own hard-earned money, was of the opinion that the University, in return, owed him gratitude and respect. Having himself never been in a university, he was unable to comprehend the students' view of the case, viz., that they conferred a favor upon the Larkin University by selecting it as the recipient of their patronage, out of the great number which were anxious to attract them. Being, however, well acquainted with Mr. Larkin's sentiments on the subject, they neglected no opportunity to disabuse him; hostilities, of a more or less overt kind, were continually being exchanged.

It was after various vain attempts to assert his authority that the old gentleman reached the spot, where the bloody hat was still an object of interested scrutiny. He had nerved himself for the ordeal, and had conquered his disposition to shudder. The general excitement had entered into his brain and pushed the personal bearing of the case into the dim background. He read the letters *A. L.* with a vague tumult of the blood, but without horror or keen regret. He touched the hat with his stout stick, turned it over, and examined it as a detective might.

"You don't remember if Aleck wore that hat when he started for the depot?" he said to Horace, who kept close at his elbow.

"No, I didn't see him start," the latter replied.

"Whether it is he or not—it is somebody has been killed."

"No doubt about that."

"And the body must be somewhere. Suppose we try to find it?"

Somebody had in the meanwhile discovered bloody finger-marks on a telegraph pole, and the intelligence was eagerly passed from mouth to mouth with appropriate comments. Instantly the crowd began to surge in that direction across the water-soaked lot, and Mr. Larkin and

Horace followed the general impulse. At every step their feet sank into the wet sod and made a sucking sound when they strove to recover them. A cold, drizzling rain was beginning to fall; the leaden skies trailed their vapory curtains along the encompassing hills, and the valley was steeped in dismal moisture and mist. Yet the enterprise of the leading spirits of the crowd was baffled by no discouragements. Tommy Colt, who had been the first to detect the finger-marks, was leading a reconnoitering party which with excited exclamations were pointing out the tracks of two men, the prints of whose boots were visible in the sod. They had apparently now dragged, now carried, a heavy body between them, and the depressions in the turf showed plainly where they had dropped and where resumed their ghastly burden. At the sight of this unmistakable evidence Mr. Larkin started forward in advance of the rest, staring with dilated eyes at the ground. Tommy Colt felt himself superseded, but dared not demur. The old man paced across the half-submerged meadow, now sticking in the mud, now again by vigorous efforts advancing. In one place, where there were half-effaced traces of blood upon the grass, he stopped and poked the ferrule of his cane into the crimson sod. An unfeeling agitation, akin to that which seized the Romans at the sight of the gladiatorial games, had come over him, and the thought that the body which had crimsoned this sod might be that of one who had been dear to him, had no place in his mind. The tracks led toward a deep and sluggish stream (by the students called the Nile) into which two considerable creeks emptied. The Nile wound through a low and marshy delta toward the lake. Thither then poured the dense multitude under Mr. Larkin's lead, dripping with wet, shivering to the marrow of their bones, and yet bent upon losing no share of the sanguinary horror. On the banks of the stream, which was swollen from recent thaws, they came to a stop, and Mr. Larkin called loudly for boats and drag-nets. A couple of dozen volunteers rushed toward the boat-houses, and descending suddenly upon the floating pier, upset it and floundered for some moments in the icy water. When they were fished out, others proceeded more carefully to launch the boats; dragnets were procured and a systematic search began. Mr. Larkin, standing upon an inverted drygoods box which some kindly soul had brought him, gesticulated with his stick and shouted at the top of his voice. Every now and then, as he was in the midst of an important command, the exasperating University yell, sounded by knots of the students, scattered in the crowd, would drown his voice and try his temper. He felt repeatedly tempted to knock down with his cane the first student that came in his way.

For a full hour the old man stood on his drygoods box in the rain, shouting his directions to the searchers. The water dripped from his beard, from his nose, and from the rim of his hat. And yet he was not cold. The excitement hurried his blood at a quickened speed through his veins. As the drag-nets seemed to bring nothing to the surface except bull-heads and perch, a small dredging machine which lay at the mouth of the stream was ordered up, and by the noisy puffing of its steam-engine added to the turmoil and seemed to give an audible expression to the excitement. But though it brought a variety of things to the light, such as demoralized hoop-skirts, tree-roots, and various kitchen utensils from a sunken canal-boat (all of which were hailed with the University yell), it revealed nothing which had any bearing upon the mystery. Another hour passed and another. It was about noon when two boats, which had trailed a drag-net a considerable distance up the stream, struck something which by "the feel of it" might be a human body. The discovery was promptly communicated to Mr. Larkin, who started to run up the bank while the mud splashed about his ears, followed by the dripping and shivering multitude. The floating pier, again upsetting, gave an icy mud-bath to a score of people, but so great was the excitement that scarcely anybody, except the unfortunates themselves, gave any heed to it. Slowly, amid breathless silence, the net approached the surface. Anxious suspense was depicted on every face. Mr. Larkin dropped his cane and, with straining eyes and loudly thumping heart, leaned out over the stream, following the motions of the men. Now—but another moment—now—an indistinct something shimmers through the water. There—it is—it is—a body—oh, God, what is it? It is a calf! A burst of Homeric laughter rose from one part of the crowd—that part which contained the students. No one else laughed; least of all Mr. Larkin. He descended from his station of command in a wrathful mood. He thrust his cane so hard into the mud that he had to stop to pull it out. Nobody dared to speak to him; he felt a burning need of vengeance upon somebody. He suddenly remembered that a petition of the students had been shown him, some days ago, by a member of the faculty, asking for a holiday on the day following Washington's Birthday, as it happened to be a Friday, and many students desired to spend this little vacation in their homes. He remembered also that he had promptly vetoed the proposition (he rather liked to veto propositions coming from the students), and the faculty had, as usual, registered his decree. It required no great ingenuity to guess the rest. The students, in order to thwart him and get their holiday, had perpetrated this bogus murder. Learning by accident that Aleck was going to New York, they had gotten possession of one of his old hats, stolen a calf from a neighboring farm, killed it on the road to the depot, dragged it over the empty lots, and thrown it into the Nile.

To Mr. Larkin this plot had no humorous aspect. It represented the deepest depth of human depravity. He was prepared to see every man who had participated in it find his legitimate end on the gallows. If he only knew who the miscreants were, he would show them that he, too, could be a successful humorist ; and not a mother's son of them but should carry to the end of his days the remembrance of the joke he would play upon him. He meant to teach those audacious vagabonds a lesson which would cure them of all future desire to trifle with his dignity. He meditated for some moments on the practicability of cancelling the charter of the University. But that required legislative action, and would, moreover, expose him to no end of ridicule. It was, perhaps, better first to discover the guilty parties, and have them summarily punished. Only that appeared to Mr. Larkin rather a lame and inadequate retribution. To him the one was just as guilty as the other, whether cognizant of the plot or not, and he hungered for vengeance upon the whole University. While he was revolving his vindictive plans a company of students came strolling along the plank-walk. They fell into single file, and each one of them lifted his hat and greeted the founder with demure politeness. Ah, but that was a trying moment for the Hon. Obed Larkin ! He saw or seemed to see a gleam of amusement lurking in every eye that was raised to his. He faced half about, with clenched teeth and his legs wide apart, and grabbed the stout silver handle of his cane with a convulsive clutch. He felt an enthusiastic desire to assault them—to have it out with them on the spot. But at that very instant Arabella Robbins and Pussy Dallas came tripping along under

the same umbrella, and as they saw the wrathful Obed
they chirruped gayly: "How do you do, Mr. Larkin?"
That brought him quickly to his senses. He could not
afford to be seen in a free fight with the students of his
University upon the common highway. He growled an
ungracious return to the girls' greeting, swore a voluminous oath in the depth of his soul, and faced once more
toward the town. As he entered his library, his wife
handed him a telegram from Aleck, informing him of his
safe arrival in New York and his probable return on the
following day.

CHAPTER XII.

"TOMATO CATSUP."

The Hon. Obed Larkin caught a severe cold, which threatened to develop into pneumonia, in consequence of his strategic operations on the banks of the Nile. He had an instinctive feeling that the town was laughing at him, and having become accustomed to look upon himself as an august personage, he could not endure the thought that his name was being taken in vain. He had no pride either of birth or blood, but he liked to pose a little as a representative American—a self-made man, owing everything to his own ability and exertions ; and he was apt to find himself in this capacity an impressive and dignified character. His fellow-citizens had humored him in this conceit until it had become part of his being. And now, in order to shirk their own share in the foolish business, they made him their scapegoat and laughed at him with amused superiority, as if they had seen through the joke from the beginning.

When the danger of pneumonia was past, Mr. Larkin was laid up for a week with an attack of rheumatism, which he also traced to the unhappy Nile expedition. The purpose of getting even with the students had by this time become an *idée fixe* with him ; and, like the pious Æneas, he revolved a good many impious projects in his sleepless nights. He finally directed Horace to write to the Pinkerton Bureau for two expert detectives, who might enter some special department in the university, get into the confidence of the students, and procure evidence for the conviction of the guilty parties. It took Horace a week of ingenious argument and persuasion to induce his uncle to give up this unworthy scheme, and he used to say, in after years, that he had never argued a more difficult case before any court. That Aleck joined his persuasions to those of his brother had very little weight with the old gentleman, because he held Aleck's practical judgment in light esteem.

The faculty of the university had, in the meanwhile, with Mr. Larkin's consent, taken up the affair, and begun a trial, which soon degenerated into broad burlesque. A mass of the most bewilderingly contradictory evidence was elicited which would have driven to despair the astutest judge in Christendom. One rural-looking sophomore, whose mind seemed as dense as his vocabulary was limited, testified that he had frequently killed calves and knew how it was done, but disclaimed all knowledge of the present case. When asked what his character and standing were in the university, he replied that his character was licentious. Such frankness naturally astounded the learned faculty, and they were inclined to believe that they had at last caught one of the transgressors, when it occurred to Professor Wharton to ask the witness what he meant by the term "licentious." The youth replied that he had taken more license than he ought to have done, absenting himself from dull lectures and recitations, such as Professor P——'s and Professor N——'s.

"I guess I've cut you more'n anybody," he added, guilelessly, to his questioner, at which, to Professor Wharton's great annoyance, a perceptible snicker ran around the room.

There was some dispute when this young man had been dismissed, as to whether he was as innocent as he appeared. About thirty more witnesses were called, and rigidly cross-examined ; but it soon became obvious that there was a conspiracy among them to "guy" their prosecutors, and, as the latter had no judicial authority and could not punish for "contempt," they could not prevent the students from getting the better of them. A few of the professors, who were gifted with more zeal than humor, plumped right into the traps which had been set for them, lost their temper, and gave occasion for the most farcical proceedings. The only thing which was established by the trial was the fact that six students, whose names were ascertained, had met, the evening before the untimely taking off of the calf, in the so-called Bayerhof, a temperance restaurant, kept by a voluminous German named Schnabel. This Schnabel, who had formerly kept a beer saloon, was a thorn in the flesh of the good temperance people of the town ; as it was more than suspected that he was growing rich by violation of the excise law. Although the town had, at the last election, voted "no license," this impudent foreigner still flaunted a jolly

Gambrinus riding on a beer-keg in the face of an outraged community. That students visited his place in the small hours of the night for the sake of procuring coffee and lemonade seemed a little incredible, though Schnabel himself maintained, with a sober face, that such was the case.

"De yoong beoples, dey set up in de nide unt read for dem egsaminations ; unt dey get hoongry—dem poor poys —unt dey gome to me, unt dey say to me : 'Mishter Schnabel, gib us ein stück Frankfurter sausage mit coffee unt Schweitzer kase unt bretzel.' Unt mein vife unt me, ve haf to get up oud of der varm bet unt fry Frankfurter wurst for dem hoongry poys vhen deir landladies' noses snores in deir billows. For dem landladies vill not get up to gib the poys sometings to eat in de nide, vhen dey shtudy for dem egsaminations."

The plea of charity to hungry wasters of the midnight oil might have been accepted as good, if the patrons of the Bayerhof had belonged to that worthy class. But it was notorious that the young gentlemen who roused Schnabel and his spouse from their slumbers did not owe their reputations to their eminence in scholastic pursuits. When it was accordingly ascertained that six undergraduate roysterers had, on the night of Washington's Birthday, met in his saloon, the virtuous wrath of the town suddenly turned from the calf-slayers to Carl Schnabel, who, by selling them liquor, had instigated them to evil-doing. After consultation with Mr. Larkin, Professors Wharton and Dowd called upon the police magistrate and swore out a warrant for Schnabel's arrest. The trial, which was set down for the following day, was the all-absorbing topic of discussion both in town and university circles. Mr. Schnabel made an attempt, though a futile one, to secure Horace Larkin for his counsel, and finally had to telegraph for a lawyer from Rochester, as all local attorneys of any standing refused, on account of his unpopularity, to defend him. The Rochester attorney was prompt to arrive, and made haste to interview the students upon whose testimony the case hinged.

The court-house was packed with people when Mr. Schnabel was brought forward to plead. He was, of course, "not guilty ;" but there was a troubled look in his eye, when he saw the long rows of students whom the prosecution had summoned to testify against him. The first of these who was called to the witness-stand relieved, however, his anxiety by swearing that, as far as he knew, he had never drunk lager beer in Schnabel's temperance restaurant.

"Have you drunk anything there?" asked the court.

"Yes."

"What have you drunk?"

"I am not sure."

"What did you order?" queried the court, impatiently.

"Tomato catsup."

"And did you get tomato catsup?"

"I don't know."

"How is it that you don't know?"

"I could not swear that it was tomato catsup. I am not an expert on tomato catsup."

"Are you sure it was not beer you drank?"

"No."

"You are not sure?"

"No. I am not an expert on beer."

"Not an expert on beer, hm! Did it look like beer?"

"I could not tell."

"Are you in the habit of drinking tomato catsup?"

"Well, since the town voted 'no license' I am obliged to drink whatever I can get."

"Why, then, don't you drink water?"

"It doesn't agree with me. Besides, I've been told that the water in this town is bad."

"Are you willing to swear that you never drank beer in Schnabel's restaurant?"

"No."

"You are not willing to swear that? Then, you must be willing to swear that you have drunk beer there?"

"No."

"But you don't seriously maintain that you drank tomato catsup?"

"I ordered tomato catsup."

One witness after another was now called and gave similar testimony. One declared that he had never ordered anything but Oolong tea; and when asked if what he got tasted like Oolong tea, he affirmed that he was not an expert on tea. Another had a standing order for "Mocha" whenever he entered, and a third was always served with "Java." All had such profound respect for the sanctity of the oath that they were unwilling to swear that what they got was beer or was not beer; they had never made a sufficient study of beer to justify them in having an opinion. The most ludicrous answers were given with imperturbable gravity, and were greeted by the audience with uncontrollable bursts of laughter. The judge vainly hammered away at his desk with his gavel, and threatened to have the court-room cleared, in case any one dared to make demonstrations inconsistent with the dignity of a tribunal of justice. Nevertheless, he did not carry out his threat when the next funny answer occasioned another outburst of hilarity. He was quick to perceive that the sentiment of the crowd had turned in favor of the young men, and the severity of his mien relaxed. He did not question that, in a superficial sense, they were telling the truth. Each one of them had obviously agreed with Schnabel upon an *alias* for beer, one calling it tomato catsup, another Oolong, and a third Mocha. The cleverness of this dodge evidently appealed to the crowd; and the judge, who in his private capacity enjoyed a joke as well as any one, could not find it in his heart to be too severe on them. He therefore dismissed the case for want of proof, and Schnabel, with a sly wink, resumed his activity as an apostle of the cause of temperance.

CHAPTER XIII.

DIVINE DISCONTENT.

To a person who rises from a severe illness the aspect of life seems often strangely changed. Common things which before seemed worthless become valuable and significant. The convalescent returns, like a traveller from the borderland of death, and his wonted surroundings have, at first, a vague air of strangeness, and have to re-adjust themselves according to a changed standard of valuation.

It was the merciful apathy consequent upon physical exhaustion which had dulled the struggle of emotions in Gertrude's breast, and thereby saved her life at a time when the faintest gust of passion might have blown out the feeble flame of her being. As her strength returned, and her senses slowly reawakened, a light veil seemed to have been drawn over her past through which memories shone dimly with a shadowy pallor. She knew that something of a vital character had occurred between Dr. Hawk and herself, but she found it unnecessary to rouse herself to a realization of what it was. The verses of Omar Khayyam came floating toward her like a soundless melody from "an immeasurable distance," and they haunted her with a nightmarish persistency, though she could only remember a few detached but fascinating phrases. And yet to ask the doctor to repeat them would seem like an approach, on her part, and an invitation to resume sentimental relations. His comings and goings were yet matters of deep concern to her, and his voice was yet potent to charge her nerves with vibrating excitement. Her interest in him seemed to return with her returning strength ; and although she tried to keep it, as it were, at arm's length, prohibiting it from stepping too near, she was not entirely successful. The doctor's spasmodic visits, which, after long absences, were crowded into a single week, to be followed again by conspicuous neglect, occupied her mind more than she suspected. Of course she possessed the key to the interpretation of this strange irregularity, and she could not help applying it in a way that was flattering to her self-esteem. The doctor's conduct said, as plainly as actions could say it, that he was struggling with an overmastering passion, which he was combating with all his strength, suffering yet defeats which were, to Gertrude's mind, no less honorable to his character than his victories. The fact, too, that his quarrel with Aleck, which, in a distorted form reached her ears, did not impel him to break off all relations with a house in which he had suffered such an insult, argued to her a heroic streak in his temperament. Even the horrible humiliation which he had suffered in being subjected to police surveillance for half a day, he had borne in dignified silence ; and the whole ghastly farce, in which he had involuntarily played a part, had roused in him no desire for vengeance. Gertrude could not doubt that it was his love for her which furnished the explanation of this unreasonable magnanimity; and although she had persuaded herself that she did not return this love, she was yet vexed with Aleck for placing obstacles in its way.

To gain a respite from importunate thoughts, Gertrude began again ɔ sketch and to model in clay. She found her abortive ttempt at a bas-relief dried and cracked on the board, d Nettie, the chambermaid, who was sent to bring it d n from the attic lost half of it on the way. It was the head of a nun—and a very aristocratic one— who had been shut up in a convent by her wicked relatives. A nun had always appeared to Gertrude a poetic character ; and she had once had herself photographed with a hood and brow-band, to see how she would look, in case she should ever decide to become one. She felt in herself a capacity both for renunciation and for high-minded rebellion against tyranny which could only find their proper expression, if she were a nun. The fact was, she felt in herself an inexhaustible capacity for any and every emotion that for the moment appeared interesting. Having procured fresh clay, she set to work again with enthusiasm, and labored for three days, with alternations of zeal and despair, at the idea which she meant to express. But her criticism was always so far in advance of her skill that she never could finish anything without feeling a desire to smash it. She had, indeed, no doubt as to the excellence of her ideas. But there was a perverse spirit

in her fingers which made them decline to do what she
wanted them to do—which made them pervert her fine intentions into something awkward and commonplace. She
dipped into Ruskin in the hope of getting some guidance
from him, and learned incidentally that she ought to study
that which was near and familiar, and that the unspoiled
human foot was a very beautiful combination of harmonious curves. With an impulsiveness characteristic of her
ardent temperament she pulled off her shoes and stockings and began to study her feet. Yes, Ruskin was right—
they were, on the whole, quite good. Large, full generous lines—high instep—only the little toe was a trifle distorted and adorned with a corn. Gertrude became possessed with a desire to model them. She covered up her
nun with a damp cloth, and seizing her modelling sticks
carved out rapidly the shape of a foot. She drew the
hearth-rug of tiger-skin forward, put her chair and easel
upon it, and placed against the fender a mirror, in which
one projecting foot was clearly reflected. She stooped
every now and then to measure its breadth, length, and
width with a pair of compasses, and became so absorbed in
her work that she did not hear a knock at the door which
was several times repeated. She hummed and talked to
herself, making exclamations of encouragement and approval, or of criticism.

"Now, Gertie, that won't do," she would say as she eyed
a clumsily modelled form, "you know better than that."
Or again, when a little lightness of touch gave her pleasure, "Gertie, my dear girl, that was well done ; I approve of you."

She was in the midst of such a soliloquy when the knob
of the door was cautiously turned, and she saw Dr. Hawk's
swarthy face appear in the opening.

"May I come in ?" he asked, with an expression of surprise at seeing her occupation. "Mr. Larkin begged me
to pay you a professional visit."

Gertrude jumped up in confusion, and suddenly re-
membering the incompleteness of her toilet, threw herself
down on the sofa and drew her feet up under her dress.
It did not occur to her, until he had closed the door behind him, that she might have prevented him from entering.

"Excuse me," he began, as he slowly approached her ;
"but I supposed you were ill in bed. Your father told
me you had not been down to dinner."

"No, I forgot it," she answered, hastily ; "I had something to do."

"Forgot your dinner," he repeated, reproachfully. "Then your occupation, whatever it was, must have been very absorbing."

"It was—quite absorbing."

His eyes fell suddenly upon the lump of wet clay in a box on the floor, and the still uncovered foot on the stand.

"But, my dear young lady, what is this ?" he exclaimed, pointing to these surprising objects. "Are you emulating Phidias ?"

"No," she replied, blushing as if she had been caught at something disgraceful. "I am only killing time."

"Time I believe has always been your enemy," the doctor remarked.

"It is every woman's enemy, unless she knows something."

She picked up a sketch-book, and in order to relieve her embarrassment began to turn its leaves with an air of interest.

"You appear to have a quarrel with woman's lot in general," her visitor went on tentatively.

"To a woman of spirit that is all that her lot is good for."

"To quarrel with ?"

"Yes."

"Do you then find yours so unsatisfactory ?"

"Yes—I have—*the divine discontent*," she said, raising her eyes to his, and smiling vaguely.

"That is something I can't prescribe for. It is a malady which, like the gout, is painful, but confers a certain distinction."

She made no reply to this ; but seized a pencil, and began to scribble on a blank page of her sketch-book. He turned toward the easel, upon which the covered bas-relief was standing. Without asking permission he removed the cloth, and with a look of great intentness scanned the medallion. Gertrude cast glances full of veiled anxiety at his face, over the top of the sketch-book. She wished to appear unconcerned ; but a dim agitation was smouldering in her nerves.

"That's a bit of autobiography, isn't it ?" said Hawk, after a distressingly long pause.

"How do you mean ?"

"It is a sort of personification of the divine discontent."

"Is it?" she queried a little hypocritically; "I wasn't aware of it."

"Tell that to the marines," he retorted, brusquely. "That rebellious curl of the lip—I know the original of that. That beautiful scorn—the same that you find in the lips of the Apollo Belvedere—the lofty contempt for life's pestiferous little meannesses—I know, too, where that came from. The chorus of whining, droning, and buzzing dunghill insects, blending into a dull and hollow monotone, instead of lulling her soul to sleep has made her conscious of her superiority. That chin, so nobly strong and stubborn, proclaims perseverance in rebellion, defiance of Fate. The hood and the brow-band which hold all this strength and loveliness in their dull frame are Torryville—the stolid, listless, narrowly self-satisfied Torryville, where an aspiration beyond bread and butter is in man an oddity and in woman a crime."

Gertrude's sketch-book had dropped in her lap; she listened first with interest, then with rapture, and when he had finished she sprang up, forgetful of her bare feet; but flung herself instantly down again, covering her face with her hands. She was ashamed of her excitement, but could not control it. Never yet had anyone spoken thus out of her very heart. Never had she hoped to find in any one such a subtle understanding of her innermost self. A man who was gifted with so deep a vision—was he to be judged by the ordinary Philistine standard? If he was different from others, the difference was to his credit. The last shadow of distrust of the doctor vanished from Gertrude's heart. She saw with a suddenly clarified sight the grandeur of this man whom she had so long misjudged. She felt his dark, sad eyes resting upon her, as she lay there foolishly ashamed of her emotion. She became now, in turn, ashamed of her shame; and with an effort at self-mastery rose slowly to a half-sitting posture, and fixed upon the doctor a large, frank gaze, full of devotion and gratitude. Hawk, who instantly felt what this glance meant, turned his back upon the nun, seized a chair, and seated himself close to the lounge. A gentle warmth seemed to be radiating from her, and rippled beneficently through his veins. If there had been a spark of simple straightforward manhood in him, he could now have plucked the fruit which hung trembling on its stalk, ready to drop into his lap. But the flush of anticipated victory, which would have made another man happily unconscious,

made Hawk conscious to his very finger-tips. He had to
play his little comedy, even at the risk of unforeseen
catastrophes.

"Miss Gertrude," he began, in a tenderly tremulous
bass, which betrayed traces of elocution, "if I dared speak
to you as my heart prompts me to speak——"

"Why should you not speak to me?" she murmured,
blushing furiously.

"Ah, my child, you do not know me! you do not know
me!" he muttered, in a despairing voice.

"Yes, I do know you," she protested, warmly, lifting
upon him a look of affectionate reassurance. He met her
gaze firmly; but there was nothing but a cold and somewhat forced melancholy in the glance with which he strove
to respond. A dissonance—a shadow—something too im-
palpable for words to express, stole in between them.

Suddenly, like the going out of a spark, the tender light
in her eyes was quenched, leaving a chilly vacuum in its
place.

"Miss Gertrude," he said, in a voice that shook with
pleading humility; "do not judge me, do not judge me,
until I tell you all."

He rose with slow and deliberate movements, seized his
hat and stalked toward the door. A dramatic exit he did
not fail to achieve, even though the scene which led up to
it may have been unsatisfactory. No sooner had the door
closed behind him than Gertrude jumped up in a tumult
of anger, confusion, and shame, ran toward the bed and
flinging herself on the top of the counterpane buried her
burning face in the pillows. Her head was in a whirl.
She lay thus for a while in a benumbed lethargy, through
which a dull pain was throbbing. She could not make
clear to herself what had happened or whether anything
had happened; she only had an aching sense of humiliation and a dim desire to hurt somebody in return for the
hurt she had suffered. She had actually been ready to
throw herself into that man's embrace, if he had but
opened his arms to receive her. She had, under the impression that he needed encouragement, almost invited
him to propose to her—and he had coolly repelled her.
But was it really true that he had repelled her? Gertrude's heart found itself, before long, pleading the doctor's cause, trying to convince itself that he had really
meant no harm. Men had a way of misrepresenting their
own intentions by sheer awkwardness. How could he,

who knew so well her worth, who had in such beautiful
words interpreted her innermost longings, how could he
wish to repel her ?   No, it was merely his foolish loyalty,
his sense of obligation, to that wretched girl who had invested her money in him and taken a chattel mortgage on
his affections, it was this which had made him behave so
abominably.   Gertrude arose with this consoling reflection, dipped her face in cold water at the washstand, and
rang for her maid.   When her toilet was completed she
ordered her phaeton ; but after a moment's deliberation
countermanded the order, and sat down to work at her
medallion.   But, somehow, she could not summon any interest in the work.   Her nun with the disdainful lips
seemed a hideous caricature.   The more she looked at
her the more insufferable she became.   There was a revival of angry feeling in Gertrude's breast as she sat contemplating her cherished creation.   All the doctor's fine
phrases recurred to her, one by one, and her hard-won
equanimity deserted her.   In a fit of disgust she seized
the modelling sticks, and made a deep gash in the face of
her counterfeit.

CHAPTER XIV.

TROUBLED WATERS.

The sun was bright and the air was filled with the rush of many waters. Down through the deep ravines swollen creeks came tumbling, plunging with a thundering boom over the rocky precipices, hurrying heedlessly on with noisy brawl and strife, seething and swirling in the smooth, black caldrons, blowing hissing gusts of spray through the bare tree-tops, whirling, dancing, rolling, and rumbling on, hurling their great tawny torrents down the slope, winding in tortuous eddies through the plain below, and emptying through a ramified delta into the lake, where their progress was still traceable as a broad, brown current, slowly blending into the clearer encompassing waters. Up among the leafless underbrush rose a tiny chorus of rippling and tinkling murmurs—now a gay little glassy treble, now a hushed little gurgling hum—from diminutive rills that meandered at their own sweet will under the tree-roots and over the stones, uniting and separating again, vanishing under the bowlders, and glinting again in the sunlight, playing hide and seek with each other, until all of a sudden their slender lives were lost in the wildly hurrying torrent.

The air was raw, in spite of the sun. Wandering gusts of warm dampness kept careering through the atmosphere and stroked your face like a caress; but from the great icy caverns under the Drum-Head Fall, where the blue icicles yet hung in solid columns, an insidious chill pervaded the very sunlight, warning you against a rash confidence in the promises of spring.

Gertrude Larkin, having exhausted the allurements of the plastic art, had yielded to a vague restlessness in her blood, and had started out on foot toward the Drum-Head Ravine, where she concluded the trailing arbutus must now be in bloom. It seemed to her that this winter had lasted a century, and she hungered for a whiff of spring. She was weary of thinking of Dr. Hawk, with his incal-

culable capers—weary of hating, and weary of loving him
—weary of inventing reasons for his enigmatical actions—
weary of her own weariness—weary of everything. She
loathed Dr. Hawk, she loathed herself, she loathed the
whole world. But in that frame of mind she found it impossible to sit still; and driven by an impulse to move,
she had found her way to the ravine. On the bridge,
under which there was a great swash of whirling and tossing waters, she met the Rev. Arthur Robbins, who, arrayed
in a new spring overcoat and a shining beaver of the latest
fashion, was picking his way along the little dry path at
the edge of the road.

"Well, Miss Gertrude," he said, lifting his hat and shaking off a drop of water which some heedless tree had deposited on it. "I am glad to see the roses returning."

"I have not seen them yet, Mr. Robbins," she replied;
"they never come until June."

"Ah, my child, I meant the roses in your cheeks," ejaculated the parson, cheerily.

The doctor's haunting quotation, "I sometimes think
that never blooms so red the rose as where some buried
Cæsar bled," flitted through her mind; and as no appropriate remark occurred to her, she leaned over the railing
and stared at the water. Mr. Robbins, who also discovered
something to interest him in the brown torrent, put one
neatly-shod foot on the middle rail and leaning forward
followed with his eyes the swirling rapids.

"It is not quite well with you yet, Miss Gertie," he said,
after a while; "you have something on your mind—something that distresses you."

"That I have always had, as long as I can remember,"
she answered, with forced lightness; "I cannot recall the
time when I was not distressed about something. There
are some people, you know, who happen to put the wrong
foot foremost when they enter the world and are unable to
rectify the mistake by anything they do afterward. I am
one of those people."

"My dear girl," the clergyman went on, while watching
with visible interest the gyrations of a dry branch in an
eddy, "I don't know that I have any business to pry into
your secrets, especially as you have always rebuffed me.
But I can't help taking an interest in you, you know. The
life you lead is unnatural for a young girl—it is not wholesome—not as it ought to be."

There was a note of sincere friendliness in this apologetic remonstrance which touched Gertrude. Was it possible that there was help here for her trouble? She respected Mr. Robbins as an upright and kind-hearted man; but she had never suspected in him any sympathy with her own complex and intangible afflictions. Besides, she vaguely objected to him as the father of Arabella, whose airs and capers he ought to have corrected, instead of encouraging them by petting and foolish admiration. His words, however, in the present moment, appealed to something within her which responded, before she had time to reflect upon her previous estimate of his limitations. She fixed upon him her deep blue eyes with their cloudy suggestions; and they lighted up with a quickened animation.

"Tell me, Mr. Robbins," she said, quite unconscious at first of the conundrum she was about to propound; "what kind of life is natural for a girl? And is the same kind natural for all girls? Is a girl a mere specimen of her sex, and has she not, like a man, a right to decide whatever kind of life may happen to suit her?"

"My dear, we are all specimens of our sex," Mr. Robbins observed, without a shadow of combativeness.

"I know that," Gertrude responded, with kindling zeal; "but men are valuable and peculiar specimens, each one of which is labelled and studied, and not blindly lumped with all the rest."

"They are not half as valuable and peculiar as women," said Mr. Robbins, with a smile and a bow, in which there was a touch of gallantry.

"The very tone in which you say that shows that you don't mean it," she retorted, with increasing earnestness, "if the mental traits of girls were thought to be of any consequence, you and other good people would not do your best to wipe them out, and to make each as much as possible like all the rest. You would try to find out not what kind of life is suitable for girls, but for this or that girl who came to you for counsel."

"That is what I try in a humble way to do," the parson declared, with amiable neutrality. Then he shifted his position, putting his left foot up on the railing instead of the right, and looked at his enigmatical parishioner with kindly compassion.

"Ah, but you are so distressingly amiable, Mr. Robbins," the girl exclaimed, with a hint of irritation. "You don't even pay me the compliment to get angry with me.

You look at me with mild disapprobation, as you would at some inconvenient canary-bird that had taken it into his head to chirrup about the problems of creation."

Mr. Robbins poked his cane energetically into a crevice of the top rail, and loosened a knot around which the wood had decayed. Having accomplished this task, he brought his foot to the ground, and there came a look of quickened interest into his eyes. "I won't quote the Bible to you, my dear," he said, "for I don't think it would do you any good. The fact is, you are rebelling against the order of the universe ; and if I didn't have a sneaking sympathy with your rebellion, I suppose I should find the right words with which to rebuke you."

"Then you think I deserve rebuke, because I am not happy."

"No doubt you do ; only I have not the heart to administer it."

"I wish you would, if you think it would benefit me. Perhaps I should then be happier."

"Happy, my child, happy ! Happiness is an entirely pagan idea. I doubt if the word is mentioned a single time in the Bible, unless it be in the sense of heavenly blessedness."

"Then Christians, you think, have no business trying to be happy ?"

"No, I don't think that at all. I only think that little girls should not trouble themselves about things which they can't possibly comprehend."

"You mean they shouldn't trouble you with things which you don't comprehend," Gertrude, in her heedless zeal, was about to reply ; but she checked her tongue and finished : "You mean it is not good for women to think."

"No, dear, I don't know even that I have the courage to say that. On the contrary, I am aware that you think some very good things—only, as you say, they don't make you any happier. The fact is, Miss Gertie, you are too clever for your own good."

"But what would you then have me do, Mr. Robbins ?" she ejaculated, not in an emotional but in a sort of argumentative despair.

"Do ? Why, I wouldn't have you do anything, unless I could get you interested in church work, in relieving the wants of the poor, and contributing your mite toward furtherance of the cause of Christ among the heathen. That is the proper work, I think, for a girl——"

"Ah, there we have it again. That, you think, is the proper work for a girl——"

"Pardon me," he interrupted, quietly, "I was going to say, for a girl, situated as you are."

"To knit stockings for the Zulus and eat strawberries and ice-cream for the benefit of the South Sea Islanders; that, you think, ought to satisfy the ambition of a girl situated as I am."

"You have a paradoxical way of putting things, my dear; but to extend the kingdom of Christ has satisfied many a man and woman as highly gifted and as ambitious as you."

There was a sudden note of authority in this final admonition which startled the girl. By the same process by which, after having drifted with the age, he pulled himself suddenly back to his orthodox moorings, he now put all weak sympathy to flight, and planted himself squarely on biblical ground. He had had the same experience a hundred times before; but his kindly and tolerant nature could never quite learn the lesson that any parley with the spirit of the age leads only to inconsistency and surrender. And yet there was in the depth of his heart a tormenting doubt which made him linger irresolutely, although he desired to be gone. Was it his fault or was it hers that his words struck no responsive chord in her soul, brought her no help in her perplexities? He hoped it was hers; but he was by no means sure of it. And yet, he understood her so well; might have entered so deeply into her state of mind, which was not alien to him. But if he had done that, what would have become of his clerical dignity? The uneasy sense of his duty to assert himself in that and not in his personal capacity was indeed the cause of his failure in this, as in many other cases. "Were I but a priest," he sighed to himself, for the thousandth time; "had I but the spirit, the voice, and the authority of a priest of God!"

He would have liked to part from Gertrude with a strong and resonant word in which there were peace and elevation. But these organ notes of consolation, though they often haunted him and seemed close within his reach, never vibrated through his voice; never stole as an inspiration into his words and lifted them above kindly commonplace. And so, in the present instance, he could but lift his shining hat with its curling brim (it was the first hat of that fashion in the town) and express the lame hope to his perplexed parishioner that returning health would restore her wonted cheerfulness. As a grand *finale* that was wofully weak ; and Mr. Robbins's ears burned uncomfortably, as he picked his way among the mud-puddles toward the town.

CHAPTER XV.

TRAILING ARBUTUS.

A deep, gaping fissure in the earth, a record of some tremendous prehistoric convulsion, its rough edges somewhat worn by ten thousand summers and winters —that was the Drum Head Ravine. In their grand outlines the two sides corresponded, a projection in one being a hollow in the other ; but the tooth of time (which is a very hard tooth) had torn and mauled the original face of the rock beyond recognition. Wind and storm had scratched and furrowed it ; the cold had pierced to its heart and burst it, and gentle spring, who in his dealings with the rock is the hardest customer of all, had stripped it bare, nay, stripped it of its very skin and carried it, with the rest of his plunder, down to the bottom of the ravine. Summer in its pity had clothed the rock, like Joseph, in a coat of many colors—dull green moss and yellow, brown, and scarlet lichens. In a fantastic mood he adorned its head with huge plumes of fern, which grew in rank luxuriance, and were splendid to behold. But like all beautiful things they perished, and in their death became the foundation of new life. The long procession of the ages, with their grand alternations of growth and decay, passed over the face of the rock, froze it and scorched it, stripped it and clothed it, shook, broke, rubbed, and scratched it, nay, undertook a series of cosmic experiments with it which left it as you see it to-day.

Pine, hemlock, oak, and maple now keep up a silent, but fierce struggle for the possession of the rock. In many places you see the pine and the oak in deadly combat on the very edge of the precipice ; it looks as if the pine had the worst of it, for it hangs out over the abyss, while the oak with its gnarled hands seems to be holding it by the hair meditating whether it shall let it drop. With a desperate clutch the pine holds on to the rock, and if it were not for the little brook which, from pure cu-

riosity, has come rippling down among its roots—just to
see the fight—it might hold its own yet for many a year.

Gertrude Larkin gazed with unawakened senses at this
absorbing page of the earth's history. If she had known
of the tremendous forces which were wrestling, if she had
but had the faintest clue to the wonderful drama which
was in progress round about her, she would never, even
in ill temper, have called the gorge a bore. She knew
something about Cicero and Virgil (the advantage of
knowing which she never discovered); she could talk
French fairly well, and she had a cloudy remembrance
of a nightmarish something called moral philosophy.
And here she went in the spring of the year, weary unto
death, starved in spirit, because her education had failed
to open her senses and supply her with a vital connecting-
link with reality. Yet there was such a fine resonance in
her for any strong or beautiful thought. She would have
rejoiced in the story of Nature's great and relentless war
—the unending battle for the poor privilege of life—
which was being waged in the rock, the soil, the water,
and the air, had she but known the language in which it
was written.

Gertrude was thinking of what the parson had said to her,
and she heeded but, in a mechanical way, the difficulties
which the rugged path presented. She clutched now and
then a low-hanging bough or braced herself against the
trunk of a tree, when a stone rolled away from under her
foot and set a little landslide in motion, on its way to the
river. There was a resinous odor from the perspiring
pines, and the swelling buds of maple and oak also contributed a faint balsamic fragrance. The sweetbriers
spread their thorny nakedness against the sun and blushed
to the very finger-tips. The brown carpet of last year's
leaves, which was wet and mildewed below the topmost
stratum, was here and there lifted by some big, purple
bud, tightly closed like a fist, flushed with exuberant life,
and sticky with rank and ill-smelling juices.

It was a toilsome path which led by all sorts of capricious turns and windings up the rock and down the rock,
along the water's edge and over decaying trunks which
bridged temporary pools. Gertrude stopped half a dozen
times to consider whether she should turn about; but
something in her blood beat in vague sympathy with the
awakening life about her, and made her aimlessly press
on. The little basket in her hand reminded her that she

had started out ostensibly in search of trailing arbutus ;
and she stooped down among the bowlders and began to
rummage among the dead leaves. Vines she found in
plenty, but flowers there were none. Only a few white
and blue anemones peeped forth among the tree-roots and
a wake-robin balanced upon its green stalk a single large
leaf, above which the white flower was nodding. There
was evidence that somebody had been ahead of her ; for
there were fresh tracks in the loose mould ; and the upturned leaves were yet dank and moist.

"Those plaguy co-eds," Gertrude muttered ; "they scent
a flower as a dog does a rabbit."

She picked, half in disgust, the anemones and the wake-
robin and was about to return to the path, when suddenly
she discovered a stooping figure among the stones, some
fifty feet above her. It was a man, and as far as she could
see, he was alone. That a man should start out alone in
search of wild flowers seemed a curious thing, and she
knew but one man in Torryville who would be capable of
it. Did she wish to meet Dr. Hawk here, after what had
occurred between them ? But who in the world could it
be for whom he was picking flowers ? He surely was not
picking them for himself ; that would be too absurd even
for him. Was it for his mortgagee—the girl who had
pre-empted his affection against all claimants ? Perhaps
the doctor was having two strings to his bow ; perhaps he
was playing under cover with his mortgagee, and was
merely satisfying his dramatic instinct in enacting little
guarded love-scenes with his patients. Gertrude flushed
with wrath at this suspicion, and resolved to call her admirer to account. But what right had she to do that ? He
had never declared that he loved her ; never asked her to
marry him. Was it not possible that her own over-wrought
fancy had spun this entire romance by subjecting the doctor's actions to a too ingenious interpretation. That was
a possibility which was fraught with fresh humiliation.

She was anxious to avoid the doctor, and yet in the recon-
dite recesses of her mind hoped that she might not succeed. There was nothing to prevent her from going home,
and she would perhaps have done so, if she had not discovered the figure of a strange woman down on the path
by the creek. A curious reluctance to meet this woman
took possession of her ; she was often subject to impulses
of this sort, and never attempted to account for them. She
skipped quickly from stone to stone, and reached the

winding wooden staircase which leads to the upper rocky terrace. Here the water-fall kept up a perpetual booming as of heavy artillery, and the spray blew in white showers through the tree-tops. The torrent seethed and tossed with despairing contortions in the smooth black cauldron, and plunged at last with hissing noises down over the brown bowlders. Gertrude became so absorbed in this spectacle that she forgot all about the woman from whom she had wished to escape ; and she uttered a faint cry, when she suddenly discovered her standing at the foot of the staircase. Yielding to an irrational impulse of fear, she ran up twenty or thirty steps, paused to draw breath, and finally flung herself down under a pine-tree that grew close to the mill-race. There was a small mill situated here, and a dam, which was overflowing on all sides with brown water. The sun was quite warm and the steam of the earth was delicious—full of stirring life and creative ferment. Gertrude sat idly gazing at the slow currents that bore dead leaves and branches to the edge of the dam, and the spongy foam and bubbles that gathered about the stones on the shores, and got detached, sailing away on some capricious eddy. It seemed in one moment so beautiful—and in the next inexpressibly dreary. The trees stretched their gaunt hands against the sky, praying for sun and summer, and they prayed not in vain, for the strong juices were rising within them and their buds were swelling.

She became aware, while she sat thus absorbed in contemplation, of some alien presence, and turning swiftly about saw the strange woman standing at the head of the staircase, gazing at her with solemn intentness. There was an air of faded gentility about the woman, bordering on shabbiness. She wore a black gown which made no attempt to disguise its age ; a smartly cut jacket, much stained and soiled, and a rather pretentious and youthful-looking hat, of a battered and demoralized appearance. There was something indefinably rumpled and untidy about her whole attire—as if she had slept in her clothes. On her face, too, which must once have been comely, there was a blight of some sort. Her features were large, plump, and faultlessly moulded ; but the dark rings about her eyes and the deep yellow pallor of her complexion spoiled all pretence they might yet make to beauty. Only her blonde hair, which was banged and curled, had a rich tawny sheen, as if it had drained the poor head upon which it grew of its

last vigor. But what impressed Gertrude more than anything else was the woman's eyes, the pupils of which were
inordinately large, and shaded imperceptibly into the black
iris. They had a vague, burnt-out look, by turns whimsical and appealing.

A dreadful oppression came over the girl, a kind of
spell-bound calm, as if her limbs were dead or too heavy
to move. She looked away over the water, and there
seemed to be a horrible fierce persistense in its un-
ceasing currents and gyrations. She saw the woman
approach her with timid, hesitating steps, and with a
strained and withered smile which was terrible.

"You will pardon me, perhaps," she heard her say (but
her voice sounded far away and incorporeal); "I took
the liberty to follow you, because I wished to speak with
you."

The thought darted through Gertrude's head that the
woman was a blackmailer, who meant to extort money by
a threat to divulge fictitious secrets. It was a consoling
reflection, therefore, to know that she was not alone in the
ravine, and that if she could make her voice heard above
the roar of the water, she might, in case of necessity call
Dr. Hawk to her assistance. She glanced uneasily down
the gorge in the hope of seeing the doctor ascend the
stairs at the side of the falls. "You need not be afraid of
me," the strange creature continued, with the same distressing smile; "I shall do you no harm. I am a poor
woman who has seen better days—yes, my dear—that I
have—so help me God!"

She heaved a sigh and her eyes filled with tears.

"I do not see what I can do for you," Gertrude forced
herself to answer; "but if you wish to talk with me, I wish
you would call upon me at home, I don't like to have people follow me about in this way."

"It was for your own sake, my dear, that I did not call
upon you at home. You think me queer, no doubt, well,
perhaps I am queer. But you, my dear—won't you allow
me to hold your hand—just for a moment, you know——"

She had seated herself on the moist carpet of pine-
needles close to Gertrude, and, with a little hysterical laugh,
tried to seize her hand. But the girl, now thoroughly
frightened, jumped up with a cry, and would have run
down the ravine, if the steepness and the slipperiness of the
path had not made precipitous motions dangerous. So
she arrested the impulse with an effort of will; but re-

mained standing, fearful and alert, like a bird about to take flight.

"If you do not leave me," she said, indignantly, " I shall call for help."

The woman struggled to her feet with some difficulty, and Gertrude noticed, as she rose up at her side, that she was exactly her own build and height. They stood gazing at each other for a minute in silence ; the woman because she was out of breath from the effort of rising, Gertrude because she wished to discourage further communication.

" My dear," the former began, with a whimsical gesture which indicated extreme nervousness, "I am a mere stranger to you, of course—I am a mere stranger, I should say—but if you knew how I have suffered——"

She shed a couple of tears, and after having rummaged in her pocket, pulled out a soiled lace handkerchief, which she applied to her eyes.

" I am sorry that you have suffered," Gertrude answered, a trifle mollified, "and if I can do anything for you," she added rashly ——

"Yes, you can do something for me," the other inter-rupted eagerly ; "would you—would you—I don't mean to seem intrusive—but I cannot help it— If you only knew— I have suffered so much—I have prayed for death many a time as the greatest mercy—and I have been so cruelly treated—by those from whom I had a right to expect kindness and love—one to whom I gave my young heart —and he broke it and crushed it—and trampled upon it— and I am so miserable. And the only one on earth I loved he took away from me—my only child—my only daugh-ter—the only creature I loved—the only comfort that was left to me he stole away from me—cruelly—in the night."

She wept now profusely, and while the tears flowed, unhindered, dived again into her pocket, from which she presently brought to light, a much-worn, and crumpled letter. She ceased her lamentation abruptly, and with a half-embarrassed air glanced from Gertrude to the letter, which she turned over two or three times, and smoothed with her palms.

" My dear," she said, with her nervous, whimsical smile, " did you ever know your mother ? "

Gertrude felt a tightening of her throat, and in her whole body a numbness and oppression. She stared dumbly at the strange woman, with a vague expectation of something dreadful that she knew would be coming.

"You never knew her? You have no recollection of her? Well, I don't wonder. You were only four years old when you were taken away."

It was as she had feared, then. This woman had some connection with her past life ; was perhaps—no, no, she could not bear the thought—it seemed so incredible, so horrible. But still the conviction settled more and more deeply in her mind that the riddle of her origin was about to find its solution.

"My mother is dead," she forced herself to say ; " I know that she is dead."

"No, my dear, she is not dead, though she has wished a thousand times that she were," cried her interlocutor hysterically ; "look at this letter—look at it—do I speak the truth, or don't I ? What does that say ? Read it, my dear, read it. I am not afraid you should know the truth. God is the judge between me and him—I have God as my witness that he stole you from me—like a thief in the night—tore the weeping child from the mother's bleeding heart ; that he did, my dear, and God is my witness, and I am his lawful wife. I gave my innocent young love to him, and that was the way he returned it ; abused me, and struck me, and stole my child away from me——"

She continued in this strain for several minutes, accompanying her narrative with excited gestures and sobs, appealing to heaven, rolling her great, vague liquid eyes, and distorting her lax, withered features with an effort to express vivid emotions. But there was a kind of ghastly unreality about it all—something premeditated and meretricious—which left Gertrude cold. She accepted the letter which was thrust into her hands, and read it half mechanically, wondering all the while at her own callousness. The letter was dated Dayton, O., May 12, 1861, and read as follows :

"My DEAR WIFE : I have got a big contract for pontoon bridges, and expect to make a pile out of it. Denton has a quarter interest, because he did the work in Washington. I shan't be home this week, but expect to get back Monday or Tuesday. Keep your spirits up, and don't get droopy. Kiss little Gertie from her papa, and tell her to hurry up with her pesky teeth, and not keep her poor mother awake nights.

"Your affectionate husband,
"OBED LARKIN."

There was little doubt in Gertrude's mind that this note was genuine. It was her father's epistolary style, and it was very like his handwriting. The ink was faded, and there was a helpless crookedness in the letters, which had not then acquired the dignity of originality. Moreover, it was not the kind of letter which anyone would have been likely to forge, destitute as it was of endearing phrases and protestations of affection. The only intelligence which it conveyed to her was that Mr. Larkin was really her father, and that his wife was not her mother. This she grasped clearly (though it failed for the moment to awaken either joyful or painful emotions); but all the other bearings of the question she put off definitely, feeling unequal to grapple with its many perplexities. She handed the letter back to the alleged Mrs. Larkin, and stared at her again with dreary irresolution. If this was indeed her mother, whose face she had so often prayed to behold, how was it possible that she could stand thus face to face with her without a vestige of emotion—without a quickening of love, or at least of pity? It may be that the revelation had stunned her, paralyzing her nerves, and produced that shivering vacuity which was creeping over her. She felt aching and sore, as if she had been pounded; but otherwise nothing except a chilly wonder. She reflected in a dim way that a much acuter sorrow would have been visible upon the woman's face, if she were a mother, thus coldly rebuffed by her daughter, upon whom she had lavished her heart's best affection. But it was all so perplexing that it seemed utterly hopeless to attempt to unravel it.

"If you will come and see my father this afternoon at three," said Gertrude, collecting her senses by a vigorous effort, "I will persuade him to receive you."

"Your father—your father!" the woman exclaimed, with a blank gaze, as if her thought had slipped from her grasp and she was trying to recover it. "Oh, yes, Obed Larkin, you mean. Well, he is a nice father, he is. He is a lovely father—and you too, you look like him—and you act like him—that's what you do—not one kind word for your own mother—your own flesh and blood—I who brought you into the world——"

She laughed again the same wild hysterical laugh, and a threatening tone stole into her speech which awakened Gertrude from her lethargy and filled her with alarm. She pulled herself suddenly together, ran down to the mill, crossed the foot-bridge, and struck the path which leads up to the highway. Her fear grew upon her as she ran, and she dared not look behind her to see if she was pursued. As she approached the University and saw the great piles of masonry shimmer through the trees, she slackened her speed and took time to recover her breath.

CHAPTER XVI.

THE SEED OF DRAGON'S TEETH.

On the University campus Gertrude discovered her father's brown mare and the well-known buggy, splashed with dried mud. Mr. Larkin became presently visible, emerging in the company of young tutor Rodney from the new Weather Signal Station. He had examined the apparatus, the application of which he had made the young man explain to him, first because he wanted to know it himself ; and secondly because he was anxious to find out whether Mr. Rodney was competent to carry on the work to which he had been assigned. The result of his manœuvre was apparently satisfactory, for he stopped every now and then on the sidewalk talking with animation and pounding the gravel with his cane.

"You just be sure you are right, young man," Gertrude heard him say, "and then go ahead. That's the principle I have always acted on. An American can't afford to waste time on what you call the traditions of science. I tell you, sir, if I had troubled myself about the traditions of bridge-building, instead of going right ahead in my own way, I should have been working now for a boss at two dollars and a half a day. No, sir, the American brain has got to do its work in its own way, or it won't do no work at all—that's to say valuable work, that's worth taking account of. The man who can only do what others have done before him may be worth his victuals. I don't begrudge him that. But that is all. He ain't worth any more."

He cocked his head with his shrewd, self-satisfied smile, and started in on some fresh topic which afforded him another opportunity to illustrate his Americanism. He saw Gertrude approaching, but he paid no heed to her. It was not his custom to expend politeness on members of his own family. It did not even occur to him that it was an unusual thing to see her on the university campus during the hours of instruction. He did not observe the traces of excitement in her face, though they were perfectly plain to the young man with whom he was talking. There was, however, an implied recognition of her presence in the annoyance he exhibited, as Mr. Rodney saluted her, and gave no longer his undivided attention to his discourse. He had struck his favorite theme of tobacco and rum, concerning which he felt sure his opinions were novel and original. It was therefore not an amiable face he turned to his daughter, as, heedless of his preoccupation, she walked up to him and took his arm; but, on the other hand, neither was it an angry face, for the humor that lurked in it and the quaint Yankee shrewdness tended to neutralize every emotion and keep it within bounds.

"Well, darter," he said, not unkindly, "are you co-educating, or what is the matter?"

He had never known her to take his arm before in that manner, and it was that which aroused his suspicion that something was wrong. But to Gertrude, the desire to get near him, to touch him, to press herself close to him, was so imperious that she broke heedlessly through the relation which habit had established between them. She would have liked to fling herself upon his neck, to hug him and kiss him; and a single caress from him would have filled her with gratitude. It did not matter so much now whether he was agreeable or not; the certainty that he was her father invested his somewhat uncouth personality with a preciousness and dignity which it had never before possessed in her eyes. She did not trust herself to reply to his remark, for her teeth displayed an alarming propensity to chatter, and she felt the tears burning under her eyelids and ready to gush forth.

"You look flustered," Mr. Larkin went on, regarding her with his small, sagacious eyes; "you'd better ride down with me in the buggy."

She nodded, and pulled him gently away toward the curbstone where Libby, the venerable bay mare, with her shaggy head, was standing. This animal had been about twenty years in Mr. Larkin's service, and she was now turning gray, and had, moreover, the unpleasant habit of stumbling. But he had grown so fond of her that nothing could induce him to part with her. She had originally borne the august name "Liberty," but this had in time been corrupted to Libby and Lib. Some people thought, when they observed the care with which Mr. Larkin drove this hoary mare, and the coaxing, cajoling way in which he spoke to her, that it was as a companion he valued her, rather than as an aid to locomotion. He had four other horses in his stable; two of which were farm-horses, one a saddle-horse named Walter Scott, belonging to Gertrude, and one, a rather ornamental family horse named Jim, who was chiefly devoted to Mrs. Larkin's service. But the old gentleman himself, who was not much for the ornamental, professed entire satisfaction with the slow and uncertain progress of shaggy old Lib.

The great university bell in the Culver Tower struck three-quarters to one as Mr. Larkin stepped into his high buggy, and hauled his daughter in after him.

"Well, darter," he said, after having addressed a few encouraging words to Libby, "I wish you'd brace up a bit. What are ye moping about anyway? Quarrelled with the doctor again, eh?"

Libby, who evidently objected to the increased weight of the buggy, was standing, shaking her head disgustedly, and Mr. Larkin, without awaiting Gertrude's answer, tried to persuade her to overcome her objections.

"Now, don't you be cantankerous, old girl," he said, chuckling at the mare's perversity; "you don't mind Gertie, do you? Take a pull now—one, two, three! Be a good old girl, now—there goes! I knew you'd think so! Good old Libby—that's a dear old girl."

Libby, having had time to meditate, expressed her dissent mildly by shaking her ears; but concluded, on further consideration, to comply with her master's request. She walked along cautiously for a few minutes, and, after having passed the university chapel, broke into a jerky jog-trot. Gertrude, being unable to control her inclination to shiver, seized her father's arm again, and clung tightly to him. Mr. Larkin now turned half about and looked at her.

"I reckon you've got the chills, darter," he said; "it ain't time yet to be skirmishing through the gorges. It is too early in the year. You're sick—that's what you are. Now I shouldn't care to see you on your back again for another six weeks."

Gertrude was grateful for the grain of sympathy which this speech implied, and felt that she must say something, lest she should appear to repel his kindness.

"I am not ill, father," she said, breathlessly; "but—but—something dreadful has happened to me."

Mr. Larkin reined in the horse suddenly, and surprised

Libby by addressing her in very uncomplimentary language. "Now you silly old thing," he cried, "can't ye
keep still when I tell yer;" then turning to Gertie:
"Well, I thought something was up. Now tell me—what
is it?"

She glanced up and down the road before speaking;
but there was no one in sight except a small barefooted
boy.

"Father," she began, with chattering teeth, "I met a
dreadful woman in the Drumhead Ravine. She said—she
said—she is my mother."

Mr. Larkin did not answer at once; but with the whip-
lash tried to brush away a horse-fly which was hovering
about Libby's tail. "H'm," he said at last, "I guess she
was lying."

"But she had a letter from you, father," Gertie went on,
tremulously, "at least it looked like your handwriting. It
was written many years ago, and it was about pontoon
bridges and money-making."

"Well—what else?"

"It was signed—it was signed——"

She could not keep the tears back any longer, but
hugging his arm tightly pressed her face against his
shoulder.

"Hush, darter, hush," he warned, in a cool, steady voice,
"don't make a fool of yourself. We'll talk it over when
we get home. Dry up those tears now and don't worry,
or folks 'll be thinking I've been scolding you."

Gertrude obeyed this injunction as far as she was able,
wiped away her tears and forced down the sobs which
rose in her throat and threatened to choke her. Perceiving that she did not have her facial muscles under control,
he took a roundabout way home, where they would be likely
to meet few people, and made no further allusion to her
adventure. He did not stop before his front-door (it was
never his custom to do this when alone) but drove into
the yard by the back gate. There he called his "man,"
who presently emerged from the barn, and with some difficulty got out of the high and inconvenient buggy. The
groom did not dare to assist him, knowing well that such
an offer would have cost him his place. But, quite contrary to his custom, Mr. Larkin, turned around and lifted
his daughter out of the buggy, which attention was so
grateful to Gertrude that she had to exert herself to keep
from embracing him. After having ascertained that Mrs.

Larkin was out driving, he led the way into the library, and seated himself at his desk, while Gertrude sat down in a rattan rocking-chair opposite. He picked up a bronze paper-cutter and looked at it, as if wondering what it was meant for, and then began gently to tap the desk with it.

"Well," he said, looking up suddenly, "this woman you was talking about. She said she was your mother? Did she offer you any proof?"

"She showed me a letter signed with your name, in which you addressed her 'My dear wife'!"

Gertie had now so far accustomed herself to the situation, that, barring a certain tremulousness, she was able to hold her emotions in check.

"H'm! And you think the letter was genuine?"

"I do not know. But it excited me very much."

"Did she ask you for money?"

"No, she asked me for nothing; but she said dreadful things about you."

"H'm, yes. How did she look?"

"She had heavy blonde hair—bright straw-colored beautiful hair—and great black eyes, with a curious blank stare and black rings about them."

For some reason this description excited Mr. Larkin; he gave a thump with the paper-cutter on the desk; wheeled about in his revolving chair and walked over to the fire-place.

"She had blonde hair, did she, eh?" he queried, with a pinched, almost malicious look in his eyes.

"Yes."

"Then it was dyed. She had dark hair when I knew her."

"Then you do know her, father?"

The question broke from her like an anxious cry, and her face was full of quivering doubt and sorrow.

"Do I know her? Well, I should say I do."

He pulled a red silk handkerchief from his pocket and wiped away the perspiration that hung in great beads upon his brow.

"And is she—my mother?"

"Yes, God help you, child—that she is, though I would have given years of my life to have spared you that knowledge."

"Why so?"

"She is a bad woman, Gertie. She was once my wife; when I was a young and poor man—and she made my life a hell for me. The only thing that could excuse her wickedness—though, God knows, I don't see how it can excuse what she did—was this, that she was rarely in her right mind. She drugged herself early and late with opium. She had this habit long before she met me ; but she concealed it from me. She knew I wouldn't stand it. I found it out soon enough, though ; and it nearly drove me wild. When you was born, I was tied to her, and I reconciled myself to the thought of putting up with her. But it went from bad to worse ; to save your life I had to get you away from her. It is no use going over all that damnable misery again. She neglected you—she didn't care any more for you than if you had been a foundling or a puppy."

"And did you take me away from her—in the night?"

"In the night? Why, no ; I may say I bought you back from her ; though any court would have decided that she was unfit to keep you. I paid her $10,000 for renouncing her claim to you, and she took the money and parted from you without a pang. She gave her solemn promise that she would never make herself known to you, or try to see you. I got a divorce from her in Ohio in 1862 ; she didn't put in an appearance, because she knew that, in the state she was in, it was no good denying my allegations. I have paid her $1,500 a year alimony ever since, of my own free will, on condition of her keeping away from me ; though the court did not give her a dollar."

Mr. Larkin, having finished this narrative, seized the fire-tongs and began to poke the fire vindictively, for there was yet a slight chill in the air, and Mrs. Larkin, who was sensitive to cold, insisted upon having a fire in the library up to the beginning of June. Gertrude gazed at his white, stubborn head and bent old back, and her heart overflowed with yearning sympathy. It struck her for the first time in her life that there was something pathetic about him. He was quite an old man, she reflected ; and he had had much trouble. He belonged to her as no one else in the world, and she belonged to him.

When he had vented his indignation upon the fire, Mr. Larkin got up, stalked across the floor and seated himself heavily in his revolving chair. He never sauntered or paced the floor in meditation ; but had always a definite goal for his motions. He fumbled about with his right hand for the paper-cutter, without looking, and having found it, half turned to Gertrude and asked

"Where is she now?"

"I don't know.   I told her to come and see you at four."

"That was not well done of you, darter.   Though she would have come anyway, so it makes no difference."

There was a pause of two or three minutes.   Then Mr. Larkin looked up wearily and said: "Is anything going on to-day, affecting the heathen?"

He was innocent of any humorous intention in this query; nor did it strike Gertrude as in the least amusing. She saw its bearing at once, and knew that he was summoning her aid to keep his wife away from the house, while the first claimant was calling.   She picked up the *Torryville Courier*, glanced down one column and up another, and said finally:

"There is to be a Union Missionary Meeting at the First Methodist Church, which will be addressed by the Rev. Abiel Striker, D.D., who has recently returned from Syria."

"The very thing.   At what hour is it?"

"Three P.M."

"You had better tell mother about it.   But probably she knows."

"Then mother does not know of this—this woman."

"No, darter; that's where I was a fool.   It would have been much better if I had told her.   There was no disgrace about it.   But mother, being so pious and all that—I jest sorter weakened and didn't say nothing to her."

There was another pause, during which the hickory log on the hearth fired off small pistol shots, and projected pieces of glowing coal out upon the rug.   Gertrude rose and stepped upon them; and the sweet odor of the wood, mixed with whiffs from the singed tiger-rug, diverted her attention slightly from the theme of discussion.

"What do you mean to do, father?" she asked at last, rather listlessly.

He did not answer at once, but fixing a keen glance upon her, spoke with a voice which sounded like the rasping of a saw.

"I want you to promise me this, Gertie, that you will never try to see this woman again, or allow her to communicate with you.   You must choose between her and me."

"You know I choose you, father."

"And you promise?"

"Yes."

"I shall give her more money, of course.   That's what

she is after. I thought I had bought all my letters back, long time ago; but it appears she has kept some back, to be used in an emergency. I don't want you to talk to her or have anything to do with her."

"I have no wish to talk to her."

"So much the better."

10

CHAPTER XVII.

AN UNPLEASANT VISITOR.

Mrs. Larkin, being unable to resist the allurements of the heathen, started off to the Union Missionary meeting, full of pleasant anticipations. She had not the faintest suspicion of the momentous events which were taking place behind her back, nor had she any perception that the air about her was charged with dumb excitement. It was no uncommon thing in the Larkin household to sit through a dinner in silence; and no one, therefore, took any note of the solemnity that prevailed at the table. Admirable and estimable people as they were, they were not sufficiently high in the scale of civilization to put themselves out, habitually, for the sake of being agreeable. Mr. Larkin, who was indeed ready enough to speak to people whom he expected to impress, had somehow less confidence in his authority at home, knowing that his stories and teachings had there long since lost their novelty. He did, to be sure, sometimes address to Horace observations about business matters and political affairs, which the latter answered with monosyllables, or with some dry and commonplace comment; and when he was in particularly good humor, he joked his wife on her interest in the heathen, and asked her whether the shirts she had sent to the Zulu-Kaffirs were a good fit. But, as a rule, he deprecated conversation at meals as interfering with the more serious business of the occasion.

Horace and Aleck returned, as was their wont, to the office on Main Street, as soon as they had finished dinner, and, besides the servants, Mr. Larkin and his daughter were the only persons in the house when the unwelcome visitor arrived. Gertrude walked about as in a trance, not knowing whence she came or whither she was going. The consciousness of this great tragic event in her life preyed upon her. It unsettled her thought, raising up new standards of right and wrong; making her uneasy and agitated. She was sitting before the fire, staring into a book, which failed to convey the slightest idea to her mind, when the door opened, and Nettie announced that there was a lady in the hall who wished to see Mr. Larkin. There was nothing unusual in such an announcement, for Mr. Larkin had the common experience of all rich men, of being persecuted by the unfortunate.

"Show her in," said Mr. Larkin.

He heard the door open and shut; but kept his eyes persistently fixed on the desk. When, at last, he raised them, he saw a tall woman, with a yellow face, dressed in shabby black, stand before him. The most noticeable thing about her were the great black rings about her eyes. Mr. Larkin, though not a sensitive man, almost shuddered as his glance met hers.

"H'm," he said, with a grunt, "you are there again, are you?"

A whimsically appealing smile, which was anything but mirthful, distorted her features, and her great, dark, cloudy eyes, which were passionate and unintelligent, seemed to have nothing to do with it.

"I suppose you have spent the last money I sent you," Mr. Larkin went on; "and you have come for more."

The woman, with a wild gesture, flung herself at his feet and embraced his knees.

"Oh, Obed!" she cried, with a sudden flood of tears; "how can you speak so cruelly to me—I who gave you my young heart——"

"Shut up," he commanded, harshly, "none of your capers now. You can't fool me. I know them all from old times. Name your figure; and be quick about it—— "

"Obed, I want you to listen to me," she wailed, raising herself theatrically on her knees, and flinging back her hands.

"No, I won't listen to you," he broke out in a rasping whisper; "you and I know each other too well to be up to any comedy-acting. It won't go down, I tell you. So behave yourself and let us proceed to business."

Gertrude who at that moment caught a glimpse of her face was amazed at the suddenness with which its expression changed. It was as if, finding the mask unsuccessful, she deliberately dropped it and exchanged it for another. She seized hold of the desk to assist her in rising; sat down in a chair and smiled. Gertrude could now see the reflection of her face in the glass, and it affected her most unpleasantly. She saw her pull the same soiled letter from her pocket, unfold it, and smooth it out as before.

"How much do you suppose that is worth, Obed Larkin?" she asked, holding it out at arm's length. There was an attempt at something resembling coquetry in her air and gesture—a faded pathetic coquetry which was sadder than tears. Gertrude could endure it no longer. She arose and moved toward the door.

"You needn't go out of consideration for me," said Mr. Larkin ; "I have no objection to your staying."

"I prefer to go, father," she answered.

"Ah, yes, you are a chip of the old block, I see that plainly enough," the visitor exclaimed with feverish vivacity ; "you think you can afford to trample upon a mother's heart—just because he does it—you think I have always looked as I do now—but it was his maltreatment that made me what I am—my face was quite as red and white and rosy as yours is—and my family was as good as any in England—but he has no more pity than a stone—only look at his mouth, how hard and cruel it is—and those green cat-eyes—ha, ha, ha!—that I ever could have loved him—that's what I wonder at now."

Gertrude heard these phrases hurled after her as she walked the length of the floor toward the dining-room door. She took this course chiefly because she had a dread of meeting any of the servants who might read her agitation in her face. She escaped thence into the empty parlor, and having ascertained that the coast was clear, ran up-stairs and flung herself upon the lounge in her bedroom. As was often the case, when her nerves had been subjected to a prolonged strain, she began to question the reality of the cause of her emotions, and at last the emotions themselves. A cool mist laid itself over her thoughts, and lulled their intensity. Her mind seemed a chilly vacuum, which was invaded every now and then by silly and irrelevant fancies. Why did her mother dye her hair, and what kind of dye did she use ? Probably her hair was turning gray and she had enough vanity left to wish to conceal it. She had once known a girl who washed her hair daily in champagne, to take the color out of it. She had become engaged to an engineer who fell in love with her hair, and would have broken the engagement when he found out that it was dyed, if she had not threatened him with a breach-of-promise suit. Thus her thoughts rambled drearily on, until she brought them

back forcibly to the all-absorbing discovery. But in spite
of her effort to realize its seriousness, an intolerable sleepi-
ness overcame her, and she could not, however much she
tried, keep from yawning.

She had lain thus for fifteen or twenty moments, when
a sluggish sense of duty awakened within her, and it occurred to her that she had not acted rightly in leaving
her father, when he had hinted at his desire to have her
stay. She accordingly rose to her feet, paused before the
looking-glass and bestowed a few decorative touches upon
her back hair which had become somewhat rumpled.
Again she drifted into abstraction, for the question urged
itself upon her : " Do I look like her ? Have I inherited
her viciousness and her hypocrisy ? "

She could not avoid seeing that the shape of her face
and its outline hinted at the relationship ; but here, as
far as she could judge, the resemblance ceased. She took
comfort in the reflection that she had her father's blue
eyes, though clouded over as it were, and modified, by
some alien admixture.

There was a knock at the door, and without waiting
for an answer, Nettie, the red-haired chamber-maid, entered.

" Mercy on us, that was a quare woman was a-callin'
upon Mr. Larrkin, Miss Gerrtie," she said, with her broad
Irish brogue.

" Is she gone ? " asked Gertrude.

" Yes, that she is, Miss Gerrtie, and thanks be to God,"
Nettie replied, seating herself upon the edge of the bed
and brimming over with communicativeness. After having vainly waited for encouragement to proceed, she let
her eyes range through the room and observed vaguely :

" Lor' knows what ye want to do with all thim naked
arrums and ligs on yer winder-coortins, Miss Gerrtie.
Thim things brings bad loock, sure, child, or me name
ain't Nettie O'Harrigan."

" You don't understand that, Nettie ; and it would be
no use for me trying to explain it to you."

" Och, but Oi know what Oi am a-talkin' about, Miss
Gerrtie, sure Oi do ; fur a modest gurrel loike you to have
men's hind ligs hung up on yer walls—and naked troonks
—and hids, with all the skin off, loike a pealed potatoe—
that ain't as God meant it to be, Miss Gerrtie ; and it
don't bring ye no good loock at all, at all."

" You needn't trouble yourself about it, Nettie," Ger-

tie observed rather loftily, seating herself in a rocking-
chair and picking up a sketch-book.

"But that woman, Miss Gertie," Nettie burst out un-
dismayed by her chilly reception, "she was droonk, or
crazy, and that's what she was, Miss Gerrtie."

"Well, Nettie, what does it matter ?"

"Didn't ye hear her holler ? She was after black-mail-
in' Mr. Larrkin, that's what she was afther. But he's an
old birrd, Mr. Larrkin is, and he don't walk into them
koind of traps."

"Well, Nettie, I suppose he is. But it isn't very nice
for you to speak of him in that way. And now I wish you
would leave me. I am tired and I don't feel well."

"Humph, and it's prroud ye are, and ye hould yerself too
hoigh and moighty to talk with a simple gurrel ; but ye
h'aint got so much to brrag off, yer own self, Miss Gerrtie, though ye carry yer nose so hoigh, and bad loock to
yez, now."

With this parting shot Nettie flounced out of the room
in high dudgeon, and Gertie was quite relieved to find
that her listening at the door had availed her so little.
For if she had obtained any specific knowledge of a compromising kind she would have been sure to blurt it out
when her ire was aroused. She had, like most servants in
Torryville, been spoiled by being treated as an equal, and
permitted to disburse her fund of gossip for the edifica-
tion of the ladies of the family. Mrs. Larkin was not
above enjoying the piquant items of personal history
which leaked through from kitchen to kitchen ; and Nettie was justly indignant at Gertrude for pretending to be
any better, in that respect, than her mother.

CHAPTER XVIII.

MISS KATE VAN SCHAAK.

Business is a blessed relief to him who has an uneasy conscience. Mr. Larkin, to be sure, flattered himself that he was on very good terms with his ; but for all that he did not like to be alone with it, and preferred almost any companionship to that of his own thoughts. As it happened, he had a lawsuit involving large sums of money, in Michigan, and sent Horace to Detroit to represent him as counsel. There was a chance of compromising on favorable terms ; but Mr. Larkin would listen to no conciliatory proposals. He threw himself into the contest with a stubbornness and pugnacious zeal which surprised even his prudent attorney. He joyfully wasted his substance in telegraphing letters of one and two hundred words, and received despatches of similar length in return. And the result was that Horace returned, at the end of ten days, with a decision in his favor, worth some $250,000, and a fee for his own services which made him expand with an agreeable sense of prosperity. He had intended to charge his uncle $1,000 ; but when he named this sum to the old gentleman he pretended to grow very wroth.

"Stuff," he exclaimed, "you know as well as I do that I couldn't have gotten another lawyer, who was worth his grub, to do that work for me for less than $3,000."

"Perhaps," his nephew assented, thoughtfully ; "but in his own family, you know, it is a ticklish matter for a man to rate himself at his full marketable figure. You took me when I was much below par, and you are entitled to your discount."

"Don't talk slushy sentiment to me, boy," cried Mr. Larkin, with assumed gruffness ; "if you are worth $3,000 you shall have $3,000, and not a cent less."

And so the end of it was that Horace deposited $3,000 to his credit in the Torryville National Bank, which sum he converted, a week later, into a farm mortgage, bearing six per cent. interest. He had in him the stuff that millionaires are made of; nothing gave him so much pleasure as a successful financial operation, except perhaps a crisp and clean-cut argument before the bar, that riddled his opponent through and through, with logical thrusts and citations of impregnable authorities. His cool sagacity, coupled with a wholly unsentimental view of human relations, enabled him to see and seize his opportunity before anybody else had discovered that the opportunity was there. It was often his custom when he was alone in the office to take out his mortgages and securities from the safe and look them over just for the pleasure of the thing. He liked to handle them, for they conjured up pleasant visions of power, influence, and recognized success. They footed up about twelve thousand five hundred dollars, which was a modest sum, to be sure ; but it represented actual earnings, self-denial, and shrewd calculation.

There was another reflection, too, which had a close connection with these financial meditations. He had concluded, some time ago, that it would be for his advantage to marry; and he had more than once made up his mind, that, all things considered, he would never be likely to meet a girl who would suit him any better than Arabella Robbins. He was fond of her, in his way ; and he rated it a high merit in her that she was still fonder of him. He tested his feelings for her in various ways, and surprised himself at finding how much deeper they were than he had been willing to acknowledge. Thus he had to admit that it would give him pain in case she were to marry any one else. It would be something more than wounded vanity. He was not wildly and desperately in love with her, but it would be absurd, on his part, to expect any such feeling to invade his sober and well-regulated life. You could not imagine a Coriolanus or a Julius Cæsar, even when in love, pining and breathing amorous sighs to the moon like a Romeo. They would love warmly, no doubt, but yet temperately and with dignity. Horace liked to fancy that he was temperamentally akin to the former gentlemen rather than to the latter.

His relation to Bella had been drifting gradually into something closely resembling an engagement. People had accepted it as a settled matter that they would some day marry. They were " as good as engaged," the gossips asserted ; and I do not mean to be invidious when I say that the young lady, who had indeed never resented allusions to such a *denouement*, had, at last, by the transparent hypocrisy and flattered gratification with which she denied the engagement, come to confirm the general impression. Mr. Robbins, who more than half-suspected that the young people kept their secret from him merely because he was supposed to disapprove, held himself in readiness (after the proper amount of coaxing and tearful entreaties, to bestow his parental blessing, and was prepared to make the best of a son-in-law who, whatever his merits, could never acquire the crowning one of being agreeable. It was and remained a mystery to him that his daughter could find him so fascinating; but this was of slight consequence, of course, as long as he was in every way estimable and had a fair chance of becoming a leading citizen of the State. But for all that, it was a thousand pities that Aleck, who was so infinitely more agreeable, had not (in spite of a few gentle hints) taken it into his head to fall in love with Bella. Mr. Robbins murmured feebly and impotently against the Lord, through the blue cigar smoke, when he meditated upon these things; but concluded sagely, when his wrath was spent, that he should only muddle matters still worse if he attempted to interfere.

This was the state of affairs when Horace, one evening in the latter part of May, found himself seated on the sofa in the parlor of the parsonage. The Rodents had taken flight the moment they saw him, and even the parson had discreetly retired to his study. He sat and talked about his plans, and Bella listened with an enthusiasm which seemed all out of proportion to the importance of the subject. But then she had a way of thinking that everything Horace said was brilliant, and if he observed that the weather was unpleasant she assented to it with such evident delight that he could not help suspecting that he had said something remarkable. She raised him constantly in his own estimation, made him feel clever, masculinely superior, and amiably patronizing. And so it happened, as they sat there in the twilight, that he felt impelled to ask the fateful question, for which she had been waiting for five years. She was almost hysterical with joy, and she embraced and kissed him with a vehemence which made him uncomfortable—a little bit bashful, as it were, on her account. They went together into her father's study and announced the engagement. But Horace had a sense of awkwardness and irritation during that trying interview which was only carried off by Bella's touching delight. He thought he had never seen Mr. Robbins appear to less

advantage, and Mr. Robbins, with an internal writhing and
squirming, went through the ordeal, but reflected all the
while that his son-in-law was one of the most unpleasant
men with whom he had come in contact.

It was in the early part of June, when this affair had not
yet lost its novelty, that Miss Kate Van Schaak, of New
York, a niece of Mr. Robbins, arrived at the parsonage. Miss
Van Schaak was a tall and slender brunette, with handsome,
regular features. The only thing which detracted somewhat from her beauty was a certain lofty and disdainful
air, and an expression about her nose and mouth as if she
sniffed an unpleasant odor. It was only when her face
was in repose that this expression was apparent; animation had the effect of softening the rigidity of her features,
and transforming her, as it were, into an entirely different
woman.

Everything about her was clear, distinct, and definite.
Her lips had firm, clean curves, which were drawn with
exquisite precision, every line, every feature was refined,
and hinted at centuries of civilization. She was, moreover,
so obtrusively clean as to make the cleanliness of others
seem to be of an inferior quality. She seemed clean
straight through. This remarkable young woman could
be apparently anything she liked to be; could charm or
repel with the same deliberation, and chose to do the
latter quite as frequently as the former. She had friends
who adored her and enemies who detested her; but
neither the praises of the former nor the vituperations
of the latter caused her for an instant to lose her superb
equanimity. She had birth, she had wealth, she had social
position; in fact all that heart could desire and fortune
bestow upon this side of the Atlantic. Why need she,
under such circumstances, be weakly and democratically
amiable? She felt herself in the position of a sovereign
for whose favor thousands sue in vain; and she did not
mean to cheapen its worth by a too lavish bestowal. She
was conscious at times of a certain fierce sense of exclu-
siveness. She experienced a pleasure in keeping her doors
closed against all the vulgar throng without, which, she
fancied, were dying to be admitted. And there was no denying that society encouraged her in this belief. She held
herself in such high esteem that others had no choice, if
they desired her acquaintance, but to accept her own valuation. It was those who most successfully expressed this
fact in speech and action who rejoiced in her good graces.

But even here, a certain reservation had to be observed, for Miss Van Schaak had *esprit* and demanded a flavor of wit or fineness of appreciation in the homage which she received. A blunt knock-down compliment she resented; but an implied compliment, deftly turned, filled her with pleasure. She had the kind of nose which in middle life becomes a vexation of spirit. Now it was only aquiline and rather handsome. It looked high-bred and a trifle haughty. But Miss Kate was very sensitive on the subject of noses, and liked no allusion to that organ in general. She had a suspicion (though an ungrounded one) that her beauty was somewhat marred by its prominence, and often stood with a hand-glass contemplating her profile, trying to settle this vital question.

I believe this was the only doubt which ever troubled her and it was not serious enough to interfere with the superb ease and security of her bearing. She had seen a good deal of the world, spent two years in a French convent, and had visited all the capitals of Europe. One German baron and two Italian counts had placed their names and titles at her disposal; but she had politely, but firmly, declined to avail herself of their kind propositions. If she ever married, she was wont to affirm, it would have to be a man whom she was afraid of. As she had never during the twenty-two years of her existence encountered such a man, she was reconciled to the thought of single beatitude. She had no objection to matrimony *per se ;* she only objected to the men who had so far honored her with proposals. Of course she was fully aware of the attractive force of the four or five million dollars which rumor placed to her father's credit ; but she was altogether too polite to refer to motives of that sort. In fact, she never spoke of her money ; and she disdained vulgar show of diamonds and gorgeous attire as incompatible with her Knickerbocker dignity. She dressed, indeed, magnificently ; but the splendor of her attire revealed itself fully only to the connoisseur. A certain quiet richness, faultless fit, and chaste elegance always distinguished her costumes. They were the wonder and the despair of those less favorably situated ; they aroused evil passions in tender bosoms, wherever they appeared. They extinguished all with which they came in contact as effectually as a snuffer extinguishes a candle.

The Van Schaak family had grown rich in a comfortable and leisurely way, without any great exertions on their part. They had happened to own some pieces of land in the neighborhood of Fifth Avenue and Twenty-Third Street ; and while deploring the influx of foreigners and the disappearance of the ancient New York, sat still and scooped in their millions. They held on to their fine old homestead on Twenty-third Street with true Dutch tenacity ; and raised hens, and cultivated cabbages and hyacinths, on land worth several thousand dollars a foot. I believe they took more pride in this piece of bravado than in any other circumstance in their family history. Mr. Adrian Van Schaak, Kate's father, used to send baskets of green peas and grapes around to his friends, and inform them, afterwards, as a good joke, that the peas cost him about ten dollars, and the grapes, fifty dollars .a piece. And like a Cato besieged by the Carthaginians, he held his ground with splendid obstinacy ; and felt with quiet satisfaction how his grapes and cabbages were growing more preposterously valuable with every day that passed. He was contemplating, as a further challenge to the enemy, the digging of a duck-pond or artificial basin, and the raising of fancy poultry, which would still further emphasize the rural character of the oasis he was cultivating for his own private delectation in the midst of the noisy marts of trade. In the meanwhile the Carthaginians were impotently roaring without his gates by night and by day, little suspecting that that roar was their most formidable weapon. For Adrian Van Schaak was a poor sleeper. He appealed vainly to the mayor and the police commissioners to have the nocturnal noises, which disturbed his slumbers, stopped. But the mayor laughed in his sleeve, and the police commissioners laughed without the least pretence of concealment, and told Mr. Van Schaak that they could not interfere with the laws of trade, and that it was time he moved his *lares* and *penates* into a quieter neighborhood. And through the long night, with short intervals, a procession of milk-carts, street-cars, drays, and ambulances, rattled with the most diabolical racket under Mr. Schaak's windows ; keeping still just long enough to enable him to doze off, then with an infernal delight plunging forward and giving him a start, which rippled down his spine and set all his nerves quivering. Mr. Van Schaak kept up his noble fight as long as he saw any chance of success, but one day, when his son Adrian, Jr., with a pointed intention, read him Sidney Smith's speech about Mrs. Partington and the Atlantic Ocean, the old gentleman perceived that his allies were deserting him, and worn out as he was with sleeplessness and impotent irritation, he struck his flag and surrendered. A month later he bought a fine double mansion on Gramercy Park ; and his house, duck-pond, and stables, and cabbage garden, vanished in a jiffy, giving place to deep excavations, steam derricks, heaps of bricks, and blocks of granite. No one knew exactly how much the old Knickerbocker cleared by that operation, for he was extremely discreet about his money affairs, and liked the mystery of large and vague figures which piqued and baffled vulgar curiosity.

Mr. Van Schaak had but two children, Adrian, Jr., who at the time of this narrative was about twenty-six years old, and Kate, who was four years younger. Mrs. Van Schaak was a cousin of the late Mrs. Robbins, whose personal un-attractiveness had been somewhat mitigated by her blue blood. Bella Robbins, who was accordingly a second cousin of Kate Van Schaak, had repeatedly visited the family in New York, and always returned tremendously impressed with their grandeur. It was a source of much satisfaction to her to have such fine relatives ; and she was aware, too, that it added to her prestige in the town. But, those Torryville people were a queer lot, and she was careful not to brag (except in the most cautious and inferential way) for fear of arousing their animosity. And, moreover, now that Kate was in Torryville, actually visiting at her father's house, people could of course see what she was, and form their conclusions as to the *entourage* which must have been required to rear so rare and splendid a flower.

CHAPTER XIX.

A CONTROVERSIAL DINNER-PARTY.

The question which agitated the parsonage after Miss Van Schaak's arrival, was whether they ought to give a reception or a dinner in her honor. The former would of course be the easier ; but then they would have to invite the whole congregation, and when Bella reflected what that would mean, her heart failed her. She knew perfectly what such a reception would be ; she could fancy all the queer and awkward specimens of grocers, dry goods men, druggists, and country lawyers with their wives passing in review before her cousin, and she could imagine all the dreadful speeches they would make, and Kate's rigid condescension, when she grew tired of being amiable ; and her high-nosed scorn when she grew tired of condescending. All that would cause talk, of course, and arouse ill-will, from which, in the end, she and her father would suffer. That was, after all, the most disagreeable side of her position as a parson's daughter, that she had always to keep her finger so anxiously on the public pulse. On every conceivable topic which divided the congregation she had to balance herself on the fence as ingeniously as if she had been a presidential candidate. Because her father was undiplomatic and easy-going, she had to be doubly wily and circumspect ; and she often had hard work in explaining away some of his hasty speeches.

Mr. Robbins had given his verdict in favor of the dinner and against the reception, chiefly because he liked to eat good dinners and hated receptions. To him the question of how to dispose of the four Rodents was a very simple one ; while to Bella it was one of hopeless intricacy. It was impossible to give one gentleman to each Rodent, and moreover reserve one for herself ; first because it would look too utterly absurd, and secondly because there were not dishes and forks and glasses enough to go around. She had cold shivers when she thought of presiding at a dinner in the presence of her critical cousin; and when the vision of the exquisite and unsurpassable feast that had been given for her in Gramercy Park flitted before her fancy, she sank into the depths of misery. She even wished that Kate had remained a New York sun-myth and never descended into the Torryville world of fact. But that was rank treason, of course; and Bella was ashamed of her sentiments. The dinner had to be given; there was no help for it. After a deal of wretched scheming it was settled that two of the Rodents were to be taken ill—for a suitable reward, and the two others were to go visiting in the country. As the dinner set (after the breakage of twenty years) just sufficed for eight, it was fortunate that the number of strictly eligible young people which the town contained fell below that number. There were first Horace and Aleck Larkin, and Miss Gertrude; then Dr. Hawk, who was supposed to have seen something of society abroad, might pass muster at a pinch, and Pussy Dallas, who had been to school in New York, presented a fairly creditable appearance. Invitations accordingly were sent to these favored few, and were promptly accepted. Councils of war were held nightly in Mr. Robbins's study, and excitement reigned in the house. Wines, terrapin, and game were telegraphed for to New York; two oyster forks were in the last moment found to be missing; and a finger bowl and a champagne glass were found to be broken, but had been insidiously glued together by the delinquent chambermaid. Then more misery and more telegraphing. And to cap the climax of vexation, it occurred to Bella that she had in her excitement forgotten the enmity between Aleck and Dr. Hawk, and that very likely their strained relations might occasion some unpleasant incident or tend to throw a damper upon the spirits of the rest. However, there was nothing to be done about it now. She felt when the fatal evening arrived, like a foolhardy skipper who puts to sea with a cargo of explosives, and thinks the chances even as to whether he will reach port or not. Nervous and high strung as she was, she had fretted herself to death with all the minutest details of the arrangement; while her father laughed good naturedly and told her to take things easy. It was not until she retired to her room to dress that she discovered how haggard she was; her hands trembled when she took down her hair, and she had to send one of the sick Rodents down to ask for a thimble-full of cognac ; otherwise she feared she would have to absent herself from the dinner.   Mr. Robbins on receiving this message came running up-stairs in his shirt sleeves with a brandy flask in his hand and his suspenders dangling at his heels ; but he could not be admitted to the virgin bower, and had to vent his solicitude in anxious queries through the door, which was at last cautiously opened and the flask passed in through the crack.

To dress for dinner without a maid is an achievement to which few women in this age are equal.   But necessity is the mother of invention ; and it is astonishing what feats a woman can accomplish when she knows that there is no extraneous help to fall back upon.   The one servant of the house who, in cases of emergency, acted as lady's maid, had been summoned, early in the afternoon, to Miss Van Schaak's room, and remained there until that imperious damsel, radiant to behold, descended into the parlor. Bella, who had to put up with her clumsy and rather ill-disposed Rodent, collapsed two or three times on her bed, and would have wept, if she had not known that tears leave traces behind them.   When, at last, her toilet was finished, she swore a solemn but inaudible oath that before she gave another dinner party she would have to take leave of her senses.   She found her father standing outside of her door, handsome, glossy, and *distingué*, but with a face full of anxious interrogation marks.

"Oh, don't you worry, papa, I am all right," she said, reassuringly ; and then, when, with gratified relief, he kissed her, she cried, with hysterical laughter :

"Oh, papa, you dreadful man, you are covered all over with rice-powder ! "

To remove the traces of this unpremeditated embrace, both had to retire for a few minutes to their dressing-rooms, and when they reappeared they had to restrain their affectionate impulses.

"Why, how lovely we look ! " cried the parson, knowing well what was expected of him ; "how perfectly charming ! "

"Now, papa ! " ejaculated his daughter, with feigned displeasure, " don't be horrid.   You know I look perfectly hideous."

"Well, if you look hideous, my dear, I am no judge of beauty."

"Now, honor bright, papa !   Don't I look dragged, and worn-out ? "

"Why, my sweet child, you look as fresh as a rose," he exclaimed, unblushingly.

"As a wilted rose, you mean?"

"No, a Maréchal Niel rose, fresh plucked, at a dollar and a half a piece."

He had not lived so long with women without learning to compromise with his conscience, and distinguish between benevolent and malevolent mendacity. It was important that his daughter should think she looked well to-night, and the torments of the Inquisition could not have wrung from him the admission that anxiety had left its traces in her delicate face. Sincerity is, after all, in civilized society, a questionable virtue.

Bella had, perhaps, a vague suspicion of her father's hypocrisy; but she was grateful for it. It left her in a doubt, which, by the complex action of her mind, might be coaxed into a flattering certainty.

"Papa," she said, gazing up into his face with eyes in which moisture was gathering, "you are perfectly lovely."

"I," he cried, gayly; "good gracious, daughter, an old fellow like me. You evidently think I was fishing."

"No, papa, but you are just sweet."

"All right, dear. What a charming family we must be! And here we are standing, recklessly wasting our sweetness upon each other. Isn't it about time for us to go down-stairs?"

She took his arm with nervous trepidation, and leaned on it perceptibly as they descended to the parlor floor.

"I wish I could be dead for the next four hours, papa," she whispered, tremulously.

"My dear, sweet child, now do be sensible," he answered, with a tenderly coaxing intonation; "you know everything will go well. But, if anything should go wrong," he added, after a pause, "then remember this: Don't apologize for it. Laugh it off; make a joke of it."

She listened, with a far-away look, as if she but half heard what he was saying.

"Something will happen to make us wish that we had never brought these people together," she murmured.

The parson caught a dim little glimmering of an idea; but it was not one capable of discussion, and he held his peace. He heard the rustle of starched skirts and voluminous draperies above him, and glancing upward saw Kate in all her gorgeousness bearing down upon him. Something like a pang nestled in his left side when this splen-

11

did apparition placed itself next to his tired and nervous daughter, and eclipsed her, as it seemed to him, with cruel triumph. I fear, however, that he did Kate injustice. It did not even occur to her to compare her rare and finished self with her excitable little cousin. She looked cool, fresh, and self-contained, because she felt that she had nothing in the world at stake at this dinner, and had consented to it as a mild diversion, and because it would have been rude to show how supremely indifferent the whole affair was to her.

The company was prompt in arriving except Miss Dallas and Dr. Hawk, who had an impression that it was fashionable to be a little late. Horace, looking a trifle uncomfortable in his dress coat, was the first to be introduced to Miss Van Schaak, and assure her that he was happy to make her acquaintance. She noticed that he bowed with his neck and not with his hips, and that he wore a satin necktie. The little sneering smile which was frequently lurking about the corners of her mouth curled her fine lips, but she suppressed it instantly. Gertrude, in a cool, sea-green satin, of a most delicious tint, advanced and shook her hand, but dispensed with the introduction, as they had met before. Kate's feminine lynx-eye took in all the details of the costume, and decided that it was very nice and picturesquely effective, but lacking that supreme touch of style which one rarely sees outside of New York. The parson, on the other hand, who had more appreciation of beauty than of style, heaved a long, audible sigh of admiration.

"Isn't this rather wicked of you, Miss Gertie," he said, with his sly, kindly smile, "to be laying snares for an old gentleman like me?"

Gertrude raised her languid blue eyes to the pastor's face, and a slow, reluctant smile spread over her features.

"You know, Mr. Robbins," she said, "it has always been my ambition to captivate you, but you remind me of the wily old fox that kept sniffing about the lion's den, making complimentary speeches, but refusing to enter."

"I have no recollection that the fox in question made complimentary speeches."

"Why, yes, don't you remember his saying that all the tracks led toward the lion, and none away; and if the lion, as I imagine, was a lioness, she must have felt immensely flattered."

They talked on in this bantering strain for ten or fifteen minutes, until Dr. Hawk and Miss Dallas made their appearance. Dinner was then announced, and each gentleman gave his arm to the lady who had been allotted to him. Bella had long contended for unsealed envelopes, to be handed to the gentlemen by a butler in the dressing-room, but her father had insisted that so much style would be sure to shock the congregation, and give his enemies a handle against him in the meeting of the board. Accordingly he assumed himself the rôle of the butler and gave the needed hints. He offered his arm to Kate, and led the way into the dining-room ; Dr. Hawk followed with Gertrude ; then came Aleck with Pussy Dallas, and Horace and Bella brought up the rear. Mr. Robbins said grace in a short and business-like way, and the hired butler began to pour golden sauterne (which would have done honor to King Belshazzar's feast), into Bohemian glasses, transparent as air and light as bubbles. The Blue Points were despatched without much conversation, except some mildly jocose remarks, addressed by the host to the table in general. The sherry, rich, soft, and darkly amber-colored, was of a rare, old vintage, and Mr. Robbins was sorely tempted to break the etiquette and tell his guests what precious stuff they were drinking ; but he held himself in check, though it made him wince to see Horace drain his glass with no more sentiment than if it had been Milwaukee lager.

In spite of all efforts of the host to make the conversation general, the tone at the table during the first half hour remained stiff, and no one, perhaps with the exception of Kate, felt completely at his ease. Horace made two or three abortive efforts to engage Bella in conversation, but she had her eyes on the butler and her thoughts in the kitchen, and answered him in a random and distracted manner which showed that she had not been listening. Now and then she gave whispered orders to the butler, and laughed nervously at her partner's soberest remarks, simply because she had to make some demonstration of interest, and laughter, as a rule, is more appropriate than tears. Horace, being unaccustomed to such neglect on her part, and being too obtuse to appreciate the situation, was inclined to retire into his shell and keep his brilliancy to himself. He had been placed (alas, he never dreamed with what deep design) on the same side of the table as Miss Van Schaak, with Gertrude and Dr.

Hawk intervening, and he had therefore no chance either of seeing or conversing with the guest of honor.

A rather awkward silence was beginning to settle upon the company when the parson, in his desperate straight, hit upon literature and mentioned a popular authoress whom he professed to admire.

"Don't you think her 'Tuscaroora' is a charming piece of work," he said, addressing himself to Miss Van Schaack.

"Yes, I think it is very nice," she answered, with some animation ; "but do you know what I heard about her the other day ? She has a brother who is a tailor."

All expressed their astonishment at so anomalous a circumstance, except Horace, who leaned forward so as to catch a glimpse of the young lady's face and said : "Well, is he a good tailor ?"

This brought a laugh, of course, in which Kate heartily joined. "Why do you want to know?" she asked, merrily ; "do you wish to employ him ?"

"No," Horace replied in his dry, matter-of-fact way, "but I do not see why it should be to anybody's discredit to have a brother who is a tailor ; for my part, I would rather have a brother who was a good tailor, than one who was a poor lawyer or a mediocre doctor."

"Now, don't let us be personal, please, Mr. Larkin," cried Dr. Hawk ; "your brother might object."

There was a jarring note there and everybody felt it. Aleck colored a little, and ran his fingers through his hair ; but refused otherwise to notice the challenge. But Kate felt suddenly exhilarated. The strong, positive voice which had the courage to enunciate what appeared to her a most paradoxical opinion, aroused in her a spirit of controversy, and set her thought in rapid motion. "May I ask you, Mr. Larkin," she began, "what makes a man estimable in your opinion ?"

"The degree with which he understands how to adapt himself to his environment," Horace replied, promptly.

"Oh, dear ! Isn't that rather formidable ? I am afraid I am an awfully inestimable creature then."

"Permit me to disagree with you. I do not know your environment, but seeing you, I have no difficulty in forming my inferences. I should say that you are the most perfect product of a charming environment that I ever beheld."

He had finished this rather ponderous remark in a voice as if he were addressing a jury, and was about to revert to his *filet de bœuf*, when he met a pair of large terrified eyes fixed upon him. "Why, Miss Bella, what is the matter?" he inquired, a little conscience-stricken, "if you take me to task like that, I shall have to be mum."

Kate was a little bit too overcome by the compliment to answer immediately. She was accustomed enough to flattery, but the scientific flavor of this compliment and the tone of conviction with which it was uttered gave it a novel and not unpleasing impressiveness. Mr. Robbins in the meanwhile seized the opportunity to interpose his demurrer.

"What you say then, Mr. Larkin," he began a little doubtfully, sipping his wine with visible gusto, "don't it amount to saying that the most successful man is the most estimable."

"Yes," said Horace, unflinchingly. "Success is after all only adaptation to environment. Is it not?"

"Certainly."

"Would you say that the pickerel, who eats all the other fishes in his lake, is the most estimable fish?" the doctor put in, anxious to display his intellectual acumen.

"Yes, I would. In the conditions under which he lives he has but the choice of eating or being eaten. I respect him for taking a clear view of his situation."

"And that translated to human conditions," the parson resumed, "would lead to the doctrine that the most estimable man was he who robbed most successfully. The longest paw and the strongest jaw, that is what commands your respect."

"Well," Horace replied with superb sangfroid, "I do respect a strong jaw and a long paw, and so do you, only you have not the courage to admit it. The predatory condition, though much mitigated, is not yet obsolete. If the alternative is presented to me to be a beast of prey or a beast preyed upon, I prefer to be the beast of prey. But the law, of which I am a humble representative, exists for the purpose of restraining man's predatory instincts, and as far as possible saving the prey from the preyer."

"I thought it existed for the purpose of strengthening the strong jaw and lengthening the long paw," Kate ejaculated with the liveliest interest.

"It is applied for that purpose quite frequently," Horace admitted with the same calm superiority; "but it was not designed for that purpose."

"You mustn't listen to him, Miss Van Schaak," ex-claimed the doctor ; "he is an inveterate cynic."

"It is my brother's hobby," Aleck remarked, leaning a little forward over the table, "that Providence has played a trick on us in putting us here, with instincts and passions which we imagine have been given us for our own per-sonal happiness and gratification ; when all the while they subserve only some general purpose, such as the pres-ervation of the race and the welfare of society."

"Look here, Aleck, aren't we getting into rather deep waters ?" the parson interposed, with vague apprehension.

"No, pray, Uncle ; do let him go on," Kate begged with sparkling eyes ; "I am intensely interested."

"I retire in favor of the junior member of the firm," muttered Horace, turning his attention to his long-neglect-ed plate.

"Well, ladies and gentlemen," sighed the parson, "I give in.   But you shan't have any Madeira as long as you bother about the riddles of existence.   Champagne you can't have anyway, because this is a clerical house, where the flesh has to be mortified."

He hoped to give a new turn to the conversation by this playful threat, and he was partly successful.   For five or ten minutes the problems of creation were allowed to rest, and a discussion was started regarding that ever fresh and inexhaustible theme—matrimony.

"Now, love," Bella observed from the lower end of the table (it was the first time the poor child had ventured to take her mind off the succession of the dishes), "love surely is personal.   Who ever heard of any one falling in love for the welfare of society ?"

"Nobody ever heard of it, perhaps," Horace replied ; "but everybody does it."

"Do you mean to say that you would do it ?" ejaculated Bella, who was herself nothing if not personal.

"I couldn't escape doing it.   I should probably not go and propose to a young lady for the welfare of society, or, at least, I shouldn't tell her that I did ; and I might even cheat myself with the belief that I was doing it purely to please myself—or the young lady."

"Aren't you horrid ?" she cried, petulantly.

"Well in that case I might not succeed in pleasing the lady in question," he repeated, soberly ; "but that is irrel-evant."

"Did you say it was irrelevant whether you succeeded in

pleasing the lady to whom you proposed?" queried Kate, with her handsome eyebrows raised.

"Yes, ma'am," the imperturbable Horace made answer, chuckling inwardly at the delightful paradox; "it has nothing to do with the question." There was nothing he enjoyed so much as to tease with an air of logic and judicial sobriety.

"I think you would soon find out that it had," Miss Dallas broke forth in her shrill treble.

"I fear you misunderstand me, ladies," he resumed, taking a sip of claret,. and wiping his moustache with his napkin; "what I assert is that the man who supposes he marries for his own gratification or pleasure is a deluded fool. He cherishes certain delusions, which it is very fortunate, from the social point of view, that he should cherish, but which nevertheless are delusions. It is essential to the existence of society that he should have children, and that he should take good care of them—adapt them well to their environment. No institution could be more admirable for that purpose than marriage, as it now exists. If he gets tired of his wife, he might think that it would conduce to his happiness to put her away and take another. But society comes and says to him : 'No, my dear fellow, you can't do that. You have got to stick to your bargain whether you like it or not!' I think society is perfectly right in saying this ; but nothing can persuade me that it is out of regard for the man's happiness that it makes the demand. No, it is for its own preservation."

"But society says nothing of the sort," Mr. Robbins protested, earnestly ; "it permits a man, when it is no longer for his own good or that of his wife that they should remain together, to separate ; on condition that he shall continue to support her and his children."

"Very true ; but it attaches such severe penalties to this violent resumption of liberty, that a man must be very reckless to venture it; and, moreover, it is in most States only under certain humiliating conditions that divorces are granted. But, as I have said, I am not finding fault with this state of things. I find it perfectly proper. Only I think it is wise to have a clear view of the terms before signing the contract."

"I presume then, Mr. Larkin, that you never intend to marry."

"Yes I do, Miss Van Schaak ; but I also intend to secure as favorable terms for myself as practicable."

"And would it be indiscreet to ask what you would consider favorable terms ?"

"First health, then wealth ; and last but not least a sweet temper !"

"And in return for all these fine things, what do you intend to offer ?"

"My own valuable self, Miss Van Schaak," he replied, with a rhetorical gesture ; "the worth of which no one knows better than I ; a man," he continued, burlesquing amusingly his own manner, "who feels his superiority to the common class to the tips of his toes and fingers, and to whom no achievement in the line of his ambition is unattainable."

A burst of laughter greeted this eulogy ; and under cover of the laughter Mr. Robbins found occasion to say, *sotto voce*, to Kate :

"You may think that is a joke ; but I assure you he means every word of it."

"Indeed ! What an interesting man," Kate murmured in return ; and in the depth of her heart a feeling of deep respect and admiration for Horace Larkin began to assert itself. He looked a trifle uncouth as he sat there at the corner of the table, square, rugged, and jovially challenging, but he was, for all that, tremendously impressive. And she did not doubt that, in case she should ever decide to regard him in the light of a suitor, she might civilize him and polish off his most glaring angularities.

"I hope you will succeed in finding a lady who will share your own sentiments in regard to your worth," she said, smilingly.

"Oh, no danger about that, ma'am," he laughed, with an evident intention to shock ; "I know bushels of them."

"But if marriage is what you say it is," piped Pussy Dallas, blushing at her own audacity, "I shouldn't think you would have anything to do with it."

"What did I say it was ?" Horace queried, nodding encouragingly to the girl as he would to a diffident child.

"Didn't you say it was a contract ?"

"Yes ; and usually a pretty bad one."

"That reminds me," said Aleck, "of what Mike Maginnis said to Uncle Obed the other day. You know Mike has just returned from the prison at Sing Sing, where he has spent four years for homicide. 'Well, Mike,' Uncle Obed said to him, 'how did you like Sing Sing ?' 'Divil a bit,

Misther Larrkin,' Mike answered ; 'I didn't loike it at all, at all ; and I tell ye this, Misther Larrkin, that if they don't make it more sociable and home-loike soon, be jabers, no dacent man will want to go there.' It is very much so with matrimony, according to Horace's definition ; it stands in need of improvement, or no decent man will want to go there."

"But if marriage is such a bad thing," Bella observed, when the laughter again had subsided, "why do so many people suffer from unhappy love ?"

"I didn't know so many people did," Horace replied ; "but perhaps you are right. I once knew a man who suffered from an unhappy love for himself."

"An unhappy love for himself !" Kate exclaimed. "How was that possible ?"

"Well, he was an intensely vain fellow ; head over ears in love with himself ; but in his soberer moments he knew perfectly well that he was an inane wind-bag, inflated beyond his capacity. He loved himself, but he was unable to return his own affection."

Horace let his glance slyly glide toward Dr. Hawk, while he related this incident ; but he refrained from making the application sufficiently pointed to be detected by anybody else.

The conversation now lapsed into commonplaces ; but the tone grew more and more animated, and it was evident that every winged moment was charged to the full with pleasure. Even Gertrude, who was usually subdued in company, lost her listless air, and became engaged in a playful controversy with the doctor. The ice-cream unhappily had been taken out of the freezer a little too early and not too skilfully ; and Bella, who was just congratulating herself on the absence of accidents, began to cudgel her poor brain to invent a joke with which to mitigate this disaster. But she found she was unequal to anything in the humorous line, and her father was eating in the most absent-minded way, without discovering that anything was wrong.

"I am afraid, ladies and gentlemen," she said at last, with a happy inspiration, "that this ice-cream has suffered somewhat from your eloquence."

"How so ?" asked Mr. Robbins, with masculine obtuseness. "I find it very good."

"How does eloquence affect ice-cream, anyway ?" inquired Dr. Hawk.

"It makes it soft," said Bella, hoping to be explicit.

"How extraordinary," ejaculated the doctor ; "I have known eloquence to make me soft, but that it could thaw ice-cream——"

"We have talked too much, and the ice-cream had to wait," cried the daughter of the house, in laughing despair. "Do you understand that, now?"

"You mean I have talked too much," Horace remarked, dryly ; "for I believe it's I who have done most of the talking."

"You couldn't talk too much if you tried," she murmured, confidingly, fixing her big, dreamy eyes upon him in undisguised adoration. They told the tale they had told so often before, and they told nothing that he was not perfectly well aware of. But this tender message, which had always before found a slight response and never failed to cause a flattered gratification, made him now uncomfortable and vaguely uneasy. Instead of making a lover-like acknowledgment, as he had often done before, he bent over his plate and pretended not to observe the significant glance. He thus missed seeing the hot blush of humiliation that poured itself over the girl's neck and cheeks, and burned in the tips of her pink ears. The coffee had in the meanwhile been served, and Mr. Robbins gave the keys of his precious cabinet to the butler, who presently returned with three boxes of carefully sorted cigars. The gentlemen made their selections, and the ladies seized the opportunity to withdraw into the parlor. They would have liked to remain, but lacked courage to make the proposition. Their departure was the signal for increased hilarity in the dining-room, while in the parlor an awkward silence prevailed. Each felt so curiously alien to the rest ; a chill stole in between them ; and nobody could think of a remark which did not seem glaringly artificial.

"Girls," said Pussy Dallas, at last, in her shrill staccato, "I think cigars are just horrid. Either men ought to stop smoking, or women ought to take it up. It would just serve them right."

"You must be awfully dependent upon gentlemen's society, Pussy," Gertrude remarked. "I don't object to their smoking as much as they like."

"Well, I don't mind if I do say it," Miss Dallas declared. "I think it is much better fun to talk to gentlemen than to ladies. There's no excitement, somehow, in talking with girls. It doesn't matter what you say to them. Nothing ever comes of it."

Pussy Dallas had earned for herself the nickname "The Students' Comfort," by her undisguised devotion to the masculine sex, and particularly that part of it which frequented the university. It was told of her (though of course it was base slander) that she made it a rule to be engaged to at least one man in each class. She had a delicate, blonde, dimpled face, and looked the picture of flirtatious innocence. She was always ready for anything that promised "fun;" a very type of laughing, irresponsible, American girlhood. Life was to her a prolonged "lark," with no more serious troubles than such as arose from bad weather or a gentleman's failure to keep an engagement. Her fresh pouting lips seemed made to be kissed, and, unless rumor belied them, fulfilled their destiny. She revelled in nonsense, and had felt herself a little constrained this evening by the dignity of the company and the vague awe she entertained for Horace Larkin, who was the only younger gentleman in Torryville with whom she could not flirt.

It was a relief to the four damsels when the scraping of the chairs upon the hardwood floor announced that the session of the "tobacco council" was adjourned. As soon as the folding doors were pushed aside, Horace walked with a thoughtless impulsiveness, which seemed wholly unlike him, to the lounge where Miss Van Schaak was sitting, and taking his seat at her side calmly ousted the doctor, who had anticipated his intention. Hawk was standing in front of her, with his Hamlet look upon his brow, and his eyes beaming with melancholy admiration. He made two or three onsets to say startling things, but presently wilted under Horace's pitiless gaze, became incoherent, and withdrew in confusion. Kate smiled with evident amusement, and womanlike, turned her undivided attention to the conqueror. A bond of sympathy seemed to have sprung up between them at the table, and each was conscious of the other's goodwill. They talked with great animation for half an hour, until the sound of wheels outside and the snorting of the horses reminded them that it was time to break up. It is not improbable that the rest of the company hailed the signal with pleasure; but Horace, surpassing himself in brilliancy, talked on more eagerly in order to have an excuse for remaining. He liked, of course, to hear himself talk. What good talker does not ? But what he liked much more was to watch the effect of his speech upon Kate. She was not in the least demonstrative ; did not explode or exclaim at his witticisms and startling paradoxes. There was a stately composure in her attitude even when she was animated ; and a charming suave dignity which was the perfection of good breeding. She made him feel, in an indefinable way, that the attention which she bestowed upon him was a precious thing, which was not lightly accorded to anybody ; and he was more flattered by this reserved and qualified approval on her part, than by the excited enthusiasm of the damsels who daily flung themselves at his head. He was, after all, uncertain whether her affability was anything more than the natural desire of every woman to please, reinforced by perfect manners and much experience in the arts of society. And it was this doubt which tormented him when he rose to take his leave, and to remove which he had so long postponed his departure. But it was still there when he walked with his brother through the dim moonlight, and it got in some vague way mingled with the fresh, damp smell of bursting buds and sprouting leaves, which careered in warm gusts through the night. "I do like a woman who doesn't fly off the handle," he said to Aleck, in a tone of deep conviction.

But in the parsonage, when all was still, and Kate had ascended to the upper region, Bella stood and gazed at her father with a little strained smile and a pathetic pretence of light-heartedness, which, however, did not deceive him. She looked pale, and weary unto death ; a strange gray tint became visible about her eyes, which burned with a feverish brightness.

"My sweet girl, what is the matter?" he asked with affectionate solicitude.

" Oh, papa, I was only congratulating myself that everything went so well," she chirped in a faint unnatural treble, and without a moment's warning swooned in his arms.

CHAPTER XX.

PENELOPE'S SUITORS.

It was astonishing what a centre of attraction the parsonage became during Miss Van Schaak's sojourn in Torryville. Dr. Hawk was almost a daily visitor, and it became rumored in the town that he was more than willing to desert the mythical mortgagee of his affections, if the dazzling maiden from Gramercy Park could be induced to take her place. He ordered roses by express from New York, and sent them, accompanied by some heart-rending lines from Omar Khayyam, to the parsonage ; and when they failed to make any perceptible impression he sent original poems, steeped in the blackest melancholy. He even made a personal visit to the metropolis on some mysterious errand, and knew on his return more of the Van Schaak family, both as to its financial and social standing than any other man in Torryville. He tried the rôle of every heroic figure known to the poets, in order to win Miss Van Schaak's favor ; but came at last to the conclusion that she was a sordid, earth-clogged soul, without any higher outlook or appreciation of nobler things. It took him fully a month to make this discovery, and it would have taken him longer, if he had been able to detect the faintest will-o'-the-wisp of hope in the thorny path before him. But there was no use disguising the fact that Miss Van Schaak treated him, as Horace would have said, like "a yaller dog." She was extremely "sniffy," and those peculiar lines on each side of her nose, which made one suspect the presence of a bad smell, were apt to become quite visible when the doctor's name was announced. She laughed at his fine sentiments, called him an absurd little village beau, with his poor little theatricals, and crushed him completely by occasionally correcting his random quotations. She was as discouraging as it was possible for any woman to be to a man who makes it evident that he is willing to place his name, his heart, and his other assets at her disposal. It was, of course, flying in the face of providence, when, in spite of all these unfavorable indications, he made her a formal proposal of marriage, and received a prompt and unequivocal refusal. For all that, the doctor could not even then reconcile himself to the inevitable. He valued himself so highly that he could not comprehend how anybody could fail to perceive what an exceptional and superior character he was. He found himself so profoundly interesting, and had been so spoiled by the worship of the Torryville damsels, that he could only explain Miss Van Schaak's freezing indifference on the supposition that some one (probably Horace or Aleck) had slandered him, or that the lady's affections were already bespoken.

It was odd, but as far as appearances went, Professor Ramsdale was the one of Kate's admirers who, to use the local phrase, "had the inside track." He had this to recommend him, that he was rather a bashful man, and cut no capers in order to make himself interesting. He had been so definitely and inexorably dismissed by Gertrude, in spite of his perseverance, that he might well be excused if he began to consider the prospect of finding consolation in other quarters. He had, indeed, on one occasion, declared that, if she refused him seven times, he would persevere even unto seventy times seven; but I fear that fidelity, if carried to such extremes, would cease to be a virtue; perhaps Ramsdale himself detected a Quixotic strain in his constancy. Altogether his first and chiefest title to consideration in Kate's eyes was not his endurance as a rejected lover, but the fact that he was a good horseback rider. He not only had a good seat, but he had the muscles of a Hercules and could manage any horse that was to be found in that part of the State. Horseback riding was the only amusement that Torryville afforded which did not tire her, and as Ramsdale was the only available cavalier for such excursions, she must have been blind to her own interests if she had failed in a mild way to cultivate him. There was something honest and sturdy about him, which inspired confidence and made brilliancy seem odious. He was restful and comfortable, a very haven of refuge from fatiguing incidents and intellectual effort. He had the rare accomplishment of being silent without appearing stupid, and permitting his companion to be silent, without embarrassment. They rode together mile after mile, up one hill and down another, without opening their mouths, except for an occasional remark about their horses or the weather. If her saddle-girth was too tight he loosened it ; if it was too loose, he tightened it. He swung her off and into her saddle with a beautiful unsentimental precision, as if she were a nice boy whom he had taken in charge. If the horse was uneasy or "didn't act right," he lifted up its hoofs, one after another, picked out a pebble that had got wedged in under the shoe, lengthened or shortened the bridle, patted and talked to the animal like an old friend. There was no longer a doubt in Kate's mind that men of this type have their uses, and that a woman might do worse than select one of them as her life-long companion. And yet (so contradictory is woman's nature), when Ramsdale, encouraged by her favor, ventured to make an excursion into the territory of sentiment, she felt offended, as if he had abused her confidence, and froze him to the core of his heart by her chilly remoteness. The Professor, taking warning, dropped the dangerous theme and lapsed stolidly back into his rôle of gentleman groom and thus saved himself from further humiliation.

It was somewhat of a disappointment to Kate, though it did not perceptibly affect her spirits, that Horace Larkin held aloof and did not join the circle of her adorers. She had heard the rumor that he was as good as engaged to her cousin Bella ; nay, that the day of their marriage was already fixed upon. But he surely did not trouble Bella with his attentions, and if he was in love with her, he deserved credit for the success with which he disguised his sentiment. Bella had, to be sure, thrown out a very distinct hint, the day of the dinner party ; but Kate was of opinion that it was her wish to be engaged to Horace, rather than the accomplished fact, which she signalized by her awkward little exclamation. Or, very likely, it was intended to warn trespassers off the premises under the penalty of the law.

"How do you like Horace Larkin?" she had asked, with an air of indifference which would have been misleading, if it had not been a trifle overdone.

"I like him very much," Kate had replied, with thoughtless directness. "I think he is a very clever man."

"O, I am so glad you like him," her cousin had cried, with sudden ardor ; "I think as you do, that he is immensely clever."

It was, of course, difficult to tell how much intention there was in this apparently guileless declaration ; but

Kate refused to take it seriously, or allow herself to be in any way influenced by conjectures. It piqued her, however, more than she would admit, that the one man in Torryville whom she had honored with her preference had the impertinence to make himself precious, and seek no opportunities to deepen the impression which he well knew that he had made. Women, she thought, had a monopoly in that kind of tactics, and it was beneath the dignity of a man to rival them in intricate demeanor. She heard a rumor that Horace was "laying pipes" for his fall campaign, and that he already had a sure thing of it, if he desired to go to the Assembly. But it seemed inconceivable that anyone could find such business more important than the cultivation of her valuable favor. She did not in the remotest way betray her solicitude on this subject; but for all that, she occupied herself a good deal with meditations concerning the motive and intentions of this enigmatical young man, who could afford to throw away an acquaintance worth millions of dollars, as if it had been a burnt-out match.

It was while her vanity yet suffered under the inferences she was obliged to draw from Horace's conduct, that he surprised her, one afternoon, by calling with the high family buggy, and the ornamental Jim, and inviting her to take a ride. It seemed an odd thing to do—especially climbing into that uncomfortable vehicle, which brought you into such unpleasantly close contact with your escort; but she concluded, after a moment's hesitation, that she was too interested in knowing what he would do next, to forfeit the chance by straining a point of etiquette. So off they started together, making a sensation in every street where they appeared (though there was little external evidence of excitement), and sending clouds of dust out over the unmown meadows. Though the weather was perfect, being neither too warm nor too cool, and the sun shone with the most genial moderation—as if he had no wish in the world but to make himself agreeable—her companion seemed to be a little distant at times, and found fault with the horse without the least visible pretext. He was neither brilliant nor conspicuously amiable, but was exerting himself with fair success to be polite. He pointed with his whip to the various farm-houses they passed, told who lived there, and the noteworthy circumstances in the lives of the inhabitants. One farmer had been suspected of poisoning his first wife, though nothing was ever proved against him ; another had made life a burden to his consort, and had, with admirable courtesy, furnished her with a rope when she threatened to hang herself ; a third had objected to his daughter's marriage to a neighbor's son, whereupon the young people had taken a horse and buggy, and clasped in each other's embrace, had killed each other with a pistol, and the horse, from old habit, had taken the homeward way and carried them straight to the relentless father's door. There was much more of the same sort ; and the conclusion he drew from it was that it was a great mistake to suppose that the worst crime was confined to the city. In the United States as in Russia, people often committed crimes from sheer boredom ; on the whole he didn't blame them. If nothing else of interest happened in his life—if he had no ambition to furnish him with a definite object in living, it was not improbable that he might take to beating his wife, in order to furnish incidents and relieve the monotony of existence for himself as well as for her.

Kate liked this badinage well enough, but was impelled to object in order to keep the conversation going.

"But suppose your wife objected," she said, "what would you do then ?"

"I intend to have her so well disciplined that she won't object," he answered, with his serio-comic air.

"I am afraid you'll make some unpleasant discoveries after your marriage," she ejaculated, laughing.

"Perhaps. But I'm equal to dealing with them. Marriage, you know, is a contract of mutual disagreement——"

"I should rather call it a compact of mutual concession."

"Oh, no, that would never do. Disagreement is inevitable. Concession on the man's part would be fatal to the domestic peace. There must be a certain amount of despotism—wise, paternal despotism, if you like—in a well-regulated family. Civilized people agree to disagree, and disagree amicably ; savages disagree and fight about it."

"Then you class yourself among savages ?"

"Oh, yes ; I shouldn't wonder if I had a good deal of the savage left in me."

"Then I hope you'll also marry a savage."

"I doubt that ; for I'm just civilized enough to have a keen admiration for a civilized woman."

He turned and looked at her with sudden intentness ;

12

and whether it was the unexpectedness of the glance or
its evident significance, she felt a vague tumult of heart,
and gazed out over the lake in order to hide her blushes.
Such a thing had never occurred in her previous experience. She had never met a man before who had thrown
her off her base and made her lose her stately composure.
She knew the symptoms of love from novels, and suspected that this was one of them. But the golden calm in
which her days had been passed had never before been
invaded by any emotion strong enough to ruffle her superb
equanimity.

Horace Larkin, conscious that he had scored a point,
whipped up the horse, and for a while they spun rapidly
over the smooth road along the lake shore. The water
shone like glass, and a fisherman who was rowing out to examine his traps sent long diverging undulations shoreward
from his bow. A few stray gulls, who had really no business in an inland sea, kept soaring silently above him, and
occasionally dipped in his wake in order to make the acquaintance of their mimic selves which floated up to meet
them from below. Ugly little boat-sheds, rugged tree-root
fences, and maples, pines, and locusts seemed to be running
a race for life toward the swift-footed Jim and the occupants of the buggy, and Kate felt the exhilaration of the
speed and breathed with deep contentment. She sat
leaning backward, regarding her companion furtively, and
endeavoring to analyze the impression he made upon her.
She had nearly recovered her wonted calm ; though there
was yet a centre of disturbance, as the weather reports say,
deep down below the surface, where the heart roots inter-
twine in the soul's primeval dusk. He was right, Kate
thought, or more than half right in calling himself a savage ; and she was not quite sure but that it was the savage
in him which attracted her. She was conscious of that
dim fear which, in a woman of her type, may be the beginning of love ; she knew that if he made up his mind irrevocably to make her his wife, she would in the end have
to surrender. She almost hoped with a hidden dread lest
her hope might be fulfilled, that he would dismiss the
thought of her and let her lapse back again into her trivial
existence, and go his own way without her. She had always
thought that she would marry a handsome man. He was
not handsome ; rather, perhaps, the reverse. The very
way he sat in the buggy, half relaxed, leaning forward with
his elbows on his knees ; the crude strength of his feat-

ures, the haphazard fit of his clothes, the general lack of finish in his whole appearance, all showed how remote he was from her sphere of life. He was not a thoroughbred ; she came very near insinuating that he was not, according to her former standard, a gentleman. And yet there was that in him which made every man she had ever known seem insignificant by comparison. He was a man—every inch of him—and he gave the correct measure of himself when he said that nothing in the line of his ambition was unattainable to him.

When they had driven six or seven miles along the lake shore, a road was found which led back to the town over the hills and which afforded a much more extended view of the landscape. The slope was rugged, and often the overgrown boughs of the sycamores reached half-way across the highway and dashed their moist leaves into the faces of the occupants of the buggy. This occasioned a little excitement and unforeseen collisions and contacts, to which the proper Kate, if they had happened to anyone but herself, would have applied the severest adjectives. But somehow she failed, in this instance, to resent the impertinence of the boughs, and her spirits rose with her agitation, until she fairly surprised herself by her gay laughter and senseless, unrestrained mirth. This was surely not the Kate who left New York three weeks ago—whose glacial propriety had frozen the courage of all but the most adventurous candidates for her hands.

It was about six o'clock in the afternoon when they reached the University campus, and drove slowly past the great piles of gray sandstone with their long, regular rows of windows, in which the afternoon sun was burning with a fiery glow. They met companies of students who came from the laboratories, carrying their books and luncheon baskets, and a few coeducational damsels who carried tennis rackets. The broad gravelled avenues were planted on either side with young elms and maples, which promised ample shade to future generations, and a glaringly red brick chapel pointed its spire against a glaringly blue sky. Along the road lay, at short intervals, professors' cottages, of all shades of architectural pretentiousness and simplicity ; and below these were seen two rather large and handsome buildings, which were the chapter houses of the secret Greek letter societies. Horace was explaining the character of these latter institutions to Kate, as far as his pledge to respect their secrets would permit, when suddenly a flag was run up on the roof of one of the mysterious edifices.

"What does that mean?" she asked, with the liveliest curiosity.

"It is a greeting to you," he answered; "it is my society."

"How very nice of them. Do they receive visitors?"

"Certainly. I shall be happy to show you the house if you care to see it."

"I should like to very much. But tell me first what you do there."

"Oh, we practise horrid midnight rites that would make every individual hair upon your head stand on end like the quills upon the fretful porcupine."

She laughed while he helped her out of the buggy; Jim seized the opportunity to shake himself so that the harness rattled, but consented, without further remonstrance, to be tied to the stone hitching-post. Half a dozen students, anxious to do the honors of the house, appeared on the piazza without waiting for the door bell to be rung, and were introduced by Horace to Miss Van Schaak. There was one young man named Lovel, who looked pleased and bashful, and another named Cottrell, whose cheerful self-confidence and loudly fashionable attire proclaimed him a denizen of the Pacific coast. These constituted themselves a committee of reception, and exhibited, with much pride, the handsome appointments of the house.

"And now," said Kate to Cottrell, who, with superfluous courtesy, insisted upon her taking his arm, "I should like to see some of the mysteries."

"I regret to say that we are not permitted to admit strangers to the Chapter Room," the Californian replied, with sudden solemnity.

"Who forbids you?"

"Our laws and traditions."

Kate had to laugh again and turned to Horace, whom she begged to exercise his authority. The door was then thrown open to a large and sunny room with a beautiful outlook upon the lake and the valley.

"Will you do me the honor to enter?" said Cottrell, with a hospitable flourish of his hand; "this is my humble abode."

The room was bright and cheerful, and furnished in rather a luxurious style. A scent of cigars pervaded the atmosphere. The walls were covered with engravings and sketches, all representing nude nymphs and goddesses, ancient and modern, and in the spaces between the frames were nailed a multitude of actresses in tights, and in a variety of piquant attitudes. There were Ledas, Galateas, Danaës, Venuses rising from the foam of the sea; and Lydia Thompsons, Maude Branscomes, Mary Andersons, and other histrionic celebrities without number rising from nobody knew where. Over the mantel-piece hung a large framed embroidered motto whose legend was: "Coeducation is the Thief of Time;" and between the windows was seen the familiar one, "God will Provide," in embroidery, to which was added in ornamental script, "Cigars."

Kate was, at first, shocked at the young man's depravity, but was too much of a woman of the world to betray her displeasure. For all that, Cottrell detected an air of constraint in her face, and remarked, apologetically:

"You know we all have our specialties, otherwise there wouldn't be any fun in living. My specialty is girls; Lovel's there is postage stamps."

The bashful Lovel blushed to his ears at this base slander, but failed to make an intelligible rejoinder.

"Go into his room and see," cried Cottrell; "his walls are covered with envelopes so that you can't see an inch of the woodwork."

"That's not for the stamps," the blushing youth stammered; "it is for the autographs."

"He has got Gladstone and Bismarck and Grant and the Emperor of Germany, and no end of big guns," the Californian declared, leading the way to Lovel's apartment.

His description proved correct; the walls were literally hidden up to the very ceiling under envelopes bearing the autographs of famous persons. From the sitting-room Kate got a glimpse through the open door of the bedroom, where there was an ash-tree bureau, with mirror of the Eastlake pattern, to the frame of which were pinned about a dozen photographs of the same young girl (and a very sweet girl it was); and over the mantel-piece there hung a delightfully awkward family group, with the father and the mother in their best finery in the middle, and three sons and four daughters, some with their hands resting at right angles upon the other's shoulder, some with their legs crossed, and all looking as glum and forlorn, as if they had lost their last friend.

While Kate was reading the character and history of the young man in his environment (and though she was not poetic, she did not fail to perceive a certain touching quality in it), a mellow brass gong was sounded, and Cottrell invited her with much ceremony to honor the society with her company at supper. She referred the question to Horace, who declared that he could see no objection. They accordingly were ushered into the dining-room, which was adorned with colored wood engravings representing scenes from German university life, such as the "Landesvater," "Fuchsritt," "Gänsemarsch," etc. There was also a large picture of a man who was eating clam-chowder with ecstatic enjoyment, and on the glass was pasted a slip of paper on which was written : *De Profundis Clam-av-i*, which, as Cottrell explained, means, being interpreted, " I have a clam out of the depths."

Kate became, in the course of the supper, so interested in these twenty-two young men, who surrounded the two tables, that she almost forgot to eat. She liked to see their envious admiration of Cottrell's audacity in entertaining her, in such a free and easy way, and their ineffectual imitation of his loud and swaggering California manners. It had never occurred to her before that boys, during that amphibious age when they are neither children nor men, had any redeeming qualities whatever ; but she concluded now that there is no age which has not its charm. To be the only woman in such an assembly, to feel their shy worship of her womanhood — *das ewig Weibliche* — was a novel and delightful experience. She had never felt so motherly in all her life before, so consciously exalted and superior, so tender and tolerant of masculine absurdity and folly. Their sudden explosions of mirth, their telegraphic communications by glances and grimaces, and the irrepressible monkey tricks of a few of the younger ones, which she appeared not to observe, made her realize the characteristics of the genus boy as never before. The quick blush which sprang to the cheeks of those who found courage to address her ; their anxiety to conceal their embarrassment from their comrades, and their heroic feeling when they had acquitted themselves creditably, seemed as good as a play. Her presence was an event to them ; roused the chivalrous instinct in them, and incited them to helpless demonstrations of gallantry which they lacked courage to carry out in quite the bold style in which they were conceived.

When Kate drove down the hillside with Horace Larkin, after this charming adventure, she was so adorably gentle, simple, and amiable, that even his cool blood was kindled and his eyes rested upon her with undisguised admiration. A sense of well-being crept over him; the world, in spite of its imperfections, seemed more nearly right than it had ever seemed before. There was a luxury in living, and each breath seemed fuller and warmer, and came from deeper down, and stung the blood into a richer and stronger pulsation. He half marvelled to himself that his conscience troubled him so little; for it was an unscrupulous game he had played with a certain tender and fragile heart which had beat unwaveringly for him for many years. He knew that this ride must have made Bella miserable, and he tried to persuade himself that he was sorry for her; but was, in the end, constrained to admit that he felt heartlessly and outrageously comfortable.

When Horace parted from Kate at the gate of the parsonage, he was conscious of having made great strides in her acquaintance, perhaps in her good-will. He was too careful a man to draw rash conclusions; for he had an overpowering sense of the millions which Kate represented, and of the dignity they conferred upon their prospective possessor. But this fact did not in the least lessen his sense of his own worth. If he should, upon mature deliberation, conclude to marry Kate Van Schaak, he would set about it rationally; and there was nothing which seemed beyond his power to achieve if he concentrated his mind upon it. He was, however, by no means sure that he wished to marry Kate; she belonged to another world than his, and might not adapt herself with readiness to the conditions which to him were natural and satisfactory. The question was certainly debatable, and he determined to debate it exhaustively.

That night, when Kate Van Schaak had disrobed her lithe virginal form, and the light mists of slumber were gathering about her neat and compact brain, gentle strains of melody stole up to her window and mingled with her dreams. She dreamed that she was being borne by twelve strong eagles over the tops of the sun-gilded forests, and that suddenly the eagles burst into song—the most blissful and ecstatic song that had ever rung in her ears. But gradually, as they sang they grew dimmer and dimmer, and melted away in shreds of golden vapor, while the song, draining their life and substance, grew stronger and at last filled the wide space round about. She awoke, and sitting up in bed, listened intently. There could be no doubt of it. Somebody was singing; and not one, but many. She heard distinctly a tenor, trembling on the high G, calling her darling, imploring her in one moment to awake, and in the next to slumber sweetly; and a sub-dued chorus of baritone and bass voices were expressing their approval of his sentiments and joining in his demands. She had to rub her eyes repeatedly before the situation became clear to her; for she had never been serenaded in her life, and was not aware that that mediæval cus-tom had survived in university towns into the present century. But when the sentimental quartet ceased and the midnight air was startled by the abrupt and irrelevant query:

> " Said the bullfrog to the owl :
> Oh, what'll you have to drink ? "

she knew that her serenaders were the members of the Greek Letter society who had entertained her during the afternoon. The reply of the owl:

> "Oh, since you are so very kind
> I'll take a bottle of ink,"

struck her as being so delightfully comical that she burst out laughing and jumped out of bed. She did not know what the etiquette of the occasion required her to do; but after a moment's hesitation she flung a dainty blue cash-mere wrapper about her, opened the window, and stood for a moment listening. Then she seized a bouquet of roses which stood in a vase on the mantel-piece, smelled it, and tossed it down to the singers. "I thank you, gen-tlemen," she said, and closed the window.

But underneath there was a tremendous scramble for the possession of the roses.

CHAPTER XXI.

THE ALMIGHTY DOLLAR.

It had been perceived by several members of the house of Larkin that there was a cloud upon the family horizon. The Hon. Obed, who was not usually subject to the blues, had, since the visit of the mysterious woman in his library, never quite recovered his spirits. He had succeeded beyond expectation in keeping the secret of this woman's claim upon him ; for no gossip connected with her visit had found currency in the town. But the mere knowledge that there was somebody in the world who, if she would, could injure his reputation, troubled him and made him nervous and uneasy. Of course he had done nothing of which he needed to be ashamed ; nay, he had acted not only honorably but even generously. But for all that, his folly in concealing what there was no need of concealing gave an ugly look to the affair, and would make people suspect that there was something under it which would not bear the light. Few would believe that his principal motive for keeping his first marriage secret was his dread of losing the affection of the present Mrs. Larkin, who stood on strictly biblical ground as regards the remarriage of one who had been divorced. He had, indeed, sounded her upon the subject a few weeks before their wedding, and had found her uncompromising. That his first wife, as soon as she had used up the money he had given her, would make a second descent upon him, and perhaps in pure wantonness expose him, seemed more than likely ; and the probability that she would continue these tactics as long as she remained above ground, destroyed his zest in living and made him (as a mere provisional measure) inclined to prepare for the end. The only consoling circumstance, to which he clung with tenacious hope, was the prospect that her vice might, when indulged without restraint, soon quench her baneful and unwholesome existence. He surprised himself again and again, praying that this might soon come to pass—wishing with a vengeful ardor that she might be come up with in the next world, and suffer tenfold (as he did not doubt that she would) the miseries which she had inflicted upon him. For a deacon and pillar of the church, these were, of course, not very laudable sentiments; and Mr. Larkin, who was a stauncher believer than his pastor, was often frightened at the rank growth of hate and wickedness which he discovered in the depth of his heart. He comforted himself, however, easily with the thought that, as men go, he was, on the whole, a fairly creditable specimen of his race, and considerably above the average as regards moral worth. If God, who was merciful toward the errors of His children, should draw the line so as to exclude him from His presence, He would have a very insignificant remnant left to be partakers of His glory. Mr. Larkin had a faint suspicion that this line of reasoning was not strictly Christian; but he found himself pursuing it, half automatically, whenever he looked back upon his life, which, if it had been investigated by the committee presided over by the Recording Angel, would have revealed several incidents which could only be made to look well by the most unblushing partisanship.

It was while this mood was upon him that Mr. Larkin, one day early in June, dropped in upon Horace at the office where the latter was seated, tilted back in his chair with his heels on his desk, smoking a strong cigar. He did not change his attitude as his uncle entered, but nodded to him over his shoulder and begged him to find himself a seat. The old man, with a troubled expression about his eyes and the corners of his mouth, pulled forward a chunky, black-painted chair, placed his feet upon a table by the window, and began thoughtfully to pick his teeth with a quill. He sat long in silence, letting his eyes wander over the long rows of law-books, bound in calf, with red or black labels for the titles, and no sound was heard except the clicks of his toothpick. The office consisted of an outer and an inner room, the furniture of which was old and rather shabby. There was a small iron safe under the desk, four or five chairs, a couple of spittoons filled with saw-dust, and a table covered with briefs tied together with blue and red ribbons.

Having exhausted the uses of the toothpick, Mr. Larkin pulled out his pocket knife, which looked old enough to be an heirloom, and began to clean his nails.

"Why do you smoke that vile weed?" he asked, addressing himself apparently to the top of the bookcase.

"It's a fifteen-center," Horace replied, "but if it is disagreeable to you, I will throw it away."

He flung the half-smoked cigar into the spittoon, rose, and began to rummage among the papers in an open drawer.

"Will you be alone for about an hour?" Mr. Larkin inquired, listlessly.

"Yes, if you wish it; I can give orders to Lawson that we are not to be disturbed."

"All right."

Horace went into the outer office, spoke to his clerk, and returned, locking the door after him.

There was another pause of five minutes, during which Mr. Larkin devoted all his attention to a troublesome hang-nail.

"I have been thinking," he began, staring at the tips of his fingers, "that I shall have to make a new will. I tore up the old one this morning."

"I am at your service, sir," Horace observed, carelessly; "it is never good policy to sleep over night intestate for a man who has as complicated interests as you have."

Mr. Larkin made no answer to this, but clinched the hang-nail close to the root, and looked much relieved.

"I want you to note down on a piece of paper the bequests and other items," he said; "then write the thing out in due legal form, and I will wait here and sign it."

"Very well. I'm ready."

"To my beloved wife, Mary Louise Larkin, in case she survives me, the income of $200,000, the capital to revert, at her death, to my nephew, Horace Larkin; to my wife, also, the house with fixings, horses, and carriages in trust during her lifetime. Have you got that?"

"Yes."

"To my beloved daughter, Gertrude Larkin——"

Horace glanced up from his paper with a lively interrogation in his face.

"Do you mean daughter or adopted daughter?" he asked; "you know you make yourself liable to have the will contested, if either name or relation is inaccurately stated."

"I mean what I say," the old man rejoined. "To my beloved daughter, Gertrude Larkin—have you got that?"

"Wait a minute. Yes, now I've got it."

"One hundred and fifty thousand dollars in bonds and stocks of Chicago and Northwestern, New York Central and Hudson River, and stock of Torryville National Bank."

Mr. Larkin here pulled some papers from his breast pocket, and examined them carefully.

"My nephew, Horace Larkin, son of my deceased brother Ezekiel," he went on, pausing thoughtfully at every other word, "I make the trustee—of the property —to be held in trust—for my wife, during her lifetime, and to revert to him at her death."

The dreariness of his expression was illuminated by a gleam of shrewd scrutiny as he uttered these words. He knew well that Horace had for years regarded himself as his probable heir, and had planned his future on a scale befitting the possessor of millions. He was curious now to see how he bore the shock of his disappointment. Scratch—scratch—scratch—went the quill, as steadily as ever ; and the coarse, somewhat tumbled hair, with the stiff bristly tuft that always grew straight up from his crown, looked irritatingly stubborn and unconcerned. Mr. Larkin, who was just the man to appreciate such stoicism, began almost to waver in his resolution ; he felt an admiration for this masterful, but self-restrained nephew, which he would have liked to express, if he had not feared to confuse again his carefully matured plans.

"Horace," he said, "would you care to know why I have left things that way ?"

"I should not presume to ask you, sir ; I don't question your right to do with yours as you see fit."

"I know that. But you had expected that I would treat you more handsomely, I reckon."

"Perhaps I had, sir. But it's all right. You need have no fear of my making a row about it."

"No ; and that reminds me that I want you to put in a clause, declaring that if any of my heirs or legatees contest my will, he or she shall forfeit all benefit accruing to him or her under that instrument."

"All right. I think that's quite proper."

The old man pulled the stump of a lead pencil from his vest pocket and began to figure on the back of an envelope. "Horace," he said, while yet absorbed in his figures, "you may scarcely believe it ; but—but—it is for your own good that I intend to leave you no money—until you are so rich that two hundred thousand more or less will make no difference to you."

"That time may never come," said Horace, plunging his hands into his pockets, and rattling with his keys and small change.

"Stuff. I know a man when I see him. You will go to Congress; you'll rise high in public life. I won't say you'll become President, because that is more or less of a lottery. If I gave you half a million dollars outright, as I once thought of doing, I should be taking away from you the chief incentive to ambition. I should be compelling you to waste your life taking care of your money, when you might be doing something better. I tell you, the fun that's to be had out of money is in getting it, not in spending it. A million is a hard task master. I mean to leave you your own master. I began as a poor boy myself, with two empty hands; and I never should have been the man I am, if I had started at the top. I believe it is a calamity to a man of your ability to commence his career with his pockets full of money."

"To be consistent, then, you ought to leave your money to an enemy," Horace observed, after a pause.

"No," Mr. Larkin answered, "I intend to leave it to my University. There it will do good. You may put down one million dollars to the general endowment fund of the Larkin University. The residue of the estate, after all bequests have been paid, is to be applied to the purchase of machinery for the department of mechanical engineering."

Mr. Larkin enumerated a dozen other bequests to charitable institutions in various parts of the State; $50,000 to the Hampton College for the higher education of colored people, and $20,000 to the Carlisle School for Indians. Altogether he disposed of something over two million dollars. He named Horace Larkin and William Dallas executors of his will, with an annual salary of $4,000 for two years.

Horace seated himself again at his desk, and in the course of an hour had composed a document in legal form, satisfactory to the testator. He read it aloud, made a few changes of expression at Mr. Larkin's suggestion, seized the pen to dot an i or cross a t, and finally attached the seal. He called his clerk Lawson in to witness the signature, but begged him to wait until two other witnesses could be procured; for, as some of the property was situated in Western States, where the law requires three witnesses, it was thought best to run no risks. Horace himself stepped across the street to the Post-office, and returned in a moment with the postmaster. Mr. Gleason, the druggist, who was also a discreet man, was unhappily not in ; but was expected every minute. He therefore left word with the prescription clerk to send him over as soon as he arrived. But as he re-entered his office, he found Dr. Hawk seated there, conversing with his uncle.

"I came here on a little private business," the doctor explained. " I want to know if you'll collect a bill of $56 for me."

"Oh, yes," Horace answered; " small favors thankfully received."

"You needn't do it, you know, if you don't want to," cried Hawk, a trifle huffed.

" I know that. I am not in the habit of doing anything, unless I want to."

They talked on for a few minutes, and Horace agreed to collect the claim. Mr. Gleason, in the meanwhile, did not arrive, and the postmaster was getting uneasy.

"Well, there is no use waiting for him," Mr. Larkin observed, rubbing his bristly cheeks with his hand ; "here is the doctor ; he'll do just as well."

Horace, from behind the doctor's back, sent his uncle a warning glance ; but the old gentleman failed to perceive its meaning, and continued :

" I have been making out a document of some little consequence, gentlemen ; in fact, it is my last will and testament, and I want you to witness my signature."

He moved toward the desk, took the will out of the drawer where it had been temporarily concealed, seized a pen which he tried on the back of an envelope, and wrote slowly and carefully,

OBED LARKIN.

The postmaster executed with due solemnity an awkward and rickety signature in the place which Horace indicated ; and the clerk, Lawson, made some flowing and ornamental flourishes in the style of Gaskell's Compendium. When the doctor's turn came, he found difficulty in getting properly seated ; pulled the leather cushion of the chair first one way and then another ; and finally asked Horace if he didn't have a stub pen, as he could not write with any other kind. By the time all his preparations were finished, Dr. Hawk had managed to glean nearly the entire contents of the will. The words "To my beloved daughter Gertrude Larkin, I give and bequeath the sum of $150,000 " burned themselves into his memory, and followed him about, after he had risen, like a writing of flame. Gertrude, Mr. Larkin's daughter! Well, if he had known that before, much would have been different. He had been excessively stupid not to have suspected it. But that venerable old gentleman, that pillar of the church, who would have thought that he had skeletons in his closet? The doctor left the office of Larkin Brothers in a state of excitement which he had not experienced since the day he saw the strange woman with Gertrude in the Drum Head Ravine. He began to put two and two together, and soon he had in his mind the material for a full-fledged romance.

"It wasn't very smart of you, uncle," said Horace, as he handed Mr. Larkin the fateful document, "to have that loon, Hawk, as witness of signature. Didn't you see me scowl at you?"

"Why, no. What's the matter with Hawk?"

"Well, he's a sort of fancy chap. Too many frills to be honest. I wouldn't trust him with a dollar, except on first-class security."

CHAPTER XXII.

A DELICATE SITUATION.

A man cannot add a cubit to his height, the Bible says, however much he taketh thought thereof ; but it seems sometimes as if he could take a cubit off. Horace Larkin felt himself distinctly a smaller man, when he walked home from the office after having executed his uncle's will. It was as if he had been reduced from six to five feet three. He had never realized before what an important aid to his self-esteem the prospect of that million was. He could not deny that he was grievously disappointed, but he was yet fair-minded enough to credit the old man with the motive which he professed. He was not at all angry with him. If there was anybody with whom he was out of patience, it was that omnivorous young monster, the University, which could not be satisfied with the million it had already gobbled up, but must needs devour the remaining one too.

Horace Larkin walked about for three days in a state of intense preoccupation, pondering this question in all its possible bearings. There was one phase of it which had presented itself to him at the first moment, but which he lacked courage to contemplate clearly. Was his first duty toward himself or toward Bella? Would it kill Bella if he broke with her ? Was not her violent affection for him rather a pathological than a psychological phenomenon ? Was it not a direct result of her hysterical condition—an attendant symptom of poor nerves? With no money, and a penniless wife, without distinction of any kind (unless her love for him might be counted a distinction), what fate could he rationally look forward to ? Ten or twenty squalid years of toil, slow and gradual rise, politically ; many setbacks, no doubt, and perhaps in the end a cheap, moderate success, or perhaps even failure. He had never been aware before how inextricably that million had been interwoven with all his plans for the future, and entered into the very foundation of the daring tower of fortune

which in his dreams he had erected. Then (shall I confess
it ?) there was one humiliating little suspicion which had
recently insinuated itself into his mind, and that it was impossible to get rid of. He was, after all, a mere village
character, and had never measured himself with strong and
brilliant men on the great arena of life. Kate Van Schaak
had come to him as a messenger from that greater world
with which he was wholly unacquainted, and had made
him in a dim way feel his limitations. She had raised his
standard of womanhood, and had made him regret his
choice by casting his *fiancée* cruelly into the shade. For
an ambitious and proud man to have this conviction, that
the companion of his life was "a little below par"—would,
in the eyes of the fine society which he would one day
enter, cast discredit upon him instead of adding to his
lustre—was a haunting torture, heavy and hopeless like
a nightmare. Then again, to imagine himself marching
down the long radiant years by the side of the stately
and gracious Kate, commanding homage, looking down
amiably upon the multitude, feeling the distinction of
wealth and fame and power in every fibre—that was a
vision that drew his eyes and his whole soul with irresistible fascination. There was no help for it—succeed he
must ; and money was essential to success. Life would be
a burden to him without success, as with a mean success ;
he could afford to take no risks. He would break with
Bella, and he would bend all his energies to marrying
Kate.

He had at first a forlorn hope that Bella might possibly
be induced to give him his *congé.* He had conspicuously
neglected her while Kate had visited at the parsonage,
and expected to be taken to task for his unlover-like conduct. But Bella, conscious of the worth of the prize she
had secured, refused to risk its loss by too great exaction
on her part. She chose the safer course to confide in
Kate and trust to her honor. She had, indeed, promised
Horace to keep their engagement secret until he consented
to her making it public. But in the first place it was more
than flesh and blood could bear to conceal the distinction
which such a relation conferred upon her in the eyes of
the town ; and secondly, publicity gave an added sense of
security which was not to be despised in the case of a
cool and slippery lover. It was the day before Kate's return to New York that Bella took this great resolution ;
for, she reasoned, a girl like Kate would be no less for-

midable a rival in New York than in Torryville. Distance
would not destroy the enchantment of her millions, and
the trail of luminous memories she left behind her would
not soon lose its lustre.

With her heart in her throat Bella knocked at the door
of her brilliant cousin, who was standing in the middle of
the room, directing Tillie, one of the Rodents, who, with an
air of flattered importance was folding up a gorgeous dress
which was spread out upon the bed. Bella, excusing her
intrusion, asked if she could not help her pack.

"No, I thank you," Kate replied, "Tillie is doing quite
well. Now, put that bonnet in the box, Tillie, and put it
into the lid of the trunk."

Tillie grinned with pleasure. She had never felt so
highly honored in all her life. And to be preferred to her
favored sister—that was a joy which made her almost dizzy.
Her brown, alert eyes flew about the room like those of a
jubilant mouse ; and she cast demurely triumphant
glances over at her sister, who had wearily seated herself
at the window. The excitement of the last weeks had
visibly told on Bella's health, which had, indeed, always
been delicate. The rings about her eyes were darker than
usual, and that gray undertone in her complexion, which
never was visible except when she was distressed, spoiled
the beauty of her clear and well-cut features. Curious
little tremors and twitchings appeared about her eyelids
and lips, and she tapped her little slippered foot against
the floor, being utterly unable to sit still.

When, at last, the trunk was packed and Tillie could find
no further excuse for lingering, the confidential mood had
left her, and she would rather have cried for sheer nervousness and vexation. Kate, who was in radiant humor,
walked about from the bureau to the bed and from the
bed to the trunk, humming the air "Landlord, fill the
flowing bowl," and it seemed impossible to open a serious
conversation to such an accompaniment. And yet, Bella
could not let the opportunity slip by ; it might never
return.

"Cousin Kate," she began at last, tremulously, "I am
so sorry you are going."

That was not, perhaps, strictly true, but it was one of
those white lies which custom has stamped with its approval.

"Well, dear, I am sorry too," Kate hummed to the bac-
chanalian air.

"I wonder if this weather is going to continue," observed Bella, after a pause, looking out of the window.

"It is usually best when it does not continue," answered Kate, facetiously.

"I don't see what I shall do when you are gone, Kate ; I shall simply die."

She lied now from sheer vacuity ; only to fill up the pauses, and by some circuitous route to lead up to the all-important topic.

"It is very kind of you to say so, dear ; but I am heartless enough to think that we shall both survive it," Kate replied, with smiling equanimity. "You know, we belong to a long-lived family."

There was just the needed note in that reply—a little caressing touch, as it were—for which Bella had waited. She could not walk into Kate's room and fling her tender secret down before her as a clerk tosses a piece of goods on a counter for the inspection of a customer. No, she had to have a bit of a melodious prelude, through which she could glide naturally into the grand and soul-stirring theme.

"Kate," she said, with burning cheeks and throbbing temples, "you have been so sweet to me that I can't bear to have you go away without telling you something—which—which——"

"Well, which what!" cried Kate, not unsympathetically.

The tears trembled in Bella's eyes. She could not go on.

"Well, dear, you are going to be married, isn't that it ?" queried her cousin, fixing her bright brown eyes upon her with a smile which seemed a little strained.

"Yes," Bella faltered, making a gigantic effort to suppress her tears. "Will you come to my wedding, Kate ? You know it's not to be this year, but probably next."

She felt immensely relieved that Kate took it so coolly ; and her quiet, superior smile made her positively grateful. She had done her cruel injustice in her thought, and was longing to do penance.

"But before I congratulate you," Kate observed, putting a couple of ivory-handled brushes into their places in the silver toilet-case, "you must tell me who it is. It must be somebody who has my approval. Otherwise, I shan't come to the wedding."

"Who it is ? Why, don't you know that ?" cried Bella, in a sort of wild falsetto ; "can't you guess ?"

"Why, no, I haven't an idea."

Miss Van Schaak had a very distinct idea ; but for some occult reason she chose to appear obtuse. She was dimly displeased that Horace Larkin had gone and thrown himself away on so insignificant a little body as her cousin; and she was not going to make it easy for the latter to divulge that unpleasant fact. She had no notion that she wished Horace for herself ; nay, she thought the probabilities were that, do what he might, he could never win her ; but for all that, she disliked having him lower himself in her estimation, and that was what he had done in accepting the sordid commonplace lot of a village lawyer, married to a poor little hysterical village belle. The "desire of the moth for the star" was, to her mind, a laudable desire, even though it did the star no good and diverted the moth from his proper sphere of usefulness. But the desire of the moth for the moth she regarded with unutterable scorn.

Bella had risen to her feet. She stood in her loose pink wrapper with a lace cascade, supporting herself against the back of a chair.

"Why, dear Kate," she ejaculated, with her anxious smile, "you surely know it is Horace Larkin—who else could it be ? "

"Well, I am sure he's very nice," Kate replied, a little listlessly ; "you have my best wishes, dear."

"Oh, I'm *so* happy, Kate. You can't imagine how happy I am."

And to demonstrate how happy she was, she flung herself upon her cousin's neck and sobbed. Kate, though she did not feel extravagantly sympathetic, respected herself too much to be unkind ; so she smoothed the girl's hair, kissed her cheeks, and begged her to compose herself. But Bella had been too long pent up with her misery to forego now the luxurious relief of tears. She wept as if her heart would break ; wept so that her whole frame shook ; and then suddenly remembered that if she kept on, she would lose control of herself and go into hysterics. So, with an odd abruptness she choked down the last sob, released Kate from her embrace, and walked blindly to the window, where she stood long leaning on her hand against the frame, pressing an absurd little ball of a handkerchief against her eyes, and heaving now and then a shivering sigh.

Kate presently selected from her homœopathic medicine

case a bottle with the proper number, took from it two pellets, which she put into a glass of water and forced Bella to drink. Whether among the panaceas of that convenient system there is one for disappointment in love or a broken heart, I do not know ; but Kate, who had great confidence in her pellets, felt sure that they would go to the right spot and effect a cure. She had a pleasant sense of having done her duty when this task was accomplished. There was a quiet satisfaction in her handsome and intelligent face, which was like an advertisement of a good conscience. It was, perhaps, by way of further indulgence to this good conscience that she sprayed Bella with a very expensive cologne, of rare virtue, and cajoled her into a rocking-chair, where she had to submit to further amateur doctoring until, in sheer self-defence, she declared that she felt perfectly well.

"Well," said Kate, " I want you to keep this phial. It never fails to relieve a nervous headache and an unstrung condition generally."

There stood on the bureau a small battery of cut-glass bottles, with pink and blue ribbons about their necks, containing the most marvellous liquids and essences.

Kate took up one after the other, allowed her cousin to smell it, and initiated her into its uses. And Bella, in spite of her sorrow, grew more and more interested, and began to feel an affection for Kate which she had never felt before. Each wonderful bottle, as it was opened and smelled, increased her humility and her admiration for her cousin. Life was evidently a more complicated affair than she, in her innocence, had dreamed.

And so the *tête-à-tête* which began with love ended with perfumery.

CHAPTER XXIII.

THE RAVINE PARTY.

While Horace Larkin was struggling with the problem how to get rid of his *fiancée* in the most decent and unobtrusive manner, Dr. Hawk was endeavoring to reconquer the affection of one whom he had alienated. He had frequently been on the point of proposing to Gertrude during the last two years, and would probably, by this time, have settled his fate one way or another, if Kate Van Schaak had not appeared on the scene. The doctor was not in the least ashamed of himself that he, like so many others, had gone to worship the strange goddess ; but he was at his wit's end to invent a plausible lie by which this dance around the Golden Calf might be made to appear compatible with unswerving loyalty to the true and only idol of his heart. He could not, of course, go and tell Gertie the unvarnished truth, that he had for two years dawdled with the idea of marrying her, but had been deterred by the uncertainty of her position in Mr. Larkin's house ; that recently he had gotten a glimpse of her father's will (which had in the most satisfactory manner settled all his doubts), and that accordingly he was now most anxious to make up for his past delinquencies and lead her straight to the altar. The only lie he could think of had a stale and unprofitable look, and he scarcely knew whether Gertie was gullible enough to be caught in so simple a trap. That he had flung himself at Kate's feet in a fit of despair, because of Gertrude's cruelty and wanton rebuffs—well, as a naked bit of prose, such a statement might excite derision among men, but when properly acted before a young and impressionable woman it might easily prove effective. Moreover, he had Aleck's hostility to fall back upon as a last resort, and further in the background complications with his mythical mortgagee, remorse for past wickedness, feeling of unworthiness, and other picturesque sentiments which might easily be dressed up so as to be extremely impressive. Gertrude had been

incautious enough to betray her resentment of his attention to the great heiress, and that was an encouraging
circumstance. If she had been clever enough to seem
indifferent, he would have had less hope of success.

There was a fashion in Torryville, originated, it was
said, by Professor Ramsdale, which had of late become
quite popular. In England people are invited, in the early
summer, to garden and lawn parties, where they drink tea
and catch cold in distinguished company. In Torryville
there were no lawns of any consequence, but there were
ravines that rivalled in picturesqueness those of the Yel-
lowstone. It therefore occurred to Professor Ramsdale
to agitate the question of giving ravine parties. The
ladies of the faculty who were not very enterprising
frowned upon the proposal, but the undaunted professor
started off one fine day with some younger tutors and half
a dozen "co-eds," improvised a co-educational boat-race,
made coffee and fried fish over an out-of-door fire, sent up
rockets and Roman candles which looked beautiful against
the nocturnal sky, and managed to have such a delightful
time, that those who had pronounced ravine parties improper made haste to explain that they had meant something entirely different, and would be charmed to accept
the next invitation.

One afternoon during Commencement week, Gertrude
and Dr. Hawk found themselves, by some chance, *tête-à-
tête* on a floating pier down on the Nile, and presently discovered that they were there for the same purpose. The
rest of the party, consisting of Ramsdale, Tutor Rodney
(a slim, bashful, but competent-looking man), Pussy
Dallas, and a dozen others, mostly co-educational damsels,
soon arrived, carrying wraps and luncheon baskets, and
were packed into four boats which were pushed out, as
soon as they were loaded, from the insecure pier. The
day was warm and clear, and the sky dazzlingly blue. The
young wheat, with its fruitful ears yet folded in glistening
sheaths, grew in long, bright-green belts down the slopes
toward the water, and made the darker green of the
meadows, with its brownish undertone, look shabby by
comparison. Here and there a square patch of buckwheat
relieved with its white bloom the monotony of green ; and
shingled and slate-covered roofs, with their whitewashed
chimneys, peeped forth among the scant foliage of apple
and cherry orchards. But the maples and chestnuts reared
their abundant crowns against the sky, and flung their

grateful shade over the farm-houses, whose small windows and white-painted walls gleamed with a snug and sheltered contentment among the gray colonnades of their trunks.

Gertrude and the doctor had not much to say to each other, as they stood there on the pier waiting for the company to get ready. For, without any agency of their own, they had been assigned to the same boat. Ramsdale and Rodney, in white flannel shirts and knickerbockers, were working like beavers getting the dories afloat ; while Hawk, in a new and rather modish summer suit, stood blandly looking on, offering them no assistance. They had just gotten the last dory safely launched, when the 'Varsity Eight appeared on their pier, carrying their light paper boat, which with the utmost care they deposited upon the stream. They were dressed in red and white skull-caps, sleeveless jerseys, and tights. The muscles on their arms and legs swelled magnificently under the sun-browned skin, " as slopes a brook over a little stone," and they walked about with a paradisaical immodesty which brought back the golden days of athletic sports in ancient Greece. It was a beautiful spectacle to see them all seated motionless, with oars uplifted, in the frail shell, awaiting the signal of " the stroke," while their inverted images trembled under them with the ripples on the stream. And when the sharp and brief command sounded, with what splendid precision they struck the water, and with what arrowy speed they shot down the Nile and out into the open lake. The girls in Ramsdale's party gave them a cheer on the way and waved their handkerchiefs after them. But within a few minutes they looked small and far away, darting through sunshine and shadow, and the captain's commands which re-echoed from the shore faded with a muffled ring in the distance.

Gertrude was conscious of a strong repugnance to the doctor when he seated himself at her side, in the stern of the dory, and she was not very responsive to his first efforts to re-establish confidential relations. He chose to appear somewhat distracted and melancholy, and the remarks he made all bore the mark of some hidden and mysterious distress. He could not speak freely, of course, in the presence of so many, but he managed to throw out some vague hints which tormented and worried her. While the co-eds and the gentlemen sang college songs, whose noisy chorus drowned all other sounds, he heaved deep sighs and muttered, "Life, life, life!" with a heart-rending intonation.

"Whom did you get all this off on, last time?" Gertrude queried, with a mocking laugh ; but for all that, her conscience was uneasy and she was more impressed than she chose to show.

"That from you, Miss Gertie ? That from you ?" sighed the doctor, as if his injury was really too deep for words. "Have I deserved that from you ?"

"That, and much more than I shall ever have a chance of repaying," said Gertrude, heartlessly.

"Well, life is a hard school. It hardens one to bear things which it would seem impossible to survive."

"Oh, I have no fear of your not surviving. I really believe you grow fat on love affairs. I have been told that you make love to every woman you meet."

"Alas, alas ! If you but knew," he whispered, tragically, and bowed his head like an injured creature that disdains to ward off the threatened blow.

But just at that moment the song stopped, and Gertrude found it unsafe to pursue the subject further. It was quite a relief when the stalwart Californian, Cottrell, who was also of the party, engaged her in conversation, and courted her in a florid and masculinely condescending style which was quite amusing. It was half-past three or four o'clock when they arrived at their destination. A fire was made at the entrance to the ravine, and both gentlemen and ladies engaged in a search for fagots and dry branches with which to keep it alive. The gorge was wide, almost flat in the bottom, and covered on both sides with an irregular growth of underbrush, from which loomed up here and there a great storm-twisted and weather-beaten pine, or an oak, that, losing its footing in the shallow soil, had become top-heavy and grew almost horizontally out from the overhanging cliffs. A stream, which fell from a height of two hundred feet and meandered with serpentine windings through the underbrush, had shrunk to a mere brook under the warm rays of the June sun ; and the slate quarry at the upper end of the ravine, which depended upon the water-power for its activity, had suspended operations until the autumn rains again should stimulate the lagging pulses of nature.

The co-educational boat-race, for which some burlesque prizes had been provided, did not in the least interest Hawk ; but he saw in it a chance of getting rid of an inconvenient rival who, with youthful insolence, was monopolizing Gertrude, and ignoring all hints that his presence

was desired elsewhere. Accordingly the crafty doctor
suggested to Ramsdale that Cottrell would make a capital
umpire, and the unhappy youth, though he saw through
the ruse, could find no excuse for declining.

"Miss Gertie," began the doctor, when his diplomacy
had triumphed, "I have been wanting to ask you for a
long time why you treat me so shabbily."

"How long?" asked Gertie with crushing sarcasm.
"What a capacious heart you must have, Doctor," she
added, lightly. "I wish I could rival your beautiful impartiality."

They were strolling along the bank of the brook, where
there was a path, now broad enough for two, now choked
up with raspberry brambles.

"I knew it was there the shoe pinched," he said, with a
touch of irritability; "but it seems almost too silly to
merit an answer."

"Then you mean to deny that you ran after Kate van
Schaak early and late."

"Oh, no; why should I deny it? But I supposed you
were clever enough to suspect what my motive was."

"Well, I am not; unless it was her five millions!"

The doctor turned his head with a weary despair, but,
instead of answering, fixed his large, dark eyes, full of
mute reproach, upon the girl. Then a slight dimness
obscured his sight, and he started up the path with long
strides, leaving Gertrude behind. She arrested her steps,
in a tumult of feeling, irresolute whether she should follow him or return to the lake shore. But, seeing the objections to the one course as well as the other, she seated
herself upon a large bowlder under a dead tree, whose
weather-bleached limbs traced themselves in vivid detail
against the sky. She sat there for a good while, determined to be angry, but feeling her wrath insidiously ebbing away; a still, small voice rose out of the depth of her
heart, defending him against her own accusations. She
had treated him shabbily; there was no denying that.
And he looked so miserable when she spoke harshly to him;
and those great sincere eyes of his, they were incapable
of hypocrisy. She was so eager to belittle his offence,
and to find excuses for it, that the gravamen of her charges
finally turned against herself, and the more she reviewed
her own conduct, the more heartless and hideous it appeared. Where could she find another man so chivalrous,
so delicately considerate of her feelings, so capable of deep

devotion and intellectual companionship as the doctor?
If he had really devoted himself to Kate, out of pique—
was not that a perfectly natural thing to do, and ought not
she, who was the cause of it, to be the last to resent it?

Gertrude sat for a long while pondering these perplexing questions, and was gradually arriving at the conclusion that it was she who had sinned against the doctor
and not the doctor against her. The brook gurgled its
pleasant music in her ears, and the crickets filled the air
with a perpetually pulsating chorus of sound. Every moment was charged to overflowing with whirring, gurgling,
chirping, warbling voices, inextricably blended together,
now faint and tremulous, now throbbing with a sudden access of strength; vibrating with a strange intensity through
heart and brain, encroaching with a sweet, wild insistence
upon her conscious life, and drawing her back into the
Nirvana of great universal nature. Emotions, whether
joyous or sad, become half impersonal in such moments,
and lose their acutest sting. Down in the golden-brown
depths of the pool swift shadows darted to and fro, and in
the cool shade of the bowlders long-legged water-bugs
skipped hither and thither, and a glittering fly came sailing down the current and got caught in a ball of foam,
whence there was no escape.

Some may contend that it was heartless in Gertrude to
get interested in these insignificant phenomena, when the
decision of her own fate was trembling in the balance.
But, sensitive as she was to every impression, she conld
not ward off this pagan semi-absorption in Nature—this
irresistible sympathy with the teeming, abundant, myriad-
voiced noon-day life of summer—the strong, eternally destroying, eternally creative heart-beat of mother earth.

Gertrude was awakened from her reverie by the creaking of branches close by, and glancing up saw Hawk
stand before her. She had to collect her thoughts forcibly,
before the situation became clear to her. A wild look,
like that of a startled bird, gleamed in her eyes as they
were first fixed upon the doctor.

"I suppose you didn't expect me back," he said, taking
off his straw hat and wiping its inside with his handkerchief.

"I haven't thought anything about it," Gertrude answered.

She had no intention to be cruel; nay, had, on the contrary, resolved to be conciliatory; but the thoughtless

words were out of her mouth before she had time to consider them. The doctor began to scratch the ground with his stick, tossed back his picturesque Hamlet-lock, and heaved a deep sigh.

"Miss Gertie," he said, with a sort of desperate recklessness, "I suppose I ought to take that as final and call it quits. I wish to God I could."

"Why can't you?" she asked.

She was unkind now from sheer perversity, and wondered vaguely at her own pitilessness. She knew, in a kind of impersonal way, that she loved him and would like to encourage him; only the loving mood had unaccountably departed, and she could not bring it back by a mere effort of will. "And you pretend then that you don't know that I love you," he continued, bitterly; "that I have loved you from the first moment I saw you?"

"How could I tell," she ejaculated, "when you didn't seem to know it yourself? You have too hospitable a heart, doctor, you love too many."

She spoke lightly; but her voice was unsteady, and she felt a dull heartache, which gnawed and burrowed among her vitals. She was disgusted with her flippancy, but scarcely knew how to abandon the tone she had once assumed. Then, perhaps, the impulse of vanity more than anything else urged her to persevere, for she wished in a confused way not to be too easily won. The doctor deserved to be punished for the pain he had inflicted upon her; and there could be no harm in making him suffer a little in return for all he had made her suffer.

"I suppose then, Miss Gertie, that all is over between you and me," he muttered, sadly; "we shall have to part and be nothing to each other."

She was on the point of answering that she was not aware that they had ever been anything to each other; but instead of that she said, softly:

"That depends upon you."

He looked up with glad surprise and drew a step nearer.

"Then you will listen to me?" he queried, with wary tenderness.

"Yes."

The tremulous insecurity of that "yes" emboldened him; he seated himself at her side on the big stone and seized her hand. His touch imparted a light shock to her and the blood surged into her face.

"Gertie," he said, in a low, beseeching murmur, "why should you and I quarrel? You can't make me believe that you don't care for me. A love so strong as mine for you would melt a heart of stone.

> "I arise from dreams of thee
> In the first sweet sleep of night,
> When the winds are breathing low
> And the stars are shining bright;
> I arise from dreams of thee,
> And a spirit in my feet
> Has led me—who knows how?
> To thy chamber window, sweet!"

The doctor was a master in declamation; he breathed forth Shelley's exquisite impassioned lines in swooning sighs, and Gertie had never listened to anything so wondrously rich and alluring. It was like a heavy delicious odor, the inhalation of which caused a sweet oppression. He repeated, after a pause, the second and the third verse with the same insinuating ardor. The landscape seemed to grow dim and more richly green; a strange magic inundation of light broke across it; her heart throbbed in slow, full beats which almost shook her frame. She felt his arm about her waist, his kiss upon her lips—but she made no resistance. There was a luxury in complete, unreasoning surrender; there was a glorious flood-tide of being—a deeper breath, a swifter pulse, and dim vistas of unrevealed bliss. After a while, she became conscious that he was talking, though she did not distinctly hear what he said. He was speaking about himself—he always spoke so beautifully about himself—and he was quoting more poetry; he always quoted poetry on supreme occasions. She saw his deep melancholy eyes light up with an intense animation; but all of a sudden she became conscious of a vague alien presence which roused her with a pang, and an uneasy sense of guilt. She looked up and down the ravine, but saw only the waving of the tops of the underbrush far away, and heard gay voices in high keys, and shrill laughter. There was for an instant a curious unreality in the scene, and she half expected to see it dissolve and change like the pageant of a dream. It seemed as if she had seen it all, to the minutest leaf and twig and tinge of light, years ago—in some previous existence perhaps—but unmistakably—without shadow of doubt. There was an anxious suspense of silence in the air, and through this silence came, like an accusing voice,

the thought of that other girl—the claimant, the mortgagee whom she had defrauded. She had, after all, a
prior claim ; she had spent her all in educating him ; in
helping him to reach the eminence for which he was
destined. She shrank from him with outraged modesty,
as she imagined how often he must have sat with that
other one, encircling her waist, calling her sweet names,
protesting his gratitude and affection. For a moment she
almost loathed him, and she loathed herself too ; but above
all she loathed that unending tiresome repetition of the
stale incidents of love, birth, death without hope of respite, through all the dizzy eternities. A paltry little
puppet, with eyes and nose and joints, pulled by unseen
wires, bowing and kissing and loving and suffering through
four or five hackneyed acts to the more than hackneyed
end—that was a woman's lot, and man's, for that matter,
was scarcely a whit better.

I would not assert that the feelings that agitated Gertrude's soul were as distinctly formulated as they necessarily have to be in the present narrative. But they were
acutely felt ; and prompted impulsive action. She leaped
down from the stone upon which they had been sitting,
and stood with flaming cheeks gazing at Hawk, yet scarcely
seeing him.

"But," she cried, with a queer little grating in her voice,
"the girl—the girl—who loved you ?"

The doctor, truth to tell, had actually forgotten the girl
who had loved him. He might, perhaps, be excused for
having forgotten what had no existence. He had not deliberately invented this romance ; but he had allowed it to
grow and take shape about him, and he had encouraged it
by mysterious hints, and sighs, and guarded admissions. He
felt now that it was so much a part of him that he did not
dare repudiate it. He had in him a Byronic repugnance
for the tame and commonplace lot, and a taste for picturesque wickedness. He was not above imitating the crude
heroes of Cherbuliez and Wilkie Collins, and though he was
too prudent to risk collision with the law, he satisfied his
romantic craving by mourning for maidens whom he never
lost, and suffering remorse for sins which he never committed. It was, however, a little cruel to have one of
these imaginary maidens turn up at the present inconvenient moment. The disagreeable query took the doctor
by surprise. He returned Gertrude's gaze with a confusion which no dramatic brazenness could conceal.

"Why don't you answer me?" she demanded, impetuously.

Hawk in his desperate strait had a sudden inspiration.

"She is dead," he answered, drawing a deep sigh of relief, but looking the picture of gloomy self-accusation.

"Is she dead?" Gertrude exclaimed, wondering. "Did she die of grief?" she added, in a soberer tone.

"I wish you wouldn't speak to me about it," cried Hawk, tossing his Hamlet lock in impatience. "I should think I had suffered enough already for that youthful folly. I was true to her, I tell you, though I never loved her; I once thought I loved her, but from the moment I saw you, I knew that I had deceived myself. There was consumption in her family, and nothing could have saved her. So you need have no scruple on her account."

There was something so flattering and pacifying in these assurances that Gertrude began to reproach herself for her doubts. She took the doctor's arm, and for a while they walked in silence along the bank of the brook. There was after all (though she would scarcely have admitted it) something deeply gratifying in having for a lover a man for whom there had been such a spirited scramble, as long as he was yet unfettered. Even the deluded faith, the sickness, and the death of the consumptive claimant had a charming air of romance in it, and removed their relation so high above the mere commonplace loves of commonplace people. She began to feel herself drawn toward him again; and as she looked at his dark, interesting face, the soft black mustache and beard, the red sensuous lips, and the fine straight nose, an overwhelming sense of his worth—his rare and radiant preciousness—took possession of her. She did not see that he had too high a forehead and too little back head to make a well-balanced, successful man; and she could not see, through the dense silky beard, that he was also rather deficient in chin. A very silly thought, which she hesitated to utter, was worrying her; but she knew she would have no peace unless her curiosity was satisfied.

"Was that girl, who loved you, dark or blonde?" she asked, with bashful haste.

"Dark," said the doctor, gloomily.

That was a great relief — to know that she was not blonde.

"And—and—what was her name?"

"Mary."

That, for some reason, also seemed satisfactory ; though it was hard to imagine why.

"Tell me," she began after a while, taking advantage of his amiability, "is it true that you had an affair with a high-born lady while you studied in Vienna ?"

"My dear child," cried Hawk, with a fine assumption of impatience, "how can that possibly interest you ?"

"Everything about you interests me."

"That's very nice, I'm sure, but you must excuse me. I'd rather not talk about that."

"If you only knew how unhappy it would make me—that you have secrets which I am not to know——"

"Well, well" (with superb masculine condescension), "if you insist. But I assure you there was nothing so very dangerous about that affair."

And he related with many piquant details how he had had the misfortune to attract the attention of a high-born Russian lady, the Princess Alexandra Grabowsky, who was as rich and beautiful as she was eccentric. How the Princess's father, who was the Russian ambassador in Vienna, had offered him a large sum of money, if he would return forthwith to America, and promise not to correspond or in any way communicate with his daughter ; how Hawk had spurned this offer, etc., etc.

There was a flavor of "Ouida" about this little romance which, however, Gertrude failed to detect. Next to Mrs. Spofford, whose "Amber Gods" the doctor held to be the greatest modern novel, he regarded the much-slandered "Ouida" as the most luminous light of contemporary fiction. He detested George Eliot, and had no patience with Thackeray ; and among the poets his favorites were Byron and Swinburne.

Rarely has a young girl been more impressed with the heroism, the beauty, the transcendent magnificence of her lover, than Gertrude was, after her excursion with Dr. Hawk up to the slate quarry. She forgave him (oh, how readily) all that he had sinned against others, and felt so deliciously confident that, after all his amatory aberrations in the past, he had now found his safe and final anchorage. He and she had been guided by an eternal destiny toward each other ; and it was delightful to trace through a multitude of apparently insignificant incidents this providential intention to bring their groping and yearning hearts together. This discovery, which was proved beyond possibility of doubt, filled her with a jubilant security and per-

haps also a slight sense of superiority to the rest of her
sex who had vainly striven to win this rare prize which now
was hers. There was passion and there was innocence,
there were tenderness and delicacy and a touching simplicity in the pure depths of this strong and sweet nature ;
and though she was swayed by moods, which often an-
tagonized each other, there was a fundamental nobility in
her which dignified even her vacillation. Like Desde-
mona of old, like Chrimhild and Brunhild, like every
sweet and wholesome girl in all times and ages—she had
sat waiting for her hero ; and believing him to be a hero,
she sang her pæan to him, and clasped him to her heart,
never suspecting what a blackamoor she held in her
arms.

Hawk and Gertrude, on returning to the camp, found,
to their surprise, that their absence had not caused any un-
easiness ; nor did their return cause any sensation. The
youths and maidens, under the lax supervision of a young
married lady who feigned the rôle of a chaperon, had all
strolled off in pairs up and down the lake shore after the
mock boat-race was at an end, and no one was missed because there was no one to miss him.

At about seven o'clock in the evening, after a frugal
supper, consisting of coffee and hard-boiled eggs, the
party broke up and started homeward. The twilight
spread over the lake, and the rockets which whizzed up
from the boats exploded with a resonant bang under the
silent skies, and dropped down their showers of many-
colored stars. The moon rose large, red, and sleepy behind the eastern hills, and showed the dark and jagged lines
of the forest in luminous relief. A stray swarm of mos-
quitos danced away over the still water, sang for an instant their angry little tune in the ears of the picknickers,
and whirled out of sight. There was something touchingly primitive in the frankness with which personal preferences were shown and recognized, and in the dropping
of coquettish airs, as the twilight grew softer and dimmer,
in the sweet instinctive response to the great universal law
which was from the beginning of the world, which holds
creation together in its innermost care. They did nothing very indiscreet ; but there were pressures of hands
which the twilight shielded ; there were audacious whispered compliments, and tender avowals which to-morrow
would appear to be forgotten. They meant nothing except a shy tentative yielding to the dim attraction be-

14

tween youths and maidens, and they were not taken seriously. They were mere phenomena of the spring-time—of the grand re-awakening of nature. The sun-god, the daring wooer, kisses the slumbering earth, and she awakes, blushes, and returns the kiss.

CHAPTER XXIV.

A NOBLE ROMAN.

There were various festivities during Commencement week in which neither Hawk nor Gertrude chose to participate. Mr. Larkin appeared, as usual, being, beside the Governor of the State, the chief dignitary of the occasion. He made his annual speech, which was the same every year, and which never lost its novelty; and its unfailing success convinced Mr. Larkin that it could not be improved upon. It was short; for Mr. Larkin made no pretence to being an orator; and it ran as follows :

"FELLOW-CITIZENS : Some of us can talk and some of us can act ; but it ain't often the same man can do both well. Some of you can remember, I reckon, the time when this town had barely 2,000 inhabitants, no gas, bad water, and plenty of ague. The streets was unpaved, and it took a foolhardy man to cross them on foot in bad weather. That was the way it looked here when I first come here. There was two churches—one Methodist and one Presbyterian. I won't talk about how it looked on the hill. That was a howling wilderness. Now, fellow-citizens, I don't want to brag, but I ask you to look about you and tell me what you see. The stately spires of seven houses of worship meet your eyes ; shops of every description, abounding with costly wares, line our streets. We have a reservoir which has killed the fever, and we have first-class drainage ; we have gas to illuminate our streets ; and our town had at the last census 11,249 inhabitants. What, now, fellow-citizens, has brought about this great change ? *I say the Larkin University.* (Thundering applause).

"The universities in this country until this institution was founded were places for the rich man's son only. I wanted to found a university for the poor man's son. (Applause.) No high living, no frills and flummery, no Oxford gowns—no nothing which a poor man couldn't afford to buy. I hope to live long enough to see the day when a thousand young men and women shall be climb-

ing this hill in the noble pursuit of learning. If I don't
see it some of you will. I am a plain man, I didn't have
much schooling when I was a boy ; but I always felt the
want of it. And when God blessed my labor and gave me
wealth, my first thought was to give the opportunities of
an education to the many thousand boys in the country
situated as I was. That's what I have tried to do ; and if
God will continue to prosper the work, I reckon, with His
help, we may call it a success."

The members of Mr. Larkin's family had heard this
speech so frequently that it had ceased to interest them.
Gertrude always listened to it with burning ears, and a
sense of discomfort. She felt as if it were herself who
was speaking and lapsing into bad grammar. Aleck was
ashamed of its rhetorical faults, and the obvious inference
people must be drawing from it, that his uncle had founded
his university as a real-estate speculation, or to advance
the commercial prosperity of the town. But somehow,
people were slow to draw such an inference, and at any
rate they were not disposed to assume a critical attitude
toward the old man. They knew he meant right, whatever he might say about it. Horace was the only one
under Mr. Larkin's roof from whom a criticism on the
speech would not have been taken amiss. But Horace,
seeing how American it was, and how characteristic of its
author, liked it without reserve, and refused to suggest
improvements.

On the evening of Commencement day Mr. Larkin gave
a dinner to the governor and the Board of Trustees. Mr.
Robbins was there to say grace, which he did with the
elaborateness which the occasion required.

The founder's dinners were, however, puritanically
frugal and flavorless. Wine there was none ; and Apolli-
naris water seemed too suggestive of medicine and de-
rangement of digestion to be acceptable as a substitute.
Cigars were likewise tabooed, and the governor himself,
who was very dependent upon his post-prandial smoke,
was obliged to go out on the piazza to enjoy it. For Mr.
Larkin understood no hints where his convictions were
involved, and lost much of his respect for the governor's
character when he saw how he relished the noxious weed.
The magistrate, on the other hand, departed with an increased admiration for his host, but this was due to an incident which occurred before the cigars were in order.

The assembled dignitaries had just despatched the

soup and were testing the quality of the lake bass, when the waitress handed Mr. Larkin a telegram. He opened it, read it, and without a change of mien, put it in his pocket. The conversation which turned chiefly on university matters, continued without a break, and no one had any suspicion that anything extraordinary had happened. When the meal was at an end, however, and the guests had entered the parlor, Mr. Larkin beckoned to Horace and handed him the telegram. It read as follows:

SAGINAW, MICH.

All twelve mills and lumber yards burned this afternoon. Cause of fire unknown. Send representative.

HAWKINS.

Horace knew that this meant a loss of upward of half a million dollars. For Mr. Larkin never insured. He insisted that it did not pay. If there was any profit in it to the insurer, he contended, there could be none to the companies; and, as the companies usually got rich, he argued that the insurers usually were duped. He preferred to take his own risks and reap his own profits. His saw-mills at Saginaw were, at present, his pet enterprise, and had yielded him a handsome percentage on his investment.

"You had better take the 10.15 train," was all he said to Horace; and, "All right," was all that Horace answered.

They were a laconic lot, but they understood each other so perfectly that words between them seemed superfluous. There was the same lumber in both of them, and their mental processes worked in conscious sympathy. Horace could not, however, deny himself the pleasure of letting the governor know what a fine old Roman the head of the house of Larkin was. And the governor, who was a democrat, was reminded of Thomas Jefferson, who, walking with a celebrated Frenchman, fell and broke his arm, but continued the walk, talking brilliantly, and making no reference to the accident.

In spite of Mr. Larkin's love for his University, there had developed of late years a latent animosity between him and the faculty. The old gentleman, with all his benevolence, was a trifle overbearing; and could not be made to understand that the professors, who would have been nowhere but for him, were not responsible to him personally, and removable at his pleasure.   He was apt to make his influence felt in an emphatic fashion in all the business concerns of the University, and his voice was understood to be decisive in the appointment of every officer, from the president to the janitors and the charwomen who scrubbed the halls.   He would have no cavil in such matters, and the trustees and faculty contented themselves in the end with finding excellent reasons for agreeing with him.

The students, too, gave Mr. Larkin great trouble.   He loved them collectively, but he detested them individually. It was not quite untrue, as Professor Dowd (who was the founder's pet aversion) remarked, that Mr. Larkin loved his University but disliked nearly every one connected with it.

CHAPTER XXV.

AN EXCITING ENGAGEMENT.

People bore the summer weather in Torryville, as they bore other visitations of Providence, with grumbling submission. They did not run away from it, first, because it was not absolutely unbearable, and, secondly, for lack of funds. The Larkins, who were an exception to this rule, stayed at home from habit, and because they had comforts at home which no money could procure them elsewhere.

Gertie had made Dr. Hawk promise to keep their engagement secret until she gave him permission to make it known. She had exacted this promise chiefly because it seemed such a delightful thing to have something to conceal, and perhaps also because she disliked to grieve Aleck, who would, undoubtedly, take the thing very much to heart. She had a dim notion that Aleck was fond of her, and she knew, too, that she was very fond of Aleck. But there had always been something between them like an invisible wall, and she began to suspect that this something was Hawk. The thought had flashed through her mind, two or three times, that Aleck's love for her was not of the fraternal kind, but that he was prevented by his semi-fraternal relation to her from revealing the true nature of his affection. She had noticed, particularly, of late, how sad his glance was, when it rested upon her, and how full of mute reproach. She did not doubt that he knew already all that she might have to tell him; but this, somehow, seemed an additional reason for sparing him the incontrovertible knowledge. Not that she regretted her choice, or had the least misgiving as to its wisdom. But she had a little soft spot in her heart for Aleck which ached whenever she thought of the pain which he must suffer on her account. He was so kind and good and reliable; almost too good, she feared, for if he had had a dash of wickedness, or at least a mysterious circumstance or other in his antecedents, his handsome appearance and polite manners would have been more appreciated. For

Gertrude held, with the majority of her sex, that goodness unadulterated was not interesting.

Her engagement remained quite an exciting affair even after the edge of novelty had worn off. For Hawk was a creature of moods, one day blithe and gay (though there was always a touch of theatricals in his mirth), and the next oppressed with a weight of gloom. He was always wrestling with the problem of existence ; forever (judging by the tensity of his mental attitudes) grabbing the sphinx by the throat, forcing it to give up its cherished riddle. Sometimes he distressed Gertrude by declaring that the quintessence of human wisdom was summarized in the word resignation. That seemed a queer thing for an engaged man to say, surely, and she cudgelled her brain to remember what she had done or said which had displeased him. The story of her mother she had felt in duty bound to tell him ; and it troubled her to think that, perhaps, he repented of his engagement after having discovered the complications into which it might lead him. Was she right in surmising that she was less desirable in his sight on account of this unfortunate mother ? He had, indeed, scarcely betrayed any surprise, when she related the circumstances of the meeting in the Drum Head Ravine ; and she could not quite get rid of the suspicion that he knew the whole story before, nay had perhaps overheard the conversation. This was the drop of bitterness in her cup of joy. She could not credit the idea— nay she would have scorned it if it had been suggested to her—that the doctor performed his little private theatricals for the pure love of them ; and because he was a dramatic character who could not resign himself to commonplace behavior. She sought always in her own words and conduct for reasons for his moods, when really they had no reasons at all. Yet he encouraged this sense of accountability in her, and reproached her in a tender, emotional voice for things which he had never thought of until she herself by her anxious queries suggested them. He was sad and gloomily resigned, on general principles ; but was ungenerous enough to accept her imaginary offences as the specific causes of his discontent. And she found no fault with him for exacting of her an impossible standard of conduct. She had a dread, no less anxious than his, of the common humdrum lot ; and the perpetual suspense in which his varying moods kept her gave a certain zest to life and compelled her to keep her own moods in abeyance. She could not afford to yield to every impulse of weariness and depression, when her whole future happiness was at stake; and in her eagerness to conciliate him she tried to remodel herself in accordance with what she conceived to be his ideals, renouncing her selfish habits and foregoing every luxury, except that of being pleasing in his sight. She did not possess the knowledge of the world to see and judge him as he was. He seemed to her a hero; the glory of his speech thrilled and intoxicated her, and his discontent seemed only the expression of his superiority. She felt exalted in humiliating herself before such a man; she alone had had the eyes to see and appreciate the nobility of this rare spirit; and a heart lofty enough to beat in unison with his.

Nothing of any consequence happened in Torryville during the summer months. Mrs. Larkin had recently withdrawn her sympathies from the Mohammedans, who, she was informed, pretended to be interested in Christianity for the sake of the medical knowledge which they acquired in the Beirut mission, and afterward relapsed into the worship of the Prophet. She had now become convinced that Madagascar offered the most fertile field for missionary effort, and was actually equipping a gentle, blear-eyed young man for an expedition to the Hovas, whose souls were pining for the light. She was growing more peevish and plaintive as she grew older, and was getting harder to associate with. She was quick enough to perceive the doctor's attentions to Gertie, and interpreted them as a wilful affront to herself. She suspended all her ailments for two months; and was half inclined to call in the obnoxious Dr. Sawyer. But this seemed almost too radical a measure. She could not quite give up the expectation of luring Hawk back to his allegiance. His present aberration she could then afford to forgive, considering his youth and his many admirable qualities. That he was engaged to Gertrude she could not believe; for that would argue a black-hearted ingratitude with which she could not credit her favorite.

To enliven the summer dulness, and give vent to her own overcharged feelings, Mrs. Larkin got up a little breeze in the church, and forced poor Mr. Robbins to take sides with her, although she had a suspicion that his sympathies were on the other side. Mrs. Larkin contended that the spirit of the world, the flesh, and the devil was getting the upper hand in the church; and she adduced in proof of this, the luxurious toilets in which women (who could really not afford such extravagance), came into the Lord's house, rustling with silks, clinking with jet, flaring with gorgeous ribbons and feathers! There was, indeed, a time when Mrs. Larkin had herself not been without aspirations as regards dress. But somehow she seemed to have been so made that no dress would fit her; creases would appear in the back and over the shoulders; and about her ample waist her gowns had a wry and twisted look, which was a source of annoyance to her until she discovered a sanction for it in the Bible. She came to the conclusion that well-fitting dresses were of the devil, and argued loss of grace. She upbraided Mr. Robbins for his laxity, and finally induced him to preach a sermon against vanity of attire, which was regarded by Mrs. Dallas as a personal attack, and prepared the good man no end of difficulties. Mr. Dallas, who was not a man to be trifled with, came forward as the champion of his wife's and daughter's honor, called the parson to account, and, as it was rumored, received from him a private apology. But as Mrs. Larkin refused to credit this, she still plumed herself on having vindicated her authority and made the devil lower his banner.

CHAPTER XXVI.

A SERIOUS CONTRETEMPS.

The burning of the saw-mills came not inopportunely to Horace, as it compelled him to be much away from home, and enabled him to charge his delinquencies as a lover to the score of business. Mr. Larkin, after having ascertained the extent of the damage and approved the plans for rebuilding, left everything in his hands, and chuckled over the shrewdness he displayed in penetrating shams and detecting frauds. He tested every item in the estimates that were submitted to him with a practical sense and sagacity which filled his uncle with delight. It was rumored, too, that as the Torryville car-wheel factory had suspended operations for the summer season, Horace selected some two hundred or three hundred naturalized citizens of Democratic proclivities among the factory hands, and shipped them to Michigan, where he gave them employment in rebuilding the saw-mills. A man would have to be blinder than a bat not to see the meaning of that; for those two hundred or three hundred Hibernians would be back before November, and then they would pay the price of the bargain by voting for Horace Larkin.

Rumors of these proceedings did not fail to reach the parsonage and cause Mr. Robbins much annoyance. He regarded such performances as little less than dishonorable, and could not sufficiently reprobate the furtive admiration with which they were viewed by the people in general. Bella repeatedly got herself into difficulties with her lady friends by championing Horace's integrity and giving the lie direct to those who ventured to asperse it; but felt ill repaid when he laughed at her zeal, and told her jocosely not to burden herself with the responsibility for his misdeeds. She sometimes felt out of patience with his eternal joking, which indicated either lack of confidence or lack of respect; but she was careful not to let him suspect the faintest shade of disapproval. For, of course, she could not force him to confide in her ; she had to take thankfully whatever he offered. And she loved him with an absorbing affection and fervor which (when her impatience had spent itself) made all that he said seem brilliant, and all that he did perfect. She persuaded herself then that there was nothing which she desired or could desire that she did not find in him. She surrendered herself to his cool and rare caresses with an impassioned tenderness and a luxurious self-extinction which many a time planted a pang in his heart, and made him shrink from the intention which lay, perfectly formulated, in the background of his mind, waiting for its opportunity. He was well aware of the atrocity of this intention ; but palliated it with the reflection that it was for her sake, not for his own, that he let the relation drift on. He had no idea of keeping her as a *dernier ressort*, in case Kate should reject him ; for, in the first place, he did not in the least doubt his ability to win Kate, and, secondly, he would have regarded it as ignoble to play under cover and abuse her confidence while yet coveting it. He held it, on the other hand, to be perfectly fair and square to burn his bridges behind him ; to break an engagement which he had entered into with a false or imperfect understanding of the case ; but he was yet unable to steel himself against an occasional access of pity or self-contempt. For all that, his resolution remained unaltered ; he would accomplish his purpose with all due kindness and consideration, inflicting as little pain as possible. He was only waiting for a favorable moment ; and an excuse or pretext that might afford him, at least, a shadow of justification.

In the meanwhile the preparations for the fall elections were rapidly being pushed by the political managers ; and the nomination for the Assembly was offered to Horace as he had expected. In fact he had "laid his pipes" as the phrase is, so shrewdly, that there was no escape from nominating him, without courting defeat. Knowing, however, that his resources were ample, the managers demanded an assessment of three thousand dollars, which after some deliberation he agreed to pay. He knew perfectly well that they were afraid of him, foreseeing that the day he grasped the helm, their power would be at an end. He had, indeed, an ideal equipment for a political boss, being a keen judge of men, endowed with sagacity, unruffled by temper, unburdened by superfluous scruples.

Unhappily he had his money so well invested that he

preferred to borrow the amount of the assessment rather than sell any of his mortgages or bank stock. It occurred to him, too, that he would be doing Aleck a favor in withdrawing some of the latter's bank deposit from circulation; for Aleck was conspicuously lacking in the financial sense, and squandered his funds in nothings, in a way that made his brother's heart ache. It was therefore with a half benevolent impulse that he approached him with the proposition for a loan.

"I have got about $500 in cash," he said; "and if you can help me out with $2,500, I shall be much obliged."

Aleck, who was sitting in his shirt sleeves in the office, smoking, and reading a popular magazine, looked up at his brother with his most engaging smile and exclaimed: "Why, certainly; I shall be most happy to let you have all I have got. My bank account has been in an uncomfortably plethoric condition since I gave that able opinion which was really yours, in the case of McTavish *vs.* Henley."

"Perhaps," said Horace, "I ought to tell you what I want it for."

"Not unless you prefer to."

"Well, there's no reason why I shouldn't tell you."

There was possibly a tinge of malice in this candor; he wanted to make Aleck *particeps criminis*—an accomplice in something of which he disapproved. He imagined that he needed a good many lessons of this sort before he would be equipped for success of a practical kind. His sensitive conscience needed to be battered until it became pachydermatous.

"You know," Horace continued, "I am going to be nominated for the Assembly at the convention next week. I've got the thing dead sure."

"No, I didn't know it," said Aleck guilelessly; "and you are willing to accept the nomination from the Machine?"

"If you can tell me of any other organization in this county from which a nomination is worth anything, I will consider it."

Aleck flung his magazine on the table and smoked for a while in silence.

"Horace," he ejaculated with ardor, "you know as well as I what a lot of infamous tricksters those men are. I should think you would respect yourself too much to enter into partnership with them."

"Well, my dear fellow, you have got to take the world as you find it. I can't undertake to reform it in one short life-time. Anyway I have no taste for martyrdom. I mean to achieve something definite, and in order to do that, I have got to use the tools which I find handy. If I were to construct my own tools, beside destroying the old ones, I should get no further."

Aleck did not answer at once, but sat again looking thoughtfully out of the window. A blue-bottle fly was bumping boozily against the pane, tumbling down upon the sill, and again flinging itself, with a persistence worthy of a better cause, against the invisible but unyielding substance. Aleck, after having watched its desperate and futile struggles, got up, opened the window, and let it out.

"Why," he asked, impulsively, "do all the world's influences conspire to break down a man's honesty?"

"Because the average man is not as yet particularly honest," Horace replied, promptly; "he is moderately honest when it pays, but no more. The world or society is but the expression of the average man's morality; and it is what he is."

"Then it is the duty of those who are in advance of the average morality to raise their banner high, and try to make the rest follow it."

"Well, I have no objection to anybody's doing that, if his tastes lie in that direction. But he does it at his peril, and ten to one, he forfeits his chances of any but a posthumous success. Even Christ, idealist as he was, recognized that fact when he said, 'Make ye, therefore, friends of the mammon of unrighteousness.'"

"But the beauty, the exaltation, the delight of such a work, I should think that was worth more than even what you call success."

"I may be deficient, but I can't see the beauty of butting your head against a stone wall, and that is what it really amounts to."

"But in the course of time your head, though it be sore, may make an impression upon the wall."

"Yes, but in the meanwhile, the wall will have made a very much deeper impression upon your head."

"But suppose the wall hid a grand and beautiful view and debarred mankind from its ennobling enjoyment, would it not be worth a broken head, nay, a thousand broken heads, to have it destroyed?"

"It might be worth your head, but it is not worth mine. As long as someone else does the butting, I have no earthly objection. I am even willing to applaud, and privately bandage his head. But in the end it amounts to this : it is folly to attempt the impossible, even if it be ever so sublime."

"He who never attempts the impossible will never achieve the possible," replied Aleck, with superb enthusiasm.

Horace, who had been seated in the revolving chair, with his back to his brother, got up, and began to saunter about on the floor. He struck a match, lighted a fresh cigar—a black, strong, high-flavored Havana—and puffing the fragrant smoke against the ceiling, planted himself in front of Aleck.

"It is no use talking," he said ; "we shall never agree on that point. You know you are awfully headstrong, and opinionated. But let me have your check for $2,500, and I'll forgive you your heresies."

Aleck pulled out a drawer, rather hesitatingly, and took out his check-book.

"Horace," he said, coloring to the edge of his hair, "do you know what this money is to be used for ?"

"I suppose so."

"And it isn't a trick you want to play upon me ; as you did a year ago, when you advised me to hire buggies and use the family influence to make votes for Wolf."

"Stuff! Don't be a fool. I want the money, and I want it to-day."

"To pay for your nomination ?"

"Call it that, if you like."

"Then I wish you would borrow of somebody else. I don't like to be made a party to such a transaction."

Horace was not an irascible man ; his wrath kindled slowly, and it glowed and smouldered long before it blazed forth.

"Say that again," he demanded calmly, gritting his teeth.

"I think you heard what I said," his brother replied, struggling to master his excitement ; "I can see no reason for repeating it."

"And you don't want to lend me the money ?"

"No."

"You think I'm little better than a scoundrel, eh ?"

"Those were your words, not mine."

"And you presume to set yourself up as a judge of my actions, eh ?"

He spoke yet with outward composure, but his voice shook with suppressed anger; and his eyes had a pinched and ugly look.

"I can't help judging," Aleck rejoined; "it was yourself who challenged my judgment."

"And are you such a blasted fool as to suppose that it makes the slighest difference to me whether you lend me your paltry pennies or not?"

"No; but I am fool enough to wish to keep my honor unstained. I want to live uprightly—not tolerably uprightly, or moderately uprightly, but absolutely uprightly. If you have supposed that all my professions on this subject are mere phrases, I shall have to disabuse you. If we must part company, as I fear we must, then don't think any harder of me than you have to."

Horace, pale, sullen, and determined, stood with his chin upon his chest, chewing his cigar and gazing through his pinched eyelids at his brother. His anger, which kept working like a subterranean fire within him, was a clear, flameless glow which sent up no smoke to obscure his judgment. The phrase "If we must part," kept humming in his ears; it had often occurred to him before that it would be for his advantage to dissolve the partnership with Aleck, but he had never supposed that Aleck would be fool enough to make the suggestion; nor had he ever expected to make it himself. He loved Aleck as well as he was capable of loving anybody; and he had always had a sense of fraternal protectorship over him which is apt to foster affection. Moreover, there was a cordial companionship between them which neither the one nor the other had ever established with any other man. They were, in spite of all differences of taste and temperament, congenial. Horace might deplore Aleck's fondness for poetry and fiction, which, he contended, interfered with professional success, but he did not fail, in a dim way, to perceive what a sweet and noble nature revealed itself through these alleged aberrations, and to round out his own culture vicariously through his brother's conversation and reading. But all these considerations, if they occurred to him, were overborne by an instinctive greed to take advantage of a moment which might never return. It was anger and outraged dignity which prompted his words, but then there was also a still small voice of calculation as he strode toward the door and looking back over his shoulder cried out: "You fool, you have thrown away your life."

CHAPTER XXVII.

A PAINFUL PARTING.

Aleck, feeling that the breach with his brother was irreparable, determined to leave the town. He discussed the matter with his uncle, who was somewhat surprised, but offered no serious objection. Only he insisted that his nephew must put poetry and that sort of stuff out of his head, and start out, as he expressed it, to make an honest living. Journalism was, on the whole, not a bad profession, and if Aleck wished to try his hand at it, Mr. Larkin would give him letters to prominent editors in New York, who might give him a chance to distinguish himself. There was a kind of benevolent indifference in his manner while he spoke, which hurt Aleck and made him want to be gone as soon as possible. He had dreamed for years of tearing himself away from the uncongenial practice of the law, and by some startlingly magnificent novel or poem which some day he meant to write, to make his fame and his living as a man of letters. He therefore accepted his uncle's recommendations, hoping through the portal of journalism to make his entrance into the temple of literature. His ambition was hot within him. The world lay shimmering in the flush of dawn at his feet, and dimly radiant visions beckoned him from afar.

There was only one thing that pained him. He must take leave of Gertrude. She was the only young woman whom he had known well, and yet he sometimes felt as if he did not know her at all. She appealed to the chivalrous instinct in him, and made him vaguely aglow with tenderness and sweet unrest. He would have liked to play the part of the young Lochinvar to her ; conquer her at first, if need be, rudely, and then afterward woo and win her by gentle speech, deep devotion, and the gradual revelation of all the wealth of affection and intellect which she never suspected. He wished that he were a

15

stranger to her; so that he might meet her face to face and soul to soul, with no distorting superficial acquaintance or relationship. He had gotten into a false attitude toward her, as a sort of jocose and amiable brother, who could be abused and petted *ad libitum.* Again and again he had made the attempt to get nearer to her; but always this hateful character, which he did not know how he had acquired, clung to him like a strait-jacket and made him seem unnatural both to himself and her. Then again Hawk, whom Aleck detested and despised, stood between them like a menacing shadow; and drove them into talking artificial commonplaces in order to avoid talking about him. The opinion which each knew that the other entertained of Hawk was an insurmountable bar to confidence.

For all that, Aleck could not find it in his heart to leave town without making one more effort to remove this barrier. This time he meant to speak freely of Hawk, and take the consequences. For he foresaw that, without his warning, their relation would drift, sooner or later, into an engagement. He found Gertie in the garret, which she had covered with rugs and draped with curtains of mummy cloth, until it bore a resemblance to a studio. She pulled a burlap over the figure upon which she was working, as he opened the door; and was busy for some minutes pinning it to the wet cloth which was wrapped about the clay. Then she rolled up hastily a sheet of tinted paper upon which he detected two or three unmistakable likenesses of Dr. Hawk. When, at last, she was obliged to face him, her cheeks burned, and she bit her lip as if to conceal a slight confusion.

"Why, Aleck," she cried, breaking into an embarrassed laugh, "what possesses you to come and see me here?"

"I am going away," said Aleck, gravely; "and I want to say good-by to you."

"Going away? Where, if I may ask?"

"To New York."

"How long are you going to be gone?"

"I can't tell; probably forever."

"What has happened?" she cried, with vague surprise. "Is—is—is it the doctor?"

The color again flared into her face and she turned away toward the window and began to pull up the shade. It struck him that there was something almost heartless in the way she uttered these words. The note of sympathy was so glaringly absent that her voice jarred upon his ears like a discord. He noticed, too, as she stood before him, with the great clay-stained apron covering the front of her dress, a certain buoyancy in her bearing, quite different from her usual listlessness. She held her head with *empressement* and in her features there was an animation which made him ill at ease. Was she crowing over his defeat ; trying to assert her superiority, or was she merely relieved at his disappearance from the scene ? She perceived that she had wounded him by her manner, and repeated her question in a more subdued tone.

"What is the matter, Aleck ?" she asked ; "you look as if you had lost your last friend."

"Oh, there's nothing the matter," he answered, being forced into insincerity by her indifferent manner. "I have thought of going away for a good while ; and it is just as well that I should go now as at any other time."

She was not in the least deceived, of course, by such a reply ; but believing that Hawk was at the bottom of the difficulty, was in doubt whether she should invite further confidence.

"Well, Aleck," she said, taking off her apron and adjusting the skirt of her dress with a few shakes and pats, "I shouldn't wonder if you are right. There's really no field for a man of your talents here in Torryville. I really wonder how you have been able to stand it so long."

He made no reply to this, but seated himself upon an inverted dry-goods box which was draped with flowered chintz. She took her seat opposite to him in an ancient arm-chair and began to turn over the leaves in her sketch-book.

"What was that you were working at as I came in ?" he queried with pretended indifference.

"Oh, I was just amusing myself," she answered, evasively.

"Pull off those rags and let me see it."

"No, you must excuse me, Aleck, I would rather not," she said, looking up at him with an air of mild defiance.

"Well, you needn't if you don't want to," he responded after a pause, sadly ; "and I suppose it is too late, now, to warn you against the original."

"The original of what ?"

"Of your bust."

"Aleck, I'd like to know what you mean !"

There was a sudden, impetuous challenge in her voice, which told him the whole story.

"I mean this," he said in a tone of commiseration, "that sooner or later you'll find out your mistake."

"Aleck," she cried, threateningly, "I don't allow anyone to speak to me like that."

She had risen and stood before him, flushed and imperious.

"You'll have to make an exception in my case," he answered in the same gentle voice; "it may be a long time before I see you again—and—and—I have no wish to give you pain needlessly. It's only this I want to say, that when you find out that my judgment of him is right—when he fails you in the moment when you most need him—for he's bound to do that—then remember that I have loved you, or rather forget it, if you like, but remember that I warned you."

He rose and held out his hand to her; but she appeared not to see it.

"You are very kind, indeed," she said, with chilling hauteur; "but I should prefer if you would keep your predictions to yourself. I may as well tell you that I am engaged to Dr. Hawk and expect to be married to him soon. I knew, of course, you didn't like him, but I believed you to be too generous to come here and malign him to me."

"Very well, Gertie, don't let us talk about it any more," he murmured, with mournful resignation; "I shan't bother you any more, dear. Only permit me to say this: I am very, very sorry."

"I don't see what pleasure it can give you to be standing here and tormenting me," she cried, with a voice of blended anger and grief; "you know I don't want to be unkind to you, Aleck, but you try me so terribly."

"Well, I'll try you no more. Good-by!"

He reached out his palm once more, and she looked at it, as if in doubt whether she could afford to relent or not. Then with an impulsive movement she put her hands upon his shoulders, looked at him with a tearful brightness in her eyes and said cordially:

"Aleck, I am so fond of you—you have been so good to me—that I could cry to think—that you could speak that way of the man I love."

"It cannot be helped, dear," he answered, returning her gaze with a dismal smile. It came over him with a chilly sense of desolation that this girl, who was so dear to him, who had been so large a part of his life and thought, must henceforth belong to another, and be as nothing to him and he nothing to her. And never had she appeared so lovable, so supremely desirable in his eyes as in this moment. She was so tall and fair and innocent, so nobly virginal, so full of fresh, pure, unwasted sentiment. And to think that this rich and sweet affection was to be lavished upon a cool, calculating knave, who had not a spark of true and wholesome feeling in him, who had deluded her inexperienced heart by an impressive bit of acting—that was the acme of bitterness. It seemed heartrending that such a wrong, so fruitful in misery, though foreseen, could not be prevented. And yet how touching was this resolute blindness of hers, this invincible loyalty to one who was so unworthy of her ; who, if it were for his advantage, would throw her off like a worn-out garment. Aleck, as these thoughts flitted through his mind, prayed that such a situation might be brought about soon, before the irrevocable step had been taken. If he were not going away, and above all, if he were not a rival, whose motives were scarcely disinterested, he would bend all his energies to unmasking the doctor, or rather contrive a situation in which the doctor would inevitably unmask himself. But these were both disheartening "ifs." As they seemed more insurmountable to Aleck the more he thought of them, he packed his trunk with a heavy heart, and departed on the evening train for New York.

CHAPTER XXVIII.

A DEMORALIZING RUBBER SHOE.

The first result of Aleck's departure was the removal of the sign-board over the office-door, bearing the inscription in big gilt letters :

LARKIN BROTHERS,

ATTORNEYS AND COUNSELORS AT LAW,

and the appearance of a new and smaller one, in which the firm was reduced to :

HORACE LARKIN,

ATTORNEY AND COUNSELOR AT LAW.

About the beginning of October the Republican Convention met, and the gentleman thus designated was, in accordance with his expectation, nominated for the Assembly. He had no idea of making an active canvass, as there were no great issues at stake, and he felt tolerably confident of his election. Nevertheless, a ratification meeting was called at Tappan's Opera House, toward the middle of the month, and Horace was put down for a speech. It was a great and enthusiastic gathering, which would have carried consternation into the ranks of the Democracy, if an incident had not occurred which was much magnified by the opposition paper and furnished material for no end of squibs. Horace was pretty well launched in his eloquence, and was giving a moving picture of the lamentable condition of the poor Southern negro, who was not allowed to vote, and whose life was altogether too sad to be contemplated without tears, when suddenly a rubber shoe, flying through the air in the direction of the speaker, struck the gas fixture and brought two glass globes down upon the heads of two venerable bald-headed citizens. One of these, being an irascible man, seized the missile, hurled it at random in the direction whence it came, and hit Professor Dowd in the nose with such force that he upset his chair and fell backward into the lap of an old farmer. Some students, who were probably responsible for the first flight of the rubber shoe, took care to keep it in motion, and while the speaker, who affected to ignore the disturbance, was in the midst of a tremendous tirade against the rebel brigadiers, the damp flabby thing, in its unforeseen gyration, hit him in the mouth, and nearly knocked him off the platform.

It was the first time in his life that Horace lost control of his temper. " The darned fool, who threw that rubber," he cried, with a face white with wrath, " is—is——" but then he suddenly remembered that he was addressing the electors, who had the power to make or mar him, and with an abrupt moderation of tone he finished : "is not a gentleman."

The unintentional humor of that exclamation struck the audience with irresistible force. A loud guffaw in shrill youthful trebles and old husky basses, drowned the orator's voice, as he attempted to continue ; and every time he opened his mouth a fresh wave of laughter would break forth and sweep over the crowd, until the windows shook and the gas globes trembled. Horace, knowing that it is impossible to argue against laughter, rapidly retired from the platform, and was followed by Mr. Dallas, who gave him rather a cooler endorsement than he had expected to do, because he saw in this rubber incident and the subsequent laugh an indication that possibly he had over-estimated his popularity. Horace was not slow to perceive this note in the manager's remarks ; and he saw, too, a possibility that he might be knocked out of the race by this same unlucky rubber. He had to retrieve himself ; that was obvious, or his prestige would suffer. Accordingly, when Mr. Dallas had finished his remarks about the Republican " Pairty " and worked himself up into a tremendous state of excitement, Horace stepped smilingly forward and begged leave to tell a story. The chairman had a good mind to deny him the privilege, but, on second thought, gave a reluctant consent.

" I am reminded by this rubber, which closed my mouth for one instant," he began, in an easy conversational tone, " of an incident which occurred during the late War of the Rebellion. A gaunt, rheumatic Yankee, well up in the forties, had enlisted in the first flush of his enthusiasm for

the Union cause. He took part in the first fight at Bull
Run, and during the forced marches in the terrible July
heat became utterly exhausted. To make matters worse,
his boots, which were a bad fit, had gnawed a big piece off
his heel, and he would not have been able to keep up with
his company, if a charitable soul had not presented him
with an old rubber. So he limped along for a while the
best he could ; but after a while fell again behind.

" 'Hurry up now, old man,' cried the sergeant to him ;
'no time now to stop for refreshments.'

" The old man, with a supreme effort, hobbled on ; but
fell again behind.

" 'Look here, old chap,' shouted the sergeant, punching
him in the back, 'if you don't stir your stumps, you'll be
taken prisoner.'

" The poor fellow turned a sallow face, full of patient
suffering, toward his captain (from whom I have the
story), and said : 'Cap'n, I'll be d——d if I ever love another country.'

"Now, fellow citizens, that's exactly my case. That man
spoke out of my heart—and out of every loyal man's heart.
Though never put to so severe a test as he, I yet exclaim
with him, 'I'll be d——d if I ever love another country.' "

The transition from this to a stirring patriotic harangue
and a scathing indictment of the Democrats, who, the
speaker contended, did not love a united but a disunited
country, was quite easy. Horace was himself aware that
he was perverting the meaning and point of his anecdote ;
for the old soldier of whom he had spoken had evidently
intended to imply that his love of country had gotten him
into a bad box ; but there was no one present who was
subtle enough to make such a discrimination. And, moreover, Horace gave them no time to be critical ; feeling
that his career was at stake, he fairly surpassed himself in
stirring and impassioned rhetoric. He lifted the people
off their feet, and made them wild with bellicose enthusiasm. When, at the end of half an hour, he sat down, smiling and perspiring, the managers thronged about him and
obsequiously pressed his hands, the crowd cheered him,
stamped with their feet, and pounded the floor with canes
and umbrellas. It was a triumph indeed, in spite of the
demoralizing rubber.

The second result of Aleck's departure was scarcely less
important than the first. Gertrude, having already inflicted
upon him the pain which she had wished to spare him, saw

no further reason for keeping her engagement secret. She accordingly released the doctor from his promise, and advised him to seek an official interview with her father. The doctor professed great satisfaction at this arrangement; but was, nevertheless, not quite so delighted as he wished to appear. The fact was, he had no stomach for an interview with the old man. He knew that the Honorable Obed was a stranger to polite circumlocutions. He was not apt to lose his temper, but he had a way of hitting hard, without being in the least agitated. Hawk shrank from an encounter with his brutal sincerity; and determined, by way of testing his disposition toward him, first to divulge his secret tentatively to Horace. The incident with the will made him feel sheepish and awkward; for, of course, he knew that Mr. Larkin would attribute unworthy motives to his wooing, and tell him squarely to his face that he was a speculating fortune-hunter, if not something worse.

It was the day after the ratification meeting that he dropped into the office on Main Street, where he found Horace, sitting in his shirt sleeves, dictating letters to his clerk. He looked up interrogatively as the doctor entered, and responded to his greeting with a careless nod.

"Is there anything I can do for you, doctor?" he inquired, coolly.

"Well, no, I don't know that there is," Hawk replied, in a tone of good comradeship, "but I tell you what, old fellow, that was a magnificent speech you made last night. You struck just the right note. I was completely carried away with it. I just thought I'd drop in and congratulate you on your triumph."

He was quite effusive, and in spite of the lawyer's unresponsiveness, insisted upon grabbing his hand. As soon as he had released this member, Horace, with an exaggerated effort, put it in his pocket and hauled out his pocket-book.

"Well," he said, gravely, "let us have it. What is it you want? Do you want to borrow money?"

Hawk, though his impulse was to take offence, smiled faintly at this grim joke, and exclaimed with forced hilarity:

"You are an incorrigible wag; but really, this time, I want to see you about something, though it isn't money."

He always felt at a disadvantage in the presence of this man, whose cool insolence irritated and outraged him.

Whatever he said appeared silly to him, the moment he had uttered it ; and in order to correct it, he was apt to say something still sillier. He was like an actor who can only play well to a sympathetic audience. But he could not afford to show his pique, when so much was at stake, and therefore concealed his ill-temper under a cloak of ostentatious good fellowship.

"You may go to your lunch, Lawson," said Horace to his clerk ; "I shall want you back in an hour."

The clerk rolled up his papers, and took his leave.

"Well, doctor," the lawyer remarked, seating himself at his desk, and rummaging among his letters, "is it a divorce you want, or is it only a breach of promise suit?"

"It is neither," Hawk replied with an uncomfortable laugh, "it is, in fact, exactly the opposite."

"Then you had better go to the parson, I am a justice of the peace, to be sure, but I have never yet tied the nuptial knot."

"Now, don't make it so deucedly hard for a fellow. You may have noticed, perhaps—or perhaps you have not —that I have been very much devoted to your cousin, Miss Gertrude."

"Oh, yes, I have noticed that you have had something going on in that line, since you witnessed my uncle's will."

"Now that's rather more than I can stand, Mr. Larkin. I assure you, I have loved her for years——"

"Yes, but you only found it out after you got that squint at the will. However, I don't blame you. A couple of hundred thousand is apt to make a girl particularly lovable."

The doctor bit his lip, and turned red with anger. Horace sat imperturbably, with his back to him, still rummaging among his papers. After a while, he struck a match on the sole of his boot and lighted one of his strong black weeds.

"You don't seem anxious to congratulate me," Hawk resumed, after a pause ; "I should think you might be a little pleasanter, considering that we are to be relatives."

Horace smoked for some minutes in silence. Then he wheeled round in his chair and said, with harsh emphasis : "You ought to congratulate yourself that I don't kick you."

There was nothing to be said after that ; and the discomfited doctor, with a sickly smile, which was meant to express pitying superiority, moved slowly toward the door, stumbled over a cuspidore, and betook himself away.

"Well, for cool impudence," Horace growled to himself, "he beats the Dutch." Hawk's conduct seemed so odious to him, that he could hardly keep from swearing whenever his thoughts recurred to it. But indeed we are fearfully and wonderfully made ; it did not once occur to him that he was himself engaged in a very similar enterprise.

CHAPTER XXIX.

"A BEAST OF PREY."

The interview with the old man, the anticipation of which had caused the doctor such distress, passed off rather more easily than he had expected. The Honorable Obed treated the matter as if it did not greatly concern him. He listened to all the doctor had to say with a non-committal expression, as if it were a business proposition the profits of which he regarded as, on the whole, problematic. That the engagement was not pleasing to him was obvious enough ; but it was difficult to determine just how much it displeased him. He recognized his daughter's free agency in an affair of this sort with a liberality which in a man of his self-willed temper was quite surprising. If it had been a tutor in the university who had proposed to marry on an insufficient income, Mr. Larkin would have imparted his advice with much more freedom and authority. His daughter was such an enigmatical creature, and so far beyond his control, that he saw no way of opposing her with success, if she had really set her heart on marrying this man. He was accustomed to seeing girls have their own way in the selection of husbands, and it did not seem to him such a heinous offence, on Gertrude's part, that she wished to suit herself rather than him. It was not until he had discussed the engagement with his wife that he began to suspect that he had, perhaps, been too easy going ; but as he had then already given a qualified consent, he could not with honor withdraw it. Mrs. Larkin, of course, was of a different opinion. Her husband's apathy and the doctor's foul desertion affected her so seriously that she had to go to bed and make the house redolent with strong medicines. As she lay in her bed with her large plump hands on her breast, and groaned and sighed whenever anyone came within earshot, she looked the saintliest and most abused creature in the world.

Mr. Larkin had during the first years of his marriage

been greatly alarmed by these sudden and unaccountable
attacks. But experience had made him callous. He now
took them very coolly, humored his wife's whim so far as
to inquire two or three times as to her condition, but
chuckled at her "capers," as something darkly and in-
scrutably feminine, which men have got to put up with,
even though they did not profess to understand it. He
was inclined to regard every woman as a bundle of such
intricate and mysterious peculiarities; and therefore not to
be taken seriously, but humorously petted and tolerated.

The November elections resulted, as had been expected,
in a Republican victory ; but what provoked more comment than the party triumph was the fact that Horace
Larkin ran five hundred and forty-eight votes ahead of
the ticket. Such a majority in a closely contested Assembly district was quite phenomenal, and was not to be
legitimately accounted for. Some of the two hundred
and thirty Irishmen who had happily finished their
labors in Saginaw just in time to come home and vote,
were said to have been very flush during the week preceding election ; and a number of others who had not been
at Saginaw had been seen calling at the office in Main
Street, where they had declared that they were undecided
as to whom they would support for the Assembly, and had
a score of friends who were equally undecided. But
their indecision had in a mysterious manner changed to
enthusiasm, and the Democratic candidate, who had walked
in the procession wearing a green suit on St. Patrick's
day, found all his blandishments futile, and declared disconsolately that "the jig was up." When this same gentleman took a leading Hibernian to task for his treachery,
the latter indiscreetly remarked : "Yer kin ketch more
floies wid molasses than yer kin wid vinegar."

This being duly commented upon, was interpreted to
mean that Horace Larkin had bribed the patriots from
the Emerald Isle. But no admission to this effect could
be extracted from any of them.

"Yer couldn't draw a dollar from him with a derrick."
one of the visitors at the office asseverated.

"Mebbe yer could with a corruk-screw," observed
another.

"No, be jabers. He's the stiddiest man on his fate and
wid his toongue whin he's dhroonk as I iver seed."

"Ah, ye shoot yer jaw ! He ain't never dhroonk at all,
at all. He only lets on out of perliteness to yer, when ye

be boozy. He's as cool in his hed, all the whoile, as a fresh cowcumber."

It will be seen from these remarks that Horace had accomplished the difficult task of gaining the confidence of "the laboring man." He had, like other candidates for office, visited saloons, treated the crowd, thrown five-dollar bills on the counter, and refused to take change (for such practices were regarded as quite proper in a politician), but nothing more serious was proved against him. This, however, did not account for his exceptional majority or the great preponderance which he instantly gained in political counsels. He was henceforth a power which had to be reckoned with.

It was the evening of the day after the election, while all these rumors were buzzing about his ears, that Horace betook himself to the parsonage to receive the congratulations of his *fiancée*. He had necessarily neglected her somewhat during the labors and the excitement of the campaign, and he thought that this circumstance accounted for the constrained air with which she greeted him. Her father, who was also in the room, received him with rather superfluous formality, and Horace was not slow to perceive that there was something unusual in the wind. He was too secure in his self-esteem to be disquieted by any one's disapprobation, and he seated himself in his usual lounging attitude and smiled his slow, superior smile, while waiting for the parson to take him to task for his misdemeanors. There was a shaded duplex lamp upon the table and a soft suffusion of yellow light throughout the room. Round about the walls were low book-cases, with strips of maroon leather along the shelves containing theological books in plain black cloth, and the poets and novelists in tree-calf and morocco. There was an air of luxurious comfort and refinement about the appointments of the room which never failed to impress Horace whenever he entered it.

Mr. Robbins, who on such occasions usually betook himself away after a few amiable remarks about the weather, showed to-day no inclination to comply with this considerate custom. He put his book on the table, face downward, cleared his throat two or three times and seemed extremely uncomfortable. How could he—a good-natured elderly gentleman—summon courage to rebuke this formidable young man, with his massive self-confidence and his pachydermatous conscience. If he were only a

priest of God, having authority, he sighed, as so often before, how he then would speak, and how vanishing would
be the obstacles which now towered in his path ! Yet his
sense of duty would not permit him to remain silent where
his child's happiness was at stake. She had begged him
so piteously to let the thing pass without notice ; she
had wept and coaxed and caressed him ; but the more he
thought of the matter, the worse it looked, and the more
imperative seemed his duty to speak.

"I understand you have been elected, Mr. Larkin," he
began with some difficulty.

"Yes," said Horace, blandly ; "I am quite content."

"And are you sure you are quite satisfied with yourself, when you—what shall I say—when you review your
course of action in the light of God's word and your own
conscience ?"

Bella, with irrepressible nervousness, rose from her
father's side, where she had been sitting, and dropped
upon a foot-stool close to the chair which Horace was
occupying. It was as if she wished to throw in her lot
with him—signify her allegiance and mitigate the effect
of her father's words.

"Running five hundred and forty-eight votes ahead of
your ticket reconciles one to a good many things," said
Horace, quietly.

This answer for some reason irritated Mr. Robbins.

"Does it also reconcile you to eternal damnation ?" he
cried, with flashing eyes.

"Why, papa, what *are* you saying ?" exclaimed Bella,
frightened, and drew still closer up to Horace, leaning on
the arm of his chair, and fondling his hand.

"Hold on, parson," the latter ejaculated, laughing.
"Eternal damnation ! Isn't that rather rushing it ?"

"You know well enough what I mean," Mr. Robbins
replied, in a calmer tone ; "you have done things in this
campaign which no man can do without imperilling his
soul's salvation."

"Well, I'll take the risk," said Horace, with an emphasis,
as if he meant that to be final, and wished the discussion
closed.

"Great God, man, if you knew how blasphemously you
speak, " cried the parson with sudden vehemence.

The young man squared himself in his chair, leaned
forward and glanced up at the clergyman with a combative light in his gray eyes.

"Couldn't I demolish you—couldn't I grind you to dust, if I thought it worth while!" that glance seemed to say. But there was no trace of excitement in his manner as he asked :

"Parson, have you read the parable of the unjust steward?"

The query came so unexpected that Mr. Robbins scarcely knew what to answer.

"I presume you have," Horace continued ; "and you remember how the Lord commended him for cheating his master and giving a ruinous discount to his debtors."

"That does not mean that he approved of him," Mr. Robbins protested.

"What does it mean, then?"

"It means that the Lord wished to impress upon the children of light the necessity of employing as much energy and ingenuity in well-doing as the children of darkness employ in ill-doing."

"That is, in my opinion, rather a far-fetched interpretation. The whole gist of the parable is contained in these words : 'Make ye therefore friends of the mammon of unrighteousness.'"

"And so you mean to say that you have scriptural warrant for going into low saloons, drinking with all sorts of rowdies, flinging ten-dollar bills on the counter and declining to take change?"

"Now, papa, how can you speak that way to Horace?" Bella broke in impetuously. "I am sure he never did any of those things."

Horace shot her a sidelong glance in which there was a gleam of compassion.

"Don't be too sure," he said.

"There! Do you hear that?" cried Mr. Robbins, eagerly ; "he is not ashamed of what he has done. He's proud of it."

"Oh, yes," drawled the delinquent, "he's not a bit repentant."

"And you think it is honorable for a man of your standing to indulge in such practices? Have you considered that the name you bear is before long to be my daughter's name, and that it is a matter of some importance both to me and to her if you choose to put a stain upon it."

There was an anxious stillness in the room, broken only by the low humming of the lamp and Bella's staccato breathing. Horace's face grew hard, and his eyes had a cold, pinched look.

"Mr. Robbins," he said, in a harsh, incisive voice, "you have assumed more authority over me than I can possibly accord to you. If my actions throw discredit upon yourself or your daughter, it is only fair that I should release you both from your obligation to me. Good-evening."

He had risen, with lips tightly shut, and stood buttoning his coat with an air of defiant resolution. There came a low wail, followed by convulsive weeping, from the carpet upon which Bella was seated.

"Oh, Horace, do not leave me, do not go away!" she sobbed, flinging her arms about his feet and clinging to them.

"My dear," he said, stooping and releasing himself from her passionate embrace; "I am sorry to hurt you, but we must part. There is no help for it."

He passed out through the door, but heard, with an irrepressible heartache, how she called his name with a touching irrational persistence; how she wept with a sore, heart-broken grief, and how her father's voice was trying to soothe her. He remained for a while standing on the sidewalk, listening; and every time he heard his name called in that shrilly jarring, piteous note (as of a voice that had tired itself out crying) his resolution received a shock, and he could scarcely keep from going back and doing penance. The friendly yellow light streamed out through the chinks in the shutters, and seemed to beckon him back. He had done this; he had inflicted this cruel pain; and in spite of the opportune excuse, there was no use denying that he had done it deliberately. He was not proud of himself now, but there was a sub-consciousness in the midst of his self-reproach that the end was worth the sacrifice. He was a beast of prey, asserting his right of survival; nothing more. If he succumbed to sentiment (and it is far easier to succumb to it than to resist it) he would merely be eliminating himself from the battle of existence as a potent and considerable force, and consigning himself to the rear ranks. And he felt in every fibre of his being that he was born for leadership.

He sauntered slowly through the damp and cloudy November night, pondering the deep problem of existence.

CHAPTER XXX.

A DISMANTLED IDEAL.

The departure of Horace for Albany at the opening of the new year was a great relief to Gertrude and Hawk. The latter, who had found in the presence of an enemy an excuse for the most eccentric behavior, would have tired the affections of any woman less heroically devoted than Gertrude. In return, to be sure, she had tired him by making him sit for a bust which she never could finish to her satisfaction. Now it was the nose that was wrong. Now it was the mouth, or the ears, which always had a look as if they did not belong to the head, but had been stuck on as an afterthought; but the chief difficulty was with the eyes, which refused to look straight, and moreover were surrounded by unaccountable swellings, suggesting sties and bumps. If the original had been making a night of it and had come home in a demoralized condition, he might have looked somewhat as the unskilful hands of his *fiancée* had represented him.

It was a great humiliation to Gertrude when she had to abandon this cherished work, which she had begun with so much enthusiasm. She could not bear to destroy it by a well-aimed stab or blow; for it had enough likeness to the doctor to make her shrink from doing it an injury. But she put it away in a closet where it gradually cracked and fell to pieces.

This calamity had scarcely released its hold on Gertrude's mind when an incident occurred which gave her much more serious cause for disquietude. She received a long letter from her mother, without date, but post-marked New York. It was a most distressing letter, filled with complaints and accusations against Mr. Larkin, and adjurations to Gertrude to come to her at once, as she wished to see her only child before she died. She gave a pitiful description of her condition, cold and starving in a filthy tenement-house, where the snow blew in through the broken window-panes, and rats infested the rooms and even the beds, and made it dangerous to go to sleep. She be-sought and entreated Gertrude not to delay her coming, as she had an important secret to confide to her which she could not possibly impart to any one else. There were tear-stains on the soiled paper, and the handwriting, which was large and scrawling, reeled along the sloping lines with a drunken unsteadiness. The style, too, was ramb-ling and incoherent; but here and there were phrases which had a singular pathos in them, and seemed to voice a genuine distress.

Gertrude was wrought up, by the reading of this letter, into a state of great agitation. The fact that it was her mother who appealed to her thus invested every word with a strange urgency and moving power. She could not reason coolly that this mother was the slave of a de-basing habit, and utterly unworthy of confidence. The opium habit was to her merely a word with a dimly omi-nous significance; but she knew nothing of its ruinous effect upon body and mind. It was her mother who was calling upon her in her need, destitute and dying—how could she, then, decline to listen? Her conscience pricked her, too, when she thought of the coolness of her demeanor, how incredulous she had been, and ill at ease during their first meeting. She had fully made up her mind as to her course of action when she went to her father and begged leave to read the letter to him. He was sitting at his desk in the library, looking over some accounts which Horace had submitted for his inspection.

"Who did you say your letter was from?" he asked, looking at her over his spectacles with a preoccupied air.

"From my mother," she answered with tremulous insist-ence; "from my mother in New York."

He leaned back in his chair, pushed his spectacles up on his forehead, and stared at her with vaguely troubled eyes.

"I thought you promised me, darter, not to have any-thing to do with that woman," he said, with quiet remon-strance.

"So I did, father. But you surely wouldn't want me to desert her now, when she is in want and dying."

"You mean lying," he suggested, gravely.

"How can you be so unjust, father? If you would only read her letter you would soon be convinced that it is true, every word of it."

"No, I won't. I wouldn't touch it with a ten-foot pole."

"I had no idea you could be so prejudiced."

He slid the spectacles down on his nose again (they were of the solid, old-fashioned, silver-bowed kind) and began to turn over his papers with an absent-minded air. She received suddenly the impression, which she had had once before, that there was something lonely and pathetic about him, in spite of his wealth, his self-sufficiency, and his commanding position. For all that, she could not help resenting his air of dismissal, as he resumed his occupation, appearing to ignore her presence.

"Won't you listen to me, father?" she asked, helplessly.

He looked up again, laid away his pen carefully, and tilted back his chair.

"I want you to throw that letter into the fire," he said, "and keep your promises better hereafter."

"I think you are very cruel not to be willing to listen."

"That's neither here nor there. You just do as I tell you."

"But, father, won't you please give me money to go to New York and see her?" cried Gertrude, with tearful entreaty. "I shall be back again soon, and nobody need know it."

"If you go," he said huskily, but cleared his throat to recover his voice—"if you go, you won't come back at all."

"Oh, yes, I will," she ejaculated, reassuringly; "I should only be gone for a few days."

"No, you won't," he retorted with surly decision; "if you go to see that woman, I don't want to see your face again."

It dawned upon her now that he meant to throw her off—to forbid her return. "But she is dying, father," she repeated, pleadingly.

"Well, it is the most useful thing she could do," he replied, "it ain't the first time she has done it."

"Not the first time she has died?"

"No, it's an old trick of hers."

"But there are rats in her room, father."

"It don't surprise me. But that'll do now, darter, I won't hear any more talk of that sort. And I thought better of you than to break your word."

"Then you won't let me go?"

Mr. Larkin rose with cumbrous deliberation and walked across the floor to where his daughter was sitting. She remembered, for many years after, the look of pain about his firm mouth, as he came toward her, and also the loud creaking of his boots.

"Throw that letter into the fire," he commanded, harshly.

But his own spirit flared up within her in response to his voice, and she answered:

"I won't."

"Will you, or will you not throw that letter into the fire?" he repeated, with a sudden ominous gentleness.

"I will not."

They stood face to face, she with large excited eyes, quivering lips, and distended nostrils, the picture of generous youthful indignation; he calm and resolute, with the hard lines about his mouth somewhat strained, and his lips tightly shut.

"Do you know, darter, that you are cutting yourself off from house and home?" he asked, with grave deliberation.

"Yes, I do; but I wouldn't do a mean and cowardly act for anybody."

There were tears in her voice, and her eyes were slowly overflowing.

"I don't want to take you at your word, I want you to go and think of it. But don't you forget this; if you break your promise to me—if you choose her rather than me—you can't come back again and say you made a mistake. You've got to stand by your choice and take the consequences."

He spoke harshly, and without apparent emotion; neither his voice nor his language ever rose above the plainest prose; but the effort with which he thrust forth his words showed how difficult he found them to utter. He did not wait to watch the effect of his warning, but turned his back upon Gertrude and walked out of the room. He knew how easily girls lost their self-control when contradicted; and he hoped that his daughter's sound sense would assert itself when her reason was left to speak, uninfluenced by her pugnacity. But unhappily there was one element in Gertrude's character which he did not take into consideration, viz., her contempt for sordid prudence and a romantic yearning to raise herself above the humdrum reality by some great act of devotion and self-sacrifice. There was a youthful sympathy with rebellion in her heart, and quite apart from personal considerations it seemed to her a fine thing to defy paternal authority in the interest of a wronged and down-trodden creature, who, moreover, was bound to her by the most sacred ties of blood. The innumerable novels she had read were unanimous on this point, that the great herd of humanity (and fathers in particular) were in-fluenced by the meanest motives, and that it was only a few heroic souls who possessed the strength and exalta-tion of character to emancipate themselves from this gal-ling yoke of Mammon. She meant to prove herself to be one of these rare, heroic beings ; and here was her grand opportunity, which, if she let it pass, might never more return.

It was a glorious thing now that she knew a kindred spirit who would value and understand her reasonings, and support her in her lofty resolution. She could not wait for the evening, when Hawk was in the habit of call-ing, but rushed out of the room, put on her hat and jacket, and walked rapidly up the street toward his office. There were invisible wings on her feet ; she was borne along by some strong impelling force, independent of her own voli-tion. She paused for breath at the gate which led to the white-painted frame house where the doctor had his domi-cile. It was in a quiet side-street, and had a small garden in front fringed with blackened stalks of hollyhocks and sun-flowers. On the door there was a well-polished brass plate exhibiting the inscription : Archibald Hawk, M.D. There was an air of stillness and seclusion about the place, and it was intensified by green paper shades which covered windows and sidelights, imparting to them a peculiarly solemn and unresponsive stare. Gertrude pulled the little glass bell-handle and heard a shrill jingle within. A pretty maid with rosy cheeks opened the door, and asked her to be seated in the waiting-room. At the end of ten minutes, which seemed to Gertrude a small eternity, the doctor made his appearance, and with a sad and somewhat strained smile of welcome conducted her into his private library. The first sight which met her here was a skeleton, whose fleshless skull was adorned with a tall silk hat, and with a half-smoked cigar stuck between its teeth. The floor was of hard wood, and covered with rich Oriental rugs. On the walls were etchings and engravings, all good, some striking, and arranged helter-skelter, but with excellent artistic effect. A voluptuous Oriental fancy was traceable through all of them. There were beautiful women emerg-ing from the bath, or shivering on the edge of marble basins, before taking the plunge. There were allegorical ladies with splendid busts and shoulders, whom the painters, as an excuse for their nudity, had dubbed " Truth," " Innocence," " Charity," etc. But these were only for the delectation of their owner and that of cherished friends who could be trusted not to take offence. As such were few and far between in Torryville, the busts were usually hidden by a tawny silk curtain, which could be made to fall apart, as if by magic, by pulling a cord.

" Well, *dolcinella*," the doctor exclaimed, with forced gayety, tossing his Hamlet lock back from his forehead, " to what happy circumstance do I owe the honor of your visit ? "

" It is not a happy, but an unhappy circumstance," Gertrude replied. " I want you to advise me, and I have no one to go to but you."

" *Poverina !* They have been bad to you at home ; have they ? "

" No ; it is something much more serious. It is something—which—which may change my life entirely."

" *Poveretta !* " sighed the doctor.

He had been reading, by way of exercise, Manzoni's " I Promessi Sposi " during the morning, and had been struck with the beauty and richness of the endearing terms in the Italian language. But to Gertrude, who was inwardly quivering with agitation, this experimental application of a foreign tongue was distasteful. It seemed to her that he was trifling with her. He was so preoccupied with himself and the effect he was producing, that he failed to detect the note of distress in her voice. She felt rebuffed, and with the impulsiveness of a high-strung nature, rose and moved toward the door. Perceiving that he had offended her, he stepped forward, put his back against the door and said :

" Not yet, dearest. Tell me what is the matter. Whatever I can do for you, I'll do with all my heart."

There was yet a lack of sincerity in his voice ; but she forced herself to believe that she was perhaps too exacting.

" I have received a letter from my mother," she said hurriedly, in order to keep from breaking down ; " she wants me to come to her."

Hawk stroked his silky beard and looked with a pensive frown toward the ceiling.

" What does your father say about it ? " he asked guardedly.

"He says that, if I go, I shall never come back."

"Hem ! That looks bad. What do you propose to do ? "

" That's what I came to ask you about. You know, my mother is ill and dying. She has no money ; and she has to live in a wretched tenement-house where there are rats and no end of dreadful things."

The wholly unmoved air with which he listened to this passionate recital, filled her with dismay. She could not persuade herself that she was fully awake ; there was some horrible mistake somewhere. It could not be possible that he denied her his sympathy. Aleck's words : " He will fail you when you need him most," recurred to her ; and the more she strove to rid herself of them, the more persistently they rang in her ears. She followed him with her eyes, while he sauntered across the floor, stopped to arrange a bit of drapery, or to straighten a picture which hung crooked. She noted how handsome he looked with his dark hair and beard, his fine nose and his rich olive complexion ; but she noted, too, a certain constraint in his movements, and a painful indecision in his face. He was carrying on a mental debate, and was unwilling to commit himself before he had reached a conclusion. She more than suspected, in this moment, that he was influenced only by considerations of prudence ; but she could not afford to have her beautiful faith in him destroyed ; she wished to be convinced against her own judgment that he was what she had believed him to be. She yearned, she panted—though with a dismal sinking of heart—to have him prove himself noble, courageous, and true.

"Archie," she began, with breathless anxiety, " I know it must be difficult for you to put yourself in my position. I don't want you to advise me, if it is disagreeable to you. I have already made up my mind what to do. But I have hardly any money ; and I want you to lend me fifty dollars to relieve my mother's distress. I am going to start for New York to-night, and if—if—I don't come back again —I'll write to you, and let you know where you can find me."

He had stood face to face with the skeleton while she spoke, staring into the empty sockets which had once contained its eyes ; but he now turned abruptly about, and paused in front of her.

"Gertie," he said ; " may I ask if you have taken leave of your senses?"

"Why," she cried, "what do you mean?"

"I mean just what I say," he answered, fiercely; "have you gone crazy?"

She looked up into his face in speechless dismay; it was as if he had removed a mask, and suddenly showed himself as he was. There was something almost brutal in his fixed stare and in the pitiless rigidity of his mouth.

"Do you think I am crazy, because I want to help my mother?" she managed to stammer.

"But you told me yourself that she is an opium-eater."

"But she is my mother."

"But your father—how about him?"

"He does not need me. He's not in distress."

"But ought you not to have some regard for yourself? What's to become of you, if he throws you off?"

"I supposed, in either case, I was to be your wife."

This was apparently an unexpected reply to the doctor, for he was visibly taken aback. He thrust his hands into his pockets, walked across the floor and became absorbed in the contemplation of "La Vérité," the one of his goddesses to whose worship he was least addicted.

"If you are to be my wife," he said, turning half about, "I shall have to insist upon obedience to my wishes."

"Indeed. And in the present case, may I ask what is your wish?"

A note of sarcasm stole into her voice and a sudden chill into her manner. For the word obedience is to the American girl what the red rag is to the bull, and roused all her latent ire.

"I wish you to go home and do as your father tells you," he said, angrily.

"And if I don't do it, what then?"

He did not venture to say: "Then all is over between us," for he saw in an instant what consequences that would involve. He was by nature given to shuffling, and could never arrive at a resolution, except after infinite deliberation.

"I should deeply deplore your waywardness," he answered, recovering his sonorous rhetorical note.

"And you will not lend me the money?"

"I should offend your father, don't you see? And since you have taken it into your head to offend him, it's much better that I should keep on the right side of him. Then there's, at all events, a chance of things coming out right."

There flashed forth a glimpse of a paltry, calculating

soul in this speech, and it filled Gertrude with loathing.
Was it possible that this was the man she had worshipped,
idealized, adored ? Was it conceivable that this man
whom, in her blindness, she had apotheosized as an incarnation of all perfections could be possessed of a spirit
so mean, so pitifully unheroic ? She could not at once
accept such a conclusion. She must subject him to the
test once more, before abandoning her faith in him forever.

"Please tell me," she asked in a low and gentle voice ;
" will you or will you not lend me the money ? "

" I will, if you will give me your sacred word of honor
that you'll never tell your father about it."

She rose with a smile of unutterable contempt, and
moved toward the door. She had no idea why she smiled,
it was, probably, as the alternative to weeping.

"You might answer at least," he muttered, sulkily.
"Will you promise ? "

"No, Dr. Hawk, I will give you no fresh promise. I
want you to release me from one which I have given you."

" Now, Gertie, I wish you would be rational."

" I am very rational—now," she said in a strange, sad,
far-away voice. "I wish you would not speak to me.
Good-by."

He was enough of a connoisseur of women to know the
futility of argument. That sudden fainting of the voice
which had the effect of sorrowful tenderness, was rather
the expression of an internal tremulousness which with
the least indulgence would have sought vent in tears.
She was in haste to be gone because she felt that she could
not keep herself in check much longer. Oddly enough,
her present regret was not for him, that he had proved
himself unworthy, but for all the beautiful sentiment she
had wasted upon him. Her pride suffered more than her
love. She felt humiliated—debased.

Now that this gorgeous cloud-vision had faded into
clammy vapor, all things seemed nauseous, unstable. It
was like the morning after the feast, when the rosy dawn
sends its first rays into the deserted banqueting hall. The
half-burned candles—how forlorn they look ! The crumpled napkins, the half-dismantled table, the empty bottles,
the corks strewn about the floor, the smell of stale cigar-
smoke ! All that was beautiful the night before is to-day
doubly distressing because of its lost beauty.

Without appearing to notice the hand which the doctor

held out to her, Gertrude opened the door and found her
way into the street. She was conscious of a strange
numbness in her knees, and the flag-stones billowed and
gave way under her feet. This, then, was the end of her
dream. She had lavished her heart's best affection upon
a masquerading mountebank. She had invested a picturesque lay figure with all the paraphernalia of heroism
which had been supplied by her own youthful disordered
imagination.

She hurried down the sidewalk, scarcely knowing where
her feet were carrying her. The familiar street, flanked
with white and slate-colored frame houses, surrounded
by garden-patches, assumed a strangely unfamiliar look.
The sunlight smote upon her eyes with a pitiless, glaring
insistance. The blood surged vaguely in her ears and
throbbed in her temples. The dead leaves rattled about
her skirts, and she dragged a dry twig along without
observing it. A bird darted with an uneven staccato
motion across the street; and her capricious fancy
attached itself to it, following it on and on into the
terrible blue infinity. It became a plague and a nightmare, this bobbing bird—flashing through sunshine and
shadow, untiring, unresting, like an insane, sleepless
thought, that detaches itself from the brain, and flies
beyond its control.

As soon as she arrived home, Gertrude began to pack
her trunk, in a dumfounded, mechanical way. It took
her a couple of hours to get her dresses and other neces-
saries of life properly disposed within the circumscribed
space; and as she had no experience to guide her, she had
repeatedly to undo her work, after trying impracticable
experiments. It was a relief, however, to be compelled to
think of something definite and tangible, to move hands
and limbs, and knock against difficulties which challenged
exertion. She emptied her pocket-book on the table,
and found that she had about $19. This would more
than suffice to buy her ticket; but it would leave her little
with which to relieve her mother's want. But there was
Aleck! He was in New York and she knew his address.
She would go to him at once and ask his aid. He would
not fail her; of that she felt confident. His blond, gentle
face with the trusty, dark-blue eyes, full of loyalty and
devotion, rose up before her fancy, and it calmed and
comforted her to think of it. She would see Aleck; she
would talk with him, and tell him of her position. He

would not stop to consider the risks he ran, as a presumptive heir to her father's money, before extending to her his helping hand. The more she dwelt upon this thought the more eager she became for the meeting with Aleck. He assumed, by contrast, all the virtues which she had failed to find in Hawk. He had warned her against Hawk ; his own true, brave, and loyal heart had felt an instinctive aversion for Hawk's selfishness and cowardly calculation. How deluded she had been! How wofully, how cruelly deluded! She began now to doubt whether she had ever loved Hawk. She had, indeed, loved a grand and heroic soul, disguised, as she thought, in his features ; but having found that the heroic soul was not there her devotion had changed to indignation ; and her trust to revulsion and outraged dignity. Ardent, youthful, and innocent, as she was, she could not conceive of a love that was not based upon worship. Having discovered that Hawk was not worthy of her worship, she concluded, too, that he was not worthy of her love. Like most young persons she was wholesomely self-centred ; she felt sore, outraged, humiliated ; but it was for herself she was sorry, not for him.

Having finished her packing she sat down and wrote a long letter to her father and a brief curt one to Hawk. In the former she begged forgiveness for disregarding his desire, in the latter she broke off her engagement. At eleven o'clock, when the family were long since asleep, she procured a cab and started for the depot. The evening was chilly and the mists were creeping up from the lake, wrapping the hills in fleecy winding-sheets. She stopped at the telegraph office and sent a dispatch to Aleck, announcing the time of her arrival. The cabman checked her trunk for her, as soon as she had bought her ticket, and helped her aboard the car. In another moment the shrill whistle pierced the night, and with rumbling and clanking of metal and the hissing of escaping steam, the train glided out into the white sea of mist.

CHAPTER XXXI.

A MOMENTOUS DISCOVERY.

The train arrived in Jersey City at an inconveniently early hour and the occupants of the sleeping-cars were in no hurry to plunge out into the chilly morning. They made their toilets at their leisure, submitted to unnecessary brushings from the colored porter, and departed one by one as the impulse prompted them. Gertrude, who had retired with the expectation of spending a wakeful night, was half ashamed of the soundness of her sleep. She had not yet arrived at the age when grief, like the carpenter in Heine's poem, works away at your coffin through the long nocturnal vigils. She had the consoling consciousness that she was doing a fine thing in burning her bridges behind her and starting out, at the call of conscience, to rescue an unfortunate woman from misery. This dim sense of heroism buoyed her up and made her sorrows interesting and therefore easier to bear. She was standing before the mirror in the end of the car which was temporarily reserved for the ladies, when she heard some one speaking her name. She recognized instantly Aleck's voice, and her heart gave a leap. With her hair yet a trifle dishevelled she rushed into a narrow passage-way which connected the ladies' toilet compartment with the body of the car, ran against Aleck, and before she was aware of it, she had kissed him, shed a few tears, laughed in an absurdly confused fashion, and blushed to the tips of her ears. Aleck, too, was blushing, and laughing and talking joyous confused nonsense. There was no one near, so she could safely hug him once more, and cry a little, and tell him how delighted she was to see his dear, good, honest face. He had raised a prententious yellow mustache since she saw him last, and she pronounced it extremely becoming. He laughed rather sheepishly at this and twirled the article in question in mock acknowledgment of the compliment. She had never in her life been so happy to see anybody ; and she had never known anyone to look so lovely as Aleck looked to her in this moment. She was not alone in the world after all; there was one whom she could lean upon; who was ready to bear part of her burden.

He seated himself on one of the sofas and waited while she finished her toilet. In a few moments she returned, wearing a handsome Gainsborough hat with large black feathers and a tight-fitting fawn-colored jacket, which was simply ravishing. Her fresh girlish face, with its innocent seriousness like that of a child, its frank, wide open inexperienced eyes, and its expression of vague expectancy seemed to Aleck the climax of all that was fair and sweet and lovable. Her absolute trust in him touched him as much as her beauty thrilled and intoxicated him. Had he not loved her patiently and hopelessly as far back as he could remember? And here she stood before him, like a young goddess sprung from the wave to rescue him from despair and supply a new incentive to his paralyzed ambition. He knew nothing, as yet, of the rupture of her relations with the doctor; but he had a joyous conviction that his prophecy had come true; that she had found out her mistake; that Hawk had unmasked himself and been consigned to perdition.

The first opportunity for explanation came when she handed him the check for her trunk, and asked him to attend to it.

"Where do you wish it sent?" he asked.

She paused a moment before answering.

"To my mother," she said, gravely.

"Your mother?" inquired Aleck, wonderingly; "I thought your mother was dead."

"No; she is alive."

"And do you know her? Have you seen her?"

"Yes."

"And you never told me about it."

"No; father told me not to."

"I think you had better go and see your mother first, before sending her your trunk. I'll keep the check, and do with it whatever you may wish."

They walked out of the shabby, barn-like depot and boarded the ferryboat. Aleck was too astonished to be communicative. It was as if Gertrude had suddenly slipped away from him again, just as he had her so deliciously near. This mysterious kinship, of which he had never heard the remotest hint, affected him unpleasantly.

He could not quite bring himself to believe in it ; nor could he entirely disbelieve in it. But he was conscious of a dim animosity to Gertrude's mother, whoever and what-ever she might prove to be. Gertie was so credulous and romantic. Was it not possible that some scheming advent-uress had imposed upon her for the purpose of extorting money from Mr. Larkin? Aleck determined to constitute himself her protector, even at the risk of displeasing her.

They sat for some moments in silence, gazing out upon the gray pageantry of the river, until the seats, which in-sidiously concealed the steam-heating apparatus, grew so uncomfortable as to compel them to rise. They made their way out of the saloon, and came near losing their balance, as the ferryboat bumped against the tarred board-fence of the slip, before reaching its moorings.

"Where does your mother live?" asked Aleck, quite *en passant*, as they passed through the gate of the ferry house into the street.

Gertrude pulled the letter from her pocket and showed him the address.

"Do you want to go there now?"

"Yes."

"But it is only eight o'clock."

"It makes no difference."

"I hope you do not object to my going with you."

"No–o. Oh, no! Only it is a poor place, Aleck, a wretched tenement-house, with rats in it, that crawl all over you. And you mustn't be astonished at anything you see."

"No, I won't."

She felt, now that she had gotten hold of him, she could not bear to let him go again. She did not contemplate the meeting with her mother with pleasurable anticipations ; nay, all sorts of vague apprehensions lingered in the back-ground of her mind, and made her ill at ease.

"Hadn't you better come and take breakfast with me, before you—go visiting?" Aleck inquired, after a while, cautiously.

"But would that be proper?"

"I can see no impropriety in it. Emotional scenes on an empty stomach are doubly trying. Let us breakfast together at the Brunswick ; then you'll be fortified against all contingencies."

"But, Aleck, my mother is starving."

She uttered this rather impassively, as if it were a proposition in geometry, or a moral maxim, which made no appeal to the emotions.

" That's no reason why you should starve," said Aleck, with the same colorless manner ; " when I expect to have my heart wrung, I always lay in a solid breakfast."

She was glad to have her scruples overridden, and without further objection mounted the platform of the elevated railroad and boarded the cars. They took a cab at Twenty-third Street and Sixth Avenue, and were driven to the fashionable restaurant with the frescoed frieze of mediæval merrymakers, dancing through the golden space. There was a sense of adventure about the whole thing to Gertrude which filled her, in spite of her apprehensions, with a subdued joy. She had still momentary doubts as to whether she was entirely awake. To sit here *tête-à-tête* with Aleck, whose blue eyes beamed upon her with tender devotion ; to feel the delicious strangeness of everything that met her eye—the gorgeous walls and ceiling, the dainty dishes, the exquisite porcelain, the obsequious French waiters, and the rumbling turmoil of the avenue without—it was like an excursion into a fairy-tale, too charming to be wholly true. She ate, with a kind of shame-faced appetite, a goodly selection of what was on the bill of fare ; the French names tempted her to try things which she really did not want ; but the ride across the river and the walk from the ferry had created a ravenous void within her which took no account of sentimental troubles.

" Do get up, Aleck," she said, with a lugubrious laugh, "and send that dreadfully suggestive waiter away, or I shall eat you into bankruptcy."

Aleck obeyed without coaxing, though not from sordid consideration ; paid his bill in a radiant humor, and started with his fair cousin in the direction of West Sixty-fourth Street. After having walked a couple of blocks, carrying her hand-satchel, he again hailed a cab and they soon found themselves in the neighborhood indicated in Gertie's letter. It was now a little after ten o'clock, and the weather had cleared. A light wintry mist still hung over the park ; but the sun was well up over the house-tops on the east side, and illuminated the smoke from a hundred chimneys which rose straight up into the still air.

Aleck and Gertie were both surprised at the appearance of the house before which the cabman stopped. It was a large and neat-looking apartment house, in a very respectable neighborhood, and could not by any license of speech be described as a tenement, far less as a wretched hovel. Gertrude pulled out her letter once more and made sure that the numbers corresponded. Unless her mother had given a wrong address, there could be no room for doubt. She entered the vestibule with Aleck, and scrutinized the dozen or more cards over the bell-handles, giving the names of the tenants. Over the bell handle belonging to the third floor, left, was a coarsely printed card, with a crest, bearing the name Count Kharlovitz. After consultation with Aleck, she rang the bell; for there was a possibility that Mrs. Larkin had moved, or that she was living with some other family. The front door was opened by an invisible agency, and again closed behind them. Gertrude was so startled by this automatic action, that she seized hold of the knob and again tore the door open. She was flushed and excited; but seeing Aleck's wonder, began to laugh ruefully at her own absurdity. They mounted two flights of carpeted stairs and rang the bell on the left, where the card with the coronet was again exhibited.

A youngish-looking man in his shirt sleeves, with a big black mustache, opened the door, put out his head, and inquired what they wanted. He was smoking a cigar of a very fine flavor.

"We wish to see Mrs. Larkin," said Aleck.

The man withdrew his head abruptly and slammed the door. A discussion was heard inside, at first subdued, but growing louder. A querulous female treble, which Gertrude thought she recognized, was pleading for something to which a rasping bass obviously objected. Presently there was a bang as of something thrown or upset, then more tearful pleading, and at last silence. Gertrude stood listening with a sinking heart. The vision of the rats creeping all over her, which had haunted her on the way, was far less terrible than the conviction which now stole upon her, that that door hid some disgraceful secret. That she had been imposed upon she could not doubt; only she was at a loss to comprehend the motive. Her mother had perhaps not expected, judging by her daughter's previous behavior, that she would obey her summons; but had hoped by the description of her misery to extort further contributions of money.

"Well," said Aleck, after five minutes' patient waiting, "what do you say? Shall we spend the morning here?"

"You must stay with me, Aleck," she replied, tremu-

17

lously ; "I am determined to get at the bottom of this.
Ring the bell once more."

Aleck rang, and the response was something that
sounded like the clatter of dishes and jingling of glasses.
Somebody was bestirring himself apparently to put the
rooms in order ; and in a few minutes more the man with
the mustache, enveloped in the flavor of his fine cigar,
opened the door quite smilingly and apologized for having
kept them waiting. He was now no longer in his shirt
sleeves, but wore a threadbare velvet jacket. He had a
coarse face, large teeth, high cheek-bones, and a receding
chin and forehead. His cheeks glistened from having been
freshly shaved, and his thick black hair was pushed back
without a parting. His gray eyes were a trifle blood-shot
and had an indescribably dissipated look. It was difficult
to conceive of a more perfect combination of brutality and
weakness than his features exhibited. There was something in his manner—a certain flashiness and florid civil-
ity—which made Aleck conclude that he was an ex-barber
or perhaps an ex-waiter in a fashionable restaurant. "*Je
vous demande mille pardons, monsieur, et madame,*" he began,
bowing with the abruptness of a jumping jack, "ah, you
spik not French ? My vife ; she know not vhich you vas.
You come in ? It is vell. You know ze Comtesse Kharlovitz, yes ? It maque me much plaisir to see you here."

Talking and bowing incessantly, he led the way into a
rather cheaply furnished parlor, the air of which was close
and pervaded with a strong smell of opium. On a small
marble-topped table stood a dainty coffee-pot, a pint bottle
of Haute Sauterne, and other remnants of a light French
breakfast. The carpet, which was a rich Axminster, was
dusty and covered with spots. Here and there on the
floor lay champagne corks, and under a chair a crumpled
and stained napkin was visible. There had apparently
been a carousal of some sort in the room, the night before, and there had been no time to remove its last traces.

"You is Miss Larkins, yes ?" said the polite host, pointing with a large flourish to a chair, upon which Gertrude
sank down, because her knees seemed too weak to support
her. "I am Count Kharlovitz, you hear of me, yes? I
am your muzzer's us-band. You permit me to smoke ?
Ze comtess, she maque her *toilette ;* she not vell, *non*, not
vary vell," here the count shook his head mournfully and
his voice became plaintive and sympathetic. "She have
vary bad sickness. Ze pain—*c'est affreux, mademoiselle, com-*

bien elle souffre—ze pain he roll her in a knot—*oui, je vous assure* she have vary bad pain."

Gertrude had not opened her mouth during this moving recital ; she had a sensation of dizziness, she could not persuade herself that that which she saw and heard was wholly and tangibly real. She had but one feeling for the man before her ; she felt degraded at listening to him ; he filled her with disgust. Her father had been right after all, and she had been wofully wrong in rejecting his advice. This was a scheme to entrap her, to extract money from her, and it was so barefaced, so transparent, that she could scarcely understand how she had failed to see through it.

Count Kharlovitz, perceiving that his eloquence did not elicit any response from Gertrude, turned his attention to Aleck, who was seated on a chair at the window.

"You is ze *fiancé* of Mademoiselle Larkin, monsieur?" he began, interrogatively.

"Oh, no ; nothing of the sort," said Aleck, blushing. "I am her cousin, and Mr. Larkin's nephew."

"Ah, yes ; ze *cousin ;* and your positiong, if you permit me as to be so free?"

"I am a lawyer, and for the present also a journalist."

"Ah, yes, a *journaliste, je comprend.* You compose for ze newspapare. It is a *grande* positiong, that positiong of *journaliste.*"

"That depends upon how you look at it. It is grand in possibilities, but it is not very grandly paid, at least not in the branch of it where I am working."

"Ah, you maque me surprise, *mais* zose *journalistes,* zay maque grande noise. Zay sell newspapare—zousand newspapare—milliong newspapare ; zay become rich, vary rich, zay build *palais,* zay live *en prince,* yes."

"Well, I've not gotten quite to that point yet," Aleck replied, smiling. " I have to build my palaces preliminarily in the air, because that is the cheapest building material I know of."

The count failed to catch the point of this remark, but pretended, nevertheless, to find it highly interesting.

"You say ze building is chip, en *Amérique,*" he ejaculated, dubiously ; "*mais non* ze rent, *le loyer de maison* it is not chip. A man he live *en prince* in France for what he pay for house in *Amérique.*"

The same plaintive voice which Gertrude had heard before now called the count, and he arose and opened the folding doors to the next-room. With his peculiar springy

step, which expressed an exaggerated alertness, he entered
the bedchamber, and presently returned, bowed to Gertrude and said :

"Miss Larkin, your muzzer will have ze *plaisir* to see
you."

Gertrude rose reluctantly, and looked appealingly at
Aleck.

"Can my cousin go with me?" she asked.

"No, your muzzer—she have much pain ; she suffare
vary much.　She see you *seule*—how say you—she see you
wiz herself."

The smell of drugs in the adjoining room, as Gertrude
entered it, was overpowering.　The air was so close that
she felt as if she must gasp for breath.　It was a sickening
bedroom odor, dead, oppressive, and heavy.　There were
evidences round about of a hasty effort at putting things
in order ; but a mass of female attire lay in a heap on a
lounge, and everything that met the eye of the young girl
was soiled and untidy.　There was one large window looking upon a court-yard ; but the shade was drawn down,
leaving the room in twilight.　Coming from the light
parlor, Gertrude could not immediately adapt her vision to
the dusk ; and it took her some seconds to discover that
the count had closed the door behind her and that he was
himself standing at her side.　A horrible fright took possession of her ; but she had yet self-control enough to keep
from betraying it.

"Open the door, please," she said, quietly.

"*Mais* ze light, it pain ze ice of your muzzer."

"Never mind, I want that door opened, and I want you
to leave me."

"*Mais, mademoiselle,* I am ze us-band of your muzzer——"

"It does not matter ; I want you to leave me ; or I shall
call my cousin."

The count hesitated a moment, as if he would give her
time to reconsider so unreasonable a request.　Then seeing her determination he cocked his head dubiously,
spread his palms and with his expressive shoulder shrug,
said: "*Comme vous voudrez, mademoiselle,*" and opened the
door.　Gertie, as soon as he had left her, threw a glance
over her shoulder to make sure that Aleck was yet within
calling distance, and then advanced cautiously to the middle of the floor.　In a large mahogany bed she discovered
a dark human head outlined against the pillow ; and she
heard a heavy stertorous breathing.　As she became ac-

customed to the dimness, she perceived also that a pair of
dark glassy eyes were vaguely fixed upon her. With a
sense of intolerable oppression she stepped up to the bed ;
she felt as if she must cry out, but could not. All her
soul was in tumult down in the depths ; but on the surface
there was a nightmarish calm which she was powerless to
break.

"Sit down, my child;" said a stertorous whisper from the
pillows; "I have been waiting for you. I could not die
without seeing you."

Gertrude was not heartless ; on the contrary she was emotional and affectionate, and her tears came easily. If she
had not had a recollection of the lively altercation which
she had heard from the hall but a few minutes ago she
would have been all sorrow and tenderness. But having
once had her suspicion aroused she could not again lull
it to sleep. She felt convinced that this impressive *mise-
en-scène* was devised especially to move her ; and the very
illness itself and the symptoms of approaching dissolution
were pretences and lies, invented for sordid purposes. It
was a relief to her to think that it was this dreadful man,
under whose sway her mother had fallen, who had compelled her to write her mendacious letter, and who was
responsible for this last cruel mockery.

"Does your father know that you are here ?" whispered
the invalid, her dim eyes gradually kindling into a more
vivid consciousness.

"Yes," answered Gertrude.

"Did he give his consent to your going ?"

"No."

"What did he say ? "

"He said I should never come back. He does not want
to see me again."

The sadness of the situation possessed her with overwhelming force, as she uttered these words, and the tears
coursed slowly down her cheeks. Her mother sighed
heavily, but said nothing. Gertrude observed with pain
how unwholesome she looked. The black rings about her
eyes were larger and darker than ever ; and all the creases
in her face had a strange duskiness which seemed positively uncanny. Her skin between these creases had no
small wrinkles but was puffy and glassy, and the dark,
vague pupils of her eyes filled the whole opening of the
lids, blending imperceptibly with the iris.

"Give me your hand," she murmured after a pause ; and

Gertrude, though she shrank from her touch, obeyed. But she could not suppress the shudder that shook her from head to foot, as her cool healthy hand came in contact with the hot, pulpy, satiny palm of the invalid.

"I want to tell you, Gertrude," the latter continued in a plaintive murmur, "how shamefully your father maltreated me."

"No, no," exclaimed the girl, eagerly; "you told me that once before."

"I haven't told you half of what I have suffered."

"But I don't want to know it. I don't want you to speak ill of my father."

"Then you love him, do you?"

There was a sudden spiteful energy in this query, which contrasted with the die-away murmur which had preceded it.

"Yes, I love him," Gertrude answered with bold earnestness.

"O my God," sighed the Countess, reviving rapidly, "to think that I have brought a child into the world who loves her mother's murderer."

She turned toward the wall and began to weep hysterically. Gertrude, with a pang in her heart, stood gazing at her without the least stirring of sympathy. She could scarcely bring herself to believe that this was her mother, to whom she owed her very life, and to whom she was bound by the closest and most sacred ties. A dull and callous heaviness settled upon her mind, and made her impervious to all emotion. She had but one desire and that was to be gone. If she could but find an excuse for interrupting the interview, she would not linger another moment. It seemed an age since she entered this dreadful place, and she imagined that she was being slowly impregnated with its poison. She yearned to get out into the pure, blessed air, and the bright, free light of heaven. But the thought of the secret she was to learn, somehow, restrained her; and she stood irresolutely gazing about her, and wondering whether she should take courage and tear herself away. Obeying a blind impulse she went to the window and rolled the shade half way up; and the sight of the sunshiny world without kindled her energy. It became plain to her in a moment that the secret might be a malicious invention which might bring disquietude and unhappiness into her life—which, being incapable either of proof or of disproof, would furnish fresh fuel for torturing reflection. She determined to ward off this secret at all hazards. A dim sense of duty protested weakly against this resolution, but lacked vitality to assert itself. She turned again toward the bed, took her mother's listless hand and said : "Good-by."

The countess started into a half-sitting posture with an unpremeditated energy of which in the next moment she repented ; for she sank back among the pillows with a groan and whimpered :

"Oh, you must not leave me, Gertrude. You must stay with me, and close my dying eyes. I have not many days left on earth."

"I am sorry," Gertrude answered firmly ; "but I cannot."

She was anxious to cut this harrowing conversation short, and moved rapidly toward the door.

"Oh, I knew it," cried her mother after her ; "you are as cruel and heartless as your father. You are like *him ;* you trample upon a bleeding heart ; you——"

Two or three more accusations were hurled after her in a screaming crescendo, but she did not hear them. The Count, seeing that his wife was going off into hysterics, drew the folding doors tightly, and pushed forward a chair in which he invited Gertrude to be seated. But she ignored the invitation, and Aleck, who was no less anxious to be gone, rose to his feet and seized his hat and cane.

"You stay, *un moment* and spik wiz me, *mademoiselle?"* Count Kharlovitz began, with his obsequious smile.

"No, thanks," Gertrude answered, "I must be gone."

"*Mais, mademoiselle,* you put *monaye* wiz me for your muzzer? She have no monaye, *non.* I have monaye in Poland, but my bruzzer—he promeese to send, but he not send. I vait long time ; but he leave me *desolé*—no friends, no monaye, no nozzing in a stranch land."

He accompanied this speech with the liveliest gesticulations, demonstrating his grief at his brother's mendacity and his utter desolation. Gertrude, who was quite prepared for such a request, opened her pocket-book, in which there was but ten dollars. She was a little ashamed of offering so small a sum, but nevertheless dropped two fivedollar bills, half apologetically, upon the table. The Count picked them up, looked at them with acute disappointment, and again dropped them upon the table.

"*Mais, mademoiselle,*" he said in a tone of reproach and offended dignity ; "you maque me vary sad. Ten dollare, zat is not vhat I expec from a daughtare to a muzzer. She

have vary bad pain—your muzzer—and she need mediceene, vary expensive mediceene, and she have no monaye."

He addressed this plausible remonstrance to Gertrude ;
but turned every moment to Aleck, as if calling him to witness to the entire reasonableness of his position. Aleck,
however, supposed that he was being included in the appeal for further contributions, and partly to rehabilitate
Gertrude's self-respect, partly to make an end of an embarrassing scene, he added a twenty-dollar bill to the two
abashed fives. The Count, whose expectation had evidently been raised to a high pitch by Aleck's movement
to his pocket, picked up the bank-note between his thumb
and his forefinger and laughed contemptuously.

"Zay Americains," he ejaculated with a gesture of mock
respect, "zay is *grande* people. Zay have zirty dollare for
ze tears, and ze groans, and ze pains of a dying muzzer.
Zay have——"

Aleck, who found that this comedy had now gone about
far enough, did not permit the count to finish.

"I must beg of you," he interrupted, with an angry
flash in his eye, "to restrain your tongue in this lady's
presence."

"You have insolence to ask me to 'old my tong,"
cried the Polander with rising ire ; "I tich you to spik
zat vay to a nobleman."

Aleck had managed during this tirade to tear the door
open, and had gotten himself and Gertrude out into the
hall. They made haste to descend the stairs, while the
count stood leaning over the bannister, hurling the
coarsest abuse after them. They entered the cab which
stood waiting in the street, and sat gazing at each other
in dumfounded silence, while the wheels rattled away
over the pavement.

CHAPTER XXXII.

THE FINGER OF DESTINY.

Gertrude was confronted with a problem which demanded an immediate solution. If she returned home, in spite of her father's warning, would he receive and forgive her, or would he make a scandal and show her the door? After having considered the question from all sides, she could not help inclining to the belief that he would do the latter. That he was in the right and she in the wrong, she willingly conceded; but she knew that to him that was not sufficient. She ought to have accepted his judgment without submitting it to the test of experience. She remembered now (though in her excitement it had not previously occurred to her) that he voluntarily paid his divorced wife $1,500 per annum, and that, accordingly, the intrigue, of which she had been the blind tool, had been nothing but a blackmailing scheme. She bowed herself in the dust and revelled in humiliation, when she thought of the lofty enthusiasm with which she had set out on this enterprise, and its wretched and disgraceful outcome. Was it then possible that she was so ignorant of reality, so incapable of judgment, so utterly unequipped for the battle of life? What wonder that men treat the opinions of women so superciliously, if they are really so worthless as guides of action. Gertrude vowed that she would never trust herself again; never set up her own will against that of her father.

It flashed through her brain that if her father had been in the right, then she had also been unjust to Dr. Hawk. But, somehow, her fancy did not warm into sympathy with this reflection. As she thought back upon the scene of her parting with the doctor, she became doubly convinced that his conduct had been outrageous. She could not determine exactly wherein his offence consisted; but that he had been unfeeling, sordid, abominable, that was as certain as the stars in heaven. The halo had utterly faded from his head; and though, rationally considered, he had not been so absolutely wrong, she could not think of him except with a sense of resentment and outrage.

But Gertrude's inability to excuse the doctor made her only the more ardently contrite as regards the wrong she had done her father. She concluded that she would not start home without having first received his permission. She was unwilling to trust the kind of message she wished to send him to the publicity of the telegraph ; for the lady operator in Torryville was an acquaintance and former schoolmate of hers, and not distinguished for discretion. She would therefore be obliged to remain two or three days in the city, until she could obtain an answer to a letter which she would not delay writing. Aleck, who cordially coincided in whatever she proposed, introduced her, forthwith, to a lady who kept a genteel boarding-house on Madison Avenue, and before nightfall Gertrude found herself comfortably installed in a room which looked out upon a long stretch of backyards, filled with fluttering undergarments hung out to dry. She lost no time in dispatching her letter, which was written out of the fulness of her repentant heart ; and then composed her soul in patience, being confident that the reply would soon be forthcoming. Aleck in the meanwhile, with the recklessness of a millionaire, had promised to disburse out of his abundance the $18 per week which was required to pay her board, and showed in all respects a charming solicitude to remove every stone from her path. In spite of her resolution to be contrite, her elastic spirit rebounded with a humiliating ease, and she could not with her best will maintain a becoming air of lugubrious resignation. New York with its noisy turmoil exhilarated her. She walked up the broad bright Avenue with a positive sense of enjoyment, which she knew was unbecoming, but which she could not help. The endless procession of carriages going to and coming from the Park, the richly attired ladies, reclining on their cushions with majestic ease, the clatter of the horseshoes against the pavement, all the gay pageantry of life in this great metropolis filled her with a child-like pleasure. She had been in New York before, to be sure ; but then she had been a school-girl, and had to promenade in a procession with a blonde pig-tail down her back, watched over by two subacid old maids. She had seen very little then ; and the system of education of which she had been the victim had had for its object not to open her senses, but rather to close them. How much more delightful it was to walk with Aleck, who was so droll and witty, and with the enthusiasm of a recent arrival showed off the sights of the town to his rural cousin. He felt so metropolitan while engaged in this agreeable occupation, and never grew in the least angry when she twitted him on the fine air of proprietorship which he had acquired during his brief sojourn.

It was inevitable that Aleck's own affairs should sooner or later become the theme of discussion. His literary aspirations, it appeared, were as yet unrealized ; nor had his efforts to get a footing in journalism been a brilliant success. He occupied a very uncertain kind of position, as a writer on space on a leading daily; but his copy, which usually was destined for the Sunday edition, was so mercilessly slashed into by a malevolent person, named Ramshaw (who had taken an unconquerable dislike to him) that the pay amounted to next to nothing. He had spoken seriously to Ramshaw, and remonstrated against the kind of treatment to which he subjected him ; but that worthy was so drunk with power that he would listen to no reason. He had even intimated to Aleck that if he did not guard his tongue, it would afford him satisfaction to bounce him. To a man who had long been his own master and practised law with a fair degree of success, it was, of course, a trial to have to put up with such insolence. Aleck's chief consolation, amid these tribulations, was the hope that, some day, he might be in a position to retaliate. And then, woe unto Henry P. Ramshaw ! It were better for that editor if he had never been born !

The zest, the sympathy, the eager interest with which Gertrude listened to the tale of his sorrows were a great comfort to Aleck. That anybody could be base enough to persecute such a dear, droll, kind-hearted fellow as Aleck was more than she could comprehend. She had never heard anything so extraordinary as the things he told her. And her heart went out to him with a sweet spontaneity which made him almost congratulate himself on his misfortunes because they brought him such exquisite compensation. During these days which would be, alas ! too brief, he gave himself up completely to the enjoyment of his cousin's society. He was in a state of felicity the like of which he had never experienced before. He walked on air, he quaffed the cup of joy in long, deep draughts. His troubles, which before her arrival had preyed upon him and made him moody, became now mere matters of history that lost all power to annoy him. He began to nourish a hope which, a few months ago, would have seemed to him the height of madness. For, why should she be so bewitchingly sweet to him, laugh with such a delicious relish at his jokes, and accept all his attentions with such a child-like directness and ravishing grace, if she did not mean to encourage his love for her? That he loved her, she knew well enough; had, indeed, known it before he was quite sure of it himself. She was not heartless; was she, then, capable of playing with his devotion for her own amusement in order to beguile an idle hour?

It was a curious thing that Gertrude did not seriously propound to herself this query. She had, in fact, no relish for any kind of problem, for the present; and would have liked to live on from day to day, and have others decide every troublesome question, without consulting her. Although the three days in which she had expected to hear from her father were past, without bringing any response to her letter, she did not at first take his silence much to heart. She had passed through so many emotions during the last month, that it seemed as if her nature had exhausted itself and she was thoughtlessly luxuriating in indolent repose. She had no conscience for the present, and did not want any. If Aleck had proposed to her, she would have been annoyed, not necessarily because she did not love him, but because loving was more or less fatiguing, and she wished to be left in peace. She was, indeed, as she cheerfully admitted, very fond of Aleck, and was not at all indifferent to his fondness for her. But she hoped he would behave discreetly and make no scenes.

But this suspensive calm could not last forever. When ten days had elapsed without any letter or message from Torryville, it began to dawn upon Gertrude that her father had disowned her. He had kept his word; she had received due warning and had no cause for complaint. She had hoped he would relent; but had she really believed that he would? No, she had not. Her momentary abandonment to pleasure had been a mere forcible staving off of the evil hour which she knew would be coming. She could now postpone no longer the decision of her fate. But she was too wrought up, too distressed, to decide rationally. She lay awake through the small hours of the night, planning and thinking, until her head seemed on the point of splitting. She imagined herself returning,

like a prodigal daughter, and flinging herself penitently at
her father's feet ; but fine as this seemed, abstractly considered, her temperament rebelled against it; and the voice
of prudence also told her that that was not the way to impress Obed Larkin. He had no sense of the dramatic, and
could not be counted upon to play the rôle which had
been assigned to him. On the whole, she liked him better
for this very cross-grained quality in him which made him
so stubborn and unadaptable. She felt sorry for him,
knowing well that he would grieve for her ; and yet see no
way of getting her back. The thought that she might
never see him again wrung her heart with pain. She saw
him wandering desolately through the big house in his
shiny dress suit, with his ancient deerskin slippers down
at the heels, with his broad stooping shoulders, shaking
from time to time his white obstinate head in vague remonstrance against the ways of Providence. She had
never been of much comfort to him, perhaps, while she
was with him ; but she had a dim consciousness that it had
been a satisfaction to him to see her, and that he would
miss her sorely now that she was gone.

Since, then, the homeward way was cut off, it behooved
Gertrude to think of other expedients. She concluded
that she must go to work and earn her own living. There
was a kind of romantic satisfaction in this resolution
which appealed to her. It was such a fine thing for a
young woman to issue that declaration of independence
which emancipates her from her thraldom to the male sex
and entitles her to pursue, in her own way, life, liberty,
and happiness. The only trouble, in Gertrude's case, was
to decide how she should achieve this delightful independence. She ran over her accomplishments in her mind,
and arrived at the conclusion that not one of them had a
marketable value. The thing she could do best was to
draw ; but she had had no systematic training and had no
idea how to set about imparting her knowledge to others.
Her modelling was just good enough to make it distressing that it was not better ; and in music she had reached
about as far as King George III., who, as his teacher asserted, had advanced from the class of those who did not
play at all, into the class of those who played badly. It
occurred to her that she might enlist the interest of Kate
Van Schaak, who was rich and powerful and had a great
clientèle of dependents. But there her pride rebelled. To
appear before Kate as a petitioner and be patronized and

condescended to—she would rather starve than do that.
In the end there was nothing to do but to appeal to Aleck.
He had never yet disappointed her confidence.   With this
comforting reflection she finally drifted into unconsciousness, just as the dawn was peeping through the shutters.

When she woke up, it was nearly nine o'clock.   The sun
shone through the shades with subdued brightness, and
sent across her bed a shaft of unobscured light in which
particles of illuminated dust were dancing.   She reached
out for a handglass and observed her face critically.   She
could not deny to herself that it was a handsome face ;
though she suspected that Aleck exaggerated its loveliness.   But if she were to go to work now, sewing or teaching or clerking, would not this beauty rather be a disadvantage to her ?   And would she not be likely to lose it,
wasting the midnight oil, toiling for the mere pittance
she required to keep soul and body together ?   She tried
to imagine how she would look, a year hence, or two years
hence, and shuddered at the picture which her fancy conjured up.

She was interrupted in her reverie by a knock at the
door.   It was the chambermaid, who brought her Aleck's
card.   He was the same stanch standby in times of peace
and in times of trouble.

" Tell him to wait," said Gertrude, suppressing a yawn.
" I'll be down presently."

She had a strong disinclination to get up and begin in
earnest the battle of life.   The act seemed half symbolic ;
and she felt in all the joints of her young beautiful body a
delicious indolence.   However, there was no help for it ;
she arose out of her bed with a languid stateliness as I
imagine Venus must have risen from the foam of the sea.
She dressed with leisurely deliberation (she rarely was in
haste about anything), and at the end of three-quarters of
an hour descended into the parlor, where Aleck was schooling his patience, studying two atrocious portraits of the
landlady and her defunct husband in their wedding attire.

"Good-morning, Aleck," she said, in response to his
greeting, " I suppose you hate me for having kept you
waiting so long."

"Yes," said Aleck, smiling, " I have just arrived at the
point when I should like to rend you to pieces."

" All right," she answered, " I wish you would.   It would
save me a heap of trouble."

" Trouble ? " he inquired, sympathetically ; " why, I

thought we had the sea of trouble behind us, and were now comfortably landed on the shore."

"Yes, or stranded on the shore," Gertrude suggested, lugubriously.

Aleck scarcely knew what to answer. His thought reverted to Count Kharlovitz and his wife as the only source from which trouble might be expected. He shuddered at the possibility of further dealings with people so utterly lost to all shame. It was therefore a relief to him when his cousin continued:

"I haven't heard a word from father yet, and you know what that means."

"I think I do, Gertie," he said, gently.

They sat looking at each other in silence for some moments. The consciousness of his love for her pervaded him like a quickening warmth ; and the sense of his responsibility for her, and his protectorship over her, filled him with tenderness. Yet he was unable to suppress a thrill of pleasure at her absolute dependence upon him. Not that he intended in any way to take advantage of this dependence. But was not the finger of Destiny visible in this complication of circumstances which had brought them so closely together, when he had resignedly blown out the flame of hope and turned his back on his dream of happiness ? There is a kind of innocent fatalism to which we are all more or less subject ; and Aleck derived an exquisite delight from contemplating the benevolent machinations of Providence in his behalf.

"What do you propose to do, Gertie ?" he asked, taking pity on her helplessness.

"I have got to do something to earn my living. And I wanted to ask you what I had better try."

He was on the point of saying : "Try to have me earn your living for you," but a fortunate instinct arrested the words on his tongue. He knew from of old that this beautiful girl whom he aspired to make his was a bundle of incalculable impulses, and that a jarring remark, betraying an ever so trifling lack of delicacy, might ruin his cause forever. "I will do what I can, Gertie," he said, heartily ; "but you know I have few connections in this city, and none that are valuable."

They discussed the matter for half an hour, and then started for the down-town newspaper offices, and inserted advertisements. They also called at several business houses in response to advertisements for clerks and office assistants; but as short-hand or a knowledge of the type-writer were invariably required, their success was not encouraging. Gertrude then took the heroic resolution to learn the use of the type-writer; and Aleck promptly hired one for her and had it moved to her room. She made very slow progress, however, and grew hopeless and despondent. Sometimes she set out alone, with the courage of ignorance, answering advertisements; and had the most humiliating experiences. Her striking beauty, her disdainful air, and her handsome clothes, made her the subject of curious conjecture. A Sunday newspaper contained a rather disrespectful allusion to her; and Aleck, who was a little quixotic in such matters, came near making a scandal at the Press Club, when he learned by whom the squib was written. But by slapping the man's face as he had intended, he would have given Gertrude a disastrous notoriety; and this reflection sobered him before he had committed any folly.

A month passed. February was nearing its end; slush and rain lasting for weeks, depressed the buoyant metropolitan temper, and quotations in Wall Street dropped from sheer meteorological despondency. Gertrude had conceived an animosity to the type-writer which made her yearn to demolish it; and short-hand, she declared, plunged her into despair the moment she looked at it. She had the most terrific attacks of melancholy, during which she lay on her bed, stared at the ceiling, and refused to answer when any one addressed her. She seemed to be in a semi-comatose condition; nothing appealed to her; nothing interested her; nothing seemed worth the raising of a hand to avert or to obtain. Her meals, which were served in her room, she sent away untouched; and Aleck's anxious messages she left unanswered. The doctor whom he sent to call upon her had to prescribe something to save his own self-respect; but it was obvious to Aleck that he was as much puzzled as the rest. One remark, however, which he let fall became, in later years, charged with significance.

"She has poor nerves," the doctor said.

"Poor nerves!" exclaimed Aleck, resentfully. It seemed to him an impertinence, on the doctor's part, to assert that anything belonging to Gertie was poor.

"Yes, most of our young women have poor nerves," declared the leech, impassively; "some inherit a shattered nervous system, some shatter it themselves."

But, as if to refute this unpleasant insinuation, Gertrude appeared at dinner that night, clothed and in her right mind ; and showed no other effects of her fast than a certain lassitude and a weary acquiescence in everything that was said or proposed to her. Aleck was so overjoyed to see her, when he called in the evening, that he could hardly restrain his emotion.

"You have given us an awful fright, Gertie," he exclaimed, as he gazed into her unresponsive eyes, and pressed her hands, warmly.

" Whom ? " she inquired, listlessly.

" Me," he answered, flushing with pleasure, as a faint smile curled her lips.

" I hope you are very well, now."

"Yes, very well."

If she had said very ill, she could not have said it more despondently.

"Why do you speak that way, dear ? Why don't you brace up and tell me you are glad to see me ? "

" Life, life, life ! " she murmured absently, quite unconscious that she was echoing Dr. Hawk.

" Tell me why you are so sad, dear. Is there anything I can do for you ? "

"No, nothing."

Her listlessness cut him to the heart. To speak to her was like butting against a stone wall. Yet he returned to the charge once more, determined, if possible, to rouse her from her apathy.

"Don't you think, Gertie," he asked, quietly, "that I have deserved a little consideration from you ? Couldn't you confide in me a little bit ? "

She looked at him mutely, while her eyes slowly filled.

"Aleck," she cried, breaking into a storm of sobs "Don't you see what a miserable, worthless thing I am ? "

She flung herself down on the sofa, covered her face with her hands, and abandoned herself to her grief. He always felt helpless in the presence of a weeping woman ; and half guilty because of his helplessness. He stood looking at her, his gentle face distorted with acute distress. He noted how her shoulders shook, and he noted too the deep groove in her neck where the back hair was gathered up ; and he could not have told why he became possessed with an irrational desire to stoop down and kiss it. There was something appealing and childlike in that neck which brought the tears to his eyes and thrilled him

18

with a yearning tenderness.   He made no attempt to console her ; knowing that it would be vain.   But when the
first vehemence of her emotion had spent itself, he seated
himself at her side and slipped his hand into hers.   She
feebly returned its pressure, and grew calmer.   It was as
if his touch soothed and comforted her.   After a while
she raised herself into a sitting posture and began to fum-
ble for her handkerchief.   She looked persistently away
from him until she had found it.   Then she did it up into
a little ball and pressed it against her eyes.   " You mustn't
mind my foolishness, Aleck," she said, catching her
breath, like a child who has been crying.   "You know I
can't help it.   I'm so miserable."

There was imminent danger of another outbreak, but
Aleck, in his anxiety to prevent it, put his arm about her
waist and drew her unresistingly toward him, and then her
wondrous head lay upon his breast, and her warm breath
wandered over his face. Oh, how beautiful she was ! How
touchingly beautiful and precious ! The pure blue depth
of her eyes, with the strange flame-like lines in the iris,
was so innocent, so devoid of reflection.   He marvelled at
his own audacity—that he could hold her thus—feel her
heart beat against his—and yet the earth continued on its
ancient round and the sun stood unmoved in the heavens.
The stars did not break into a jubilant pæan, as they might
have been expected to do, in order to celebrate so great an
event.   The eternal, beautiful mystery of sex, which to a
pure-minded, virginal man like Aleck was doubly mysterious, filled him with reverential tenderness.   He loved this
girl, had loved her as long as he could remember.   He had
seen her and talked with her daily for many years.   And yet
there was something remote and strange about her, something divinely awe-inspiring ; because she was that wonderful, inscrutable, exquisite, and adorable thing— a woman.
Aleck was thrilled with this consciousness ; she was not
his cousin Gertie whom he had known and quarrelled
with in Torryville ; but she was a lovely embodiment of
a sublime fact of Nature.   She was born to suffer as he
would never suffer.   She was born to be loved as he
could never be loved.   She was the last and best pinnacle
of God's works ; the supreme result of God's creative intelligence.

Aleck made no attempt to formulate these feelings as
they surged through his soul.   His head was in a whirl ;
he thought with a delicious dimness ; but he felt with a

delicious acuteness. He did not speak, for it seemed a
pity to mar such a glorious fulness of feeling with poor
shrill words. This high-tide of pure emotion and noble
bliss comes but once in a life, while the soul is young and
the heart unspoiled, and to the great crowd of super-
civilized creatures it comes never at all. The golden age
survives in a few hearts, and the tree of life still yields a
noble fruit to the man and the woman whom God created,
and it can never lose its sweetness. Aleck found himself
drawn by an irresistible force closer and closer to the girl
who lay in his arms ; he bent his head over her and he
kissed her again and again. She uttered no protest, but
looked at him with eyes full of dewy brightness. It was a
luxury to her to feel his protecting arm, to see the sweet affection that beamed out of his eyes, to hear the caressing murmur of his voice, as he told her of his love. She was conscious of no wild ineffable delight such as his. There was
little of the divine flutter and agitation such as she had
experienced when she pledged herself to Hawk. She was
like a storm-beaten dove that tumbles wearily into an open
doorway and rests, rejoicing in its security. If Gertrude
had not been fond of Aleck she would not have accepted
the refuge he offered her ; but she had no clear idea of anything except an imperious desire to be rid of the responsibility for her own future. She thought, perhaps, she loved
him. The kindness she felt toward him ; the respect she
entertained for his character ; and above all her trust in his
good, staunch, faithful heart may have appeared to her
hardly distinguishable from love.

"I am afraid you have made a bad bargain, dear," she
said to him, smiling with languid radiance. "I am a poor,
useless thing, and I shan't be any help to you at all."

"My sweet girl," he cried, and it seemed as if his heart
must burst with happiness. "My darling girl !"

"Poor Aleck," she murmured, with an expression half
tender, half compassionate. "My poor Aleck !"

He did not suspect that she was thinking of Dr. Hawk,
and pitying him that he could enjoy with such rapture the
leavings from another's table. For she was no longer in
her own sight as precious, as proudly unattainable as she
had been. She could not quite get rid of an uneasy sense
of guilt, as her memory stung her with dimly remembered
scenes. Was she not defrauding this dear, guileless cousin
of hers in allowing him to quaff the turbid goblet she was
holding to his lips as if it were the bright, immortal nectar ?

And yet, why should she spoil his ecstacy ? Why begrudge him the full measure of his joy ?

She lay long passively in his arms, smiling at him with the same dewy brightness, accepting his passionate caresses, feeling the blood surge with a luxurious fulness through her veins. She arose at the sound of an imaginary knock at the door ; and then the mood was spoiled and did not return. They walked for half an hour arm in arm up and down the floor, and discussed rationally their plans for the future. It was decided that they were to marry without delay, and Aleck was to write to Mr. Larkin and ask his consent. If this consent was withheld, they concluded to notify Mr. Larkin of the marriage after it was consummated. Of course, they would have to commence their house-keeping in a small way; for Aleck was scarcely making a living for himself, nor were his prospects particularly brilliant. Gertie, with all her accomplishments, was not an eminent economist, and knew about as much of the value of money as she knew of differential calculus. The $3,200 which Aleck had brought with him from Torryville, and which constituted his entire worldly possessions, appeared to her quite an imposing sum, and the deplorable fact that about $800 had to be deducted for excess of expenditure over income since his arrival in New York made no perceptible impression upon her. She was ready for every sacrifice ; nay, gloried in the prospect of poverty and self-immolation, because she hoped in that way to make up her sentimental account with Aleck. She did not hint, even to herself, that she had taken him as a *pis aller;* but she felt that, compared to the great and rapturous love which he had flung at her feet, the sentiment which she entertained for him was a feeble and worthless thing ; and it was therefore a satisfaction that the future would afford her a chance of doing penance.

A week after the day of their engagement Aleck and Gertrude were married, without having heard from Mr. Larkin. They went to a Congregational clergyman in Brooklyn, in company with two members of the Press Club, who acted as witnesses. They went on a wedding journey on the elevated road to High Bridge and Washington Heights, and after having boarded for a week, hired a pretty flat of four rooms and kitchen in the seventh story of the Patagonia apartment house. About that time Aleck met by chance Henry Thurlow, a former classmate of his in Larkin University, who was about to found a school for boys in the region on the west side of Central Park. They had not been particularly congenial in their college days; but they now took a great liking to each other, and the end of it was that Aleck accepted an engagement from Thurlow, as teacher of English and history, at a salary of $1,200 a year. The problem of bare existence was thus preliminarily solved; if there was one man in the city of New York who was supremely happy, that man was Alexander Larkin.

CHAPTER XXXIII.

HORACE GOES A WOOING.

When the Honorable Horace Larkin heard of his brother's marriage, his first reflection was that Aleck must in some way have gotten a glimpse of his uncle's will. He could not otherwise have committed the folly of marrying so disagreeable a girl as Gertrude ; for Horace had always professed inability to discover any charm in Gertrude. On second thought, however, he receded from this opinion, first, because he did not see how his brother could have gained the intelligence he attributed to him ; and secondly because, with his generous Quixotism, Aleck would be perfectly capable of walking straight into the trap which that artfully innocent minx of a girl had set for him. She had by this time found out that Hawk was a knave, Horace reasoned, and having grown tired of him had deliberately involved Aleck in her toils. It is needless to say that the honorable legislator would have entertained a higher respect for his brother, if he had speculated in Gertrude's affection with an eye to securing her fortune. It was a great question, however, whether such a speculation would have proved profitable ; for the old man was quite capable of punishing his daughter's disobedience by substituting some other name for hers in his last will and testament. Horace was, however, for the time being, too absorbed in his own affairs to be greatly perturbed by any body else's blunders. He had scarcely been a month in the legislature before he was recognized as a considerable personage. He made very little noise ; disappointed frequently by his vote those of his constituents who had supported him because he was "a gentleman," and played a discreet but skilful game with the one view of obtaining power. The lobbyists who approached him with corrupt propositions could never quite make out whether he was too high-toned to be bribed or was holding out for a higher figure. He displayed no moral indignation ; but fenced dexterously with jokes and humorous anecdotes. Some main-

tained that he made fun of them to their faces; others
(where it served his purpose to make that impression) regarded him as a harmless, jolly dog who had gone into
politics chiefly for his amusement. For all that the impression gradually gained ground that he was too rich to
be bribed; and his colleagues were inclined to concede
that under such circumstances honesty was not a bad
policy.

It was during a legislative recess about Easter that
Horace resolved to carry out a plan which, since his departure from Torryville, had never been absent from his
mind. He had asked Kate Van Schaak, when he took
leave of her at the railroad station, whether she would
permit him to call upon her in New York; and she had,
after a moment's hesitation, granted him the permission.
Knowing well the import of this diplomatic pause, he had
concluded not to be in a hurry; and Kate began to fear
that she had overdone her diplomacy when the whole
winter had passed without his darkening her doorway.
She thought of him frequently, sometimes with pleasure,
sometimes with irritation. She found it hard to forgive
him for appearing to hold in such light esteem a privilege
which she granted to so few. She could not quite make
up her mind whether she liked or disliked him; she would
have been grateful to any one who could have settled that
question for her. He had invaded her life, as the Goths
and Vandals did the well-ordered, civilized Roman Em-
pire, and it was impossible to get rid of him again. He
was a man whom one could hate, but not ignore. Nay,
he was a man, who, if he were a little more civilized, she
would be capable of loving.

Kate was sitting with her writing desk on her lap, in-
dicting a letter to a young curate whom she permitted to
draw upon her for a stated monthly sum, in aid of his
charities. Having finished the letter in a clear English
caligraphy (which was full of character and very different
from the high-shouldered American girl's hand) she signed
a check for $250 and directed the envelope. She heard the
butler's knock at the door and bade him enter. The card
which he presented upon the silver salver bore the name
Horace Larkin. She noted the absence of *Mr.* and the
florid, Gaskel compendium style of script, which was no
longer in fashion.

"Tell the gentleman I'll be down presently," she said,
stooping to hide the blush that sprang to her cheek.

It was so contrary to her principles to betray eagerness
to see any one that she lingered for ten or fifteen minutes
before the mirror, arranging her hair, shaking the skirt of
her dress into the proper folds, contemplating her back
view in a hand glass, perfuming her handkerchief, and
judging critically the effect of each decorative touch she
bestowed upon her stately person. She wore a dress of
dull blue stuff, of perfect fit, cut with impressive simplicity, and with a royal amplitude in the train. She descended the stairs, and with Olympian serenity entered
the parlor and greeted her visitor. He had spent his time
while waiting in studying the room, the magnificence of
which he was not connoisseur enough to appreciate. It
was finished in white and gold in the style of the *directoire*.
One wall was covered with a gobelin tapestry of the most
exquisite workmanship and coloring, representing an
eighteenth century *fête champêtre* full of delightful rococo
frivolity. Every piece of furniture, even including the
piano, which was finished in inlaid work and white enamel,
carried out the same effect, uniting into an indescribably
rich and harmonious *tout ensemble*. There were pictures
upon the wall, not one of which was allowed to obtrude
itself, though there was not one which was not worthy of
minute study. There was a Jérome, a Bouguereau, and
two charming Corots.

"I am very glad to see you, Mr. Larkin," said the damsel whose taste had found expression in this chaste splendor ; "won't you please be seated ?"

She spoke with just the proper degree of friendliness,
but quietly and without effusion. He had meant to say
something significant, as he grasped her hand ; but the
cool serenity of her manner chilled him, and made him
conclude not prematurely to expose his intentions. He—
Horace Larkin—was too important a person to be trifled
with ; and you could never tell what a girl of this kind
might do.

"Political life seems to agree with you," she continued,
seating herself in a white tapestried chair opposite to him ;
"you look well; you have the air of a conqueror."

"Then my air belies me," he answered, throwing his
resolution to the winds; "for in your presence I feel like
one conquered."

"Ah, Mr. Larkin," she rejoined with her calm, beautiful smile, "you have not lost your cleverness at repartee,
I observe. But you ought to remember that I am the

cousin of Bella Robbins, and I might take it into my head to report to her some of your fine speeches."

"I have no objection," he replied with a recklessness which he was far from feeling; "though I doubt if it would be a kindness to her."

Kate looked at him for a moment with a deepening seriousness. She did not quite know how to interpret that remark.

"I suppose," she said, with an assumed lightness of manner, "that I violate no confidence if I tell you that I know of your engagement."

"Then you know more than I do. I am no longer engaged to Miss Robbins."

She sat still as a statue for two or three seconds, and not a gleam of the joy that flared up within her was reflected in her face. His engagement had not presented itself to her as a serious obstacle, if she should conclude to encourage his advances; but still its rupture seemed, in a way, providential, and cleared away a host of doubts.

"I am afraid poor Bella will take that very much to heart," she said, in her most conventional tones; "she was quite fond of you."

He was on the point of answering jocosely that she was neither the first nor would she be the last; but the inappropriateness of this became suddenly apparent to him, as he glanced about the room. That kind of frontier humor required a different setting from the white and gold *à la directoire.*

"It was a sad affair to us both," he finally replied; "I mistook her; she mistook me."

Kate got up and rustled about the room in search of something. The very noise of her skirts, somehow, seemed to him delicious. A woman who moved with such pomp and circumstance—whose simplest act bore the impress of a stately self-respect—by God's rood that was the kind of woman he would like to attach to his life, to enrich, widen, and dignify it. He began to feel a little bit ashamed of his origin, as it dawned upon him how supremely civilized and refined Kate was in comparison with him. How poor and sordid his past had been; how simple his aspirations; how crude his ideals! Rustic though he was, he did not fail to perceive that she carried her head as no other woman did whom he had ever looked upon. And how exquisitely finished she was as to ears, and nails, and hands! And could anything be more perfect in its way, than that self-contained face, with its pure and placid beauty.

Horace made these reflections while the object of his admiration went to the piano and picked up a small gold bottle of smelling salts. She had broken off the conversation just long enough to afford the painful topic time for a decent burial. As she again seated herself, the sweet faint perfume that enveloped her was wafted toward him and the impression of her rich and rare quality became overwhelmingly vivid. It was a new experience for this self-complacent, supercilious villager to entertain, as he did in this moment, a doubt of his own admirableness and a lurking suspicion that he had, perhaps, been deceived in himself ; that, possibly, he was a little crude. But such as he was, he meant to try for this prize with all his might, and if there was strength and talent and virtue in him, he was resolved to strain them to the utmost in this enterprise.

"Tell me, Mr. Larkin," Kate began with the air of introducing a new topic, " why do you think it is that so few of our young men of good family and education go into politics ? "

"It is," Horace replied in his leisurely drawl, " because they are not fit for politics. They don't know enough."

"Why, you surprise me ! Is it your opinion, then, that those individuals from the liquor saloons and the slums who do govern us are the fittest to govern ? "

"No, they are deplorably unfit, but yet fitter than Anglomaniacs and blue-blooded Knickerbockers who squander their lives in laborious and vapid amusements, in coaching, riding after hounds, yawning in club windows, and in a hundred other ways aping the English aristocracy on a small and contemptible scale. The majority of our politicians are a low-lived lot, and many of them corrupt. But they have the courage to be American—crudely and uncompromisingly American—and that is, in my eyes, a virtue which is not to be lightly rated."

"And may I ask, Mr. Larkin, what do you mean by being American ? "

"Being frankly, ably, enterprisingly plebeian. It is the plebeian after all, who shall inherit the earth——"

"I beg your pardon. According to the Bible it is the meek."

" I must differ with the Bible, then ; for the meek, in my experience, if they inherit anything, never manage to keep it. It passes, sooner or later, into the hands of the strong,

the self-assertive, the grasping. But these, as you will admit, are plebeian characteristics. A universally prosperous,
comfortable, impudent, and enterprising mob—that is the
goal toward which we are steering ; and in my opinion it
is a good and desirable one."

It gave him satisfaction to enunciate these Jacobin sentiments, in all their naked offensiveness, because he was in
this very moment in danger of being unfaithful to them.
He cherished in his heart a vague hostility to the exclusive,
aristocratic world which he was aspiring to enter ; and he
resented his own weakness in finding that desirable which
he despised. The discussion continued for fifteen or
twenty minutes ; and he managed, as before, to impress
Kate greatly with his ability, his originality, and the distinctness of his personality. It was in this latter quality that she
discovered his charm. His ruthless, slam-bang style of
argument was such an entire novelty in the tepid, well-regulated atmosphere of her quiet and well-bred existence.
She had heard no man speak like that. And she believed
that the man who could speak like that was sufficiently remarkable to achieve anything upon which he concentrated
his energies. She had an instinctive perception that she
was herself the object upon which his energies were preliminarily concentrated. And, much as she rebelled against
the conclusion, she was inclined to believe that he would
also, in this instance, prove more than a match for her.
She liked his fearlessness in making such a merciless on-
slaught on her prejudices. He was as original as a wooer as
he was in everything else. When he got up to leave, she
gave him her hand with extreme graciousness and said :
" I hope, Mr. Larkin, you will give us the pleasure of your
company to dinner, to-morrow night, at half after seven.
I should like to have you make the acquaintance of my
father and mother ; and I shall also make an effort to get
my brother Adrian and his wife. It will be entirely *en
famille*."

Horace grew nearly pink through his coarse, weather-
tanned complexion, as he uttered the conventional phrase
accepting this invitation. It was impossible, however
much as he steeled himself against the sentiment, not to
feel exceptionally favored, and rise a trifle in one's own
estimation, at having been thought worthy to breathe this
highly sublimated air in the company of such exclusive
and privileged beings.

CHAPTER XXXIV.

THE CROW DINES WITH THE PEACOCK.

The Van Schaaks always dined in state. They rarely made special preparations for guests, except to order an extra lot of flowers ; for their *chef* was an eminent man in his line, and was daily turning out culinary *chefs d'œuvre.* Old Mr. Van Schaak regarded the art of dining as one of the fine arts, and suffered the penalty of his devotion to gastronomics in acute periodic attacks of gout. He never could learn wisdom, however, and after a few vain efforts gave up the attempt. Terrapin, canvas-back, and highly spiced *patés* of a complex and dangerous composition, were to him what the world, the flesh, and the devil are to men whose susceptibilities take the normal direction. He dressed with extreme care, bestowing as much attention upon his toilet as if he had been a reigning belle. A fresh rosebud was never missing from the lapel of his coat. The curve of his hat brim was always according to the latest and most correct taste. He was five feet nine inches high, and of full habit ; his gait and bearing were rather pompous, but, like every man absorbed in little things, he was fussy and somewhat irritable. His neat, round head, which was a little flattened on the top, was covered with curly gray hair, in a fairly good state of preservation ; and his fat, serious face had an extra capillary adornment in the shape of a mustache, likewise gray, with ends carefully twisted.

Kate, who was a good judge of character, did not deceive herself with the idea that this pink of Knickerbocker propriety would take kindly to the gentleman from Torryville, whom she had invited to dinner. She had to explain her motives at some length, urging, among other things, the wealth and importance of the Larkin family, and her duty to repay the attentions she had accepted from them during her visit with her uncle. When Horace arrived in the evening, Mr. Van Schaak was therefore reconciled to his existence, though he yet found it annoy-

ing to have to dine unknown people of questionable antecedents. The fact that his guest was a member of the
Assembly was particularly distasteful to the old gentleman ; and when Horace entered with his usual *sans cèrè-
monie* air, and on being presented shook his hand with
rural cordiality, Mr. Van Schaak retired like a turtle into
his shell and was only reluctantly polite. Mrs. Van
Schaak, whose view of the world did not differ much from
that of her husband, inquired with seeming interest about
the geography, climate, and products of Torryville, as if it
had been a foreign country, and asked him when he
meant to return "to the West." She was a large and
stately lady, about fifty years of age, with gray puffs,
plump face, and a nose somewhat pronounced, carried at
an angle expressive of fastidiousness and disdain. She
was handsome, but looked as if she could be unpleasant
in private. On Horace she had a most depressing influence, and he felt a continual impulse to glance into the
looking-glass to see if anything was the matter with his
costume. It was a great relief to him when Adrian Van
Schaak, Jr., arrived with his wife ; for a fresh breeze seemed
to enter with him, and the conversation started up like a
blaze out of ashes. This was not due to the rather dull
and portly young man himself, however, but to the lively
little lady upon whom he had bestowed his name. She
played at ducks and drakes with the family dignity, in
the opinion of her elders, and in her determination to be
amused threw all other considerations to the wind. She
asked Horace ten questions before he had time to answer
one ; declared, under the impression that he came from
some remote locality, that the West was awfully jolly, and
confided to him, at the end of five minutes that she
thought Eastern society frightfully slow. It turned out,
presently, that she was the daughter of one of those great
California millionaires who had fled from the wrath to
come, when Kearney and the sand-lotters seemed in a
fair way to gain control of the State. She had diamonds
which it would have made a woman ill to look at, if her
bony neck and shoulders had not had the effect of a consolation. She was not pretty, but carried herself as if she
thought she was. Her expression after each one of her
reckless speeches was a bid for applause ; and if she
failed to get it, she showed her displeasure.

"I do hope you are going to take me out to dinner,
Mr. Harkness," she said to Horace, as soon as she had

ascertained that he possessed the gift of speech ; "you know, my father-in-law always lectures me on the error of my ways, when he gets a chance at me ; and I don't like that, would you ? "

"Your father-in-law must be very hard to please, if he can find anything to criticise in you," said Horace, with polite mendacity. He honestly believed that truth could exist only among men, and that sincerity, if practiced toward women, would wreck civilization.

"There ! didn't I say so ?" cried Mrs. Van Schaak, with vivacity ; " I am going to tell him that, as sure as you live. I have always suspected that I was an unappreciated woman, and when so great an authority as you agrees with me—that simply settles it."

A tall blond gentleman with English side-whiskers and a bald spot on the top of his head, here made his bow to the hostess and was introduced to Horace as Mr. Suydam. Mrs. Van Schaak, Jr., added, *sotto voce*, that he was immensely rich. He had inherited Broadway and Fifth Avenue property which piled up millions for him at a dizzying rate. He kept a clerk whose sole business was cutting off coupons. He was simply wild about Kate, and the chances were that sooner or later he would marry her. All this the indiscreet little lady managed to impart to Horace in less than a minute, while the company rose and each moved toward his predestined partner. A little middle-aged woman, who looked as if she disapproved of the plan of creation, had in the meanwhile made her appearance, quite noiselessly, and been presented as Miss Terhune. She found herself, by an unpleasant necessity, attached to Adrian Van Schaak, Jr., who swore inwardly, but outwardly offered his arm with irreproachable politeness. Horace, too, was inclined to rebel against Providence, when he saw the odious Mr. Suydam march off with Kate, while he himself had the honor of bringing up the rear of the procession with the hostess. It was something of a compensation, however, to find Kate his neighbor on the right, and to note the vivid regret expressed in the face of Mrs. Adrian, Jr., at her having lost him. The dining-room was palatial in its dimensions. It was finished in oak, with game pieces exquisitely carved on each panel of the wall. The ceiling, which was also of oak, was one mass of rich and elaborate carving. A corona of gas-jets with reflectors hung high up above the heads of the diners, and shed a soft radiance downward. At the windows there were deep

curtained recesses with cushioned seats, which invited to
amorous confidences. The suspicion which had been
growing upon Horace since yesterday's visit, that he was
a hayseed and a backwoods man, and that there were a
multitude of things which lay outside of his philosophy,
began again to knock at the door of his mind, and demand admittance. He was so unused to humility in his
estimate of himself that this persistent suspicion made
him uncomfortable. But the thought again suggested itself that he was a deuced lot cleverer than all these effete
gentleman put together, and he began to itch to assert
himself, so as to give them a proof of his superiority.
Dulness had so far reigned supreme at the table, the remarks falling in languid driblets, glaringly premeditated
and artificial. Mrs. Van Schaak had inquired, with a
bland reserve which would have counteracted any tendency
on his part to feel flattered by her interest, where he was
going to spend the summer, where he spent last summer,
and whether he didn't think vulgar people were a great
bore? Mr. Van Schaak had, by way of making himself
agreeable, impressed upon his daughter-in-law the importance of buying her *paté de foie gras* in big jars, not in the
small ones, because the latter contained really an inferior
article, and he was just launching into his usual prandial
lecture on the necessity of putting away and mortifying
the old plebeian Adam in her which savored of California,
and cultivating a new aristocratic Adam of Knickerbocker
reserve and propriety. Kate had been discussing the Junior Patriarchs' Ball with Mr. Suydam, and for the sake of
drawing Horace into the conversation reported to him that
gentleman's last remark.

" Mr. Suydam thinks," she said with quiet affability,
" that the Junior Patriarchs' will have to be given up, because so many objectionable people manage to intrude
there."

Horace, who was well aware that he was himself, from
Mr. Suydam's point of view, objectionable, was inclined
to accept this remark as a challenge. It irritated him to
see this vapid and self-important snob talk confidentially
with Kate about subjects from which he was of necessity
excluded. He resolved to break a lance with Mr. Suydam,
and saw here his opportunity.

"Who are those objectionable people ?" he asked, not
loudly, but yet with a kind of bugle note in his voice which
roused everyone from his apathy.

"Who are they," Suydam repeated with astonishment ; "why they are prosperous trades-people and brokers and creatures whom nobody ever heard of before."

"Excuse me if I appear inquisitive," Horace went on, "but who is nobody ?"

"Now really you quite embarrass me, nobody is—well —aw—I referred to people in good social standing like the Van Schaaks, and the Livingstons, and your humble servant, if you like."

"That is rather excessive modesty on your part, I should say. I should never have presumed to call you nobody."

It was a cheap joke, of course, and Horace was not in the least proud of it. But in that dense and heavy atmosphere of dull propriety which pervaded the social circle of the Van Schaaks, any little display of wit made a sensation. Young Adrian looked at his father, with a strong inclination to laugh ; but the old gentleman, who would countenance no such lévity, coughed into his napkin and looked more shocked than amused. Only Mrs. Adrian, Jr., gave a ringing laugh, which she suddenly checked when she perceived that no one joined in it. Old Mrs. Adrian turned her eyes upon Horace with the stare of a locomotive. In order to relieve the embarrassment, he felt obliged to say something.

"It is a curious fact," he said, with smiling ease, " how little we are capable of learning from history. The new man and the new nation that carries the future in its pocket is always objectionable to the venerable aristocracy who, as somebody has said, have their future behind them."

The remark was addressed to the company in general, but nobody seemed disposed to take it up, except Mrs. Adrian, Jr., who exclaimed gayly :

"Ah, now you are getting personal."

Her manner was so inimitably droll that Kate could not keep from laughing ; and as soon as she had given the signal, all joined with one accord. This unexpected approval emboldened Mrs. Adrian.

"I knew it," she said, "the moment I saw you that you had something weighty in your pockets ; but I didn't suspect it was the future."

"Allow me to compliment you on your perspicacity," said Horace, laughing.

"Thanks ! But from this time forth you may know that my eyes are upon you. I shall watch to see the great future rise from your pockets, like the Afrit from the jar in the Arabian Nights."

" I hope it won't be anything so frightful."

" No, but as big."

Old Mr. Van Schaak, who failed to appreciate this sort of chaff chiefly because he missed the points of the jokes, here addressed himself to Horace with benevolent superiority.

" Did I understand you to say," he asked, " that you liked objectionable people ? "

That was as near as he ever came to apprehending a complex sentiment.

"Yes," said Horace, boldly ; " I am myself a plebeian, and like my kind. America is a plebeian state, a raw, vigorous, and aggressive new-comer among the nations of the earth, and all the venerable lands of Europe therefore dislike her—find her objectionable. Why not, then, frankly recognize this as a distinction and a source of strength, instead of setting up a little mimic aristocracy of our own, which can be knocked down with the greatest ease by a few hard-shell facts gleaned from history ? "

Mr. Van Schaak was quite unequal to a discussion of this sort, and in order to curb his indignation drank a glass of champagne. But he sent Suydam a glance which was an unmistakable exhortation to put down the sacrilegious iconoclast.

" Then you mean to say," the blonde millionaire began, " that Americans ought to be ashamed of their ancestry."

"No, I was just trying to say that they ought not."

Here was another point scored, and Mr. Suydam, seeing that he was no match in wit for Horace, would have relapsed into silence, if he had not felt the exhorting glances from all sides which appealed to him to step into the breach as the champion of their cause. But the wine he had drank and his fear of discomfiture excited him unduly and made him ill at ease.

" When I hear a man talk as you do," he said, insolently, " I always suspect that his own ancestry is not much to brag of."

" There you misapprehend me again," Horace replied, with his calm smile ; " I do brag of mine ; and what I deprecate is excuses and concealment. My father was originally a saddler ; then he became a mason and something of an inventor ; my grandfather was a farmer. They lived small and sordid lives, no doubt ; and their

19

manners, I suspect, were none of the best ; but they were good, honest people, and they were part of the strength of this great new, raw-boned continent which holds your future and mine."

There was a pause of nearly a minute, and everyone ate in silence.   Mrs. Van Schaak fixed again her locomotive stare on Horace, whose superb, smiling imperturbability irritated her even more than his objectionable ancestry.   To think that she was dining a man whose father had been a saddler ; it was a disgrace which it would take her years to outlive.   She discovered suddenly a number of plebeian traits about her guest which she had not noticed before, particularly his stiff, stubbly hair, imperfectly parted on the left side, the barbaric emphasis and directness of his expression, and the redness and clumsy shape of his ears.   Then he wore a white satin necktie, which was indicative of questionable antecedents.   She cheerfully left to her daughter the task of entertaining him for the remainder of the dinner, and registered a mental vow to prevent him from crossing her threshold again.

On Kate Horace's avowal of his plebeian origin made a very different impression.   It was difficult to define her sentiment ; but she felt drawn toward him and repelled from him in the same moment.   His refusal to be dazzled by the splendor of her surroundings pleased her ; for it was not the callousness of the barbarian he displayed, but the self-respect of the man who is conscious of his strength and who is, in all respects, the reverse of a snob. It was delightful to her to see him hoist his plebeian standard and refuse to strike it before any power in the world.   Whatever else he was, she said to herself again and again, he was emphatically a man.   And among her acquaintances, how many were there to whom that title, in its full meaning, applied ?   Suydam, with his millions and his rigid propriety, faded into insignificance beside him, became insipidly blond and priggish.

She took a bud from the great bank of roses in the middle of the table and pinned it in Horace's button-hole.   It was an attention which from anybody else would have meant nothing ; but from one so chary of favors as Kate Van Schaak, it was like the declaration of intentions which precedes naturalization.   Horace, who had done his wooing so far without the least co-operation on her part, felt a glow of pleasure stealing through him, but took care to give no outward signs of elation.   Kate was conscious

too, of having made a demonstration ; but she had
intended to make it, and awkwardness was a sensation
with which she was not acquainted. She sat and talked
serenely with him of the Larkin University, of the sere-
nade the students had given her, of the beauties of spring
in Torryville, and there was something in her personality
which made the most commonplace remarks in her mouth
appear brilliant and impressive. They borrowed something from her rare and exquisite self, and thereby gained
a new flavor.

It was about ten o'clock when the cigars were brought
on a tray of beaten copper, upon which stood a winged
genius who bit off the ends, and a Pompeian lamp which
furnished fire. The ladies retired to the drawing room ;
Mrs. Adrian, Jr., making a little grimace to Horace in the
door to indicate how she envied him the pleasure of smoking. The conversation flagged, and long awkward gaps
yawned between each remark. Mr. Suydam finally tried
to give Mr. Van Schaak a description of a saddle horse he
had recently bought; and Adrian, Jr., insisted that if that
beast turned out well, he was no judge of horse-flesh.
They got into a tolerably animated dispute, in which
Horace did not participate. He was glad when his cigar
was finished, which gave him the right again to join the
ladies. After five minutes' stiff and colorless talk with the
hostess he fell again into the hands of Mrs. Adrian, who said
all the most indiscreet things she could think of and gave
him a fair insight into her domestic relations. He did nothing to encourage this confidence ; but it apparently amused
her to satirize her husband's family a trifle, in return for
their disapproval of her; and he had no means of checking
her. A little before eleven he took his leave, feeling that,
in spite of the bad impression he had made upon the old
people, he had yet allies within the fortress, and it was only
a question of time when it would surrender.

CHAPTER XXXV.

AN UNSENTIMENTAL PROPOSAL.

If Mr. Van Schaak had not been a little bit afraid of his daughter, he would have taken her severely to task for inviting Horace to dinner. But in spite of his frequent resolutions to haul her over the coals, he never brought it further than to a mild remonstrance. He fumed in the privacy of his own bosom, but in the presence of her dark, placid eyes, which read him like a book, with all his foibles and imperfections, he felt so at a disadvantage that both his courage and his wrath evaporated.

Father and daughter were seated together in the library the morning after the memorable dinner. The room was surrounded with low book-cases of carved ebony, in which were poetry, histories, and novels in superb *editions de luxe,* which, if the authors could have seen them, would have compensated them for many privations. The walls were hung with stamped leather in which large conventionalized leaves and flowers in bronze and dark blue tones predominated.

"Don't you think, Kate," said Mr. Van Schaak, looking up over the edge of his newspaper, "that we made a mistake in dining that Mr. Harkness from Torryville ?"

" Do you mean Mr. Larkin ? " asked Kate, quietly.

"Yes, Mr. Larkin. That wild man from the West, who was here yesterday."

"He is not from the West, father ; nor is he wild. "

"Bless me, daughter ; I hope you are not taking his part."

"Yes," said Kate, " I am."

"And don't you think he appeared—what shall I say— rather ill bred ? "

"No. He is not ill bred ; nor is he exactly well bred. He is unbred."

"Well, call him anything you like ; but he is not what I call a gentleman."

"Perhaps not; but he is something still better; he is a man."

"Good gracious, Kate; I really believe you—you like him."

Mr. Van Schaak let his newspaper fall upon his knees and stared at his daughter's serene countenance with a shocked expression.

"Yes," said the unperturbed Kate, "I like him very much."

Mrs. Van Schaak entered at this moment with her nose in the air, a slight morning discontent on her face.

"Mrs. Van Schaak," cried her lord in helpless despair, "do you hear what your daughter is saying? She says she wants to marry that wild Westerner who dined here yesterday." He always transferred to his wife the responsibility for Kate's existence, when he got vexed with her.

"I did not say that," remarked Kate, contemplating the toe of her dainty slipper; "moreover, he has not asked me."

"There, didn't I say it," exclaimed her parent, appealing again to his better half; "did you hear that, Mrs. Van Schaak? She says she is only waiting for him to ask her."

"What is the good of exciting yourself about such absurd things, Adrian?" asked Mrs. Van Schaak, fretfully; "now you'll have one of your bad headaches again; and then we shall all be made uncomfortable."

The consideration implied in this remark had a soothing effect upon Mr. Van Schaak. He got up, touched his hair and mustache, cast a glance into the mirror, and composed his ruffled feathers as a cock does after a fight. He picked up the newspapers and sought solitude in his private apartments. Presently he was heard to order his saddle-horse, and in half an hour descended in the appropriate attire for equestrian exercise.

This was but the first of a series of skirmishes between Kate and her father. Mr. Van Schaak was much inclined to forbid Horace the house; but was restrained from resorting to extreme measures by his confidence in his wife, whose superior diplomacy would, no doubt, prove equal to the occasion. In the meanwhile the obnoxious visitor came and went at his pleasure, and Kate received him, and took no steps to discourage his attentions. He returned to Albany, whenever his duties demanded, but made a point of spending every Saturday and Sunday in the city, in Miss Van Schaak's company. When, finally, in the early part of June, he made his proposal in due form, Kate was in no way surprised, and she gave him her answer in a perfectly cool and rational manner, without the least emotional flutter. They were seated together in the white and gold drawing-room and had been discussing Horace's political prospects, when a sudden fire lighted up his eyes and he said: "I should not have the presumption to ask you to share my life, Miss Van Schaak, if I did not believe that it would be a life worth sharing."

She liked the originality of that form of proposal, and she liked the self-appreciation it betrayed. The total absence of sentimental allusion also appealed to her.

"Why do you think it worth sharing?" she asked, in order to draw him out.

"If you have not the penetration to discover that," he answered with his ringing aggressive tone, "I shall not undertake to tell you."

She smiled and looked at him with unmistakable admiration.

"Perhaps I have discovered it," she said.

"And do you agree with me?"

"Yes, I do."

He got up, flushed with pleasure, and seized her hand. He would have liked to fold her in his arms, but there was something in her air and bearing which clearly forbade it. A slight chill stole over him; for although she had uttered no word, and made no gesture to indicate it, he felt that caresses would be excluded from their relation. It would seem an inconceivable presumption, on his part, or on any one's part, to kiss her. He was not physically attractive to her, as she was to him. For all that, the sense of her preciousness, of her rare and exquisite worth, impressed him deeply. Like a pure and fragrant pond-lily, untouched and untouchable, she floated on the placid waters of life, and what she lacked in warmth of color she more than made up for in delicacy of texture and fineness of form. He must take her at her own terms or lose her. There would be no hearts broken in either case; unless, indeed, he were to develop a heart for the express purpose of having it broken. But disappointment there would be, and resentment and baffled aspiration. The man, however, who holds the woman of his choice by such frail bonds, let him avoid risks, and let him postpone all experiments until after the wedding.

Horace was not exactly happy as he descended the

stairs of the Van Schaak mansion, after having obtained
Kate's promise to marry him. At least he was not as
happy as he had expected to be. There was something
lacking—glaringly lacking ; though he was not sure
what it was. He was certainly no sentimentalist who was
disturbed because a kiss had been denied him, and because
there had been no thrills, no gush, or tender nonsense.
And yet it seemed singularly barren and incomplete, this
engagement of his ; a little too much like a commercial
transaction. The mere feeling of gratified ambition failed
to supply the keen delights which he had anticipated. A
curious insecurity came over him ; and though he would
have been ashamed to admit it, he could not suppress a
doubt as to whether he had acted wisely. Had not Kate
appeared so supremely desirable to him, chiefly because
she seemed to be beyond his reach ? Had not her lofty
indifference stung his energies into activity, and challenged his ambition ? Had he not made up his mind to
marry her, chiefly because the general presumption was
that he could not ? He sauntered down Irving Place meditating on these questions, without pretending to answer
them. The thought of Bella obtruded itself incessantly
upon his mind, and a vague tenderness for her meekness
and her misfortune awoke within him. Was it remorse
he felt or merely an irrational regret at the necessity of
being cruel ? That was another idle query, which haunted
him with uncomfortable persistence. He straightened
himself up, and began to look about him ; the street was
deserted on the sunny side ; but on the shady side he observed a man who was walking along rapidly, carrying
some books under his arm. The figure struck him as being familiar, and a second glance convinced him that it
was Aleck. But what a change had come over him ! His
coat was devoid of style and his trousers were baggy at
the knees. There was a forward bend, as of haste or preoccupation in his walk, but not a stoop. It was the walk
of a man who has an end in view, but takes no pride in his
appearance.

Horace turned about and, crossing the street, followed
his brother at a distance. The sight of him aroused a
host of memories. How much lonelier and more selfish
his life had been since he lost Aleck. And what was
their quarrel really about ! A paltry money affair ; and on
his own part, besides, a mean calculation. He longed so
to speak to Aleck that he was eager to minimize the cause

of their disagreement. He hastened his steps, though as yet undecided whether he should yield to his impulse. They had now reached Madison Square, and Aleck, without looking right or left, plunged into the glaring sunshine.

Horace, fearing that he might lose him in the crowd of children, nursery maids, and loafers that encamp under the stately trees of the square, broke into a run and overtook him.

"Aleck," he said, laying his hand upon his shoulder.

Aleck started back and stared in blank bewilderment.

"Horace!" he cried, as the perception dawned upon him that it was his brother, and then again, with a joyous outburst:

"Why, Horace, is it you?"

"It's yours truly, large as life and twice as natural," replied Horace, taking refuge in his usual banter.

"And what are you doing here?" inquired Aleck, beaming upon him with a boyish, undisguised pleasure.

" Oh, I have something going on here in the petticoat line," said the elder brother in his jovial off-hand way. But he had scarcely uttered the rude phrase before he was ashamed of it. There was a kind of implied mendacity in it. It misrepresented his relation to the woman for whose favor he had so earnestly sued.

"Ah, a divorce suit," said Aleck ; "well, I have heard that your practice is spreading over the whole State."

" Oh, yes, it is not bad," Horace rejoined, rather relieved that his brother misunderstood him.

They walked along at a leisurely pace under the great trees, talking of indifferent things. Horace, who was aching to confide to Aleck his engagement, was unable to find the proper tone for such an important announcement ; and Aleck was haunted with the spectres of a hundred momentous things which he wished to say, but which somehow, he hesitated to utter. It was odd, but these two, who were so fond of each other, and had longed so for this chance to speak freely, talked, under a constraint which neither understood, the most artificial stuff to each other. Aleck was the first to escape from this bondage of platitude

"Horace," he said, stopping in front of his brother and taking hold of his arm, " I want to ask you if you'll come home with me. If you don't want to, just say so, and I shall not be offended. But—but—I should regard it as a great kindness to—to—my wife," he finished, blushing with happy embarrassment.

"Where do you live?" asked Horace, considering rapidly the various aspects of the problem. Would his uncle approve of his according any sort of recognition to Gertrude, after he had himself disowned her? Was it worth while imperilling his relation to his uncle for the sake of obliging Aleck? But there was also another side to the question. He was now a sufficiently important man to afford to consult his own preference. He was absolutely indispensable to the Honorable Obed, who would be too shrewd to pick quarrels with him on a slight pretext. He was about to marry the daughter of a millionaire, and his prestige would be immensely increased by the wealth and social position of his bride. He concluded to accept Aleck's invitation. The risks were too insignificant to be considered.

"I live way out of creation," Aleck was saying, while these thoughts flashed through his brother's head. "We shall have to take the Sixth Avenue Elevated. Come along!"

"Hold on a minute! Tell me first, have you got Gertrude's mother with you?"

"No, we have done with her long ago."

"Then I'm your man. I should like to see Gertie; and besides, I want to have a talk and a confidential smoke with you, as in old times."

They started across the square and down Twenty-third street toward the elevated railroad, Aleck talking joyously and telling little matrimonial experiences which were calculated to show his wife in the most charming light.

Horace scarcely knew whether it was touching or ludicrous to hear him thus guilelessly congratulate himself on having drawn the grand prize in the lottery of life, when as a matter of fact he had been a *pis aller*—a last refuge to a woman who by her own folly had gotten herself into an embarrassing situation. What could be more pitiful to a man of Aleck's talents and prospects than to teach school six hours a day at $1,200 a year, live in a stuffy little flat and grow seedy and near-sighted in the mere paltry effort to keep soul and body together? But then, *chacun à son goût!* To Horace such an existence would be worse than death.

"You don't know," the deluded enthusiast exclaimed, "you can have no idea how lovely she is to me. I am aware that you never appreciated her as I did; but then it was your excuse that you never really knew her. In fact I never did either. If I had, I should have murdered Hawk for daring to love her. Fortunately, however, that was a very one-sided affair. She allowed herself to be fascinated by his fine talk ; I can easily forgive her that, for I was myself under the spell of that humbug for a good while. But she has told me that she never really loved him. And that has made me so happy. For, I must confess, I was foolish enough to be tormented by a kind of retrospective jealousy, whenever I thought of that plausible rascal. Now, I have none of that ; for I have her own word for it, that she simply deluded herself into thinking that she cared for him. You must not imagine, however," here Aleck broke out into a soft laugh, and his eye shone with a happy illumination, "you must not suppose that she is all sweetness and light. For in that case she might evaporate in my arms into sheer luminous perfection. No, it is the touch of earth which, after all, I love the best in her. Her sweet little feminine ways, her pouts, her occasional rebellions against my authority, her irrational behavior, her bewildering feminine logic. You know, two weeks ago, she was taken ill in the most unaccountable manner, and the doctor told her she must keep on her back, and not exert herself for about a week. We had been in the habit of going out to take our dinner at a restaurant, and you can't imagine what delightfully jolly little dinners they were ! But now, of course, I had to bring the dinners to her. The first day or two she ate them, though not with much gusto ; but on the third day she rebelled, declared that everything was cold, that if I couldn't bring her a hot dinner, she wouldn't have any dinner at all. She wasn't going to stand this nonsense any longer ; the doctor was an old nightcap who was trying to run up a bill by keeping her on her back, when she was perfectly well, etc. She was going to get up, whether the doctor liked it or not, and she had made up her mind to have a decent hot meal, even if she had to walk a mile for it. Of course I remonstrated, but it was no good. I begged, I implored her to consider her health. But she laughed at me, and told me I was a ridiculous, fussy, busybody. Up she started and down four flight of stairs; the elevator was, as usual, out of order. Then in despair, I ran after her, taking four steps at a time, overtook her on the fourth landing, flung my arms about her and carried her bodily back to her bed-room. She made no resistance.

She was almost too astonished to speak. Without a word she lay down on the bed, turned her face to the wall, and refused to stir or to answer any of my questions. I offered to send to the Brunswick for a dinner; and finally, I was reckless enough to suggest Delmonico. I might just as well have talked to the wall. She was and remained dumb. At last without awaiting her consent I rang for a messenger, and procured an excellent meal from a restaurant close by. There was quail on toast, filet de bœuf, cream meringue and all the things I knew she liked. But do you suppose she relented? Not a bit of it. During the entire afternoon she lay like one dead; and I sat in the parlor, pretending to write, but really watching her anxiously in the mirror. Oh, how miserable I was! I really thought she had made up her mind to starve herself to death. I paced the floor in agony, made the most contrite speeches to her, but all to no purpose. I had about given up the battle and was mentally composing her obituary:

"'LARKIN—May 12th. Gertrude, beloved wife of Alexander Larkin, daughter of the Honorable Obed Larkin, of Torryville, in the twenty-first year of her age. Please omit flowers.'

"I had just gotten to that point, I say, when, to my unutterable delight, I saw her rise cautiously, and with a quick movement tear a leg off the quail which was on the table by her bed. I stood speechless, watching her in the mirror. She rose again, and after having made sure that she was unobserved, tore off another leg. The third time, the rest of the quail went the same way. Then the cream meringue vanished. Suddenly, when my anxiety was relieved, the ludicrous aspect of the thing struck me and I began to chuckle, first softly, then more loudly, until I burst into a ringing laugh. She lost her appetite instantly. But in the same moment I was at her side. She smiled in a shamefaced sort of way, then she hugged me and cried, and called herself silly and foolish and begged my pardon; and I am afraid I cried some myself too, and we were absurdly, irrationally, extravagantly happy."

Having got started on this theme Aleck took no note of the stations they passed and would have gone on to Washington Heights if Horace had not asked him at Seventy-second Street, if it was not time to get off. He had begun to pity Aleck from the bottom of his heart, for asking so little of Fate, for consenting to be happy at such a very cheap price, for constructing an illusory paradise for himself out of such poor material.

They sauntered up one street and down another and came at last to an enormous ten-story caravansery, of red brick with brown stone trimmings. They entered a somewhat squalid vestibule, with tesselated floor and exhibiting a multitude of brass bell handles, under each of which there was a rectangular opening containing a card. That was the Patagonia.

CHAPTER XXXVI.

"THE PATAGONIA."

Aleck tried to be gay and debonair as he opened the door from the dark hall into the room which he was pleased to call his study. But he could not disguise his excitement from his astute brother. He laughed boisterously at things which were not ludicrous, knocked the furniture about in his effort to find a comfortable chair for his guest, and skipped from one subject of conversation to another with bewildering vivacity.

" I hope you'll excuse the looks of things, Horace," he said ; " for you know we are not yet quite settled. We don't like to buy the things we need all at once ; things that we have to live with we prefer to get one by one. And I tell you, we get no end of fun out of our furniture expeditions. Gertie, you know, has about as much idea of money as the man in the moon. I have had an awful lot of trouble in teaching her to count her change when she goes shopping. 'Why, you certainly don't want me to insult the clerk to his very face,' she exclaimed, the first time I spoke to her about it, and she swept the change she got from a ten-dollar bill into her purse with a royal recklessness."

It was perhaps pardonable in Aleck that he found the peculiarities of his wife absorbingly interesting, and imagined that they could not fail to appear equally delightful to his brother. But Horace, to whom the poetry of a man's relation to the woman he loves was as a sealed book, could not repress the reflection that Aleck had degenerated sadly. He was making a complete fool of himself over this woman ; and as he had now chosen to go his own way, there would be no use in trying to open his eyes. The room in which they were sitting was about six feet by eight, and contained two tall book-cases made of stained pine boards, a lounge covered with green rep, a cherry writing desk and two cane-seated chairs. Over the desk hung crayon portraits of Aleck and his wife, the former with a curious twist to his mouth, the latter with an eye which threatened to drop out. The cipher of the artist, G. L., in a boldly ornamental style, was visible in the right hand corner. The happy possessor of these works of art could not conceal his pride in them, but had to call his brother's attention to their excellence. He then excused himself, and in making his way to the door stumbled over Horace's long legs, which stretched across the whole unoccupied area of the floor. A moment later there were unmistakable sounds of a sub-dued dispute in the next room, and the inference lay near that the lady of the house was not anxious to renew her acquaintance with her brother-in-law. The brother-in-law in question smiled, and on the whole sympathized with her reluctance. Aleck's entreaties seemed, however, in the end to prevail ; for he returned presently in a radiant humor, and announced to Horace that his wife had con-sented to see him. If it had been the Queen of Great Britain and Ireland who had signified her willingness to receive him, the tone of the announcement could not have been more impressive. He flung open the door to the parlor, much as a royal lackey does who shows you into the presence of the sovereign.

Horace made his bow to Gertrude, who met him in the middle of the room. His first thought was that she was really handsome (a fact which he had never discovered be-fore), and her first sensation was one of relief that he did not kiss her. For she had dreaded that, out of regard for Aleck, he might have found it incumbent upon him to be affectionate.

" I am very glad to see you, Horace," she said, simply.

" And I to see you, Gertie," he answered with the same degree of veracity. " You have grown so handsome that I should scarcely have known you."

Aleck, who was standing by, beaming upon his wife with a half paternal, half lover-like pride, here burst out vigo-rously : " Now, there you see ! Isn't it the very thing I have been saying to you, that you are growing more beau-tiful every day ? And you have insisted that I was flatter-ing or making fun of you."

" Now, don't be such a jack, Aleck ! " was the prompt re-sponse ; " or Horace will think you have lost what little sense you ever had since getting married. And then he will hold me responsible for your absurdity."

She flushed with a vague embarrassment and seated her-self on a chair in front of her easel. The conversation moved somewhat cumbrously from one indifferent topic to

another, and Horace had time to take an inventory of the
room. It was an unconventional parlor, to say the least.
It contained very little furniture, and that of odd shapes
and sizes. There were a sofa and three or four chairs, not
with the usual shop look, but handsome, solid, and of pleasing forms. They had obviously been carefully selected, one
by one, in down-town shops where handsome things have
not yet reached prohibitory prices. The floor was covered
with a rug of good colors, and the walls with a multitude
of unframed charcoal drawings, whose chief function was
to conceal the glaring blue and yellow wall paper. A large
home-made screen, decorated with bulrushes and flying
cranes, also in charcoal, hid the ugly fireplace and mantel,
and striking bits of drapery were effectively arranged about
the doors, the mirror, and wherever there was anything objectionable to put out of sight.

"I suppose, Gertie," said Horace, in order to make talk,
"that here in New York you have a fine chance to prose-
cute your art studies?"

It is hard to tell why the suspicion awoke in her that
he was making sport of her. She could not presuppose
any benevolent interest in herself or her work in this cold
and quizzical brother-in-law, who had always disapproved
of her, and frequently given her the benefit of his harsh
criticism.

"The best thing that could be done with my artistic
aspirations would be to smother them," she answered,
gravely ; "if you could help me to do that, I think I
should be grateful to you."

"How can you speak that way, Gertie," ejaculated
Aleck, with ardor. "I should be grieved if your marriage
were to interfere with the development of your artistic
talent. When we are better off than we are now, I intend
to have you take lessons of the best artists in the city, and
I shall be astonished if they don't agree with me in my
estimate of your genius."

"Then I fear you are destined to be very much astonished, dear," she answered, sending him a pleased glance,
full of shy gratitude and tenderness.

"She is right, Aleck, she is right," interposed the
ungallant Horace ; "not that I mean to pronounce upon
her artistic merits. But to a married woman a talent
of that sort, if it is genuine, is a source of more misery
than happiness. I am not speaking of a mere amateurish
facility in drawing ; for that might prove an amusement

and a pastime.   But genius will not put up with a divided
allegiance.   It demands the whole man or the whole
woman, and it avenges itself, if you try to put it off with a
compromise."

Aleck stood his ground bravely against the united
charge of his brother and his wife, declaring at last
sublimely that he would rather sacrifice his own life to
Gertrude, than have her sacrifice her life to him.

"Aleck, my boy, you are the same old sixpence," cried
Horace, laughing ; "but permit me to say," he continued,
more solemnly, "that nobody has a right to sacrifice himself to anybody else. If he does he simply eliminates
himself from the struggle for existence, proves his unfit-
ness to survive.   It is natural for every strong man to try
to make every other life tributary to his own ; but the
man who consents to make his life tributary to somebody
else's is from Nature's point of view a weak man ; or what
amounts to the same, a Quixotic enthusiast whom she will
refuse to perpetuate, because, in the present state of her
affairs, she has no conspicuous use for him. She may
allow him to exist in a small way ; but what is existence
without predominance?"

"Oh, Horace, you deluded sage," Aleck exclaimed,
dramatically, "do you actually mean to assert that Nature
has no use for the man who is more generous than the
average of his kind ?"

"Nature respects nothing but strength, physical and
intellectual," Horace replied.   "The man who is in
advance of the morality of his age is, for practical purposes, a fool.   It is no use quarreling with Fate ; and in
the United States the average man is the Fate that rules
us and determines our place in the world."

They were now launched on one of their old-time disputes, and for a full hour they fought hot logical battles,
each sticking tenaciously to his side of the question.   Gertrude, though she was aglow with partisanship for her
husband, and occasionally was tempted to speak, was
restrained by a certain awe of the formidable Horace.
Though his attitude toward her was changed, she yet felt
the after-effect of his contemptuous superciliousness, so
freely expressed in the past. She was on needles and
pins whenever Aleck seemed on the point of weakening, and
was eager to come to his rescue. When it became obvious to her that he was getting worsted, all her old animosity against Horace flared up, and she would have

liked to tell him how odious he was. Aleck, however, took his defeat in good part, declaring laughingly that it was all in the family, and that he did not pretend to be a match for so keen a logician as his brother. It then occurred to him that he had forgotten to offer Horace a cigar, and he made haste to remedy his neglect. Gertrude marvelled at his good nature, and was stung by a sneaking little doubt, whether it might not possibly be true that such amiability did argue weakness and was a disqualification for success. And she hungered for success with all her heart, chiefly for the purpose of bringing Horace to his knees by furnishing a practical refutation of his argument.

"I suppose," observed the unconscious object of her wrath, with an insinuating air, "that Gertie is not yet inured to smoke. How would it do if we retired to the study, where we shall not annoy her?"

She was clever enough to understand that this was a ruse to get rid of her, and she therefore made no objection. Only the unsophisticated Aleck failed to discover any such intention; because he could not imagine how a man could be constituted who would by preference dispense with Gertrude's society. He accepted, however, his brother's suggestion; but came near embracing his wife when, with a heroic disregard of her own wishes, she invited Horace to stay to dinner. A practised eye might, however, have detected a shade of relief in her wide-open blue eyes when the invitation was declined.

Horace expanded with a sense of ease and unrestraint when he found himself alone in his brother's company.

"Aleck," he said, taking some slow critical whiffs of his cigar to test its quality, "I have got something to tell you, and I shall dispense with all preliminaries. My dear boy, I am going to be married."

"I am delighted to hear that," Aleck burst out with enthusiasm; "she has been so mortally ill, and I knew you couldn't afford to have the wrecking of that poor girl's life on your conscience——"

He became aware suddenly that his brother's face had undergone an ominous change. There was a hard black look about his eyes which he knew too well from of old. He stared at him with a gaze of terrified questioning.

"I don't know what you are talking about," cried Horace, rising and staring out of the window.

"Why—whom—if I may ask—are you going to marry?" stammered Aleck, in painful confusion.

20

It was a good while before Horace recovered his equanimity. " Because you choose to throw away your life,"
he said, harshly, sending Aleck a fierce glance over his
shoulder, " is that any reason why I should go and throw
away mine ? "

" No," Aleck was on the point of answering ; " you prefer to throw away the lives of others. A man has a right
to experiment with his own life, but he has no right to
experiment with the lives of his fellow-men."

He knew, however, that if he gave utterance to this
thought, there would be an end to his pleasant relations
with his brother. And he valued him too much to sacrifice him to an epigram. The suspicion rankled in him
that it was his marriage which appeared to Horace as an
evidence of failure and a consignment of his life to hopeless mediocrity ; but even that he chose to forgive, if forgiveness for his own blunder was yet obtainable.

" You know, Horace," he began in a tone of conciliation,
"that I am a thoughtless fellow, and that my feelings
often run away with me. If I have offended you I am
heartily sorry for it."

" It is d——d easy to feel sorry ; but you are the most
left-handed chap I ever did know."

" Well, perhaps I am, but I am too old to mend my ways,
so I fear you'll have to put up with them."

" I don't know about that. Anyway it takes time for me
to get into a forgiving mood. You have spoiled my desire
to be confidential. Good-by."

" But you are not going without telling me who the lady
is whom you are going to marry ? "

" I'll tell you some other time, I can't to-day."

He had seized his hat and cane, and Aleck mournfully
opened the door for him and rang for the elevator. They
shook hands at parting, the one listlessly, the other warmly,
repentantly.

It was not the first time that the righteous has had to
apologize for his righteousness, and that the unrighteous
has exacted an apology for a criticism upon his unrighteousness.

The next day Aleck received a letter, written at the
Union League Club, informing him that the lady who was
destined to become his sister-in-law, was Kate Van Schaak.
If the roof of the heavens had tumbled down about his
ears he could not have been more astonished.

CHAPTER XXXVII.

PRELIMINARY ARRANGEMENTS.

Kate Van Schaak conducted her campaign on the Fabian plan. She refused to deliver engagements, but she adhered calmly and resolutely to her purpose, announced it now and then with neat and distinct emphasis, and allowed daily gusts of ill-temper to sweep over her with admirable equanimity. She listened to the severest reproaches without growing angry; she made judicious admissions when, as sometimes happened, the criticisms on her *fiancé* came within the line of truth; and gradually accustomed her parents to the inevitable by permitting them to exhaust their patience in futile resistance.

The four summer months were spent, as usual, at Newport, where the Van Schaaks had a charming villa. Horace, who had looked forward with much pleasure to spending part of his vacation in the old town by the sea, had his ardor considerably cooled when Kate requested him not to approach her until her return to the city in the autumn. If it had been anybody but Kate who had made such a proposition to him he would have suspected intrigues and flirtations, in which he was not to interfere, but Kate, with her clear brown eyes and placid brow, was so far above these things that they seemed unworthy of consideration. Another suspicion, however, suggested itself, and was not so easily dismissed—was she, perhaps, a little ashamed of him, and preferred not to have him near her until she had won the right to amend his appearance in accordance with her own taste? If such was the case, Horace had a good mind to descend upon her unannounced in order to test the quality of her regard for him. But in contemplating this plan he gradually acquired a realizing sense of her formidableness. She was not a person to be trifled with; and it would be extremely unsafe to subject her to unpleasant surprises.

So it came to pass that Horace spent the greater part of the summer drearily at Torryville. He communicated his intention to marry Miss Van Schaak to his uncle, and was a trifle disappointed at the manner in which the old man received the announcement.

"Well, you've had your own way pretty much in everything," he said, pursing up his lips thoughtfully ; " but mark my word, she ain't the kind of girl that it'll be easy to pull tergether with."

" I don't see what you mean, uncle," exclaimed his nephew.

" I didn't reckon you would," said Mr. Larkin, with his shrewd smile, " but you will, by and by."

" I wish you would tell me now."

" Well, she ain't broken in, neither for saddle nor harness," observed the old man, persevering in his equine simile.

" But you don't want to break girls, uncle, as you would a horse."

"Don't you, though ? Well, all I've got to say, is this ; if you don't, you'll be sorry for it by and by.   You'll want to try it when it is too late.   And then the jig is up.   Good by, John !   It ain't nice to be your own counsel in a divorce suit."

" But, uncle, fooling aside, I wish you would tell me what you have got against Kate Van Schaak."

" Bless you, I haven't got anything against her.   She only looks to me rather hifalutin.   And I ain't no judge of women if she ain't sorter hard-bitted, hard in the mouth ; good on the trot when you get her started, but mighty hard to start."

Although he was far from being a sentimentalist, Horace did not relish hearing such disrespectful terms applied to the woman upon whom he was about to confer his name. If it had been anyone but his uncle who had spoken thus, he would have given vent to his resentment in unmistakable language.   But that is the disadvantage of being a beneficiary, you cannot enjoy the luxury of unrestrained sincerity.

Among all the trials of the long and hot summer, which Horace had in part anticipated, there was one which was happily absent.   The Reverend Mr. Robbins had, in consequence of the recent severe illness of his daughter, taken a vacation, and had migrated with his entire tribe into the Adirondack wilderness.   It was said that Bella's lungs were affected, and that she had already had several hemorrhages.   Others declared that she was suffering from nervous prostration and hysteria. But whatever it was, Horace was relieved of the unpleasant necessity of meeting Mr. Robbins and his Rodents in the post-office and in the street, as he otherwise inevitably would have done ; and for this he was duly grateful.

He had, moreover, a source of consolation which, to gentlemen in his position is sanative of many ills to which lovers are heirs. He received weekly letters from Kate, which arrived with a beautiful regularity and precision. They were not in the least effusive ; but they were neatly and well written, containing sage but conservative comments upon the society about her, accounts of balls, sailing parties, and routs, and occasional allusions to their approaching wedding. Barring the latter, there was nothing, either in the matter or manner of them, which was not fit for publication. What Horace missed in them (and sometimes missed acutely), was the personal note, the note of confidence, trust, and devotion. He did not know from experience what was the proper tone of a so-called love-letter ; but he had been led to suppose that it was something quite different from the tone of mere sensible and friendly companionship which characterized the epistles of which he was the recipient. It appeared to him, though his demands as regards sentiment were extremely moderate, that they had both gotten a false start ; for the essays on contemporary history which Kate forwarded to him every Saturday, somehow forced him to respond with philosophical disquisitions and treatises on sociology. I am bound to say that some of these were quite brilliant, and well worthy of a place in one of the leading magazines. He was aware that he held his place in her esteem by dint of his intellect, and did not neglect, therefore, to display the strength of this intellect, whenever the occasion presented itself. He could not pretend that he liked this necessity, or that it satisfied his idea of the fitness of things, but he saw no way of remedying it, and therefore acquiesced.

Politics had been in a state of stagnation during the early part of the summer. But about the middle of August the Hon. Reuben Studebaker, who had represented the county in the State Senate for a quarter of a century, died of Bright's disease, leaving his senatorial shoes the object of a spirited competition. The Hon. Reuben had not been a resident of Torryville, but it was claimed by Mr. Dallas and his colleagues that by a kind of traditional rule

of rotation, the succession belonged by right to his town-
ship, of which Torryville was the centre and chief ornament.
Mr. Studebaker, it was freely asserted, had not been a model
law-maker, having been concerned in every corrupt job
which had passed the legislature since he first made his
entrance into politics.   But he had managed to keep himself in favor with his constituents by procuring for their
locality a branch of the insane asylum, canal improvements, and other legislature favors, and for conspicuous
citizens of his town profitable jobs of all sorts at the public
expense.   He had posed as the champion of rural simplicity and virtue against the extravagance and vice of New
York City, and he secured additional prestige by taking
the lead in every raid upon the treasury of the wicked
metropolis.   It was, of course, difficult to find a man
worthy and competent to succeed so useful a representative, and the press and public opinion wavered long before
arriving at a conclusion.   Then with a marvellous unanimity the Republican papers made the discovery that the
Hon. Horace Larkin was the man designated by talent,
character, and conspicuous public service to fill the place
of the late lamented senator.   The Democratic journals
vainly charged bribery and corruption, and called attention to the fact that the Hon. Obed had " pulls " on the
Republican editors, and owned stock in their papers.
However that may have been Horace loomed up as the
man of destiny, was nominated by the convention, and in
due time elected.

But before this auspicious event was consummated
another enterprise, hardly less important, demanded the
attention of the candidate.   It had been his plan originally
to hire a house on the hill belonging to his uncle and fit it
out properly for the reception of his bride.   But when he
remembered the unattainable splendor of her present surroundings, his courage began to fail him.   He could not
afford to appear mean before her.   Cherry or black walnut cabinet finish, Morris wall papers, and Axminster car-
pets, which had hitherto represented to his mind the acme
of magnificence, had, since his dinner in Gramercy Park,
grown insupportably commonplace ; it expressed a futile
aspiration to rise above respectable shabbiness.   If he had
caught the bird Phenix, he was in honor bound to furnish
a fitting cage.   After having duly pondered the ways and
means, he broached the matter to his uncle, and asked his
advice. They had a long and earnest discussion, which only

the profound respect they entertained for each other prevented from being a stormy one. Old Mr. Larkin disapproved strongly of Horace's intention to build a fine
house, on a lot he owned half way up the hill ; but ended
with offering him a loan of $25,000. And so an architect
was instantly engaged, plans were submitted, and before
the end of July the ground was broken and the foundation
laid. Half a dozen designs, all of an ambitious style, were
submitted to Kate, and she promptly indicated her preference. But the cool way in which she referred to this enterprise, which to him was an affair of the most vital importance, disappointed and offended him. Had he not for her
sake withdrawn his capital from good investments, and put
three-fourths of it into a house which was planned to suit
her taste, not his ? Had he not incurred the risk of losing his uncle's good will by proposing a scale of living
which to the frugal millionaire seemed simply preposterous ? And to these sacrifices she responded with the sober suggestion that she required very deep closets in her
private rooms and a marble bath so arranged that she
could step down into it, and should not have to climb into
it. There were a multitude of other specifications as to
light, ventilation, and plumbing, but not one word of gratitude or affection. She was honest, at least, Horace
thought bitterly ; and she was charmingly consistent. He
had exalted the prose of life and scouted its poetry ; and
life had taken him at his word. For this was prose with a
vengeance.

CHAPTER XXXVIII.

WHICH IS THE TRIBUTARY?

The wedding of the Hon. Horace Larkin to Miss Kate
Van Schaak was celebrated with due pomp and magnificence at the beginning of the winter.   All fashionable
New York was there; and some beside who rarely venture
forth into the glare of the modern day.   Decrepit old
Knickerbockers, who seem but an expiring tradition in
the city which they founded, came forth from their ancient
haunts in Stuyvesant Square and hobbled up the stately
breadth of Second Avenue, from below Fourteenth Street.
Some wore frilled shirt-fronts and embroidered wrist-bands,
and they shook their heads, either from decrepitude or
disapproval; for this wedding was to them another evidence that the world was sadly out of gear.   The Hon.
Obed Larkin and Mrs. Larkin were also present, the former sober and quiet, the latter exhilarated and excited; in
fact, the old gentleman had all he could do in keeping his
wife from making a jack of herself.   He wore during the
entire ceremony a dubious air, took his departure (in spite
of Mrs. Larkin's protests) by an early train, and remarked
repeatedly to his unresponsive spouse that this world was
a mighty queer place.   He could not understand how a
level-headed man like Horace could have made so fatal a
mistake as this marriage appeared to him to be; and the
more he thought of it, the less he understood it.   The ten
or twenty millions which Mr. Van Schaak was reputed to
be worth did not furnish an adequate explanation.   He had
refrained from making Horace rich, chiefly to save him
from the perils which he had now deliberately incurred.
He was so deeply and bitterly disappointed that he scarcely
cared to disguise his feelings.   All those upon whom he
had pinned his faith seemed bound to make a botch of
their lives in spite of his precepts.

Mr. and Mrs. Horace Larkin took the train for Albany a
little after midnight.   Kate did not quite relish this flavor of

state politics about their wedding journey, but she recognized the necessity and submitted to it. Dreading hotel life,
they had taken a handsomely furnished house for the winter, the rent of which exceeded Horace's senatorial salary
multiplied by two. But that, too, was a necessity against
which it was futile to rebel. It was a charming old-fashioned house, with a kind of solid Knickerbocker dignity,
and a warm air of having been lived and died in by succes-
sive generations. Horace hoped that Kate, who had an
eye for character, would take to it kindly, and attribute to
her husband's civilized taste what was really a lucky accident. He would have been quite as capable of being entrapped by a medley of garish splendor, fit to make a
sensitive woman tear her hair. In fact, he entered his
new domicile with fear and trembling, lest it should develop in the eyes of his wife some atrocious feature which
he had failed to discover. It was a novel sensation for
him to feel this nervous deference for the opinion of another, and a corresponding doubt as to his own compe-
tency of judgment. And one little incident which occurred
immediately after their arrival was not calculated to allay
his apprehension. He had stepped forward in a flutter
(which he had never before experienced) to assist her in
removing her wraps. She was wonderful to behold, in a
gorgeous velvet cloak, cut to her figure, and richly lined
with blue fox. As she lifted her veil, and revealed her
pure, placid face, flushed with the cold, he was conscious
of a thrill and a dim stirring of something within him
which must have been tenderness. For she was his, this
ominously beautiful and formidable piece of womanhood,
this complex and superior creature for whom so many had
sued in vain. As she stood there before him with her intelligent dark eyes fixed upon him, and that vague disdain
which was habitual with her in the curve of her lips, he
became conscious of the tremendous compliment she had
paid him in entrusting her precious self to him. He could
afford to overlook minor points in the presence of this
overwhelming fact. It was as if a new warm fountain
sprung forth in his breast, and began to flow with a gentle
murmur. For no man who is not a brute can contemplate
that touching phenomenon, which was dawning upon
Horace's consciousness, without the awaking of whatever
chivalry there may be in him. And full of this sentiment
he was stepping forward to offer his services, for the first
time in his life, as *valet de chambre.* She had herself un-

hooked the intricately wrought silver clasp under the chin
and pulled out a dagger-like needle which she seemed to
pass through her cranium without the least inconvenience,
and he had cautiously taken hold of the cloak and was
making an effort to remove it.   But by ill luck, one of his
sleeve buttons caught in her hair, and as, unaware of this
complication, he gave his pull, she turned upon him a
pair of eyes full of calm severity, and said :
    " Oh, what a clumsy baboon you are ! "
    If she had spoken in momentary anger, provoked by the
pain, he would have readily forgiven her.   But she was
not angry ; it was rather a deliberate rebuke, and its
chilling severity stabbed him like cold steel.   He felt
hurt ; so hurt that he thought he could never get over it.
What would his life be in the company of a woman who
on the morning after her wedding could address him thus ?
He was in the habit of looking facts in the face, and this
one seemed too alarming to be lightly dismissed.   The
circumstance, too, that she took everything for granted,
without the least recognition of the forethought he had
displayed in securing her comfort, was somewhat disquiet-
ing.   There were servants in the house ; and for aught he
could learn, she supposed houses were built with servants
in them.   He had telegraphed ahead for a hot breakfast,
but soon found the muffins lead, and the chops uneatable.
She made no ado whatever, but she tasted the dishes with
a critical air, and put them quietly aside.   As he sat and
looked at her across the table in amazed silence, he grew
so angry that he had to clench his teeth to keep from
blurting out some offensive phrase.   He was fully aware
that it would not do to yield to any rash impulse, for the
relations he established with his wife now would have an
important bearing upon his whole life's happiness.   Her
palate, he reasoned, had been educated up to a point far beyond his comprehension ; and he ought scarcely to object
to that high development of the senses which made her the
rare and complex being that she was.
    "You don't seem to eat anything," he said with forced
composure.
    " I am not very hungry," she answered, picking daintily
at a piece of bass, which had been a trifle scorched in
the broiling.
    " I fear you are over-tired."
    She made no reply for a while, but looked at her plate
half absently, then pushed it away.

"How long do you think you'll have to stay in this dreadful place?" she asked.

"What dreadful place?"

"Albany."

"Until the end of the session."

"And when will it end?"

"Probably about the middle of May or the first of June."

"I am not going to stay here as long as that."

He thought it prudent not to challenge her by a spirit of opposition, and therefore avoided taking issue with her.

"Why do you object to the town?" he inquired, between two sips of coffee.

"It is so unfinished, so unkempt. It has such a horrid, ragged, American look."

"American? Do you dislike it because it looks American?"

"Yes, you know what I mean. That hideous glaring newness and bareness and barrenness—you see that nowhere but in our country. I cannot imagine anything more offensive to all the five senses combined than the main street of an aspiring American village."

"But you know it is after all American; and on that account, it seems to me, we have got to improve it or put up with it."

"No, there you are wrong. And let me just tell you here, what my plan is. I want you to get an appointment as minister to some European court. It is only with that in view that I could tolerate this odious place for a little while. With my fortune we could live *en prince* in Paris or London or St. Petersburg, and your political distinction would count for much more there than it ever will here. Life is more commodiously and agreeably arranged for people of fortune there than it is here, and as long as we have but one life to live I have no intention, from patriotic motives, to make it less enjoyable than it ought to be."

A curious idea began to dawn upon Horace's mind; but he brushed it away as unworthy of consideration. It returned, however, and refused to be dismissed. This neat and perfectly finished plan, complete in all its details, was no inspiration of the moment. It was a long-cherished, well-matured purpose, the realization of which she had deliberately set about. Was it not possible, nay probable, that she had married him simply on account of her faith in his ability to carry out this scheme ? He did not delude himself with the thought that she loved him. But that he, with his determination to make her life tributary to his, had himself been appropriated with exactly the same purpose on her part, that seemed like a colossal joke— one of those jokes that seem funny to all except the one at whose expense it is perpetrated. He remembered distinctly the expression of her face at Mr. Robbins's dinner, when he told her that he regarded no achievement in the line of his ambition as being beyond his power ; and it would not surprise him if he were to discover that she concluded, at that moment, that he was the man to carry out her ambition.

" May I ask you," he said, fixing his eyes upon her with a gravely questioning look, " when that plan first occurred to you ? "

"Oh, it was long ago," she answered, carelessly. " When I was in the convent in Paris, I made the acquaintance of the Princess de Méran, who was exactly my age. We became great friends, and she once took me home with her to her father's château in Picardy. I saw with my own eyes how those people lived, and I made up my mind that it was a beautiful and dignified and enjoyable life. Being an American I could not have that life, but I resolved to choose the next thing to it that was attainable to one of my nationality. You might say that I could have chosen to marry a French or German noble, and at one time I thought of that. But their ideas of women and their treatment of them are revolting to me, and I concluded that with my American education, I should buy position too dearly at such a price."

" And then you concluded to marry me, because among the men you had met, I seemed most likely to be able to carry out your scheme for you ? "

"I married you because I had respect for your intellect."

"Doesn't that amount to the same thing ? "

"Perhaps."

"And do you not think it is a little bit imprudent on your part to show me your hand so early in the game ? "

"If you are to accomplish a thing, you have got to know what it is, and keep it in mind from the beginning."

Horace smiled sardonically. He began to doubt whether he was really awake. There sat his young wife opposite to him, and told him, as it appeared to him, with the most refreshing insolence, that she had planned his life for him, and that all he had now got to do was to bend his energies toward the accomplishment of her plans. Was it a creature of the sex usually referred to as the gentler, who was making him this astounding proposition ? She had the faculty of clear thought and definite statement in an enviable degree. There was no mistaking her purposes. She had ruled her father's house, including the father himself ; she had never been crossed in any of her desires. What, then, could be more natural than her expectation to continue in this imperial rôle and take charge of her husband's destinies as she had of those of her parents. He must, of course, in some way, hint to her that he meant to share with her the reins of government ; but it would have to be done gently, for he was resolved, if possible, to avoid a collision.

"Has it occurred to you," he inquired, quietly, "that I may have something to say about all this ? "

"Yes," she answered, lifting her dark eyes with a look of grave observation; "but I sincerely hope you will not disagree with me."

"I will promise not to disagree with you to-day," was his reply, as he brusquely rose from the table. "I intend, if possible, to exclude disagreements from our honeymoon."

He noted a subdued excitement in her manner, or the nearest approach to excitement, which he had ever witnessed in her. Yet she rose with the greatest deliberation from the table, as if to rebuke him for his haste. In fact, in the suspicious frame of mind in which he found himself, everything she did or said became a more or less cloaked demonstration of antagonism. He could not reconcile himself to the thought that he was responsible to her for his actions; yet she seemed to take such responsibility for granted. Diplomat! The idea of his becoming a diplomat, and dancing attendance upon foreign dignitaries—he who loathed the pomp and circumstance of courts, and despised from the bottom of his heart the gilded idleness which in the effete monarchies was a title to respect ! No, thank God, he was an American to his backbone, and meant to assert himself here at home and rise as high here as his opportunities and his ability warranted. Was it, after all, wise to have introduced into his life a new and wholly incalculable force, which might set itself to work to frustrate his ambition instead of furthering it ? He had never before contemplated this possibility, because it seemed, only yes-terday, so absurdly remote. But to-day it was a tangible something which had to be reckoned with.

"Mrs. Larkin," he said as his wife approached the door (it was the first time he called her by that name, and it seemed extremely odd), "if there is anything I can do for you, I hope you'll let me know."

"If you'll kindly telegraph to father for my horses and carriage and Lamkin, my coachman, I shall be obliged," she answered with a slight salutation, and left the room.

Horses and coachman and carriage—all this fuss and expense of moving back and forth, for only three or four months! Well, he had not acquired the feeling of a millionaire yet, nor the needs of a complex existence; and he was probably a poor judge. He disliked making a grand splurge with his wife's money, immediately; pre-ferring a slower and more judicious expansion. But there was her mandate, clear and peremptory, as usual. He seized his hat with a muttered oath and walked down the street to the telegraph office.

CHAPTER XXXIX.

A MATRIMONIAL PROBLEM.

It is odd how a good judge of men may utterly misjudge women. Horace had thought of marriage as an amicable partnership, to which he contributed the brains and his wife the money. That he was to be head of the firm followed, as a matter of course, and that his junior-partner, recognizing his superiority, would unmurmuringly acquiesce in his decisions, it had never occurred to him to question. At the end of the first month of his married life, he was, however, a sadder and a wiser man. His calm and well-bred Kate, who could be so very charming when she wanted to, developed also the correlative faculty of not being charming when it suited her pleasure. She displayed no preference for the latter kind of behavior, but always threw upon him the onus of disturbing their pleasant relations. She demanded his time, she demanded his thought and his services in a hundred ways ; but she made her demands politely, though with that clear and well-chiselled neatness which irritated him, in spite of his better judgment. He asked himself the question twenty times a day, whether he had sunk to the position of being his wife's business manager. She owned in her own right a dozen houses in New York, both in aristocratic and in plebeian localities, and as the leases expired, a correspondence with the agents and frequent journeys to the city became necessary, to attend to the management of the property. Besides this, Kate had railroad and government bonds, coupons constantly falling due, money to be invested, and investments requiring to be closely watched. The mere business of being her husband was sufficiently absorbing to occupy a man's entire time and thought. She had a remarkably clear head and a good business judgment herself ; but she paid Horace the compliment of thinking his better. He was obliged, whether he would or not, to neglect his work in the legislature ; and the opportunity to make his power and influence felt in the Senate slipped out of his hand before he was aware of it. Indications began to appear, before the end of the session, that he was looked upon as a rich man who was playing at politics.

Kate had a definite, preconceived idea of what a marriage ought to be ; and though it was somewhat at variance with her husband's idea on the same subject, she managed to make him live up to her ideal. If she had attempted to define it she would have said that marriage should be a rational and well-bred companionship between two people who could advance themselves and advance each other's purposes by joining forces. She had, however, a strong conviction that her purposes were by far more rational and more important than his ; and that it was his duty for the present to subordinate his interests to hers. When a man married a woman of her wealth, position, and general superiority, it was but fair to demand of him a certain appreciation of his good fortune. He might, at least, hold his own affairs in abeyance, and allow hers to take precedence. If Mrs. Larkin had formulated any such theory of marriage and propounded it to her husband, it is safe to say that he would have rebelled. But she was too clever to commit any such blunder. She quietly absorbed him and took possession of him, as a matter of course, without consulting his preferences. She treated him with respect and with a kind of friendly *camaraderie* which made it impossible to rebuff her. She enjoyed conversing with him when, as she termed it, he was in his rational mood ; liked to have him explain the position of parties on the issues of the day, and asked intelligent questions which showed that she understood him completely. But if, as sometimes happened, his admiration for her degenerated into tenderness, she grew chilly and reserved, and administered prompt rebuffs. As soon as he saw the futility of such approaches, and had conquered the sheepishness, incident upon a repelled caress, she freely forgave him, and serenely resumed her discussion.

If any one had told Horace Larkin, a year ago, that he was to become so solicitous about the favor of any mortal creature, he would have laughed him to scorn. But, if he had had the courage to contemplate his situation clearly, he could not have escaped the conclusion that he was in a mild and polite way henpecked. His wife grew more formidable and at the same time more admirable to

him with every month that passed. Only on a single
occasion did he achieve a victory over her ; and then,
like a prudent general, she only retired from an indefen-
sible position.

Bills had been accumulating to an alarming extent in
the house, and a month passed before Kate took any steps
to pay them. Horace had a certain delicacy in calling her
attention to the subject ; because legally he was the debtor,
and it seemed to him that, in permitting her to pay his bills,
he abdicated the headship of the family, and assumed a
position of subordination and inferiority. Yet he did not
have the money to defray the lavish expenses which she
incurred ; especially as the building of his house in Torryville was a heavy drain upon his resources. It was therefore a relief to him when Kate one morning, after breakfast, handed him a check book and begged him to settle up
all accounts.

"But I have no deposit in the Second National Bank,"
he said, seeing that the check book was issued by that institution.

"But I have," she answered ; "you only make out the
checks and I will sign them."

"You must excuse me," he said, firmly ; "but I cannot
agree to that arrangement."

"May I ask you why you object to it ?"

"In point of law, the man is the head of the house. I
wish to preserve, at least, the semblance of that character."

"I have no wish to deprive you of it. But I must insist
upon my right to do with my own as I want."

"Certainly ; only there is no need of insisting."

"Then what are we disagreeing about ?"

"I do not wish to pay my bills with your checks."

"I have no objection, if you prefer it, to your paying
them with your own."

There was a sting of sarcasm in this remark, which made
him wince. A slow wrath began to smoulder in his vitals,
and threatened to break into flame. She had the best of
the argument apparently, and yet he felt that he was right.
There is nothing so irritating as to be worsted in argument
by your wife. Horace could not afford to retire from the
bout except with flying colors.

"Mrs. Larkin," he said with keen, incisive emphasis, "I
will pay the bills, as you suggest. But I must insist, henceforth, on your cutting down the scale of your expenditures
and living within my income."

21

He handed her the check book and walked slowly out of the room. All his soul was aroused and his strong frame shook with suppressed anger. Had it come to this, that he must go to his wife for pocket money and advertise to the world his dependence upon her, at the same time that he sacrificed to her his career and his honorable ambition. No, he would have this thing settled now and here ; and he would not yield an inch. They must agree upon a *modus vivendi ;* otherwise life would be unendurable.

He was still passionately absorbed in this meditation as he entered the Senate chamber and flung himself into his seat. A page came up and handed him a dozen letters. He tore them open, one after another, and glanced at the signatures ; but he could not fix his mind on their contents. A bill was being languidly debated, the object of which was to remove all safeguards against fraud in the awarding of canal contracts. The representatives of the Canal Ring were there in full force, and their paid hirelings on the floor of the Senate had it apparently all their own way. Horace sat listening with a vague irritation to their thinly veiled arguments in favor of corruption, and it struck him suddenly what a wretched pass democracy had come to, when enterprising scoundrels could stand up, in the full light of publicity, and with pretences that deceived nobody, facilitate the schemes of thieves and plunderers. The wrath within him as he sat listening to these harangues gradually diverted him from his personal grievances ; and he began to itch to give these shameless fellows a whack over the head. Without a moment's deliberation he rose from his seat and addressed the speaker. A ripple of interest ran through the assembly at the sound of his voice. He had brought a reputation with him from the lower house, but had so far done nothing in the Senate to justify it. There was a rousing clarion note in his voice, when he was deeply stirred, and before he had spoken five minutes, all conversation had ceased, and the letter-writing members had laid down their pens and were straining their ears to listen. For once in his life he threw policy to the winds and spoke out of the depth of his conviction, striking right and left and caring little whom he hit. He surpassed himself in vigor and in reckless sledge-hammer eloquence. He showed up the purpose of the bill, waxed indignant over its iniquity, and tore the arguments of its defenders into shreds with a fierce vindictive delight. The doings of the Canal Ring, its composition and its whole inner history had been familiar to him for many years ; but, somehow, they had never stirred his wrath until to-day. The rumor spread through the corridors that the Hon. Horace Larkin was making an assault upon the lobby, and the galleries rapidly filled with alarmed members of the third chamber. When, at the end of an hour, the honorable gentleman sat down, the universe, as far as he was concerned, was restored to equilibrium. He had retrieved himself in his own eyes. He was yet a power in the world, whatever he might be in his own household. The air about him seemed charged with electricity. The reporters were scribbling away for dear life, preparing despatches to telegraph to all the corners of the continent. Not a soul ventured to lift his voice in favor of the bill, after the irrefutable exposure it had received, but at the voting which followed, it must be admitted, that it came within a dozen votes of receiving a majority. The Senate adjourned on the motion of some rural Solon who seemed badly frightened ; and Horace sauntered out, but was overtaken in the lobby by two so-called " dude members " from New York City, who were profuse in their congratulations. He grew shy, however, at their eagerness to claim him as a brother reformer. He was by no means sure, yet, that his path lay on that side ; and he was in no haste to commit himself.

It did not occur to Horace that his speech had the least bearing upon his matrimonial problem. The thought of meeting his wife was not pleasant to him. It was chiefly to postpone the evil hour that he walked about the city and finally found himself in the open country under a bright cold sky, with bare brown fields on either hand. He presently heard the firm, rhythmic hoof-beat of horses and the roll of carriage wheels over the smooth highway. The metallic clicking of the harness sounded close by, and in the next moment there was a great splash, as the animals struck a puddle in the road, and before he could look about he felt the mud plastering his face and flying about his ears. He stopped angrily, and was about to shout to the coachman ; but recognizing that worthy by the august dignity of his back, remained silent. He caught a glimpse, too, of Mrs. Larkin, wrapped in her precious furs, lolling in the corner of her carriage, with her air of vague disapproval of the world in general.

"Great God," he murmured with clenched teeth, as he shook his fist after the departing carriage, " if I don't get even with you——"

He contemplated his figure, dripping with mud, and merely to give vent to his overcharged feelings swore a long voluminous oath. Then he pulled out his handkerchief, rubbed his face and picked the dirt out of his mustache. A fierce resentment flared up in his heart. And yet what had she done to him to arouse such savage sentiments ? She had surely not directed her coachman to give him a mud-bath. She had simply not seen him, and if her coachman had seen him, he had not recognized him. And yet there was a symbolic significance in the act which made it atrocious, in spite of its being unintentional. It was thus she drove through life, calm and imperious, devoid of all fellow-feeling for her kind, and heedlessly bespattering the chance wayfarer with the mud from her carriage wheels. He had hoped to occupy the vacant seat at her side ; but somehow, he lacked the impudence to do it with good grace ; there was a democratic strain in his blood which made him, in spite of his equestrian facilities, a foot passenger.

He got home, under the cover of the twilight, and made his toilet for dinner. Mrs. Larkin had made the dress coat and the white tie obligatory; and though he rebelled against what appeared to him senseless ceremony, he lacked courage to avow himself in her eyes a plebeian. He resolved, as he descended the stairs, not to refer to his accident and to repress the resentment which it had excited, for he was rational enough to see that in marriage slight causes may have long and disastrous results. Having taken this woman for better or for worse, and knowing what an irrevocable fact she was in his life, he would only be punishing himself in arousing feelings in her which must make their intercourse more difficult. So he greeted her, as she entered the drawing-room, with the ceremonious stiffness which she liked, offered her his arm and conducted her to the table. He felt that in doing this he had gone far enough ; and he made no further effort to make himself agreeable.

"I was sorry you did not come home early enough to take a drive with me," she said, tasting her *consommé*, "I enjoyed it very much."

"So did I," he answered, with a sardonic grin.

"Ah. Then you, too, went driving ?"

"No, I went on foot."

The tone of these answers convinced Kate that her amiability was wasted, and she quickly withdrew her antennæ into the shell of her icy reserve. And thus they sat through a long dinner of half a dozen courses, glancing furtively at each other, while they ate their costly delicacies without the least appreciation of their choice flavors. Horace was angry and miserable ; Kate was offended and miserable, and felt that her dignity would never permit her to make another advance toward such a boor as her husband. When the meal, at last, came to an end, he excused himself and retired into the library, where he sat smoking and pondering his wretchedness until midnight.

The next morning at breakfast, the same pleasant pantomime was repeated ; and the situation seemed doubly unendurable. Horace, feeling that a crisis was at hand, determined to precipitate it by carrying out his threat in regard to the bills, discharge the superfluous servants, and enforce discipline, without regard for consequences. He spent the morning in the library, signing checks and writing letters, and was about to start for the Capitol, when Kate entered the room unannounced, and seated herself in an easy chair close to his desk. He noticed with some astonishment that she carried two New York papers in her hand, and that the severity of her expression was much relaxed.

"Have you read that ? " she asked, putting one of the papers before him on the desk ; "I thought you might like to see it." He took up the paper and read a report of his speech of yesterday and an editorial in which the ability and the courage of his performance were highly praised. He was hailed as the coming man in his party, and a great future was prophesied him.

"Why have you not told me of this ? " she asked with grave friendliness.

"I did not think it would interest you," he answered, doggedly.

"Then you do not know me, Mr. Larkin ; nothing would interest me more."

"You think it might induce the President to send me to the Court of St. James ? " he asked, flinging himself back in his chair, and smiling sarcastically.

"Not at once," she replied, with imperturbable composure ; "we can afford to wait."

He was much tempted to resume his writing and ignore her presence. His dignity seemed to demand that he should snub her ; but he was either not brave enough or not rude enough to obey this impulse, for she was a tremendous fact, this serene, beautiful woman, with her clear brow, her fine intelligence, and her firm and definite purposes. How could he help admiring her ? She was exactly the type of womanhood which *a priori* he would have judged to be most admirable. And yet she roused the old Adam in him with a frightful persistency, and made him fear that, before he was done with her, he would get to the point of striking her.

Kate, if she had any perception of what was going on in her husband's mind, was not disturbed by it. She was capable, not of forgiving, but of ignoring a great deal that was unpleasant, after having received this forcible proof that she had not been mistaken in her judgment of him.

"Mr. Larkin," she said, rising and leaning with her hand on the side of the desk, "would you kindly let me know what arrangement would be satisfactory to you, in the matter of our common expenses ? "

He was taken aback by the suddenness of the question. He was too obtuse to see the connection between this proposed surrender and the prophecies of the New York paper.

"What good will it do you to know ? " he asked ; "I shouldn't like to risk a second refusal."

"You would oblige me by telling me."

"Very well, then. My proposal is that you should hand over to me at the beginning of the year or every half year whatever sum you may see fit to contribute toward the running of our household. The administration of it must be in my name and in my hands. If you have suggestions to make, I'll listen to you with pleasure, but the deciding voice must be mine."

She gazed at him for a while in silence, and her features brightened with a look of pride and gratification.

"Would you allow me," she inquired, with extreme courtesy, "to take your place for a moment at the desk ? "

He arose, somewhat mystified, and offered her his chair.

"I'll be parboiled if I know what she is up to now," was his mental comment. He regarded her movements with the kind of interested curiosity with which one watches the gesticulations of a conjurer when anything imaginable may be the result. She took a pen, tried it on the back of an envelope, and pulling her small check book from her pocket proceeded to draw a check. It would have been hard to tell why at this point he looked away with a marked assumption of indifference. He took a little stroll on the floor, looked out of the window, and began softly to whistle. When he had finished this little farce to his own satisfaction, he found his wife standing in front of him.

"Would you kindly accept this as my first contribution?" she said simply, handing him the check ; and with a slight salutation she left the room.

Half dumfounded he stood and looked, now at the door, now at the slip of paper he held in his hand. There was not a suspicion of *éclat* or dramatic effect in her manner. But the very absence of it, the queenly simplicity of her speech and act, made you listen for the orchestral flourish which follows a climax in dramatic action.

"Pay to Horace Larkin or bearer Fifty Thousand Dollars— $50,000—*Catharine Van Schaak Larkin"*—were the words which he read, and re-read until they made him dizzy. He realized slowly what they meant. He was a victor, indeed, but for all that he felt defeated. It was Pyrrhic victory.

CHAPTER XL.

A MATRIMONIAL CHRONICLE.

The family on the sixth floor of the Patagonia consisted no longer of two but of three. A little brown and wrinkled fragment of humanity had arrived about six weeks ago, and had made no end of commotion in the household. It was, for all that, enthusiastically welcomed, and after some rather spirited disputes between his parents, it was named Obed Larkin. While he was in the vegetable state, devoting himself solely to the absorption of nourishment, his father, curiously enough, took a livelier interest in him than his mother; and it was not until he had acquired some rudimentary accomplishments, such as smiling, kicking, and putting his toes in his mouth, that the latter began to discover his charms. But then, Gertrude had been very ill, and under peculiarly trying circumstances. She was subject to unaccountable moods and, at times, the burden of poverty was so heavy that it seemed as if she must break down under it. Aleck was now part proprietor of the school; his heart was in his work, and he was looked upon as a successful teacher. But if he was successful, she argued, how could he be content with a paltry $2,500, which was less than many a clerk got, who had neither his intellect nor his culture? Aleck was entirely unable to explain this to her satisfaction, although he exerted himself hard enough. He tried his best to keep a brave heart amid all their tribulations, and he thought a hundred times, when her moods tried him beyond endurance, of the physician's saying that she had inherited poor nerves. He could not be angry with her for a physical ailment which had been bequeathed to her at her birth by Him who visits the iniquities of the fathers upon the children. And moreover, he loved her so dearly, that even when she tortured him, his heart was full of tenderness and pity, and he thanked God that it had fallen to his lot to comfort and protect her. He did not rebel against his fate, nor did he waste time in vain regrets. He had not expected a life of unalloyed bliss, and knew that he had no right to expect it. A cheerful resignation is compatible with a good deal of happiness ; and there were moments when Aleck blessed even his trials for the sweet rewards they sometimes brought him.

I may as well admit it ; the code of conduct in the Patagonia was a little peculiar. When Gertie, after a prolonged attack of the blues, sat opposite to her husband at the table, eating nothing and feeling a vague resentment of his appetite, it would occasionally happen that the absurdity of her own behavior struck her and she would give little lugubrious laughs, to which he would sympathetically respond, although he had not the remotest idea of what provoked her mirth. Only, on general principles, he was anxious to encourage any cheerful impulse she might have. Then, when the meal was at an end, she would, by way of reconciliation, rumple his hair a little in passing his chair, and he would feel as grateful for this attention as if it had been the tenderest caress. Perhaps, after the lapse of five or ten minutes she would invade his humble library, and seating herself upon his lap attribute to herself all manner of obnoxious qualities in the hope that he would contradict her.

" I have been perfectly horrid, Aleck, haven't I ! "

"No, dear, you haven't been horrid ; you couldn't be horrid, even if you tried to."

" But I have tried to, Aleck ; I have been as bad as I possibly could."

"You have tried to be horrid ? Why, dearest, I can't quite believe that."

"You don't know me, Aleck, I know myself I am perfectly detestable, and yet I can't help it. There is a kind of blue devil inside of me who makes me do and say the most abominable things to you. I would give the world to be cheerful and contented, but it is no good to try, I simply can't. And this blue devil leaves me quite as suddenly as he comes. And then I know how miserable I have made you, Aleck."

He knew from sad experience how dangerous it was to agree with her, when she was in this mood of self-accusation, or even to show the slightest disposition to concede that there was a modicum of truth in her indictment. The penalty for such an unwary admission was apt to be severer than justice demanded.

"Well, Mr. Larkin," she would say, withdrawing her

arms from his neck, as abruptly as if he had been a leper,
" if that is your opinion of me, it is a great pity you didn't
find it out before. You might then have been saved the
mistake of marrying me."

Whereupon she would rise from his lap and walk out of
the room deeply offended, and he would vainly spend the
rest of the evening in all sorts of ingenious devices to coax
her back into good humor.

Of course he soon learned his lesson. He became a
positive expert in affectionate mendacity. He could tell
to a " t " what answer she expected, and never scrupled to
give it. After a while these domestic excursions into the
domain of fiction lost all relation to his conscience. With
admirable brazenness he told her ten times a week that
she was the most amiable woman in the world, and that
she had not the remotest suggestion of a temper. And
when it suited her mood to dispute this assertion, he would
admit with a judicial mien that she had spirit, and that
he had no respect for a woman who had not.

Thus passed year after year of their married life. They
grew a trifle more prosperous and were able to move into
a better flat. Another boy arrived, and came near receiving the name of Horace, but Gertrude professed such an
aversion for this name that Aleck was obliged to change it
to Ralph. Obed had in the meanwhile grown very handsome and had developed the most fascinating characteristics. He was scarcely three years old when he began to
show (as his father thought) evidences of an unusual intellect. His pride in the boy and his affection for him knew no
bounds, and he did whatever he could to spoil him. In
the school, among his fellow-teachers, he never failed to re-
late Obed's last clever saying, until on one occasion he
happened to see a cartoon in *Puck*, representing a man
who stands alone at one end of a room, disconsolately turning over some photographs, while at the other end twenty
or thirty people are crowded together in animated conversation. And under the picture he read the legend : " This is
the fiend who tells the bright sayings of his five-year-old
son." It was a warning which he could not afford to disregard. Instead of bragging to his friends of his child's
cleverness he now kept a diary in which all the evidences
of Obed's precocity were faithfully chronicled.

Most women, after marriage, sink the wife in the
mother, or the mother in the wife. The force of their
affection flows abundantly in the one direction or the

other, but never equally in both. Gertrude, after the
birth of her children, felt a new well-spring of love opening in her breast. The old aimlessness of her life, which
had been its chief affliction, distressed her no more.
Every moment of the day had its urgent duties, and though
she did not profess to find them always delightful, they
yet filled a want in her heart and prevented her from
nursing empty griefs. She was fully convinced that, if
the opportunity had been afforded her, she would have
risen to fame as a sculptor. Her talent, as it ceased to be
actively exercised, became less a source of vexation to her
and more one of pride. It redeemed her from the dreary
commonplaceness which is the lot of the vast majority of
women. It made her exceptional and justified a height-
ened self-respect. Social position, she persuaded herself,
she did not care for ; and Aleck strengthened her to
the extent of his ability in her wholesome contempt for
conventionalities. He was innocent enough to believe
in her sincerity, when she commiserated those earth-
clogged souls who drove in carriages and had no thought
beyond fashion plates and the exchange of inane civilities.
As if there ever was a woman, from Sappho and Madame
de Staël down, who did not yearn for the conventional !

Aleck sometimes in his saner moments suspected that he
spoiled his wife. It seemed to him that the more anxious
he grew to please her, the harder she grew to please.
Occasionally when his friends, Miller and Tuthill, who
were employed in the school, told him how they managed
their wives, he resolved to take Gertrude seriously in hand
and once for all establish his authority over her. But
somehow the time seemed never opportune for beginning
this course of discipline. Either Gertrude was too charming in her perversity, or too touchingly sweet in her pouts,
or she was not in very good health, which might account
for her irrational conduct. And was he, after all, such an
exemplary fellow himself that he could afford to set himself up as a judge over her ?

It was while this question of discipline was troubling
Aleck, that Gertrude declared that she wanted a fine etching
on the wall over the sofa. Couldn't Aleck spare a Saturday afternoon and go with her on an expedition in search
of something effective and appropriate. She knew exactly
what she wanted ; but she would yet prefer to consult
him. Quite flattered at this consideration he started out
with her, and made the round of the stores which make a

specialty of etchings.   But the most hopeless diversity
of taste soon became apparent.   Gertrude would look at
nothing but dogs, while Aleck, as she contemptuously
averred, would look at nothing but girls.

"Suppose, Gertie," her husband proposed, when the
twentieth store had been visited, "suppose we strike a
compromise.   I am willing, if you say so, to take a girl
with a dog."

"As if that were a compromise," retorted Gertrude, pug-
naciously ; "then you would have your way after all."

"What, then, would you propose ?" he inquired, wearily.

"Well," she said, "I—I—would propose a dog with a
girl."

"All right, dear.   You take your choice.   I have got to
run over to Brentano's.   I'll be back in fifteen minutes."

Having finished his errand, he returned.   His wife met
him in the door with a radiant face.   She professed great
delight at seeing him, and talked vivaciously about everything under the sun.   When they got home, an hour and
a half later, Aleck was confronted with six dogs' heads set
in a panel.

"But where is the girl, Gertie ?" he exclaimed, too
amused to be angry.

"Well now, Aleck," she replied, coaxingly, seizing his
arm and gazing up into his eyes, "don't you think dogs
are a great deal nicer ?"

"Well, dear," he ejaculated laughing, "when they are
well disciplined, I almost think they are."

"So do I ; but you know, that's just the trouble with
girls ; they *can't* be disciplined."

"Are you quite sure of that ?"

There came a challenging light into her eyes, in which
there lurked yet a spark of amusement.

"If you have any doubt on the subject, suppose you try
the experiment," she said, with humorous defiance.

"No, I'll take your word for it, dear.   You know
best."

"But really, don't you think those dogs are lovely,
Aleck ?"

"Well, I can't say I do ; but I shall probably get used
to them after a while."

"Now, Aleck, that's perfectly horrid in you to say
that.   You only say it to make me wretched."

"Well, dear, to be frank, I think I am beginning to like
the picture more, the more I look at it.   You know you

can never tell at once whether you like a picture. You have to live with it."

"Yes, exactly. That's what I have always insisted. And don't you think that Collie Calypso is a perfect beauty?"

"Yes, she is really very fine. Such faithful eyes and such solemn dignity in her expression."

"Well now, Aleck, that is perfectly charming. I knew you would in the end agree with me."

For ten minutes more this discussion was continued with coaxings and playful threats, until Aleck had been induced to admit that all the six dogs were beauties, and that he liked all of them—nay, preferred them to girls. But Gertrude, after her first flush of triumph began to grow uneasy. The very completeness of her victory caused her apprehension. Dim impulses of generosity began to stir within her. When they had finished dinner and Aleck had retired into his study for a smoke, she braved his detested pipe (which since Obed's birth he had adopted for economic reasons) and seated herself upon his lap. She insisted upon his continuing to smoke, declared that she was getting so accustomed to his pipe now, that she would miss it if he were to give it up, and bewildered him by her amiability and her magnanimous proposals.

"Aleck, you poor boy," she said, "did it ever occur to you that I am not half as nice to you as you are to me?"

"No," declared Aleck, laughing; "how could anything so absurd occur to me?"

"But Aleck, it is really so. You give up to me always; and I never give up to you."

"Don't you? Why, my dear, I think you are quite wrong there."

"Tell me of a single instance.'

He pondered solemnly for several minutes and finally invented a case; but she took him up promptly, and refuted him; whereupon she embraced him with remorseful tenderness and shed a few furtive tears. But when Aleck, encouraged by her affectionate mood whispered some endearing nonsense in her ear, and responded with happy ardor to her caresses, she grew suddenly coy, lifted her face from his bosom with a little frown of guilty defiance and said in a tone of grave remonstrance:

"Now, Aleck, don't gush! Why must you always gush, the moment I touch you? You know I am a great deal too good for you; but you are the only one I have, so, of course, don't you see?"

The inference to be drawn from this declaration was by no means flattering, but he had learned by this time to interpret a great deal of what she said in a Pickwickian sense. For his love for her was like a radiant luminary which shed its warm lustre upon her every word and act, investing them with an irresistible charm. "At bottom she is good and true," he said to himself, when that fact seemed in special need of reaffirmation; "and I would not have her otherwise."

And this faith of his in her essential goodness was not disappointed in the present instance. When Gertrude rose from her slumber the morning after her etching expedition, and her eyes met the six solemn faces of the Duke of Buccleugh's dogs, she grew almost as solemn as they. She could not comprehend the mysterious change they had undergone; they had lost every vestige of beauty over night. The next day they became an annoyance, and the third day they were a positive affliction. Their grave reproachful eyes followed her wherever she went. She could endure them no longer. Without notifying Aleck, she donned her street costume, visited the dealer and exchanged her canines for one of Boughton's old-English girls, and the prettiest one she could find. When Aleck came home that evening, they had a spirited contest in magnanimity which ended with a little scene of a strictly confidential nature :

> " Teach me, only teach, love,
>   As I aught.
>   I will speak thy speech, love,
>   Think thy thought."

" But," exclaimed Aleck, not liking to be outdone in generosity; " you might at least have kept one or two of the dogs, and yet gotten me my girl."

" No, Aleck," she answered with mock gravity, "you can't expect to get more than one girl for six dogs. I should say that was a fair equivalent."

There was, however, a more serious side to the life of these affectionate triflers than appeared in these playful encounters. Aleck had never quite given up his literary aspirations, and though struggling with disadvantages of every kind, saw a will-o'-the-wisp of hope continually dancing in his path, luring him on to fresh endeavors. Several of his poems found their way into the magazines, and were extravagantly praised by a single friendly critic to whom

Aleck, in the days of his prosperity, had lent $20. It was odd, he thought, for a debtor to choose that way of getting even with him. If he had damned him with exceptional virulence, he would have been less surprised. To Gertrude, however, these drops of praise were extremely sweet. She kept the newspaper cuttings in her sewing basket (in which she also kept her purse and everything else, except what properly belonged there) and read them half mechanically to herself while she sat nursing her youngest child. It had never occurred to her that Aleck might be a great man—a great man in disguise, as she put it to herself. But if the world decided that she was wrong in her estimate of him, she was more than willing to be convinced. She hoped most ardently, both for her own sake and for his, that he might attain celebrity as a man of letters ; and that it might come to him, while they were both young enough to enjoy it. With every month and every year that passed she grew more anxious ; until one day she stumbled upon a newspaper paragraph, which informed her that literary fame was rarely attained in youth, and that Thackeray, George Eliot, and Balzac were well on toward forty before they emerged from obscurity. She cut this item out and pasted it in her pocketbook ; and whenever her heart was heavy, she took it out and set herself bravely to tracing resemblances between her husband's circumstances and those of the great authors. And when finally a little success came to him she saw in it a promise of the fulfilment of all her fond dreams.

Aleck happened one day to read an essay by Edmund Clarence Stedman, in which the assertion was made that the present age demanded novels rather than epics, and that we were living in a period of transition during which poetry was suffering an eclipse. Poetry was no longer the chief artery through which the intellectual vitality of the century was pulsing. This statement struck him forcibly, and presently started him on a journey of exploration in his own mind. Was he a poet by the grace of God—a man with whom lofty rhythmic utterance was natural and imperative ? Was he not rather oppressed by a dim creative yearning which demanded some kind of expression, and had chosen a poetic one because it seemed the most dignified and satisfactory ? Would it not be worth while to make an experiment in prose, if the rewards of authorship lay in that direction ? A plot for a short story soon occurred to him, and it cost him three sleepless nights to develop it consistently in all its details. He said nothing to Gertrude about it, until it was finished and accepted by one of the leading magazines. It was an episode of political life which he had witnessed in his youth, with a realistic rural love-story intertwined. There was a strong touch in it, and here and there great felicity of phrase. The little stir it created was very grateful to its author, for it opened the magazines to him and stimulated his ambition. At the solicitation of his wife he began a full-grown novel, entitled " The Cloven Foot;" which grew, in the course of a year and a half, to be such an absorbing topic that it blotted out half the real life about them. When Aleck came home from the school, where he did his writing in his private study, Gertrude's first question as she went to meet him was : " How is your Cloven Foot?" Then followed a lively discussion of the hero's fate and the heroine's doings and sayings, criticisms, designing of costumes, and unsparing ridicule, on the lady's part, of the toilets which Aleck had evolved from his inner consciousness. Little Obed, who sat at his father's side, listening to the conversation, created much merriment by his innocent questions concerning these fictitious personages, in whose reality he firmly believed. He heard this question : " How is your Cloven Foot," so constantly that he took it to be a normal and proper salutation, and when Mrs. Tuthill called upon his mother, he startled that lady by saying (after much vain coaxing to be polite) : " How do you do? And how is your Cloven Foot?"

Among the many plans, the realization of which depended upon the success of her husband's novel, was one which Gertrude cherished with the fondest anticipations. She wanted a house of her own. Her bad moods, which yet continued, though with longer intervals than before, she attributed to the discomforts incident upon life in an apartment house. When the steam radiators at five o'clock in the morning commenced to make a racket like a continuous discharge of musketry, and roused all man's unregenerate impulses, she contended that it required stronger nerves than she possessed to keep an even temper through the day. When the shivering old maids on the top floor demanded a temperature of eighty degrees, and the pipes, in passing through the lower flats, heated these apartments to the same temperature, it seemed as if a needless burden was added to existence, and a little profanity would have been excusable. This relief, was, however, denied to Gertrude. She had to bear her cross and be silent. But she took it out in the blues. Housewifely thrift was not among her virtues ; and everything relating to housekeeping vexed and annoyed her. She had an idea that when she got a house, all these trials would be at an end. Servants objected to flats, for obvious reasons ; but when they were given free sway in a house, she had been told that they gave far less trouble. She was anxious to try the experiment.

One trial, which at the outset of their married life Aleck had anticipated with dread, was happily spared them. Gertrude's mother, the Countess Kharlovitz, as she called herself, died about six months after her daughter's visit to her, and was buried at Aleck's expense. Count Kharlovitz, it turned out, had had some connection with a counterfeiting gang, and getting himself entangled with the police betook himself to parts unknown. His history, which was a picturesque and varied one, was published in the Sunday *World*, with sundry illustrations. Aleck read it with a quaking heart, and congratulated himself that there were some facts which had escaped the reporter's notice. The name Larkin was not mentioned in the article.

22

CHAPTER XLI.

BLIND SKIRMISHINGS.

After having served two terms in the Senate, Horace Larkin determined not to accept a renomination. His chief reason for turning his back upon the State Legislature was his wife's aversion for Albany. During his second term she refused to accompany him, and took up her residence in her father's house in Gramercy Park. He was, of course, at liberty to visit her there ; but the atmosphere of the Van Schaak family was uncongenial to him ; the old gentleman irritated him by his fussiness about all sorts of nothings, and Mrs. Van Schaak by her high-nosed condescension. He felt as if he were simply tolerated ; and that it was only Kate's authority which secured for him a certain amount of consideration. For she treated him with an almost ostentatious respect in the presence of her parents, and exacted a similar treatment from them. But, after all, it was not pleasant to be living in such a state of armed neutrality. From pure inanity and desperation he took to flirting mildly with Mrs. Adrian, Jr., who, from hunger for amusement, pounced upon him like a vulture ; but the disapprobation of the other members of the family made the air so oppressive that he lost heart for the enterprise. On Mrs. Adrian, however, this repressed condemnation had exactly the opposite effect. It stimulated her to greater audacity. From sheer deviltry she praised Horace to the skies ; professed the most extravagant regard for him, and did her best to give a perfectly harmless affair the appearance of a deep intrigue. With a mischievous air of innocence she sat at the dinner-table, saying whatever came into her head, and attributing to him the most compromising remarks, which he had never uttered. And when he, entering into the joke, replied by attributing to her some still more indiscreet utterance, she would shake her forefinger at him in playful threat, and exclaim :

"Now, Horace, I wouldn't have believed that of you. I'll be more careful next time. Never, never shall I say anything nice to you again."

At last, when this comedy had gone a good deal further than was agreeable to him, he seriously remonstrated with his fair persecutor.

"I hope you'll not take it unkindly," he said, "if I beg you not to talk of me the way you do at table."

"And what way do I talk about you?" she inquired, with mischief lurking in her eyes.

"You know that as well as I do," he answered, "not to put too fine a point on it—you—you make me very uncomfortable by—your—fanciful statements."

"Why not say lies?" she cried, gayly. "I may just as well confess it, I like to lie. It is such a relief after a long day of monotonous truth-telling."

"And might I be permitted to suggest that you choose some other subject for your fictions the next time? You may not suspect it—and, of course, I know you don't—but you put me, at times, in a very embarrassing position."

"Don't I, though?" the heartless creature exclaimed, in great glee; "why, my dear Horace, who would have thought you were so unsophisticated?"

He perceived that he must change his tactics if he were to make any impression upon her. She was absolutely irresponsible, and gloried in her irresponsibility. It was not so easy a matter as he had anticipated to extricate himself from her jewelled clutches.

"Do let us talk seriously, Annie," he said, leaning forward and fixing an earnest gaze upon her; "I know, of course, this is all play to you, but to me it may have serious consequences. My wife—you know, I should not in her present condition, wish to exasperate her."

"Ah, but that is what I should like above all things," Mrs. Adrian ejaculated, with a sudden flash of resentment in her eye; "I would give ten years of my life, if I could make Kate angry, not miffed only, you know, but real hopping mad. She has exasperated me until I have cried, not once, but a hundred thousand times—and nothing would give me more pleasure than to get even with her."

"But you must excuse me if I refuse to be a party to such a scheme," Horace replied, with a cool firmness which made her shudder; "if I must have a quarrel, I prefer to have it with you rather than with Kate."

"Well, I don't blame you. We all know on what side our bread is buttered. And still it is a great pity, for you were so amusing," she finished with a little sigh, as with a mock courtesy she left the room.

It was true; Kate had found it beneath her dignity to take notice of her husband's flirtation. If she was privately annoyed by it (as was not unlikely), her self-respect was too great to permit her to make the slightest demonstration of dissatisfaction. Nay, she even heaped glowing coals upon his head by showing an interest in his costume.

"Couldn't you find out," she said to him one evening, as he was conversing with her in the up-stairs sitting-room, "where Adrian gets his clothes. You'll not mind my telling you that his coats and trousers have a certain air of being *comme il faut* which yours have not."

"I'll go to his tailor, if you like," he answered; "though I can scarcely hope to rival Adrian in elegance."

"Yes, you can. And I want you to promise to show me samples of cloths which are fashionable, and consult me before making a choice."

When, a week later, Horace entered his wife's apartment, arrayed in the garments thus carefully selected, she looked at him critically, and with visible disappointment. That indefinable air which she found so impressive in her brother was still wanting. Horace, reading her unspoken judgment in her face, felt a kind of sheepish discomfiture which he could not shake off.

"Kate," he said, with a half pathetic laugh, "it's no good. It isn't the coat, it's the man."

She was almost inclined to admit the failure of her experiment; but it was not in her nature to concede that she could be wrong.

"I don't think so, Horace," she replied in her firm, clear voice; and in the hope to apply balm to his wounded feelings she added: "I have always maintained that you have just the style of ugliness that can be made to look like distinction."

"Thanks," he said, smiling ironically; "don't exert yourself further. You might make me conceited."

The long expected event which had kept Horace in the city during the greater part of the winter, finally took place about the beginning of March. A little black-eyed daughter was born to him. He had expected to experience some little emotion on such an occasion; but he was disappointed. The only sensation of which he was conscious was a slight

embarrassment at his utter superfluity. It appeared to be
in order to say something appropriate to Kate ; but she
was evidently expecting nothing, and perhaps he would,
in the end, only be making a jack of himself. So he betook himself away with a sense of awkwardness and
oppression. He found it hard to forgive his daughter
her sex. He felt as if she had purposely deceived him.
Both Kate and he had been confident that they were to
have a boy. However, even a girl might be made an excuse for a little paternal vanity ; and feeling a strong need
of confiding in someone, Horace walked up the Avenue
to the Union League Club, of which he was a member.
There he sat for an hour pretending to read a newspaper.
But he saw no opportunity such as he desired for a jocose
assertion of his new dignity. At last the thought of Aleck
came to him like an inspiration ; he hired a cab and drove
into the unfashionable neighborhood on Twenty-third
Street between Seventh and Eighth Avenues where his
brother's migratory household was then sojourning. It
was not the first time, by any means, that he sought Aleck
during this dreary, interminable winter. He had been quite
a frequent visitor in the huge human hive where men
swarmed like bees and crawled through long labyrinthine
passages to their appropriate cells. After many rebuffs he
had succeeded in establishing himself tolerably in the favor
of his nephew Obed, upon whom (much to his mother's
annoyance) he lavished presents. But Horace did not
have the knack of pleasing children, and to romp with
them as Aleck did, without the least loss of dignity, would
have been impossible to him. It was almost pathetic to
see how he sued for the good-will of his two pretty
nephews ; though Gertrude always maintained that he did
not care a rap about them.

The fact was, Horace felt a little awkward in his relations with his brother, because he had never been able to
induce his wife to renew her acquaintance with Gertrude.
He had used the excuse which the expectation of an addi-
tion to the family had furnished as long as it was available ;
and it had cost Gertrude the greatest exertion to listen to
the repetition of this plea with a sober face. There were
a hundred spiteful remarks which she would have liked to
make, and which she would have made, if Aleck's eyes had
not restrained her. She knew that Kate looked down
upon her, for a variety of reasons ; and it seemed hard that
she should be denied the satisfaction of letting her know

how sublimely indifferent she was to her attentions, and how entirely superior she felt herself in all respects.

It was about the middle of May, when the baby was more than two months old, that Horace again broached the perilous topic to Kate at the luncheon-table. They were to move to Torryville, where their new house was awaiting them, in two weeks ; and there could be no reason, as far as he could see, for refusing to be polite, when politeness cost so little. If it were a question of an intimacy which might in the end prove burdensome, he would be the last to urge it upon her. But Gertrude was a proud and sensitive woman, against whom there would be no need of being on one's guard. And moreover, they were to live in different cities, and their lives would of necessity be far apart.

Kate sat listening to this earnest argument with her usual placid expression. Only now and then a fine scorn, or the merest shadowy suggestion of it, would flit across her countenance.

"It is useless to discuss such a matter with you, Horace," she said, taking a sip of tea ; "for you don't know the first thing about social usages, and the obligations you incur by a call."

"But do tell me," he interposed, eagerly, "what have you against Gertrude ? You surely don't need to like everybody you call upon."

"I should hope not," she answered, emphatically, "or I should have to drop nine-tenths of my visiting list."

"That's what I supposed. What, then, is the matter with Gertrude ?"

"There is nothing the matter with her. She is very nice, I don't doubt, and all that. But if you don't mind my saying it, she is scarcely, in the strictest sense, good form, not quite *comme il faut.*"

"Not *comme il faut !* Well, I must say, I don't see it. Seems to me she looks as well as anybody, and a good deal better than most of the people who come here. Now, do tell me, why isn't she *comme il faut ?* "

"Not *comme il fau,* if you please, but *comme il fauo,*" Kate corrected, blandly ; she was proud of her Parisian accent, and rarely missed an opportunity to lord it over him, when he used a French phrase.

"Well, *comme il fauo,* then," he cried, exaggerating his accent. "But you didn't answer my question."

"I don't know that I can answer it to your satisfaction.

It would be like trying to explain the colors to a blind man."

" You mean to say that I am not *comme il faut* myself ?."

" I shouldn't like to say that to you ; but to cut short the discussion, I'll call upon your sister-in-law, as you wish."

" Thanks ! And if you'll permit me to make a further suggestion—refrain as far as you can from patronizing her. She is very sensitive."

" Anything else ? "

" No, nothing else."

At half-past three o'clock Kate ordered her carriage, and with a great rattle of wheels, clicking of metal, and hoof-beats of prancing steeds, invaded the plebeian neighborhood west of Seventh Avenue. One of the liveried footmen jumped off the box and with a profound bow opened the carriage door.

" Tillbury," she said, "tell James to drive back into Fifth Avenue and stop nowhere. Be back here promptly in fifteen minutes."

The footman made another solemn bow, and having rung the bell of the apartment house, remounted his box. He made a grimace to his colleague James, as he repeated his orders. Madame evidently had relatives of humble degree, and did not wish her conspicuous carriage to be seen waiting outside an apartment house in such a shabby quarter.

The visit passed off without any incident. Kate, with her quiet lynx eyes, took in every minutest detail of furniture and upholstery, and reflected that it was exactly what she would have expected. She made the usual benevolent inquiries regarding husband and children, remarked that the weather had been extraordinary, patted Obed's cheek with her gloved hand and hoped that Mrs. Larkin found time to cultivate her artistic talent, which she had heard was quite promising. It was all *de haut en bas*, and Gertrude was keenly conscious of the condescension which every word implied. She bristled with suppressed animosity, and would have given her visitor a hint of her sentiments, if she had not been afraid of affording her pleasure by making a goose of herself. It was obviously her best policy to be haughty in return, freezingly polite, and for each pat on the shoulder give another back. Being, however, less practised in this game than her expert sister-in-law, Gertrude felt repeatedly that she was being worsted, and an inner tremor which she could not master began to show itself in her manner. Kate, too, saw it, and having no desire to humiliate her, rose to take her leave. She was every inch the *grande dame*, and could afford to be magnanimous. There was no petty meanness in her, only a superb self-confidence and dignity. If Gertrude had consented to humble herself from the beginning, she would have liked her and taken her under her protecting wing. Now they parted with artificial smiles, and pressures of hands, and polite assurances of the pleasure each had taken in seeing the other, and a fixed resolution never to run the risk of doing it again. While the elevator bore the victorious Kate down to the level of the street, where her carriage drove up to the door at the very instant she made her appearance, the vanquished Gertrude sat hugging her four-year-old son, Obed, and shedding some perfectly irrational tears upon his blond head.

" Oh, you dear child," she whispered, " what would become of your poor mamma if she didn't have you ? "

" But you have Papa and Ralph, too, mamma," objected the literal Obed.

"Yes, dear, I know it," she sighed, and hugged him more tightly.

CHAPTER XLII.

NEMESIS.

The removal to Torryville was being delayed by a hundred unforeseen incidents. The conviction was beginning to grow upon Horace that Kate was purposely delaying it, and that she had no intention of settling permanently in the place toward which his inclinations and interests were drawing him. He was sitting in his father-in-law's gorgeous library (filled with handsomely bound books which no one ever read) ruminating bitterly upon the fate which was in store for him, if she should absolutely refuse to accompany him to Torryville, as she had once before refused to share his life in Albany. If she said no, he knew it meant no, emphatically and inexorably. The arrogant speech he had once made to Aleck, about making other lives tributary to his own, was slowly emerging, phrase by phrase, from the blue cigar smoke ; and he smiled sardonically to himself at the thought of his crude delusion. Kate was a charming tributary, forsooth ! She insisted not only upon directing the course of her own life, but of his, to boot. Unless they agreed to separate, they had no choice but to patch up some sort of *modus vivendi;* to keep on working at cross-purposes, as they had hitherto been doing, was suicidal. Their lives had got to run together and must take the course which the stronger force in the united current determined. That was nature's law, against which there was no use demurring. He had frequently announced this fact with much satisfaction to himself and to the discomforture of his hypothetical antagonist. But now—and here was the rub—a horrible misgiving clutched like a chilly hand at his heart. Was he the stronger force, or was Kate ?

Horace flung his cigar into a big Satsuma vase which stood before the empty fireplace, and lighted another. He let his eyes wander over the richly carved oaken ceiling ; took up a newspaper which lay on the floor and at-

tempted to read. But everything seemed stale and unprofitable. If he was confronted with the alternative of
spending his life as a satellite of his wife's family or living
his own life away from her, what should he do? It was
a serious question which had to be seriously weighed.
Why couldn't Kate be made to see that it was for her advantage to allow him to work out his own destiny and
pursue his own ambitions. It was indeed hard to comprehend how such an admirable woman as Kate on all
hands was conceded to be, could be so hard to live with.

He was in the midst of these despondent meditations
when the butler entered and handed him a neatly en-
graved card, bearing the name, *Rev. Arthur Robbins.* Now
that was just lacking to make his cup of bitterness over-
flow! What in the mischief could the old gentleman be
wanting of him, unless he meant to take him to task for
his past delinquencies.

"You had better take this card upstairs," he said to the
butler; "it is Mr. Van Schaak the gentleman wishes to
see."

"He asked very particularly for you, sir. He was very
particular indeed, sir, that it was you he wanted to see,
sir."

"All right. Show him in."

He repented of the words the moment he had uttered
them; but of course, if Mr. Robbins had some particular
errand for him, dodging would be useless. He arose, as
the clergyman entered, and shook his hand with a rather
stiff and colorless manner.

"I hope you are well, sir," he said, motioning him to a
seat; "Mrs. Larkin will be very happy to see you. I'll
send word to her and let her know you are here."

He was about to press the button of the electric bell
when Mr. Robbins, with some trepidation, seized him by
the arm.

"No, I beg of you, don't call her," he said, "the fact is,
—I'd—I'd rather not see her."

There was a note of distress in his voice which aroused
a sympathetic echo in his listener. Even the least emotional of us has moods when he is impressionable. Horace
noted with benevolent interest how white Mr. Robbins
had grown, how grave and wrinkled. He looked like one
bowed down with grief. Of the fine intellectual smile
which formerly lighted up his features not a suggestion
was left. There was something strained and anxious in

the lines about his mouth, and his glance was full of trouble. But his attire was still scrupulously neat, his white necktie immaculate, and his small, well-shaped feet shod with obtrusive perfection. But what impressed his interlocutor most was a certain embarrassed deference in his manner, so different from his former cheerful dignity.

They sat and fenced for a while with the usual commonplaces about the weather and polite inquiries concerning friends and relatives. Horace took good care, however, not to ask concerning the one who was uppermost in the minds of both, and Mr. Robbins was obliged to introduce her unsolicited.

"Yes, the weather has been very trying this spring, even in Florida," he was saying; then, after having coughed apologetically into his handkerchief, he continued: "You know, we have been obliged to spend the winter in the South on account of my daughter Bella's health."

"I trust her health is improving," Horace observed, awkwardly.

"No, she is dying," said Mr. Robbins, rising abruptly and walking to the window.

Horace tried to intimate that he was sorry; but the words stuck in his throat. A dim sense of reproach stole over him; and a vague discomfort oppressed him. He could not tell exactly whether it was his conscience that made him uncomfortable, or the mere awkwardness of the situation. It was quite plain to him that he had behaved villainously; but he was one of those characters to whom self-approval is not absolutely indispensable to comfort. He had acted for his own interest; but an awful query loomed up in the very wake of this reflection and a dull pang nestled in his heart. Had he acted for his own interest? Had he not rather, in his ruthless disregard of all interests but his own, deceived and outwitted himself? What would his life have been, if he had kept faith with Bella? He saw it in a flash; and her pale, pathetic face with its anxious smile, so full of eager, fervent adoration, rose out of his memory. Poor child! She had loved him indeed. And that love of hers, which he had so heartlessly spurned—he saw clearly in this moment how beautiful, how precious it was.

When Mr. Robbins had mastered his emotion, he turned again toward the man who in wrecking his daugh-

ter's life had wrecked his own ; and he did not curse him,
or threaten him with disaster and vengeance for the injury
he had done ; but he looked at him with uneasy embarrassment, gave a little cough and said :

"I came to ask a favor of you, Mr. Larkin ; Bella wants
to see you."

His voice broke pitifully and he turned again to the
window. Horace got up and began to pace the floor.
Never in his life had he appeared so black to himself ; so
mean and contemptible. There was something within
him, like a vast weight of woe, which pressed upward and
threatened to overwhelm him.

"I must have your answer now," said his visitor, huskily ; "we have not much time to lose."

Horace, without a word, went out into the hall and
seized his hat ; Mr. Robbins followed him. They walked
rapidly across the square, down Twenty-first Street to
Fourth Avenue and took an uptown horse-car. In the
neighborhood of Madison Avenue and Fifty-eighth Street
they entered a quiet family hotel and were carried by the
elevator to the third or fourth floor. Through a long carpeted corridor, at the end of which sat a sleeping chambermaid, they reached a door, marked 149, which the clergyman noiselessly opened. The air within was pungent with
the odor of medicine. The shades were drawn before the
windows ; but the bright May sunshine filtered through,
revealing the usual bare hotel room with a black walnut
table, a rep-covered sofa, and half a dozen chairs. Presently a young girl with black squirrel-like eyes and a
sharply receding chin entered, and Horace recognized one
of the Rodents named Nettie. She gave him a nod over
her shoulder, in which he thought he detected a restrained
animosity. She held a whispered conversation with her
father ; and the latter excused himself and walked on tiptoe into the adjoining room. Nettie remained standing at
the door and glowered at the visitor.

"I hope you feel good now," she said, bluntly.

Horace returned her glance, but for the first time in his
life he was at a loss for an answer. How could he blame
her for hating him ? What a monster of iniquity he must
seem to her ! For two or three minutes this distressing
tête-à-tête lasted. But nothing further was said. Then
Mr. Robbins opened the door and beckoned to Horace,
who arose and walked heavily across the floor. He was
conscious of nothing except a dull heart-ache, and a help-

less regret that he had come. What could this meeting avail
him or her, now that all was irrevocably past, and the
tears were shed and the anguish suffered ? He averted
his face, as he crossed the threshold, and waited a moment
before summoning courage to look. The door was softly
closed behind him ; a slight tremor pierced his stolidity.
As his eyes accustomed themselves to the dimness, his courage again ebbed away. He knew there was a shock in store
for him, and a painful one. But it was too late to retreat
now. With a dogged resolution he turned about and
approached the bed. He wanted it over, and the sooner
the better. He had braced himself to endure anything, but
yet started back at the sight which met his eyes. And it
was a pitiful, a heart-rending sight. Propped up in pillows,
with an unnaturally flushed face, the bony structure of
which was cruelly emphasized, lay the poor little girl who
had flung herself in his path to be trampled down by his
ruthless feet. And yet what a touching thing was this love
of hers which she had given him, almost unasked, and
which he had held in such light esteem ! He had known
her heart-secret, long before she thought it revealed ; and
he had slighted and scorned it, and yet in a momentary mood
of magnanimity given it his supercilious approval. How
bitterly he repented of this magnanimity now ; for it was
that and not his scorn which had killed her.

Horace stood long before the bed, gazing at the face,
relieved by its high color against the pillow. The wheezy,
labored breathing of the invalid filled the silence. It wrung
his heart with pity to see how fragile she looked, how
wasted by disease and suffering. Her cheek-bones were
cruelly prominent ; and even the bones in her temples and
lower jaw were clearly outlined under the tense skin.
Her hands, which lay listlessly on the coverlid, showed their
anatomy with horrible suggestiveness. Only her wavy
blond hair was unchanged, and by contrast with her emaciated face looked too heavy for the frame to which it
was attached—as if it had drained it of its last drop of
vitality. He became aware, after a while, that she was
conscious of his presence, and was endeavoring to speak
to him. But again and again her voice failed her. Her
eyelids seemed heavy, and she raised them with a feeble
effort, but presently they closed again. He fell upon his
knees at the side of the bed ; not from emotion, but because he felt her desire to speak, and was anxious to spare
her needless exertion.

"I am glad you came," were the first words he distinguished ; and then after a long pause : "Horace."

He stooped down over her and listened ; but for a long while no sound came ; by the moving of her fingers, he guessed that she wished him to take her hand, and saw by the relaxation of the tensity of her expression, that he had guessed aright.

"I wanted—to see you," she whispered, "because—because—I didn't want you to feel bad—as I—knew—you would—Horace—when I am dead."

He felt as if his heart would break. She had never known how little he had cared for her ; she had imagined to this day that he had loved her ; she had held him guiltless and given her father the blame for having driven him away. In despair, of course, and not from cold-blooded calculation, had he married Kate ; and his life had been, in a measure, blighted as well as hers. What a pathetic romance, forsooth ; and yet he was glad that she had cherished it, glad that her last days had not been embittered with the anguish of a spurned affection. A reassuring pressure of her hand was all the answer he could give her ; and a faint shadow of joy flitted across her emaciated features. In her grateful glance there was a fond proprietorship, a touching devotion.

"You know," she resumed, after another pause, "I was never quite—well. I was—sick—when I became engaged to you. But—but—I couldn't tell you—it was wrong, I know—but I couldn't. You remember what you said to me—don't you ?"

"No. I don't remember," he murmured.

The strained, anxious smile which he knew so well, or a mere ghost of it, hovered about her lips, and a sudden moisture clouded his eyes, and compelled him to turn away, lest he should distress her by weeping. But she perceived the change in his expression before he was aware of it himself.

"Horace," she repeated, "I am—so glad you came."

"But what was it I said to you ?" he asked, with a voice which sounded strange in his own ears.

"Oh, yes," she answered with brightening eyes, "you remember—you said that—when you married—you'd want first health—then wealth—and then—a good temper. I had not health—but I didn't dare—tell you—it was wrong —I know it—but—but—now—I have told you—so you needn't—feel bad for me."

She spoke with painful breaks and had much difficulty in articulating. Only by a pathetic effort did she succeed in making the last words intelligible. Her eyes closed again, and she sank into a heavy stupor. For a long while he lay on his knees, holding her small hot hands, and listening to her labored breathing. His thoughts ranged through the past, and all the scenes of his life, from his boyhood and early youth, passed in panoramic procession before his vision. And the more he thought, the keener grew the pang of regret for that which was done and that which was left undone. His soul was stirred in its depths ; and dormant emotions rose in tumult and wrestled with Fate, the inevitable, the inexorable. He had never dreamed that he had in him such capacity for suffering.

CHAPTER XLIII.

MUCH AT STAKE.

Horace walked about for some days as in a dream. He seemed to have run his head into a noose, and the more he tugged at it the more the rope cut him. At the breakfast table Mr. Van Schaak read the notice of Bella's death in the morning papers; and his son-in-law heard it with a listless stony face. A heavy numbness had taken possession of him; and it seemed to matter very little whatever happened to him or to anyone else. Kate ordered the carriage and called at the hotel with her mother; but he refused to accompany her. The letter of condolence which he attempted to write to Mr. Robbins he was unable to finish. Every phrase in it struck him as the cruelest mockery. It was like stabbing a man and then begging his pardon. During the afternoon he wandered about the city; and at last dropped down upon a bench in a public square. There he sat trying to unravel the tangled skein of his life. His strong vitality reasserted itself; and he saw the futility of his sorrow; the uselessness of regret which paralyzed action, but could not undo the wrong. In the evening he had recovered his wonted composure; and had fully determined what to do. If Kate refused to accompany him to Torryville, he would go there without her. He would offer her a separation, or a divorce, if she liked, on her own terms.

Kate, who was a connoisseur of human nature, must have read in the tense lines of his face the resolution which, at the dinner-table, he endeavored to mask with an unwonted show of amiability. For when he arose from the table, she anticipated him with a request for a confidential interview.

"You have something on your mind, Horace," she said, when they had retired to the privacy of the library; "is there anything I can do for you?"

"Anything you can do for me!" he cried with a mocking laugh; "well I like that."

"I am glad you like it," she retorted with exasperating composure; "but please tell me why you find it ludicrous?"

"It is useless to talk with you, Kate," he broke out, vehemently "you regard me as a chessman which you can move
about on the board at your pleasure, and which is there
merely to enable you to win your game. But I mean to give
you notice to-night that I intend to play a little game of
my own, no matter whether it coincides with yours or not."

"*Pas de zèle*, my dear, *pas de zèle*," she warned, in her
gentlest society accents, "we can talk to better advantage
if we do not get angry. As I understand it, you are dissatisfied with me. Please, tell me what is your grievance."

Ah, she was marvellous, that Kate. She was simply im-
mense! Health, wealth, and a good temper! She had all
three in superlative perfection. That was the thought that
flashed through his head, and instantly soothed the commotion that was raging there. Kate had seen in an instant that he was in a mood which made quarrelling dangerous, and she refused to quarrel. So clear a head, such
unerring judgment—how could he help admiring it?

"If I have not misunderstood your tactics," he said,
forcing himself to be calm, "you intend to spring a trap
upon me. You do not intend to go to Torryville."

"What I wish is one thing; what I intend is quite another.
May I ask you why you are so anxious to return to that
stupid village?"

"Because my whole career is bound up with my residence there. First, I want to go to Congress."

"Why couldn't you go to Congress from this city? I
understand from father that he is quite willing, for my
sake, to expend the money necessary to procure you a
nomination."

"I am greatly obliged to him; but I must decline. I wish
to owe my preferment in public life to my own talents, not
to your father's money."

"Ah, I see. But, apart from that, why would you decline
to go to Congress from this city?"

"First, because I should have to declare that I am a
resident, which I am not. Secondly a Republican nomination, if it is for sale, is not worth buying."

"But suppose you were a Democrat."

"Excuse me, my dear, but now you are supposing a little
too much for my patience. What you mean to say is, suppose I were a scalawag——"

"Not at all; but I understand your position. Now,
may I ask, why you have set your heart on going to Congress?"

23

" Because," he ejaculated, raising his voice again, with an irrepressible irritation, " it is my life ! Because my inclination and my talents fit me for a public career. And moreover, how am I ever to fulfil your dream of going as ' diplomat to a foreign court,' if I do not first distinguish myself in politics ? They do not pick diplomats out of the gutter."

He knew this argument was insincere. He had no intention in the world to accommodate himself to her plans ; but all is fair in love and war. If he gained his point, discussion would be in order afterward.

"Now, please, *pas de zèle*," she begged, raising her white hands again, warningly ; while her intelligent eyes scanned his face with earnest scrutiny. For two or three minutes she sat thus ; and the calm logical thoughts seemed to move almost visibly behind her clear forehead.

"You have convinced me," she said, at last, rising with fine dignity ;. " I am ready to move to Torryville, whenever you say."

" Then I say to-morrow."

" Very well ; but I should prefer the day after to-morrow."

" As you please ; the day after to-morrow."

As in all engagements of this kind Horace, though apparently victorious, felt more than half defeated. He took no satisfaction whatever in his triumph, for he knew that in generalship he was no match for Kate. The ruse by which he had brought her to terms might prove a seed of dragon teeth from which might spring no end of unpleasant consequences. She might, any day, have a disagreeable surprise in store for him. His mood was therefore anything but hilarious when, on the appointed morning, he drove up to the Grand Central Depot, with a tiger and a coachman on the box, sitting upon their folded coats, and all the pomp and circumstance of which prosperous republicanism is capable. Kate, on the other hand, was as serene as the lovely June weather, and gazed into the sunlit space with that superb indifference which no mere plebeian can hope to attain. A Swiss nurse, dressed in Alsatian peasant costume, sat on the seat opposite, holding a bundle of precious laces and ribbons, containing among other things, a baby. As they dismounted from the carriage at the entrance to the waiting rooms of the New York Central Railroad, Horace observed an undertaker's wagon, through the open door of which a long pine box was visible.

He had just stepped out upon the sidewalk and was about to conduct his wife into the waiting-room, when he met Mr. Dallas, of Torryville, and Mr. Robbins, both with black crape on their hats. Behind them came Graves, the tanner, leading Nettie Robbins, who was enveloped from head to foot in a long crape veil. Horace, with a cold chill creeping over him, was about to press on past them. But Kate stopped to speak to her uncle and to utter the conventional phrases of sympathy and condolence. He sought refuge again in his wanted stolidity ; but when the pine box was lifted from the wagon by four men and carried past him toward the baggage office, it grew black before his eyes, and the pavement upon which he stood billowed under his feet. An irrepressible anguish quivered through every fibre of his being ; his brain was in a whirl and he was on the point of losing consciousness. But with a violent effort of will he collected himself ; and with set teeth and an ashy pale face watched the progress of the four men, and Mr. Dallas's lugubrious alertness as he ran about them, warning them to be careful, and the pitiful vacuity and stunned stare of the old clergyman's face. Was he—Horace Larkin—responsible for this calamity ? Did he have this sin on his conscience ? He hoped to God that he had not. With desparing tenacity he clung to her assurance that she had always been ill, and that the end must have come soon, whether he had crossed her path or not. But what was life and what was death, after all ? What did it matter, if the one was prolonged or the other hastened by a few brief years. The sunshine, as it beat upon his eyes, seemed a mockery ; and the world a cruel, unreal sham.

It was time at last to board the train, and Kate, with decorous seriousness, bade her uncle adieu. Happily she had engaged an entire palace car for herself and her retinue ; while the mourning party was assigned to another. But hour after hour, during the long day, the thought pursued Horace of the dreadful freight which the car in front of him was carrying. His imagination conjured up the spectacle with painful vividness and with shuddering details. The old superstition of the sailors occurred to him ; that the ship that carries a corpse in its hold will be wrecked. His life would henceforth carry a corpse in its hold. Did that argue disaster ? He entered his new house, which seemed bound up with his fortune and his hopes of happiness, and he had not thought of providing a closet for a skeleton. Well, life is a curious affair.

CHAPTER XLIV.

Horace had for years been " laying his pipes" for the congressional campaign upon which he now entered. He had been practically sure of the nomination, since his only possible rival, the late representative, had, by the Larkin influence, been appointed minister to a South American republic, and after infinite trouble had been induced to accept. It seemed now that he had tolerably plain sailing ; as it was scarcely conceivable that any one the Democrats could nominate would have even a fighting chance. This was generally conceded in Torryville, when Horace and his wife made their triumphal entry into the town in the beginning of June and moved into their palatial mansion on the western hill slope. There was no disputing now, that Horace was the first citizen of Torryville. The venerable Obed was completely outshone, and, what was more remarkable, accepted his eclipse with philosophical serenity. He shook his head occasionally at the extravagance of Horace's establishment and the fast pace at which he was going ; but he still trusted him implicitly, and worked to advance his interests. Mrs. Larkin, who was in worse health than ever and determined to quarrel with Kate, was firmly held in check, in spite of her lamentations. She had a hundred grievances against her nephew's wife, who, she insisted, treated her like a pickpocket. When the elder lady (in accordance with the custom of the town) went to spend the day with Mrs. Horace in her new house and naturally expected to examine her clothes, and give advice concerning servants and housekeeping, she found herself politely snubbed. Kate was not in the least confidential, and though, after some coaxing, she consented to have her maid exhibit her wardrobe to Mrs. Larkin's wondering eyes, she professed an ignorance concerning the cost of her dresses which her visitor regarded as transparent pretence. And it was not only Mrs. Larkin who inclined to this opinion. Mrs. Dallas, Mrs. Graves, and the Professors' wives,

"She is quite—that is—I am not sure—but I will send the servant up to inquire."

It was of no use that he argued with Kate that the social tactics of the metropolis were inapplicable in a town of twelve thousand people, where everybody knew what his neighbor had for dinner. A certain amount of mendacity might be practised with impunity among a million inhabitants which among a thousand might be unsafe. Metropolitan mendacity was unsuited for country life. The special occasion which called forth this argument was an invitation which Kate had already accepted to an evening party at Mr. Dallas's. The dress she was to wear was already spread out upon the bed, and her maid stood ready to unlace her.

"Horace," she called into the next room, where he was struggling with an obstreperous bootjack, "I really can't go. You know as well as I that it is going to be very stupid."

He appeared in the door in his shirt-sleeves, perspiring, with his hair down in his eyes, and one boot in his hand.

"What is the matter?" he asked.

She motioned to the chambermaid to leave the room, and then repeated her declaration.

"You may tell Mrs. Dallas," she added, blandly, "that I am not at all well, otherwise it would have given me great pleasure to be present at her entertainment."

He stared at her for a while in dumb amazement.

"Any more lies you want me to tell?" he blurted out, rudely.

"Really, Mr. Larkin, I must decline to answer. I am not accustomed to such language."

"And I am not accustomed to hear women lie."

"Indeed" (with haughty irony); "well, you know you are not an authority on social usages."

"Perhaps not, but I have still some authority left of another kind. When I tell you that I desire you very much to go to Mrs. Dallas's; that it is of the utmost importance for me politically that you should not offend her, are you, then, going to persevere in your refusal?"

"I have told you once, Mr. Larkin, that I am not going."

"But when I command you to go?" he cried, angrily; but the words were hardly out of his mouth, before he comprehended how foolish they were. To threaten with

in fact all the ladies who had any pretension to social standing, found Mrs. Horace stuck-up and altogether disagreeable. They had all looked forward to her arrival with the pleasantest anticipations; and each one of them had determined to gain her confidence, and become her very particular friend. It was therefore doubly bitter to have their first overtures so coldly received.

The fact was, they did not understand her, and she did not understand them. It would never have occurred to Kate that this Mrs. Dallas, who said "you was," and whose father had kept a livery stable, could have the audacity to aspire to become an intimate in her house. And as for the rest, she was perfectly willing to be polite and even friendly to them, in her own condescending way, but if they presumed upon her courtesy to pry into her closets, give impertinent advice, and even converse with her servants, she had no choice but to keep them at arms' length. The time-honored country custom, to which many ladies were addicted, to drop in early in the forenoon and spend the entire day in gossip and espionage, was a special affliction to her. After having been entrapped once or twice into such a position, she grew very wary, and denied herself to visitors who showed any disposition to be importunate. She sent word by the servant that she was ill, or that she was not at home, although all the town knew of her comings and goings. For she never went out on foot; and her equipage, with its glittering trappings, was too dazzling to pass anywhere unnoticed. Its passage through the streets or along the Lake drive was an event which was looked forward to and discussed for an hour when it was past.

It was scarcely to be wondered at that Horace was much annoyed at his wife's unpopularity. He saw plainly enough that she was imperilling the chances of his election. Before the summer was half over he was credibly informed that his friend Dallas was playing him false, and was nursing a promising little boom of his own. It was of very little use that he "made himself solid" with butchers and bakers and candlestick makers, lent money on bad mortgages to influential Irishmen, and opened a free reading room for the Firemen's Association; a spark of animosity against him was smouldering in the breasts of his townsmen, and might become a blaze before the meeting of the nominating convention. An American country town is a crystallization of the Democratic spirit; it is as free from snobbishness as any aggregation of men on the face of the globe. The candidate's magnificent house, instead of making him popular, made him suspected ; and his superb carriage and flunkeys aroused open hostility. His wife's attitude toward the ladies of the town capped the climax by raising him enemies in every household. And yet, strange to say, Kate was far from divining what a storm of displeasure was raging against her in the bosoms of the Torryville ladies. She flattered herself that she had treated them very handsomely, and that they had reason to be grateful that she had unbent so far in her desire to make herself agreeable to them. When Horace intimated to her that they cherished sentiments of an opposite kind, she was frankly astonished.

"You know, of course," she said, "they could scarcely expect me to take them to my bosom and make friends of them."

"Yes, that was exactly what they expected," her husband replied.

"But surely you agree with me that such an expectation is preposterous," she exclaimed, with unwonted animation.

"No, I can't say I do."

"Would you, perhaps, have me go around and talk politics with my butcher, as you do ; and smile graciously on that absurd little bookseller Dabney, who insists upon shaking hands with me when I enter his shop ?"

"I don't see that it would hurt you to shake hands with him. He is a very decent sort of fellow."

"I must say, Horace, I have often been ashamed of you, when I have seen you flattering trades-people ; joking with them, and treating them as if you regarded them as your equals. But I have consented to overlook it, because I thought perhaps it was a political necessity. But when you demand that I, too, shall demean myself to such practices I think it is time for me to protest."

"My dear," he ejaculated with humorous despair (for he knew by this time her limitations), "I don't demand anything of you ; but only ask you not to snub people any more than you have to."

"Snub people, Horace ! Why, I don't snub them at all. If there is anything I pride myself on, it is my tact in dealing with the lower classes. I never have any difficulty with my servants because I know how to keep them in their place. I am kind to them, but I let them know where they belong."

"Yes, I see," he answered, ironically, "you *have* tact in

dealing with the lower *clawsses*" (he exaggerated her broad, English a). "Well, my dear, you are the American humorist, sure enough. I shudder to think what would have become of you if you had lived in the time of the French Revolution. The lower classes ! It is too good !"

He gave a loud, mirthless laugh, thrust his hands into his pockets, and with a desperate fling of his head paced across the floor. There was something almost pathetic in her hallucination, and in her utter alienation from the spirit of her country, and her incapacity to comprehend its manifestations. And yet, though he almost detested her exclusive and aristocratic sentiment, he had a vague sense of flattery that this high and mighty lady, who looked down upon all her kind, had deigned to honor him with her favor and confidence. He knew how easily this favor was forfeited ; how a *mal àpropos* remark, implying the remotest *soupçon* of personal criticism, or a trifling *gaucherie*, or unintentional incivility would freeze her up and make her dumb for an entire day. It was an impious desire, but for all that he could not help wishing that he possessed the power to make her one-tenth as miserable as she sometimes made him. It was not a mere vindictive desire to retaliate, but rather an assertion of his self-respect and an aspiration for that unattainable goal—marital equality.

It would make an endless chapter if mention were to be made of all the comical and tragical incidents occasioned by his desire to keep on good terms both with Kate and the town. He constituted himself her ambassador and the mediator between her and the offended community. He exercised all his ingenuity in putting the best interpretation upon her words and actions. It was especially her refusal to see people when they called which made bad blood ; and when she sent word to Mrs. Graves that she was ill, he sometimes, in order to enforce belief, himself to corroborating her statement by incidentally scribing her symptoms. Then, perhaps, fifteen minutes later, Mrs. Professor Dowd would call, and Horace would repeat to her his regrets that his wife's illness would prevent her from seeing her ; when lo ! Kate would appear fresh as a lily, and greet the visitor with serene affability. After a few experiences of this sort, he grew so wary that he refused to commit himself concerning his wife's health; and once when Mrs. Professor Wharton asked how Mrs. Larkin was he answered with embarrassment:

an authority which he could not enforce was wretched policy.

"You forget yourself, Mr. Larkin," was her reply, uttered with freezing dignity, and he knew that all further parley was useless.

But this hate—this wild hate—that flared up in his breast, when, after having closed the door, he sat upon his bed, desperately clutching his newly blacked boot, and shaking it against the ceiling! Was she going to wreck his career, merely out of caprice, or to gratify a feminine spite? That was not like her, to be sure; but she appeared to be capable of a good many things with which he had not credited her. He was fairly frightened at the wrath which seethed and boiled within him! Was all that he had lived for to come to naught, for this woman's sake? The boot which he held in his hand, and which had, by this time, blacked both his face and his shirt-bosom, flew with a bang against the hard-wood paneling of the wall opposite, where it left a deep mark. For the good-natured and amiable fellow that he had always held himself to be, this was rather anomalous behavior. But life was dealing outrageously with him, rousing all the latent violence deposited in his soul by barbaric ancestors. The holy St. Anthony himself could not have endured such conduct in his wife without wishing to strangle her. But then, to be sure, St. Anthony was a bachelor.

The thought of her who was dead came into his mind, and he grew calm; but it was a calm filled with bitterness and vain regrets.

CHAPTER XLV.

THE TRIALS OF A CANDIDATE.

One would have supposed that when such words had been spoken and such feelings aroused, life under the same roof would be impossible. But in matrimony nothing is impossible. The alternative to people who are ambitious and have children is so terrible as to be no alternative. Kate exhibited a stiff and superb aloofness for three or four days, but then she began to tire of her lonely dignity ; and at last she unbent so far as to make remarks at the table about the weather and other novel topics. Horace, though he had sworn never to be friendly to her again, could not make up his mind to snub her, first, because he lacked the courage, and secondly, because he was, at heart, more anxious for peace than she was. And so it came to pass that one day, when he was sorely harassed by the prospect of political disaster, she entered his library, and took her seat in one of the great leather-covered easy chairs. She talked politics with him in her usual clear and dispassionate fashion, asked him questions, the intelligence of which fairly startled him, and aroused again all his admiration for her beauty and cleverness. She had as good a brain as any man, he reflected ; nay, how many of his friends were there whose cerebral machinery was in such perfect order ?

"You have led me to suppose," she remarked, after half an hour's conversation, "that I have injured your political chances, and I should not wonder if you are right."

"Well," he answered, with careless magnanimity, "there's no use crying over spilt milk. You were made in a different mould from these people here, and you can't help offending them."

"Then you have given up the contest ?" she inquired, with sudden animation.

"Not at all. But you mustn't be surprised if I am defeated. My only chance is to pull through on the Presidential ticket ; for the district is Republican ; and if I am

scratched in Torryville, I may have enough of a majority
outside of this county to make up for it."

"Would $25,000 improve your prospects?"

He opened his eyes with joyous wonder. This was
help in the eleventh hour. It would have comported
better with his dignity if he had been able to conceal his
delight, but the proposal took him so entirely by surprise
that he could not disguise the sense of happy relief it gave
him.

"Kate," he cried, "I am not going to pretend to be
better than I am. $25,000 would put me on my pins again
at a jump."

"Here's my check for the amount," said Kate, handing
him a piece of paper which she had kept folded up in her
hand; "it is my contribution to your campaign expenses."

"Thanks, Kate; it is very good of you to take such an
interest in my affairs."

"Your affairs are my affairs," she declared, rising and
moving toward the door. "But perhaps," she added, fac-
ing him again with her fine quiet smile, "you wouldn't
mind telling me how you are going to use this money?"

"I am going to make friends of the Mammon of Unrighteousness," he answered, with a quizzical look.
"You've got to fight the devil with fire, and mammon
with mammon."

His wife's magnanimity in this instance quite dazzled
Horace. He had been brought up frugally, and had early
been impressed with the value of money. It almost hurt
him at times to see how lavishly she spent her wealth on
things which he regarded as utterly superfluous. Nay,
odd as it may seem, one of the trials of his new estate was
his inability to habituate himself to the scale of expenditure befitting a millionaire. From old habit he practised
all sorts of small economies, such as using a match twice,
when there was a fire in the room, tearing off the blank
half of a letter sheet, etc. If he saw a pin on the floor he
always picked it up, and stuck it into the lapel of his coat;
and though Kate frequently depleted his arsenal, by throwing the whole collection into the fire, he always started a
new one the following day. His coats and trousers, which
he found it harder to part with the older they grew, also
had a mysterious way of disappearing; and new clothes,
accompanied by preposterous bills, arrived simultaneously
from Adrian's tailor in New York. From long experience
he knew how futile it was to remonstrate with Kate on

such extravagance ; for her supercilious smile and her offer
to settle the bills were harder to put up with than his
enforced dudishness. Yet so far from giving himself airs
with his modish attire, in the presence of his simple neighbors, he was half ashamed of himself, and had a constant
desire to apologize.

It dawned upon him gradually that Kate had made up
her mind to remodel him with a view to his future diplomatic calling ; and the question seemed worth debating
how far he ought to accommodate himself to this process
of transformation.

He determined, of course, in the first instance to oppose
it with all his might ; and plumed himself not a little on
his successful resistance to her proposition to have him
part his hair in the middle. It would ruin him politically,
he declared, if he were to appear in Torryville with his
coarse bristles divided in the style of the Prince of Wales.
It would subject him to no end of ridicule, and blight his
career. As a mere joke, however, he allowed her to
experiment a little with his hair ; chiefly because it was so
very flattering to have her take such an interest in his
appearance. With a look of sheepish resignation he
stood before the mirror, while she made two stiff ivory
brushes promenade over his cranium with ruthless energy.
And he scarcely noticed, or resolutely refused to notice,
that after each such experiment, the partition crept a little
further up his skull ; his mustache acquired a brisker and
more aspiring aspect, and his whole exterior an indefinable
air of *chic*.

It is not unlikely that these concessions to his better
half injured Horace in the campaign in the active preparation of which he spent the entire summer. He soon
found that it would be dangerous to rely upon his old
popularity ; but he acquired instead the reputation of being a master in " organization, " which is a euphemism for
all those agencies and influences which can ill bear the light
of publicity. The nomination, which came within an inch
of slipping through his fingers, he secured by "organization;" and during the months of September and October
his agents worked up the district with a thoroughness
which had never before been equalled. It was virtually a
house to house canvass ; with arguments, both material
and intellectual, in each case adapted to the character of
the elector. The candidate himself appeared but twice
during the campaign in public, and made then the neces-

sary revision of his exterior, wearing ill-fitting clothes and
restoring his hair to its pristine rusticity. This was in response to the many allusions in the Democratic press to
his aristocratic proclivities and princely style of living.
The speeches he made were brief and made no particular
sensation. They were merely a vehement reiteration of
the party programme. He was no longer in touch with
the people as he had formerly been ; he missed their spon-
taneous roar of applause and even the affectionate disrespect with which, of old, they were wont to greet him.
Altogether he was in an unpleasant frame of mind and saw
omens of disaster in every insignificant incident. Thus, one
day, he felt the cold perspiration start on his brow, while
overhearing a conversation between two Irish politicians
who were supposed to control a considerable portion of
"the liquor vote."

"Larrkin," said the one, "he's gone back on the byes,
begorra ; and it's the byes 'll go back on him on eliction
day."

"Oh, ye be blamed," retorted the other, in whom
Horace recognized a chronic pensioner, "ye talk loik a
fool. It's savin' his money he is fur eliction day."

"Oh, the divil he is," shouted the first with a derisive
laugh ; "if he's a-savin his cash, its because he knows he's
goin' to be bate."

It then occurred to Horace that, in his attention to the
remoter parts of his district, he had perhaps neglected
Torryville ; and a check for $10,000 which he procured
from his father-in-law, was during the next week diffused
among the Hibernian clubs. An organ was presented to
the African Methodist Church, a hall was rented and fitted
up for the local German Turnverein, and several hundred
volumes of books were added to the Larkin Town Library.

While the candidate was thus absorbed in his political
labors, his wife amused herself as best she could. It had
not been her choice to spend the summer in Torryville,
but she had recognized the necessity, and gracefully acquiesced. Having exhausted the pleasures of driving and
horse-back riding, she was persuaded by Professor Ramsdale to try sailing, and when Horace marvelled at her being
able to spend an entire afternoon in a boat with that "stupid, fish-eyed lunkhead," she declared that she did not
find it difficult, because "she liked dumb animals."

In the beginning of October Mr. and Mrs. Van Schaak
arrived, and there were a series of dinner-parties. But

these afforded no relaxation to the harassed candidate, but rather an additional annoyance. Kate had established a standard of brilliancy for him to which he was bound to live up ; and if he showed a disposition to rest upon his laurels, she spurred him up by questions and direct appeals. She absolutely demanded that he should, so to speak, vindicate her wisdom in having married him on evèry occasion ; and in every phrase he uttered demonstrate the possession of the intellect with which she credited him. Now it is quite possible that during the fatigue and worry of this vexatious campaign he had not his faculties entirely at his command, and in endeavoring to come up to her requirements made unsuccessful attempts at being funny. Kate's face, like the most sensitive barometer, showed him then the state of the atmosphere, and the weather probabilities for the next twenty-four hours. It was observed by the quiet Ramsdale, that after a dinner at which he had not shone, the Honorable Horace seemed never anxious to get home. And this was scarcely to be wondered at ; for Kate proved herself, on such occasions, the mistress of a certain scant, but cruelly cutting vocabulary, which sometimes wounded her lord's self-respect to the quick. He could never quite comprehend this contradiction in her character ; that from others she demanded for him the utmost respect, while she herself, in private, was capable of treating him like a school-boy or a pickpocket.

" Mr. Larkin," she said to him, when after the Honorable Obed's dinner-party they found themselves together in matrimonial solitude ; " I was ashamed of you to-night. For an intellectual man, I thought you made a very poor show. You appeared as heavy and poky as if you had not a spark of wit."

" But my dear," he answered with unwonted meekness ; "didn't you tell me, the night before last, after our own dinner, that when I made jokes, I appeared undignified and silly. To-night I thought I would not run that risk ; and so I introduced serious topics of conversation ; and as it appeared to me I held my own very creditably."

" No, you did not, Professor Dowd routed you entirely in that discussion about the duty of the state to care for the weak."

" You must excuse me, but I don't think so."

And now followed a recapitulation of the argument, ending in personal recrimination.

" My idea of table talk," Kate finished, summing up the

case in her clear and dispassionate way, " is that it should be neither silly nor profound. A certain lightness of touch is essential. People don't go to dinner-parties to be instructed, but to be amused. If a man has wit he can discuss almost anything and make it entertaining. I remember once reading of Gladstone, that he was heard discussing, between the oysters and the coffee, French cookery, translations of Homer, the excavations at Nineveh, Parisian bonnets, college athletics, the early church in Great Britain, horse-racing, and Egyptian hieroglyphics, and that he appeared to be equally at home and equally felicitous on all these topics."

It may have been in consequence of the unusual exertions attendant upon these dinner-parties, that Mrs. Obed Larkin suddenly died of an apoplectic stroke in the latter part of the month. She had a funeral that would have rejoiced her heart, if she could have witnessed it ; for out of respect to the Founder, all the faculty and students of the University accompanied her to the grave, forming a procession which covered half a mile of the road from the town to the cemetery. The gloom which this sad event cast over the family was not relished by old Mr. Van Schaak, who therefore returned to New York without awaiting the issue of the election. As it was, moreover, a presidential year, he was half inclined to depart from his usual habit and honor one or the other of the candidates with his vote. He had a long private interview with Kate before taking his leave ; and it must have been an exciting topic which they discussed, for the old gentleman looked as red as a lobster when he issued forth from his daughter's apartments.

The week preceding an election is never a pleasant one to peace-loving citizens. Brass-bands, fish-horns, and discordant cheering made the night hideous ; bonfires were burnt on the public square, and parades and torchlight processions imparted an unwonted animation to the quiet village streets. Men in fantastic regalia rushed about with sooty perspiring faces, yelling for their favorite candidate, and the ubiquitous small boy formed the tail of all processions and cheered impartially for all candidates. When finally the first Tuesday in November made an end of this pandemonium, all the community drew a sigh of relief. The average citizen, strong partisan though he was, smiled at his zeal and was reconciled to any result, provided it was decisive. Only Dallas and his little gang,

who were suspected of " knifing " their own congressional
nominee, the Honorable Horace Larkin, were so chagrined
at his election that they forgot to rejoice in their national
victory.   It was small comfort to know that the obnoxious
gentleman ran 2,800 votes behind his ticket, and that his
majority was but 101.   This had so obviously been the
occasion to kill him off and relegate him forever to obscurity ; and to have come so near to this result, without yet
attaining it, was doubly bitter.

CHAPTER XLVI.

"THE CLOVEN FOOT."

Aleck Larkin's novel, "The Cloven Foot," after many vain wanderings, found at last a publisher. Like a madman the happy author rushed home on the day when he received the letter informing him of its acceptance. He spent an evening of absurd hilarity with his wife and children, talking the most rapturous nonsense and embracing promiscuously every one who came in his path. It was only Gertrude's timely warning which saved him from demonstrating his joy in the same impressive manner to the chambermaid. At dinner he cracked a bottle of champagne and made a speech, which was a triumph of unconscious humor. To Gertrude, however, it seemed beautiful, eloquent, and perfectly rational. She felt more convinced than ever that Aleck was a great man ; and she began to swell agreeably with an historic importance, like Tasso's Leonora or Dante's Beatrice. Life had yet something in store for her. When the novel was published, nobody could fail to see what a wonderful work it was. She had told Aleck so, all along, encouraged him when he lost heart ; and by her sincere praise spurred him on toward its completion. How often he had told her that, without her, the book would and could never have been written ! And she knew that this was true ; and some day, perhaps, the world too would know it ; and then her title to glory would be secure. The time might even come, a hateful little afterthought suggested, when she might return her sister-in-law's patronage with interest ; and she saw herself move with queenly dignity through gorgeously lighted apartments, distributing benevolent nods and smiles, *à la* Kate, to a respectfully admiring multitude.

It was three months before Christmas that the book appeared ; and although it caused no great commotion in literary circles, it yet had something more than a *succès d'estime.* The influential magazines and papers, as a rule, spoke well of it ; one or two reviewers (among whom Aleck's

24

journalistic debtor of long ago) indulged in extravagant prophecies regarding his future ; and some pitiless humorist, seeking whom he might devour, fell foul of him and held him up to ridicule. He entirely lacked the heart to show this latter production to his wife, and feigned a feverish hilarity, in order to conceal from her the pain which it caused him. But he was only moderately successful in this pious fraud. Seeing that something was wrong, she put him to bed in spite of his protests, and clapped mustard leaves on his feet. She had read in the papers that there had been several cases of typhoid in the neighborhood and she feared that Aleck had made himself liable to an attack by overwork and excitement. When the fever failed to declare itself, the next day, he was permitted to get up ; but for a whole week he was treated like an invalid and pampered with delicacies and anxious tenderness. After that, he vowed he would show his wife the unfavorable as well as the favorable criticisms, but when the next of the latter order fell into his hands, he came to the conclusion that she would inevitably exaggerate its importance ; and that it would be cruel to inflict upon her needless pain. There was especially one sneering and supercilious notice from a very authoritative journal which burned in his pocket and caused him untold discomfort. It seemed, for a while, a duty to show this to Gertrude, lest she should form an exaggerated idea of his success. But he knew so perfectly well that, in her mind, it would blot out all her pleasure in the book ; it would convert his fair success into the most abject failure ; nay, he feared that it might open her eyes to the undeniable weaknesses of his performance and damn it irretrievably in her estimation. She was not capable of moderate judgments. He was in her sight either a genius or a miserable bungler. There were no intermediate degrees. And who will blame him for refusing to exchange the former character for the latter ? He found it so pleasant to be a hero in his own family ; to have incense burned to him ; to have his modesty deprecated by a fond conviction, on his wife's part, that it was but the crowning adornment of greatness.

The final awakening, if awakening it was, from this delightful dream of fame occurred six months after the publication of " The Cloven Foot." Then the publisher's statement arrived, showing a sale of six hundred and fifty-seven copies. As, according to the contract, the author was to renounce his copyright on the first one thousand copies sold, there was not a cent due to him ; and as, more-over, he had rashly guaranteed a sale of one thousand, he had the further prospect of paying one or two hundred dollars for his courtship of the muses.   He spent two weeks of absolute torture before he could make up his mind to confess this humiliating state of affairs to Gertrude ; and he was prepared for tears, reproaches, and accusations, all of which he was resolved to bear with guilty resignation.   But how great was his amazement when the incalculable Ger-trude, instead of the rôle of the accuser, assumed that of the comforter.   She seated herself upon his lap, and while twirling his mustache with a thoughtful air, told him all manner of charming things about the inability of the world to appreciate true greatness, about the tragic fate of genius in general, and the ultimate bitter-sweet revenge of a posthumous renown.   She spoke of Keats and Shelley, and although he failed to see any similarity between his lot and theirs, her words yet aroused in him a sense of meri-torious martyrdom.   He saw his imaginary works em-balmed in dignified library editions, which were much praised but seldom read ; and usurped for the nonce a chapter in some future History of American Literature among those writers whose illustrious gifts had only se-cured recognition, when it could benefit them no more.

It did not occur to him that her contentment was simu-lated.   That she too had been building castles in the air, which now came tumbling down about her ears, never once entered his head.   He did not possess the ingenuity to connect certain mysterious letters he had received from real-estate dealers with any project of hers, which now must come to naught.   He had thought it rather odd that people of whom he had never heard should beg to inform him that they would be happy to rent him an admirably situated, and completely furnished country place at Islip, or Irvington or Bar Harbor, with stable, carriages, etc., for the very moderate sum of $4,000 or $6,000 or $8,000, as the case might be.   But he ascribed this eccentricity, on their part, to the zeal of their agents, which often outran their discretion.   If he had dreamed that Gertrude, out of the proceeds of his book, had expected to rent a pleas-ant summer home, where they might live in freedom and contented isolation, the financial failure of his enterprise would have grieved him more deeply.   For he knew well what a trial the summer was to her, in second-rate Long Island boarding-houses, crowded with vulgar and

aggressive people, whose one aim seemed to be to prove
to you that they were quite as good as you were, and
probably " a blamed sight better." She was refined and
sensitive ; not given to be autobiographical, and receiving
autobiographical confidences on short acquaintance with
a certain reserve which aroused animosity. She was a
solitary nature and had never quite acquired the tone of
easy intercourse with her own sex. The awful democracy
of the summer boarding-house seemed therefore positively
infernal to her in its capacity for inflicting suffering.

It was far past the usual hour for retiring when Gertrude, with a lugubrious enjoyment of her unsuspected
sacrifice, rose from her husband's lap, smoothed her hair
before the mirror, and declared with a laugh that she
wanted no more nonsense, and that it was time he should
" behave." It was her habit to charge to his account all
" foolishness," by which was meant undignified demonstrations of affection ; and though at times he knew himself innocent as to the initiative he never demurred against
such charges. For, as has been hinted, she was terribly
sensitive ; and, if he was to be trusted, had the most perverse memory in the United States. The student-lamp
upon the table was growing dimmer, and threatened to go
out. A cold February rain was beating against the window-panes. Then, with startling distinctness, a loud bark
re-echoed through the house, half like the crowing of a
cock, half like the baying of a hound. Gertrude's face
grew suddenly rigid and her eyes dilated with fear.

" What is it, dear, *what* is it ? " he cried, jumping up and
seizing her hand.

" Croup ! " she whispered ; " run for the doctor."

She disengaged her hand from his grasp, and recovering
her composure hastened to the nursery. There she found
her four-year-old boy Obed standing on the floor in his
night-gown, holding on to the bed, while the terrible cough
shook his little frame from head to foot. The steam
heater, that assassin of innocents, had, for some inscrutable
reason, known only to the janitor, raised the temperature
to eighty-five degrees. The child, perspiring and uncomfortable, had kicked off its coverings (in spite of safety
pins), rolled out of bed, and sleeping there in a draft from
the window, which was lowered a little at the top, had
caught the dangerous malady. The nurse, whose duty it
was to watch him, was, as usual, having company in the
kitchen. The doctor arrived in half an hour, took the boy's

temperature, listened to his breathing, and left directions
for his treatment. Aleck begged to be permitted to watch
over him, but was peremptorily refused. When, in spite of
the prohibition, he lingered at the door, Gertrude impatiently motioned him away.

"What is the good of our both losing our sleep?" she
asked; "you go to your room, and take Ralph in bed with
you; and see that he does not kick the blanket off."

"I will," he answered, "if you will promise to call me at
two and let me watch till morning."

"Very well! But I don't want you to talk now; he is
falling asleep. Hush-sh-sh."

He had no choice but to obey. With a heavy heart he
undressed, but resolved to stay awake, so as to be at her
beck in case of need. For an hour or more his son Ralph,
who, with all his charming qualities, was not a pleasant
bedfellow, assisted him faithfully to keep this resolution;
but at the end of that time unconsciousness stole over him,
his thoughts became incoherent, and he drifted away into
dreamland. He scarcely knew how long he slept; but it
must have been about five o'clock when his son awoke him
with this timely query:

"Papa, which is the strongest, the lion or the eagle?"

Aleck, seeing the light peeping in through the closed
shutters, jumped up with a guilty conscience. Flinging
his dressing gown over his *robe de nuit* he started for the
door of the nursery. Gertrude, pale, almost haggard in
the morning light, sat at the bed holding the sick child in
her lap. Her large blue eyes were full of anxiety; there
was trouble in her face; and something sweetly maternal,
like the shimmer from an inner radiance, illuminated
her noble features. Aleck, seeing in this the divinest gift
and highest vocation of womanhood, gazed at her with a
heart overflowing with tenderness.

"How is Obed?" he asked a little shamefacedly; for
he was aware that he must look irritatingly fresh and rested
after five hours' sleep.

"How is he?" she answered, with quivering lips. "Come
and see."

Aleck walked on tiptoe across the floor, feeling all the
while her reproachful eyes fixed upon him.

"How do you feel, darling?" he said to the boy, laying
his hand on his hot forehead; "papa is so sorry you are
ill."

The child smiled feebly, but did not answer; his poor

little breast was heaving painfully, and his breath came with a distressing piping and stertorous sound through the obstructed little throat.

"I am ashamed of myself, Gertie," Aleck continued, turning to his wife.

"I should think you ought to be," she replied, curtly.

"I had determined to stay awake ; but sleep overcame me. But why did you not call me, as you promised ?"

"If you did not care enough for your child to be kept awake by anxiety for his life, I did not want your assistance," she retorted, with terrible severity.

"How can you speak so to me ?" he broke out, deeply wounded. "Do I not care for my children ?"

"Oh, yes, as long as it costs you no trouble, you care for them."

"Gertrude," he exclaimed, gazing at her in sudden alarm, " what do you mean ?"

"Oh, you are an unfeeling brute," she cried, bursting into a flood of tears. " Here your child is dying, while you are sleeping."

If she had struck him a blow Aleck could not have been more astounded. Was this his gentle, considerate wife, who only last night lifted a burden from his heart by her sweet confidence and affection ? In hopeless bewilderment he stood staring at her. She had put the child in its crib, and had flung herself prostrate at the foot of the bed, clutching the blanket with her fingers. Her frame was shaken by convulsive weeping. He could not bear to take her to task for her injustice to him, while her heart was wrung with anguish for her child. Suddenly he remembered the words of the physician who said, years ago, that she had poor nerves. This reflection, as on a former occasion, brought him infinite relief. She had watched while he had slept. Her nerves were unstrung, her head was racked with anxiety and pain. The suspicion pierced him like an arrow that perhaps her love for the child was deeper than his. How often he had felt a glow of satisfaction at the thought that he was a good and affectionate father ! And yet his affection had not been strong enough to keep him awake while his boy's life was in danger.

He was interrupted in these reflections by the arrival of the doctor. Gertrude arose, wiped away her tears, and, struggling for composure, gave an account of the night. The physician, after having examined the child, declared that only tracheotomy could save its life. Another phy-

sician was accordingly called in and the operation successfully performed. The day passed amid feverish fluctuations
of hope and fear. In the middle of the afternoon there
seemed to be a great improvement ; the boy's temperature
went down ; his breathing became easier. Gertrude was
then induced to take a little rest, and Aleck undertook to
stay with Obed. He received meekly a hundred instructions, promising to carry them out to the letter. The child
was sitting up in bed propped up in pillows. With his first
relief from pain, his liveliness returned, and he made pathetic attempts to play with his father, putting his finger in
his mouth, pulling his hair down over his forehead, and nip-
ping at his mustache, and after each prank giving a soundless laugh, which was touching. When he began to tire of
these diversions, Aleck brought him a box of colored Christmas candles, which served to amuse him for another half
hour. Presently he signified by signs that he wanted them
lighted, and Aleck, not having the heart to refuse him,
struck a match and lighted a candle. The little boy puck-
ered up his lips and tried to blow it out, but could not ; as he
yet breathed through the tube in his throat. He soon discovered, however, that by putting his finger over the opening of the tube he could make the flame flicker. The great
success of this experiment led to its repetition. But the
third time the candle was blown out, he was seized with a
violent coughing fit, and fell back, choking, turned black
in the face, and as his mother appeared, pale with fright,
in the door, he made a pitiful attempt to call her name.
She seized him in her arms ; his little struggling fists grazed
her cheek, and fell down limply on his breast. It was a
dead child she pressed to her heart.

But oh ! the misery of the following days, the alternations of keen pangs of anguish and a mellow, tearful sadness and half wondering resignation ; the hopeless loneliness of sorrow, and the union of hearts under a common
loss ; the impotent rebellion against God's inscrutable
ways, and the anxious peering behind the veil of eternity ;
the awful sense of our insignificance ; the callousness of
exhausted emotions—it were vain to describe it. It is
hinted at in Omar Khayyam's terrible verse :

> "When you and I behind the veil have passed,
> Oh, but the long, long while the world shall last,
> Which of our coming and departure heeds
> As heeds the seven seas a pebble cast."

Aleck, having wrestled with his grief until he no longer knew whether he or it had conquered, set about making arrangements for the funeral. He inserted an obituary notice in the papers; not because there was anyone he wished to notify (for he had but few acquaintances in the city), but simply in conformity to custom. When the day of the funeral arrived, there were, besides the clergyman and the undertaker, but six people in the room; all associates of Aleck in the school. The white coffin was standing on a table in the middle of the parlor, and Gertrude, gazing with tearless eyes upon the lovely little face, marvelled that this little form, which, but a few days ago, was so instinct with restless life and activity, could now be so strangely still. The clergyman had just opened his prayer-book, and was about to begin the service, when there appeared at the door a tall, gray-haired man. He walked up to the coffin, and stood for some minutes staring at the dead child. Gertrude, who knew his step before she saw his face, arose and went toward him.

"Darter," he said, huskily, grasping both her hands, "I want to take little Obed home."

She tried to answer, but could not utter a sound. Her tongue seemed paralyzed, and there was a lump in her throat.

"Darter," the old man continued, gazing at her solemnly, "I want to take you home, too."

"But Aleck—father," she managed to falter.

"We'll take him along, too."

It was very still in the room. The bright winter sun poured in at the windows, and falling upon her head, burnished her hair with a faint golden sheen. The mantel clock ticked away busily in the silence. The clergyman stood with his open book, glancing from one to the other, anxious to begin the service. Aleck, in the meanwhile, had come forward, and was holding his uncle's hand. Their eyes, by a common impulse, sought the dead child, whose placid face the sun was illuminating. And a cruel pang shot through Gertrude's heart; no rosy translucence, no vivid play of features responded to the glare of the light. The bloodless pallor, the sunken, lustreless eyes revived the pain; and an awful sense of desolation and loss overwhelmed her. And when the clergyman's clear voice rang out upon the stillness, "I am the Resurrection and the Life," a great wave of emotion swept through her soul; she flung herself upon her father's breast and wept.

The service was soon at an end ; the woful moment came when the coffin was closed and given into strange hands ; and all the terrible tragedy of mortality, with its solemn riddles, was suggested to their sorrowing hearts. But in some vague way it was a comfort to them that the child was to be taken to the family vault in Torryville, and not to that dreary necropolis, that awful democracy of the dead, on Long Island.

At noon they boarded the Torryville train and arrived late in the evening. They were met at the depot by Horace and Kate, in whose carriage they were driven in state to the old Larkin mansion. And after supper, when they were all gathered in the large library, the old man walked up to the fire, and while poking it in an aimless and hap-hazard way delivered himself of this speech :

"I want you to understand, darter, that this is your house. I had meant to give it to you, Horace. But I'll cancel my mortgage on your house ; so it'll amount to the same thing. I am going to stay with Gertie and Aleck as long as I last. And I want you to be good friends, boys ; and have no rows about property, nor nothing else. I'm a-goin' to leave everything in ship-shape ; for human nature is human nature, and I don't want to take no risks. For you, Aleck, I'm going to get a berth in the University. Having written a book, you'll do, I guess, for Professor of English ; and it so happens that we have just got a vacancy in that department, and if we didn't have one I'd make one. And your little boy, Obed—God bless his dear soul—well—all I've got to say is this—he didn't live nor die—for nothing."

It was about a week after this conversation, when his new sense of proprietorship in the great mansion had become a trifle blunted, that Aleck overtook his uncle walking along the road that skirted the lake. The old man had never been much of a pedestrian ; but the state of his digestion gave him trouble, and his physician had ordered him to take a daily walk of an hour. There he was striding along with his ponderous gray head bent, and his eyes fixed on the ground ; and every now and then, when he espied a piece of frozen horse-manure, he thrust the peg of his cane into it, and flung it across the fence into the neighboring field. Aleck noticed that the surface of the snow on the right side of the fence was black with this useful fertilizer, while on the left side it was merely gray from the dust and the soot of passing railway trains.

And he could not help smiling, as he reflected that the field on the right side belonged to the Larkin estate, while the strip of land between the lake and the road belonged to Mr. Dallas. And this man of millions—this great philanthropist—actually occupied himself during his morning walks in spearing frozen horse-manure and fertilizing *en passant* his own field rather than his neighbor's. Aleck, it must be admitted, felt ashamed on his uncle's account, and regretted having caught him at so undignified a task. For he was anxious to admire him in sincerity—which in the past he had often found it difficult to do. He therefore affected not to observe the frequent employment of the cane as a manure fork, as he caught up with Mr. Larkin, and they walked along together.

They talked for a while of indifferent things in a haphazard, fragmentary, and constrained way. They had never been quite congenial. The habitual attitude of years could not (however much they both desired it) be suddenly altered. It was a matter of feeling; not of reasoning. At the end of five minutes they reached a hill, from which the University buildings could be seen, with the sunshine glittering in their long rows of windows.

The old man stopped, thrust his stick into the ground, and stood gazing with meditative satisfaction at the massive row of rectangular edifices. "Aleck," he burst out suddenly, while his face lighted up with a rare enthusiasm ; "if God spares me I hope to live long enough to see the day when a thousand young men and women shall climb that hill in pursuit of learning."

He pointed energetically at the group of sandstone barracks, as he uttered these words, and fixed upon his nephew a glance full of craving for sympathy. Aleck, however, upon whose mind the horse-manure episode had left an unpleasant impression, answered, perversely :

"But, uncle, what would you do with such a mob of scholars ? The country, in the end, would be embarrassed by the cheapness of higher education."

The old man was evidently unprepared for such an answer, but he shook off its suggestion, as he would a troublesome insect, and remarked, in a voice of deep conviction :

"No, Aleck, no. No man is ever embarrassed by his learning, but by his ignorance he is embarrassed. I know that. I was a poor boy, and had no chance for book-learning. I always thought I should have amounted to something in the world, if I had had it. I don't want any poor boy or girl to suffer, as I did, for the want of a chance to learn ; and then feel, as I do, what he might have been. That is the reason that University stands there on the hill-top, Aleck, and if I don't live to see a thousand students there, I am sure you will."

He took off his rusty beaver, wiped its inside with his bandana handkerchief, replaced it upon his head, and resumed his slow, ponderous walk. Aleck remained standing in the middle of the road. A flash of insight pierced through his soul, and broke with a swift illumination over his countenance. He saw the pathetic side of his uncle's life ; its failure in the midst of its success, and the fundamental nobility of the character which it revealed. When he rejoined the old man, there was a new light in his eyes, and in his voice a warm cordiality which made Mr. Larkin look up for a moment, but with no betrayal of the pleased surprise which he felt. That was the beginning of their new relation, which the years have ripened and deepened.

CHAPTER XLVII.

ENCHANTMENT AND DISENCHANTMENT.

The Hon. Horace Larkin and his wife were seated in their great drawing-room on the first floor, discussing that harassing problem, where and how to spend the summer. Their house, which was built of white sandstone, in a semi-ecclesiastical style, a kind of domesticated Gothic— was not only the finest in Torryville, but one of the finest in the western part of the State. It commanded a superb view over the lake and the valley, and traced itself, with its high gables, in strong relief against the dark pine forest and the green fields, planted with tulip-trees, elms, and shrubbery. In front of the mansion, the whole slope toward the lake was carefully graded and decorated with flower-beds, gravel walks, and well-trimmed hedges. A wide carriage road, bounded by young trees and white-washed bowlders, wound up from the highway, with graceful curves, to a wide, resonant archway in front of the main entrance. The house within, if a daring figure may be permissible, was an esthetic revel in three acts and some twenty-five scenes. The parlor, which was finished in white and gold, was but a variation of that of the Van Schaak mansion in Gramercy Park. But the drawing-room was an independent creation of Kate, upon which she prided herself. It had a superb spaciousness, and with its high ceiling and wide doors gave an almost palatial impression. The exquisite woodwork, the grand piano in the style of the *Directoire*, the rich and harmoniously blended draperies of doors and windows, the Japanese cabinets laden with costly bric-à-brac betrayed a fastidious taste and artistic skill in the smallest detail.

It was in deference to his wife's wishes that Horace spent the hour after dinner, in her company, in this sumptuous apartment. He never felt at home there ; he never got over the feeling that he was only visiting Kate. He was afraid to sit down on the chairs, lest he might soil or break them. They were apparently not made with a view to service ; and as they stood there in dainty minuet attitudes, they impressed him with a sense of alienism which habit did not blunt. He longed for his big, ugly, office chair with the well-worn leather cushion, one caster gone, and one arm in a state of chronic decrepitude. It was, moreover, a trial for which he held the magnificence of the room responsible, that he was forbidden to smoke in it. His post-prandial cigar seemed, from long habit, absolutely essential to his comfort; but Kate had no pity on such reprehensible habits; and in the end he had to conform to her demand. It was odd, that, in spite of her disapproval of him, she was very dependent upon his society. Without scolding and without being anything of a shrew, she had a knack of asserting her authority; and for lack of other subjects she probably enjoyed asserting it over him. He had already made up his mind to sacrifice his own predilections in this question of a summer residence ; because experience had taught him that it never paid to triumph over Kate. A victory over her was always a temporary affair, which in the course of time would resolve itself into a disguised defeat. If he went to a place which she did not like, his summer would be a prolonged martyrdom. The more was the pity that they disagreed so radically concerning what constituted the desirable qualities of a place of summer sojourn. There was Newport, which suited Kate to perfection, but to Horace was a synonym for everything that he held in detestation. Bar Harbor he found scarcely less objectionable ; and there may have been a *soupçon* of truth in Kate's assertion that what he would have preferred above all would be to stay where he was, regarding nothing but his own indolent pleasure. It may have been observed by some that a latent acidity had begun to develop itself in Kate's temper ; and though she was placid and dignified as ever, her quiet words had often the stings of scorpions. She had a way, when she was crossed, of giving him neat little lady-like stabs in every phrase she uttered. When the evening mail arrived, putting an end to the domestic debate, Horace was boiling with suppressed irritability. Yet he said nothing to indicate his state of mind, for wives have this advantage in matrimonial disputes, that they care nothing for the consequences, while husbands as a rule do. Though Kate might wound his self-esteem, he never wounded hers in return. And I fear she had just a little contempt for him on this account, mistaking his chivalry for lack of ability. It seemed often incomprehensible to her how he had risen to the eminence he had reached, with his very moderate

gifts ; and she could only account for it on the supposition
that men as a class were much inferior to women. She,
for her part, was quite prepared to take up the gauntlet
against any of them. And there was no disputing in her
husband's mind that her impregnable conviction of her
own superiority, apart from other considerations, made
her a formidable antagonist.

The mail this evening was very large ; and there was
among the twenty or thirty letters a large franked one of
an imposing official aspect. Kate could not quite conceal
her interest in this letter ; nor her chagrin when her husband, with an instinctive impulse to thwart her, pushed
it aside with ostentatious indifference. He tore open
envelope after envelope, smiled, grunted, pulled his mustache, forgot his ill-humor and laughed outright. As a
member elect of Congress, and a potential power in the
State, he felt his importance. Petitions of the most inconceivable sorts were raining down upon him. He was
courted and cajoled by every interest dependent upon
legislative favor. Human nature was exhibiting itself to
him in some of its most contemptible aspects. Horace
had rapidly perused half a dozen petitions and one or two
veiled offers of bribery, when he put his hand in due order
on the official envelope. He broke the seal, which was
that of the Department of State of the United States ; and
as he glanced down the page, his features lighted up with
a sudden animation.

"Kate," he said, forgetting his grudge, "here is something that'll please you."

"What is it ?" she asked, looking up from her newspaper with a well-simulated air of abstraction.

" How do you like the Czar of all the Russias ? "

"A man after my own heart," said Kate ; " a little wholesome despotism, that's just what we need in this pestilent
democracy of ours."

"You'd better tell him that."

"If I had a chance I would."

" Well, you may have the chance ; here is a letter asking me if I will accept the appointment as minister to the
court of St. Petersburg."

"Ah ! how very nice ! I hope you will accept."

"I don't know."

Here another debate followed, but a much more amicable one. In his heart of hearts, Horace had already made
up his mind. The honor, coming unsolicited, was too

great to decline. There were a hundred reasons why he should not decline. But, wishing to put Kate under obligation, he yielded to her argument inch by inch and with seeming reluctance acquiesced in her conclusions. By some mysterious process his aims and ideals had altered. The position of a diplomat seemed no longer so contemptible to him as it had done in the days when he ran for the legislature. He could even imagine himself dancing attendance upon the rulers of the effete monarchies without democratic compunction. Half unconsciously his bearing changed, as he listened to Kate's subtle flattery (for it suited her purpose, just then, to flatter), and he paced the floor, holding his head high, with a tentative diplomatic air. Envoy Extraordinary and Minister Plenipotentiary of the United States of America! It sounded extraordinarily well! A man could afford to sacrifice a good deal in return for such a dignity.

His acceptance of the appointment was accordingly telegraphed to Washington, and the next day all the newspapers of the Union were commenting upon it. Thus the vexed summer question was happily solved. Instead of going to Newport or Bar Harbor, Kate consented, without persuasion, to go to St. Petersburg. But her spouse, the minister, was far from suspecting the depth of exultation and triumph that dwelt in her heart when he showed her the imposing official document which constituted his credentials, and the tickets for Liverpool, on the Cunarder Servia. For Kate was too wise to boast ; she had builded patiently and silently for many years, and here the structure of her ambition stood complete.

On the night before the Servia sailed, Mr. and Mrs. Adrian Van Schaak, Sr., gave a dinner at their residence in Gramercy Park in honor of their son-in-law, the Honorable Horace Larkin, and his wife. It was a brilliant dinner, and many distinguished persons were present. The newly appointed minister sat at the right hand of his mother-in-law, who no longer paralyzed him with her locomotive stare, but beamed upon him a gaze of maternal pride and admiration. On the other side of the minister, enveloped in an exquisite, tantalizing perfume, sat his sister-in-law, Mrs. Adrian, Jr., embarrassingly *decolletée*, charmingly *naïve*, indiscreet, and brimming over with mischief.

"Horace," she said to the guest of honor, "do you know I once thought you were the cleverest man I had ever known?"

"That was very nice of you to think," he responded; "and may I ask to what I owe the forfeiture of your good opinion?"

"Oh, well, no—it's scarcely worth while, only I'll say this; now I think that your wife is the cleverest woman I've ever known."

"To which I agree, most cordially."

"Ah, well, you'd better, or I shouldn't like to be in your shoes," cried the lady, laughing.

"Hush—sh—sh, my dear child!" Horace warned, disguising his annoyance; "do remember there are people round about us who have ears."

"But they are such very long ears," laughed Mrs. Adrian, with her gay, irresponsible air; "look at Adrian's there, for instance; he is the safest man in the world to say things to; in fact he never gets anything right, so you can always contradict him, and he never gets angry any more because he knows it's no good."

"Well, I wish his wife were as discreet as he."

"Do you really? Well, now, you do me injustice. To-night, I am the soul of discretion, I am just dying to tell you something, and I asked mamma to put me next to you, so that I might have the chance. But I haven't whispered a syllable about it simply because I didn't want to spoil your dinner."

"I appreciate your kindness; I hope your good resolution will last till the coffee."

"Now, Horace, that's simply abominable. I am going to punish you for that; I am going to tell you now and make you sea-sick before you've finished the *filet*."

It was futile that he resolved to pay no attention to her hints. That she had some unpleasant revelation in store for him was evident. Nor could he hope that she would spare him; for she hated Kate with all the hate of which her kittenish, inconsequent nature was capable. And she had a grudge against Kate's husband because he nursed her pride by advancing her fortunes.

"Well," she resumed after a pause which had been devoted to a *paté* of sweetbreads, "Kate made a diplomat of you, after all."

"I don't know why you say that Kate did it," answered Horace, with a sense of relief, for he was under the impression that this was an entirely new topic; "the appointment came to me unsolicited from the President. And that is what I chiefly value about it."

" Unsolicited, oho ! " cried his fair tormentor, her eyes
dancing with mischief ; " and that's what you value about
it ! Well, my dear brother-in-law, if you won't take it
amiss, may I be allowed to ask you a question? Aren't
you a little bit fresh ? "

Horace colored to the edge of his hair. This certainly
passed the limit of permissible banter. And yet, if there
was something behind her words besides a desire to tease,
he had better know it, even at the expense of his pride.
Laughter and animated conversation sounded about them,
and remarks were frequently addressed to him which he
had to answer. In order not to attract attention, he
artfully involved Mrs. Adrian in a dispute with the Russian Minister from Washington, and himself with some
winged platitudes wooed the favor of her ladyship with
the fine shoulders and the gorgeous diamonds who was the
minister's wife. But when the dinner was at an end, and
the company had broken up in little groups scattered on
chairs and *chaises longues* in the large *salon*, he approached
his sister-in-law once more and asked her to explain her
delphic utterances.

" I want you to tell me without reserve," he said, gravely,
" has anyone, as far as you know, asked this appointment
for me ? "

" I don't know," she answered.

" Then what did you mean by your insinuation ? "

" I meant this," she retorted, a slight coldness stealing
into her manner, " that Mr. Van Schaak paid $20,000 out
of Kate's money and $25,000 of his own to the Republican
campaign fund, on condition that you should have this
appointment."

She was surprised at the effect of her words. He
turned quite pale and stared with a look of intense resentment toward his wife, who was sitting in an easy-chair accepting the homage of the Russian Minister. In a flash he
saw the whole plot, with its skilful half-revelations and
concealments, and the consummate sagacity and patience
with which it had been advanced and developed from stage
to stage. What had he been but a dupe and a marionette
in his wife's hand? She pulled the wires ; he performed
the part and arrogated a semblance of independence.
But in the midst of the bitterness of his resentment, there
awoke a feeling of profound respect and admiration for
this marvellously cool and daring woman, who conceived
such long plans and carried them out so ruthlessly.

25

"One thing more, Annie," he said to his sister-in-law, as she made a motion to leave him, "are you absolutely sure that you have told me the truth—I mean that you have not been deceived?"

"I can show you a letter from Q—— which will convince you."

"And you mean to say that this arrangement was made with the President?"

"No, not with the President; but with some one very close to him who claimed to speak for him."

"Thank you. And now, Annie, do me the favor not to tell Kate that I know this. I'll make it worth your while. Ask anything you want of me in Russia, and you shall have it, if it is in my power to give it."

"Agreed. I'm coming over next year with Adrian to be presented at court in a dress that will make Kate ill. That shall be my reward."

The next morning at seven, when the Servia steamed out with the tide, a tall gentleman, extremely *comme il faut* in his attire, was seen walking up and down on the deck, holding his chin well up, and with a certain diplomatic reserve in his bearing. His hair was parted in the middle, and his mustache had a premeditated curl, which hinted at wax. At his side walked a handsome lady, with a cool and contented air and something in her look and bearing which indicated the *grande dame*. They were talking together in a serene and undemonstrative way, apparently unconscious of the sensation they were making.

Leaning against the bulwarks on the starboard side stood an aspiring novelist, rejoicing in the company of the pretty young girl who yesterday became his wife.

"Do you know who that is?" he asked, with a toss of his head toward the distinguished promenader.

"No," she answered; "who is it?"

"It is Mr. Larkin, the newly-appointed Minister to Russia."

"He is not handsome."

"No, but he dresses well."

"And he is so *distingué.*"

"Yes; he has the walk of a Minister Plenipotentiary and Envoy Extraordinary."

"How proud his wife must be of him!"

"Yes; and he of her."

THE END.